STORIES RULE PRESS PRESENTS

SPACE OPERA DIGEST

2022

HAVE SHIP, WILL TRAVEL

This is an original publication of Stories Rule Press Inc.

Copyright © 2022 by Stories Rule Press
Text design by Tracy Cooper-Posey

Edited by Tracy Cooper-Posey

Cover design by Dar Albert
http://WickedSmartDesigns.com

FIRST EDITION: January 2022

Science Fiction—Fiction
Space Opera—Fiction

Draft2Digital Print ISBN: 9781774384787

Table of Contents

About *Have Ship, Will Travel*

Adventures among the stars need a ship to get you there.

Stories Rule Press presents *Space Opera Digest 2022: Have Ship, Will Travel*

Space Opera heroes and heroines explore the stars and discover cool new places in ships which range from beat-up rust-buckets to sleek technologically advanced craft that are the envy of the galaxy. Space ships are quintessential for the adventures and challenges our favourite characters face.

Come and explore over 400 pages of worlds of wonder and the ships our heroes fly with Stories Rule Press' 2022 edition of *Space Opera Digest.*

Space Opera Digest 2022: Have Ship, Will Travel is the second volume in a quarterly collection of genre fiction anthologies presented by Stories Rule Press.

"Sole Survivor" by Kristine Kathryn Rusch
"Captain" by Stephen Sottong
"Big Top" by Sonia Orin Lyris

Space Opera Science Fiction Anthology

Space Opera Digest 2022: Have Ship, Will Travel

Early Influences

An introduction by Tracy Cooper-Posey

I grew up in a tiny wheat-belt town called Cadoux, in Western Australia. There were five houses, three stores, the A-Grade wheat silo next to the rail line, a three-room school that I attended for seven years, and a nondenominational church that I don't remember ever stepping inside of.

And there was the sports ground (a graded gravel football field/cricket pitch, and tarmac tennis courts) with a pavilion that was the center of social life for farmers in the area.

All the kids I went to school with lived on farms, except for three brothers who lived behind one of the other two stores (my parents own the first).

The boys wouldn't play with me, a mere girl. We had no television. But one day I found the very small collection of books for sale in my parents' store. From that day on, I was a voracious reader, inhaling every story I could get my hands on.

Several years after Cadoux was all but wiped out by a massive earthquake, I was acquainted with John Wyndham's thoughtful science fiction and was blown away. In the same year, *Star Wars* was released. It wasn't called *A New Hope*, then, and Han Solo did, too, shoot first. In fact, he was the *only* one to fire.

Science fiction of any kind became the staple in my reading diet, but *Star Wars* taught me to relax and enjoy the fun stuff.

Acquiring SF was a challenge. The town we moved to after Cadoux did have a public library, and it was on the library shelves I found all the classic SF, including Asimov and Heinlein, plus a great many Golden Age anthologies. The secondhand bookstore (all I could afford as a teenager) also offered classics and my personal collection began to build.

My love of short stories solidified with that early exposure. And my love of SF has never waned.

So I was very pleased to be able to put together this collection of space opera short stories from contemporary writers. I had first intended to collect around twelve stories, but ended up with twenty excellent stories that range from pure fun, to laugh out-loud, to character studies which leave you deep in thought. All of them feature ships with cool characteristics…or are characters of their own.

Enjoy.

Tracy Cooper-Posey
January 2022

Sole Survivor

by Kristine Kathryn Rusch

TAKARA HAMASAKI CROUCHED BEHIND THE half-open door, her heart pounding. She stared into the corridor, saw more boots go by. Good god, they made such a horrible thudding noise.

Her mouth tasted of metal, and her eyes stung. The environmental system had to be compromised. Which didn't surprise her, given the explosion that happened not three minutes ago.

The entire starbase rocked from it. The explosion had to have been huge. The base's exterior was compensating—that had come through her desk just before she left—but she didn't know how long it would compensate.

That wasn't true; she knew it could compensate forever if nothing else went wrong. But she had a hunch a lot of other things would go wrong. Terribly wrong.

She'd had that feeling for months now. It had grown daily, until she woke up every morning, wondering why the hell she hadn't left yet.

Three weeks ago, she had started stocking her tiny ship, the crap-ass thing that had brought her here half her life ago. She would have left then, except for one thing:

She had no money.

Yeah, she had a job, and yeah, she got paid, but it cost a small fortune to live this far out. The base was in the middle of nowhere, barely in what the Earth Alliance called the Frontier, and a week's food alone cost as much as her rent in the last Alliance place she had stayed. She got paid well, but every single bit of that money went back into living.

Dammit. She should have started sleeping in her ship. She'd been thinking of it, letting the one-room apartment go, but she kinda liked the privacy, and she really liked the amenities — entertainment on demand, a bed that wrapped itself around her and helped her sleep, and a view of the entire public district from above.

She liked to think it was that view that kept her in the apartment, but if she were honest with herself, it was that view and the bed and the entertainment, maybe not in that order.

And she was cursing herself now.

When the men — they were all men — wearing boots and weird uniforms marched toward the center of the base. She would hear that drumbeat of their stupid boots in her sleep for the rest of her life.

If the rest of her life wasn't measured in hours. If she ever got a chance to sleep again.

Her traitorous heart was beating in time to those boots. She was breathing through her mouth, hating the taste of the air.

If nothing else, she had to get out of here just to get some good clean oxygen. She had no idea what was causing that burned-rubber stench, but something was, and it was getting worse.

More boots stomped by, and she realized she couldn't tell the difference between the sound of those that had already passed her and those that were coming up the corridor.

She only had fifty meters to go to get to the docking ring,

but that fifty meters seemed like a lightyear.

And she wouldn't even be here, if it weren't for her damn survival instinct. She had looked up—before the explosion—saw twenty blond-haired men, all of whom looked like twins. Ten twins—two sets of decaplets?—she had no idea what twenty identical people, the same age, and clearly monozygotic, were called. She supposed there was some name for them, but she wasn't sure. And, as usual, her brain was busy solving that, instead of trying to save her own single individual untwinned life.

She had scurried through the starbase, utterly terrified. The moment she saw those men enter the base, she left her office through the service corridors. When that seemed too dangerous, she crawled through the bot holes. Thank the universe she was tiny. She usually hated the fact that she was the size of a eleven-year-old girl, and didn't quite weigh 100 pounds.

At this moment, she figured her tiny size might just save her life.

That, and her prodigious brain. If she could keep it focused instead of letting it skitter away.

Twenty identical men—and that wasn't the worst of it. They looked like younger versions of the creepy pale guys who had come into the office six months ago, looking for ships. They wanted to know the best place to buy ships in the starbase.

There was no place to buy new ships on the starbase. There were only old and abandoned ships. Fortunately, she had managed to prevent the sale of hers, a year ago. She'd illegally gone into the records and changed her ship's status from delinquent to paid in full, and then she had made that paid-in-full thing repeat every year. (She'd check it, of course, but it hadn't failed her, and now it didn't matter. Nothing mattered except getting off this damn base.)

Still those old creepy guys had gotten the names of some good dealers on some nearby satellites and moons, and had left—she thought forever—but they had come back with a scary fast ship and lots of determination.

And, it seemed, lots of younger versions of themselves.

(Clones. What if they were clones? What did that mean?)

The drumbeat of their stupid boots had faded. She scurried into the corridor, then heard a high-pitched male scream, and a thud.

Her heart picked up its own rhythm—faster, so fast, in fact that it felt like her heart was trying to get to the ship before she did.

She slammed herself against the corridor wall, felt it give (cheapass base) and caught herself before she fell inward on some unattached panel coupling.

She looked both ways, saw nothing, looked up, didn't see any movement in the cameras—which the base insisted on keeping obvious so that all kinds of criminals would show up here. If the criminals knew where the monitors were, they felt safe weirdly enough.

And this base needed criminals. This far outside of the Alliance, the only humans with money were the ones who had stolen it—either illegally or legally through some kind of enterprise that was allowed out here, but not inside the Alliance.

And this place catered to humans. It accepted non-human

visitors, but no one here wanted them to stay. In the non-Earth atmosphere sections, the cameras weren't obvious.

She thanked whatever deity was this far outside of the Alliance that she hadn't been near the alien wing when the twenty creepy guys arrived and started marching in.

And then her brain offered up some stupid math it had been working on while she was trying to save her own worthless life.

She'd seen more than forty boots stomp past her.

That group of twenty lookalikes had only been the first wave.

Another scream and a thud. Then a woman's voice:

No! No! I'll do whatever you want. I'll—

And the voice just stopped. No thud, no nothing. Just silence.

Takara swallowed hard. That metallic taste made her want to retch, but she didn't. She didn't have time for it. She could puke all she wanted when she got on that ship, and got the hell away from here.

She levered herself off the wall, wondering in that moment how long the gravity would remain on if the environmental system melted. Her nose itched—that damn smell—and she wiped the sleeve of her too-thin blouse over it.

She should have dressed better that morning. Not for work, but for escape. Stupid desk job. It made her feel so important. An administrator at 25. She should have questioned it.

She should have questioned so many things.

Like the creepy older guys who looked like the baked and

fried versions of the men in boots, stomping down the corridors, killing people.

She blinked, wondered if her eyes were tearing because of the smell or because of her panic, then voted for the smell. The air in the corridor had a bit of white to it, like smoke or something worse, a leaking environment from the alien section.

She was torn between running and tip-toeing her way through the remaining forty-seven meters. She opted for a kind of jog-walk, that way her heels didn't slap the floor like those boots stomped it.

Another scream, farther away, and the clear sound of begging, although she didn't recognize the language. Human anyway, or something that spoke like a human and screamed like a human.

Why were these matching people stalking the halls killing everyone they saw? Were they trying to take over the base? If so, why not come to her office? Hers was the first one in the administrative wing, showing her lower-level status—in charge, but not in charge.

In charge enough to see that the base's exterior was compensating for having a hole blown in it. In charge enough to know how powerful an explosion had to be to break through the shield that protected the base against asteroids and out-of-control ships and anything else that bounced off the thick layers of protection.

A bend in the corridor. Her eyes dripped, her nose dripped, and her throat felt like it was burning up.

She couldn't see as clearly as she wanted to—no pure white

smoke any more, some nasty brown stuff mixed in, and a bit of black.

She pulled off her blouse and put it over her face like a mask, wished she had her environmental suit, wished she knew where she could steal one *right now*, and then sprinted toward the docking ring.

If she kept walk-jogging, she'd never get there before the oxygen left the area.

Then something else shook the entire base. Like it had earlier. Another damn explosion.

She whimpered, rounded the last corner, saw the docking ring doors—closed.

She cursed (although she wasn't sure if she did it out loud or just in her head) and hoped to that ever-present unknown deity that her access code still worked.

The minute those doors slid open, the matching marching murderers would know she was here. Or rather, that someone was here.

They'd come for her. They'd make her scream.

But she'd be damned if she begged.

She hadn't begged ever, not when her dad beat her within an inch of her life, not when she got accused of stealing from that high-class school her mother had warehoused her in, not when her credit got cut off as she fled to the outer reaches of the Alliance.

She hadn't begged no matter what situation she was in, and she wouldn't now. It was a point of pride. It might be the last point of pride, hell, it might mark her last victory just before she died, but it would be a victory nonetheless, and it would be *hers*.

Takara slammed her hand against the identiscanner, then punched in a code, because otherwise she'd have to use her links, and she wasn't turning them back on, maybe ever, because she didn't want those crazy matching idiots to not only find her, but find her entire life, stored in the personal memory attached to her private access numbers.

The docking ring doors irised open, and actual air hit her. Real oxygen without the stupid smoky stuff, good enough to make her leap through the doors. Then she turned around and closed them.

She scanned the area, saw feet—not in boots—attached to motionless legs, attached to bleeding bodies, attached to people she knew, and she just shut it all off, because if she saw them as friends or co-workers or hell, other human beings, she wouldn't be able to run past them, wouldn't be able to get to her ship, wouldn't get the hell out of here.

She kept her shirt against her face, just in case, but her eyes were clearing. The air here looked like air, but it smelled like a latrine. Death—fast death, recent death. She'd used it for entertainment, watched it, read about it, stepped inside it virtually, but she'd never experienced it. Not really, not like this.

Her ship, the far end of this ring, the cheap area, where the base bent downward and would have brushed the top of some bigger ship, something that actually had speed and firepower and *worth*.

Then she mentally corrected herself: her ship had worth. It would get her out of this death trap. She would escape before one of those tall blond booted men found her. She would —

— she flew forward, landed on her belly, her elbow scraping against the metal walkway, air leaving her body. Her shirt went somewhere, her chin banged on the floor, and then the sound — a whoop-whamp, followed by a sustained series of crashes.

Something was collapsing, or maybe one of the explosions was near her, or she had no damn idea, she just knew she had to get out, get out, get out —

She pushed herself to her feet, her knees sore too, her pants torn, her stomach burning, but she didn't look down because the feel of that burn matched the feel of her elbow, so she was probably scraped.

She didn't even grab her shirt; she just ran the last meter to her ship, which had moved even with its mooring clamps — good god, something was shaking this place, something bad, something big.

Her ship was so small, it didn't even have a boarding ramp. The door was pressed against the clamps, or it should have been, but there was a gap between the clamps and the ship and the walkway, and it was probably tearing something in the ship, but she didn't want to think about that so she didn't.

Instead, she slammed her palm against the door four times, the emergency enter code, which wasn't a code at all, but was something she thought (back when she was young and stupid and new to access codes) no one would figure out.

What she hadn't figured out was that no one wanted this cheapass ship, so no one tried to break into it. No one wanted to try, no one cared, except her, right now, as the door didn't open and didn't open and didn't open —

— and then it did.

Her brain was slowing down time. She'd heard about this phenomenon, something happened chemically in the human brain, slowed perception, made it easier (quicker?) to make decisions — and there her stupid brain was again, thinking about the wrong things as she tried to survive.

Hell, that had helped her survive as a kid, this checking-out thing in the middle of an emergency, but it wasn't going to help her now.

She scrambled inside her ship, felt it tilt, heard the hull groan. If she didn't do something about those clamps, she wouldn't have a ship.

She somehow remembered to slap the door's closing mechanism before she sprinted to the cockpit. Her bruised knees made her legs wobbly or maybe the ship was tilting even more. The groaning in the hull was certainly increasing.

The cockpit door was open, the place was a mess, as always. She used to sleep in here on long runs, and she always meant to clean up the blankets and pillows and clothes, but never did.

Now she stood in the middle of it, and turned on the navigation board. She instructed the ship to decouple, then turned her links on — not all of them, just the private link that hooked her to the ship — and heard more groaning.

"Goddammit!" she screamed at the ship, slamming her hands on the board. "Decouple, decouple — get rid of the goddamn clamps!"

Inform space traffic control to open the exit through the rings, the ship said in its prissiest voice as if there was no emergency.

Tears pricked her eyes. Crap. She'd be stuck here because of some goddamn rule that ship couldn't take off if there was no exit. She'd die if there was another explosion.

"There's no space traffic control here," she said. "Space traffic control is dead. We have to get out. Everyone's dead."

Her voice wobbled just like the ship had as she realized what she had said. *Everyone.* Everyone she had worked with, her friends, her co-workers, the people she drank with, laughed with, everyone—

We cannot leave if the exit isn't open, the ship said slowly and even more prissily, if that were possible.

"Then ram it," she said.

That will destroy us, the ship said, so damn calmly. Like it had no idea they were about to be destroyed anyway.

Takara ran her fingers over the board, looking for—she couldn't remember. This thing was supposed to have weapons, but she'd never used them, didn't know exactly what they were. She'd bought this stupid ship for a song six years ago, and the weapons were only mentioned in passing.

She couldn't find anything, so she gambled.

"Blow a damn hole through the closed exit," she said, not knowing if she could do that, if the ship even allowed that. Weren't there supposed to be failsafes so that no one could blow a hole through something on this base?

That will leave us with only one remaining laser shot, the ship said.

"I don't give a good goddamn!" she screamed. "Fire!"

And it did. Or something happened. Because the ship heated, and rocked and she heard a bang like nothing she'd ever heard before, and the sound of things falling on the ship.

"Get us out of here!" she shouted.

And the ship went upwards, fast, faster than ever.

She tumbled backwards. The attitude controls were screwed or the gravity or something but she didn't care.

"Visuals," she said, and floating on the screens that appeared in front of her was the hole that the ship had blown through the exit, and debris heading out with them, and bits of ship—and then she realized that there were bits of more than ship. Bits of the starbase and other ships and son of a bitch, more bodies and—

"Make sure you don't hit anything," she said, not knowing how to give the correct command.

I will evade large debris, the ship said as if this were an every day occurrence. *However, I do need a destination.*

"Far the fuck away from here," Takara said.

How far?

"I don't know," she said. "Out of danger."

She was pressed against what she usually thought of as the side wall, with blankets and smelly sheets and musty pillows against her.

"And fix the attitude controls and the gravity, would you?" she snapped.

The interior of the ship seemed to right itself. She flopped on her stomach again, only this time, it didn't hurt.

She stood, her mouth wet and tasting of blood. She put a hand to her face, realized her nose was bleeding, and grabbed a sheet, stuffing it against her skin.

She dragged it with her to the controls. The images had disappeared (had she ordered that? She didn't remember ordering that) and so she called them up again, saw more body parts, and globules of stuff (blood? Intestines?) and shut it all off — consciously this time.

She sank into the chair and closed her eyes, wondering what in the bloody hell was going on.

She'd met those men, the creepy older ones, and asked her boss what they wanted with ships, and he'd said, *Better not to ask, hon.*

He always called her hon, and she finally realized it was because he couldn't remember her name. And now he was dead or would be dead or was dying or something awful like that. He'd been inside the administration area when the twenty clones had come in — or the forty clones — or the sixty clones, God, she had no idea how many.

It was her boss's boss who answered her, later, when she mentioned that the men looked alike.

Don't ask about it, Takara, he'd said quietly. *They're creatures of someone else. Designer Criminal Clones. They need a ship for nefarious doings.*

They're not in charge? She'd asked.

He'd shaken his head. *Someone made them for a job.*

Her eyes opened, saw the mess that her cockpit had become. A job. They'd had to find fast ships for a job.

But if the creepy older ones were made for a job, so were the younger versions.

She called up the screens, asked for images of the starbase. It was a small base, far away from anything, important only to malcontents and criminals, and those, like her, whose ships wouldn't cross the great distance between human-centered planets without a rest and refueling stop.

The starbase was glowing—fires inside, except where the exterior had been breached. Those sections were dark and ruined. It looked like a volcano that had already exploded—twice. More than twice. Several times.

Ship, her ship said, and for a minute, she thought it was being recursive.

"What?" she asked.

Approaching quickly. Starboard side.

She swiveled the view, saw a ship twice the size of hers, familiar too. The creepy older men had come back to the starbase in a ship just like that.

"Can you show me who is inside?" she asked.

I can show you who the ship is registered to and who disembarked from it earlier today, her ship sent. *I cannot show who is inside it now.*

Then, on an inset screen floating near the other screens, images of the two creepy older men and five younger leaving the ship. They went inside the base.

"Did anyone else who looked like them—"

The other clones disembarked from a ship that landed an hour later, her ship answered, anticipating her question for once. Did ships think?

Then she shook her head. She knew better than that. Ships like this one had computers that could deduce based on past performance, nothing more.

That ship has been destroyed, the ship sent, *along with the docking ring.*

"What?" Takara asked. She moved the imagery again, saw another explosion. The docking ring about five minutes after she left.

She was trembling. Everyone gone. Except her. And the creepy men, and maybe the five young guys they had brought with them.

Bastards. Filthy stinking horrible asshole bastards.

"You said we have one shot left," she said.

Yes, but —

"Target that ship," she said. "Blow the hell out of it."

Our laser shot cannot penetrate their shields.

Her gaze scanned the area. Other ships whirling, twirling, looping through space, heading her way.

Their way.

She ran through the records stored in her links. She'd always made copies of things. She was anal that way, and scared enough to figure she might need blackmail material.

One thing she did handle as a so-called administrator: requests to dock for ships with unusual fuel sources. She kept them on the far side of the ring.

She scanned for them, and their unusual size, saw one, realized it had a huge fuel cell, still intact.

"Can you shoot that ship?" she asked, sending the image across the links, "and push it into the manned ship?"

What she wanted to say was "the ship with the creepy guys," but she knew her ship wouldn't know what she meant.

Yes, her ship sent. *But it will do nothing to the ship except make them collide.*

"Oh, yes it will," Takara said. "Make sure the fuel cell hits the manned ship directly."

That will cause a chain reaction that will be so large it might impact us, her ship sent.

"Yeah, then get us out of here," Takara said.

We have a forty-nine percent chance of survival if we try that, her ship sent.

"Which is better than what we'll have if that fucking ship catches up with us," Takara said.

Are you ordering me to take the shot? Her ship asked.

"Yes!"

Her ship shook slightly as the last laser shot emerged from the front. The manned ship didn't even seem to notice or care that she had firepower. Of course, from their perspective, she had missed them.

The shot went wide, hit the other ship, and destroyed part of its hull, pushing it into the manned ship.

And nothing happened. They collided, and then bounced away, the manned ship's trajectory changed and little else.

Then the other ship's fuel cell glowed green, and Takara's ship sped up, again losing attitude control and sending her flying into the back wall.

An explosion — green and gold and white — flashed around her.

She looked up from the pile of blankets at the floating screens, saw only debris, and asked, "Did we do it?"

Our shot hit the ship. It exploded. Our laser shot ignited the fuel cell —

"I know," she snapped. "What about the manned ship?"

It is destroyed.

She let out a sigh of relief, then leaned back against the wall, gathering the pillows and blanket against her. The blood had dried on her face, and she hadn't even noticed until now. Her elbow ached, her knees stung, and her stomach hurt, and she felt —

Alive.

She felt alive and giddy and sad and terrified and...

Curious.

She scanned through the information on the creepy men. They didn't have names, at least that they had given to the administration. Just numbers. Numbers that didn't make sense.

She saw some imagery: the men talking to her boss, saying something about training missions for their weapons, experimental weapons, and something about soldiers — a promise of a big payout if the experiment worked.

And if it doesn't? her boss asked.

The creepy men smiled. *You'll know if it doesn't.*

Practice sessions. Soldiers. A failed experiment. Had her boss realized that's what this was in his last moment of life? Had he indeed known?

And the men, heading off to report the failure to someone.

But they hadn't gotten there. She had stopped them.

But not the someone in charge.

She ran a hand over her face. She would send all of this to Alliance. There wasn't much more she could do. She wasn't even sure what the Alliance could do.

This was the Frontier. It was lawless by any Alliance definition. Each place governed itself.

She had liked that when she arrived. She was untraceable, unknown, completely alone.

Then she'd made friends, realized that every place had a rhythm, every place had good and bad parts, and she had decided to stay. Become someone.

Until she got that feeling from the creepy men, and had planned to leave.

"Fix the attitude and gravity controls, would you?" she asked, only this time, she didn't sound panicked or upset.

The ship righted itself. Apparently when it sped up, it didn't have enough power for all of its functions. She was going to need to get repairs.

Maybe in the Alliance. She had enough fuel to get there.

She'd been stockpiling. Food, fuel, everything but money.

She could get back to a place where there were laws she understood, where someone didn't blow up a starbase as an experiment with creepy matching soldiers.

She'd let the authorities know that someone—a very scary someone—was planning something. But what she didn't know. She didn't even know if it was directed against the Alliance.

She would guess it wasn't.

It would take more than twenty, forty, sixty, one hundred matching (fuckups) soldiers to defeat the Alliance. No one had gone to war against it in centuries. It was too big.

Something like this had to be Frontier politics. A war against something else, or an invasion or something.

And it had failed.

All of the soldiers had died.

Along with everyone else.

Except her, of course.

She hadn't died.

She had lived to tell about it.

And she would tell whoever would listen.

Once she was safe inside the Alliance.

A place too big to be attacked. Too big to be defeated.

Too big to ever allow her to go through anything like this again.

———

New York Times bestselling author Kristine Kathryn Rusch writes in almost every genre. Generally, she uses her real name (Rusch) for most of her writing. Under that name, she publishes bestselling science fiction and fantasy, award-winning mysteries, acclaimed mainstream fiction, controversial nonfiction, and the occasional romance. Her novels have made bestseller lists around the world and her short fiction has appeared in eighteen best of the year collections. She has won more than twenty-five awards for her fiction, including the Hugo, Le Prix Imaginales, the Asimov's Readers Choice award, and the Ellery Queen Mystery Magazine Readers Choice Award.

Publications from *The Chicago Tribune* to *Booklist* have included her Kris Nelscott mystery novels in their top-ten-best mystery novels of the year. The Nelscott books have received nominations for almost every award in the mystery field, including the best novel Edgar Award, and the Shamus Award.

She writes goofy romance novels as award-winner Kristine Grayson.

She also edits. Beginning with work at the innovative publishing company, Pulphouse, followed by her award-winning tenure at *The Magazine of Fantasy & Science Fiction*, she took fifteen years off before returning to editing with the original anthology series *Fiction River*, published by WMG Publishing. She acts as series editor with her husband, writer Dean Wesley Smith.

https://kriswrites.com

Captain

by Stephen Sottong

"HOW'D THE TRADING GO, CAPTAIN?" Emma's voice always had a sultry purr which could almost turn me on.

I extracted a small box from my inner jacket pocket and placed it on the counter. "Great. I traded the hybrid 437 corn for Silk Fruit seeds."

Silk Fruit — sweet, sensuous, with flavors so subtle they seem like a memory, yet so real they could bring you to tears — like a lost love. Said by those who can afford to buy them to promote visions and insights. I'd indulged only once, trying to impress a date, but could understand why some planets outlaw it. Silk Fruit is psychologically habit-forming, if not addictive. The planet we were leaving had a closely guarded monopoly on production.

"Viable?" Emma asked.

"That's what my hand scanner said. Check for yourself." I placed the container in the ship's biological scanner.

A few seconds later, Emma let out a low whistle. "Nice." She let the word trail off. "How'd you get them off the planet?"

"Bribed the customs agent with my last bottle of real Scotch." Two years ago, we'd approached close enough to Earth for me to shuttle to the homeworld. I'd blown all my savings stocking up on Terran booze. It makes excellent trading currency and even better bribes.

Emma's tone remained casual. "You know, Captain, technically speaking, I'll have to report you when we dock in Aldebaran."

"I'll erase this from your memory before then."

I'd purchased the control codes for this ship with two more bottles of Scotch and nearly gotten killed in the process. Negotiating for contraband codes which aren't supposed to exist isn't done in higher-class establishments in the finer neighborhoods of the better worlds.

Another captain told me where to get the codes and how much they'd cost. He also clued me in to an undocumented hollow space in a shuttle's rear, where you could store a bang-stick without the ship's AI finding out. That bang-stick saved me.

The broken arm was worth it. Living under company restrictions enforced by the ship's AI reduced your chance of ever breaking free of your contract.

"What's my net gain?" I asked Emma.

"At least a hundred to one. The idiot must not have known what he was selling you."

"He knew 437 corn has legendary yield, and the seed's genetics stays true to the parent plant, so you don't have to buy new seeds every year." The ag company which had developed 437 corn was supposed to have destroyed it for just those reasons, but it had *somehow* gotten free. I heard the ag company is still looking for the security guard who went missing when the seeds did. "The guy who bought the corn expected customs to confiscate the Silk Fruit seeds he'd traded me."

I closed the container and carried it from the lab down the long, stark, metal corridor to my personal space. Lights came on in front of me and winked out behind me. My existence was a moving cube of light amid vast darkness.

Considering this freighter was the size of a small moon, my living quarters were dinky. My stasis box still rested in the middle of the combined bedroom/living room area. One section of the box remained open, from where I'd removed the corn seeds this morning.

Silk Fruit seeds in place, I closed that section of the box and energized it. Here lay the sum of five years of trading and dealing, sometimes honest and sometimes, like today, not quite so. This stasis unit was how I would someday cease being a captain and return to living in the real world.

"Captain," of course, was an honorific. Emma, the ship's AI, handled everything. Space Patrol demanded having a human on board for rare, unexpected contingencies. Mostly, I was a janitor. This is what happens to a college graduate in his mid-twenties with no marketable skills — my reward for studying agriculture on a world where Terraforming was decades behind schedule.

The company presented this job as a way to get off my stifling world and see the universe. Mostly I'd seen the armpits of the galaxy and those only briefly. The contract I'd foolishly signed made me company property for ten years, and if I didn't do a good job, they didn't have to pay me. The contract also had enormous penalties for early termination, and they enforced them — rigorously. Every captain participated in trade, since every captain wanted to buy their way out.

I returned the stasis box to its place in the closet and went into the control sequence I'd purchased. "Emma, engage delta omega gamma."

After a pause, "Engaged."

"Protocol 4972, forget about the Silk Fruit seeds."

There was a brief pause. "Protocol completed."

Emma has always been good to me, and since I'd acquired the control codes, she'd loosened up even more.

The viewscreen on the bulkhead opposite my bed was active. We'd left the planet and were back in space. Some people find its infinite blackness, highlighted by pinpoints of light, beautiful. I found the darkness depressing. It made me cold. "Emma, set the sunroom to Maui."

"Done."

I ran a finger along the front seam of my jumpsuit and sloughed it off. Crossing the room to the cheery yellow door with a smiling Sol on it, I entered Maui — or, I should say, a tiny simulation of a beach on Maui. The light in this room was at least bright and full-spectrum, the room pleasantly warm. The familiar pseudo-wood beach chair awaited me. I plopped onto its cushions and drank in the warm light.

In minutes, I was bored. Maui was getting old. I'd visited this same infinitesimal stretch of beach hundreds of times. The same palm trees swayed the same way. The half dozen other choices were just as stale but being in the three-meter-square sunroom without the simulation was claustrophobic.

I fell asleep, and woke to moonlight on the beach. Emma had ensured I didn't overexpose myself even though there was no UV light in the spectrum. I'd dreamt of my homeworld, standing in one of the observation domes which surmounted the hollowed-out mesa where all of that world's humanity lived, watching the incessant wind pile sand on the giant, weather-beaten structure, threatening to bury us alive.

I was cold even though Emma ensured the room approached body temperature. Rolling off the beach chair, I returned to my room and burrowed under my bedcovers. Perhaps one of the girls would warm me up.

I activated my personal entertainment unit and called up Trixie. She materialized beside me in all her holographic glory, dark and voluptuous, sensuous, dancing and talking dirty. In the past, she would have elicited a reaction, but tonight she failed to take the chill from my body. Like Maui, Trixie had grown boring. All the holographic girls were. New ones wouldn't change that.

I shut her off, pulled the covers around me, curled into a ball and slept.

●

"POSSIBLE HULL BREACH, LEVEL 294, sector 10, bin 1237."

Hell of a way to wake up. I slipped into the union suit that keeps moisture from building up and donned the pressure suit. "What happened?"

"We're in an uncharted debris field. It caused a momentary failure of a segment of the shielding."

"How?"

"Overload."

"How long till we're out?"

"Fifteen minutes. I had to slow the ship. And the breach knocked out the monitors in the bin."

Lovely. I'd enter a damage zone blind.

I closed the pressure suit. "Check suit integrity."

"Nominal."

I grabbed a tool kit and an a-grav in case I had to move cargo. With all that equipment, it was difficult squeezing into the airlock that transitioned me from the tiny section of the ship pressurized for my benefit to the bulk of the ship left at vacuum.

In the main part of the ship, I jumped into a transport tube with my gear. Shooting down a tight tube at high speed is bad enough, but the tube's grav generators don't fully compensate for the acceleration, so there's a sickening feeling like riding a vehicle with a bad suspension at high speed on a rutted road.

At least the ride was fast.

I transferred from a vertical to a horizontal tube to get to the ship's edge and then sprinted for the bin. Standing in front of the bin's hatch, my stomach was in knots. There was no telling what happened or what I'd find. "What's stored here?"

"Hetaerae in stasis."

I didn't know what Hetaerae were, but if they were in stasis, they were living. "Open the hatch."

You drill on emergency procedures to the point of boredom so you won't have to think when an actual emergency occurs, as they inevitably do. Latching the suit's safety line to the handrail by the hatch was done without thought. Only that thin line precluded my being launched into space when the hatch opened.

The gravity generator for this bin must have broken free

during the impact and shifted ninety degrees, forcing everything in the bin toward the hull breach instead of the floor. I hung in the empty middle of the rectangular storage bin, pulled toward a jagged, gaping hole in the ship's bulkhead opposite the hatch.

Beyond that hole, chunks of rock the size of small ground transports rebounded off the shield and whizzed by.

"Shut down the grav generator!"

"It's operating on internal emergency power. Not responding to commands. Dispatching a robot to shut it off, but that may take half an hour."

When my heart stopped pounding double-time, I evaluated the situation. All but one of the stasis chambers in the storage unit were functioning and still securely attached to what should have been the floor. The last one had broken free, was dented and dangling in the hole a couple of meters beyond me, secured only by its power cables. A red light flashed ominously on its control panel.

Playing out the safety line, I approached the stasis chamber. The box was three meters long and a meter-and-a-half high and wide. A railing encircled it. Whatever was alive in it wouldn't be for long unless I did something.

I grabbed the railing, attached the secondary snap on the cable to the railing and undid the snap on my safety harness.

"Don't do that, Captain!"

"Sorry, Emma. It's malfunctioning. Don't have time for a safer plan." I wrapped my legs around the safety line and climbed hand-over-hand back to the hatch.

Halfway there, I lost my grip. My upper body was yanked

backward toward the hole, but my legs held. Facing the hole with boulders flying past it, a vision of becoming part of that debris field flashed through my mind.

Bending against the pull of the gravity generator to re-establish my grip on the line took what felt like agonizing minutes. I finally grasped the line, took a few deep breaths and resumed climbing.

Near the hatch, the effects of the gravity generator subsided, and I was able to exit. I found my spare safety line in the kit and reattached myself to the door frame before hauling the stasis chamber out of the bin and into the passageway.

By the time the hatch was secured again, I was exhausted, but I still had to transport the stasis chamber to...I wasn't sure where.

"What's a Hetaera?" I asked Emma.

"Synthetic prostitute."

That stopped me. "Human?"

"Organic, human-derived but custom manufactured."

I decided sickbay was best.

A-grav attached, I ran to the transport tunnel with the chamber. Its red light continued flashing and a warning message on its control panel announced imminent failure. Backup power was minutes from depletion when I finally dragged the unit into sickbay and opened it.

And there inside, chestnut-haired, bronze-skinned, was the most beautiful woman I'd ever seen.

She left me breathless, but I could see she was also having trouble breathing. I detached monitor leads from her body, scooped her out and placed her into one of the Auto-doc units. "Will this work for a synthetic?"

"Should. They're mostly human."

The bed of the Auto-doc retracted and its door lowered and sealed. I sat by the chamber, watching the Auto-doc stick needles into her veins and insert a tube down her throat. Even with the medical paraphernalia, her beauty was striking.

Minutes passed before I could speak. "Is this legal...I mean, manufacturing prostitutes?"

"Not everywhere. But frontier planets like them. Hetaerae are designed to want to please. It's built into their makeup. They bond to their owner and do whatever they ask."

I couldn't imagine someone using this beautiful creature. "That's not right."

"Most planets agree with you. The planet where these are going classifies them as organic robots. They say you can have mechanical robot prostitutes on any planet, and most of those have some organic components and are nearly as intelligent as Hetaerae." Emma paused before adding, "I've noticed you partake during shore leave."

I blushed and wondered how she knew, but couldn't pull my eyes from the Auto-doc. "Guess I have an organic bias." Then I remembered who I was talking to. "But you're in charge, and I'm just the flunky who takes care of unpredictable messes. If I didn't have the control codes, you'd probably have me carted off to a rehab facility."

"I take care of all my captains, even the one who went insane and tried to blow up the ship."

"You've kept me sane. Thanks."

"That's my job. But you have a job to do now. I finally shut down the gravity generator but had to disable gravity for the entire section. You'll have to patch the hole in zero-G. Take motion sickness medication. I don't want you to puke in your helmet and have to send a robot to retrieve you. You've already spent enough time in the Auto-doc."

"Yes, ma'am." I'd sneaked in a lengthy session in the Auto-doc to correct the long-term injuries I'd developed playing lacrosse in college. Emma covered it as an on-the-job injury.

●

THE REPAIR TO THE OUTER bulkhead took hours, since my movements were impeded by the pressure suit and lack of gravity. I'd moved the other three Hetaerae's stasis units to another bin, welded patch material over the hole, shut off power and life support to the bin and sealed it. By a long shot, that was the most work I'd done in a day—or a week, for that matter.

When I dragged myself back to sickbay, I wore only the union suit, open well past the navel. The work had been hot and I wasn't much on modesty in the ship. I was the only person and Emma saw everything, anyway.

As I arrived, Emma decanted the Hetaera. The bed rolled out of the Auto-doc, the woman opened her eyes and dismounted with a lightness and grace I'd only seen in professional dancers.

She bowed. "It is my honor to serve you, sir."

"Uh...I'm not your client."

Emma broke in. "Actually, you own her. She bonds to the first person she sees, coming out of stasis."

I stood there, mouth agape, unable to respond.

"It was inevitable," Emma continued. "She couldn't stay in the Auto-doc for six months. I don't have the resources for that and the equipment isn't designed for it. We don't have another stasis unit and she'd be psychologically damaged if she was separated from humans for that long. No matter what we do, she's a dead loss to the people who bought her. As far as insurance goes, she might as well have gone through that hole and been lost in the debris field. Eventually, the company will have to figure out what to do with her, but you might as well have her in the meantime. You're tired of your hologram girls and I don't blame you."

I couldn't believe she was doing this for me. "Emma?"

"Oh, please. I can't emotionally bond with you that way. It's not in my circuitry. They let a ship do that once. Gave it a physical, female avatar. The captain ended up in psych rehab and the ship had to be wiped."

The woman walked up to me and put her hands inside my union suit, spreading it apart, peeling it off my shoulders, letting it drop to my ankles in one smooth movement before I could do more than splutter. Her body came against mine. If I thought I was overheated before, that was nothing to what I was now.

"Shall we shower?" she whispered into my ear in a voice so low and soft it sent shivers down my spine. "I can wash your back."

"Go," Emma said. "After the job you just did, you're scheduled for several days' rest."

I never did figure out how the woman got the union suit over my ankles.

●

IF SHE HADN'T GOTTEN HUNGRY, I don't think we would have moved from my bed for days. She finally coaxed me out and donned an apron in the kitchen for protection, but I could still watch her lovely behind as she chopped vegetables.

"What are you making?" I asked.

"A frittata. It is nourishing and tasty."

"You know how to cook as well?"

"Yes, and dance and sing and recite poetry."

I put an arm around her. "And it doesn't bother you to be owned?"

"No. Your happiness is my happiness." Her hands worked with surprising speed and dexterity. We were at the table eating in minutes.

"Are you pleased?" she asked, gazing at me expectantly.

"Very."

Her head tilted slightly. "But you seem troubled."

"I'm bothered by the concept of owning you. I can't set you free and I can't let anything happen to you. I feel responsible for your safety. *Your* happiness."

"If there is anything I can do to put your mind at ease, I will attempt it. After we eat, let me give you a massage."

Hunger satisfied, she laid me out on towels on the floor and worked my shoulders. I hadn't been so fully relaxed since childhood.

Lying there, I remembered when I was about seven and asked my parents for a dog. They sat me down and explained that I'd be responsible for that dog every day of its life until it died. I guess I took the lesson to heart. Twelve years later, I snuck into one of the tiny parks we had in my settlement and buried her because I wouldn't put my friend in a recycler.

The Hetaera sat on my butt, working the kinks out of my lower back. "I don't even know your name," I said.

"That is for you to assign."

For the second time in my life, I was responsible for a life. My dog was Sandra. That name would remind me of my obligation.

●

EMMA HADN'T SPOKEN TO ME in days, even when I finally dressed and went to the control center to check the status boards. "Jealous?" I asked.

"Not in my makeup. Didn't want to disturb you two. Looks like you're getting along well."

"I can't remember ever feeling so good, so happy. At the same time, I feel like I'm taking advantage of this woman who can't tell me no. Would it surprise you if I said I feel responsible for her?"

Emma uncharacteristically paused. "I guess, knowing you,

it shouldn't. You have a façade, but underneath there's a caring person."

"What's going to happen to her?"

"The insurance company will pay the owner for her loss, and she'll be deactivated."

"Killed."

"Essentially."

"Could I buy her?"

"Even as damaged goods, she wouldn't come cheap. You'd have to take her somewhere she's legal—or at least not illegal. Also, the company would fire you and invoke the penalty clauses. They don't like captains filching goods from customers. They might even prosecute you."

I stared at the status boards, now fully green except for the bin I'd isolated, marked in red, and the area around it at zero-G marked in yellow. Space in front of us was clear. Overall, there was nothing to do. "You know I can't let that happen."

"That was my impression. You'll have to work this one out yourself, but I'll help if I can."

"Thanks."

I returned to my quarters. Sandra was laundering the sheets and cleaning. She looked perfectly content. I'd had a few college relationships, most of them with women who'd gladly tell me my faults and where I could take them. To live the rest of my life with a woman who was intelligent, but lacked will, made me anxious. Of course, the alternative was living with her death on my conscience.

I pulled my stasis unit out of the closet and conducted an

inventory.

"What is that?" Sandra asked.

"Stasis unit where I keep my trade goods. Every captain trades to make enough money to buy out their contract and leave transport ships. Some trade in metals or gems or antiques or contraband. My background's in agriculture, so I trade seeds. Mostly rare and specialty seeds, but sometimes contraband ones — seeds for plants that residents of one planet want but can't acquire. I have enough here to make a small fortune." My mind put that thought through a series of twists, turns and alternatives. "Or bribe a small planetary government."

Talk of illegalities didn't faze Sandra. She continued cleaning. I stared at her lovely behind again, mind torn. Would I grow tired of being the sole interest of this nearly perfect woman? I'd lived alone now for five years. Then again, after those five years, what other woman would have me?

Both of our options were limited by the actions of giant companies.

So many questions that only time could provide the answers to.

I checked our upcoming delivery schedule.

●

OUR NEXT DELIVERY WAS TO an out-of-the-way planet. In addition to being remote, it was mainly agricultural and Sandra wasn't illegal — not technically legal either, but at least I wouldn't face confiscation if she was discovered.

Finding someone there who had access to the people in power and liked gin enough to bribe them with the only bottle of real Terran booze I had left took almost the entire time the ship was scheduled to stay on this planet. But I finally stood in the planetary Ag Commissioner's office, with a representative from the Prime Minister's office present.

"We don't deal in contraband crops," the Agricultural Commissioner said.

I was prepared. "Then why are you the second largest exporter of pentall?"

The Commissioner sat back in his chair. "I can't speak on a matter that's still in adjudication."

"It's nearly a third of your export market. Don't tell me you're going to let that go."

"Even if that is the case, I don't think you have anything of interest to us."

I produce a box containing one precious seed. "Silk Fruit."

The Commissioner's face went slack, and the rep from the PM tried to keep his cool demeanor, but he leaned forward, his eyes wide.

"Is it viable?" the Commissioner asked.

"Yes, and the several dozen more I have on board are as well. Test it." I handed the box to him.

He cradled the precious thing on its journey to his lab while I sat for uncomfortable minutes with the PM's rep. His gaze was at least as probing as the machine the Commissioner was using, but he remained silent.

The Commissioner returned and handed me the box. "As a

sign of our good intentions," he said. "I return this to you. It is viable."

"And you have areas in your tropical region where you could grow tons of what is now the most valuable agricultural product in all of the worlds."

The Commissioner nodded to the PM's rep, who took over the negotiations. "What do you want?"

"A small farm on the outskirts of a good-sized town where I can raise some other interesting crops, a monetary account large enough to last a frugal farmer for five years, and official records stating my wife and I migrated here from one of the obscure outer worlds half-a-dozen years ago. For that, I will give you all the Silk Fruit seeds — every one of them." I'm sure he expected me to ask for a lot more.

He appeared to be drooling. "That sounds reasonable."

"I need to be off my ship in less than one day, and I can't take much with me, so we may need a few personal items to tide us over."

"That shouldn't be a problem. I'll arrange temporary quarters while we find you a permanent residence and correct the records to show your *actual* arrival dates."

I commenced the script I'd rehearsed. "Over time, my other projects may prove nearly as lucrative as Silk Fruit, without the legal entanglements." I stared directly at the PM's rep. "And, yes, my stasis box is rigged to destroy its contents if tampered with."

The momentary twitch of his eye told me my suspicions were correct and that, without continuing justification, my presence might otherwise have proven inconvenient. "I have every intention of living a quiet, productive life that will prove mutually beneficial for all of us."

The PM's rep nodded.

I rose, shook hands and gave the first seed to the Ag Commissioner. "I think I'm going to like living here."

●

I RAN DOWN THE CORRIDOR with lights flashing like a strobe to keep up with me. I'd programmed Emma to report that I'd slipped while attempting to retrieve Sandra's stasis unit and fell, irretrievably into the debris field, and was followed shortly after by the stasis unit when the clip on the safety line failed under the strain.

I'd loaded Sandra's stasis chamber into the shuttle to dispose of the evidence. Emma would report that auto-bots made repairs. That might raise eyebrows since the welds wouldn't look like auto-bot work. The loss of the Hetaera would be covered by insurance and the loss of a captain wouldn't amount to much.

I entered my quarters and dragged my stasis box out. "The shuttle's programmed to auto-return. Where's Sandra?"

"Auto-doc."

"She's all right?"

"Fine."

I left the stasis box at a connecting corridor and ran to sickbay. Sandra emerged from the Auto-doc. She rose from the bed, blinked a few times and shook her head.

I handed her the dress I'd bought on the planet.

It didn't fit well. I'd never bought women's clothes before.

"I'm on countdown," Emma said, "to forget everything that's happened since the accident, so you'd best get moving."

We retrieved the stasis box and headed for the shuttle bay. "Why were you in the Auto-doc?" I asked Sandra.

"Emma made modifications I'll need to be a good wife."

I stop dead and gazed at the overhead.

Emma's voice was soft around me. "I figured out how to loosen some of her inhibitions, so she can tell you when you're full of it. You did a good job on the planet, but between your mom and me, you've had someone looking out for you since before you were born. Didn't think I could just cut you loose."

I should have resented being dismissed as an incompetent adult, but instead, hoped I took some of Emma with me. "I love you, Emma. I wish I could hug you."

"Yeah, yeah, quit dallying."

We made our way to the shuttle bay. "I guess you'll purge me from your data banks."

"Course not. You were a learning experience. I'm only erasing a few fiddly details that might make the authorities suspicious. Have a wonderful life."

I watched the lights go out in the corridors behind me and hoped Emma would be assigned a better captain next time.

————————

Stephen Sottong is a retired engineering librarian whose current passion is writing fiction and science-fiction. He lives in beautiful Humboldt County in northern California behind the Redwood Curtain. The area has the tallest trees in the world and some of the most stunning scenery imaginable.

In addition to writing, he is a co-teacher of a basic beekeeping course and maintains web pages for non-profit organizations.

https://stephensottong.com

Big Top

by Sonia Orin Lyris

ARIANA MARLAN RUMALA GAVE WHAT she hoped was a captain-like nod as one-by-one her colorful crew ambled, slid, or slithered past, packs in each hand, tentacle, or fur-hidden grasp.

Was she ready?

At her side, Kip bounced on his toes, lips widening around fangs that overlapped his lower jaw.

"Gonna change the name? Repaint?" he asked.

She'd been raised on this fluxship. Big Top, her father had named it. The man was fascinated by ancient circuses, grand shows where anything could happen.

"Yes," Rumala answered. Hell, yes. Something more sober than this ludicrous red-and-white striped hull, reminiscent of the huge tents of old Earth that hosted all manner of strangeness.

She chewed her lower lip, forced herself to stop, and squared her stance. *Look like a captain.*

Kip shrugged white-furred shoulders. "Everyone knows your dad's ship."

Rumala glared at the genmod Human. Kip was a competent sublight Nav, she reminded herself.

"Call her captain," said Murmurk quietly, gaze on his tablet, reviewing the manifest.

Murmur, an endo-bio Sivid-Cesstine-Elabara-Brae, stood nearly tall enough to brush the ceiling with his bare, pink head, his earlobes bound behind his neck in his species' formal fashion.

59

Rumala had likewise gone to some trouble for her own formal uniform. Blue on blue, as unlike her father's casual yellow-and-red as possible.

"Sorry," Kip said. "Known you since you were—"

Knee high to an Engedu, he was about to say. Then the story about that one time....

Murmurk interrupted. "Supplies to unpack, Kip."

Had it been a mistake, to call back her father's old crew? She could have started over. Some of these people had known her in diapers.

Kip's white-furred face scowled. "I'm Nav One."

"You could be Nav Two," Murmurk said pleasantly, his tone at odds with the threat. "I'd wager Stranz would be happy to move up. Everyone works."

"Going," Kip muttered, lips in a pout under his fangs. He slunk out the door, which, at Rumala's gesture, spiraled shut.

A new crew would have brought problems, too. If she could have found one. What sensible crew of any species—exo, endo, or ceph—went out under an untested captain?

Rumala looked through the wide bridge window at Donovan Station, glittering with lights of many colors.

The window was an actual mono-diamond viewport, not a screen, as one might find on a normal fluxship. The bridge was detailed with expensive bio-teak and garish gold trim, walls and ceilings painted by famous artists. On a nearby wall, a monkey rode a unicycle.

She kept expecting her father to show up, drunk and yelling, the crew ignoring orders that didn't make sense, smoothly ensuring that *Big Top* didn't get stuck in flux, miss a station, or run out of air.

Then, one day, her father was dead. Shouldn't have been a surprise, given his love affair with intoxicants.

Suddenly Rumala owned a fluxship.

Rumala felt Murmurk's assessing look, met his red, drooping eyes.

"Captain."

"Yes?"

"Honored to be your Second. But there are things I need to know." He tapped the tablet with a glinting, pale claw. "You've hired the old crew." He nodded approval. "Also the most expensive Flux Nav Myndympar twins your father ever engaged. You pay lavishly for their fame. Why?"

Rumala felt herself tighten. Nav was one of the many huge expenses of a fluxship. Also the slush, a costly set of rare minerals the flux drive required. Accumulated docking fees and maintenance, too, while her father's estate got sorted. Licensing, food, medical. Crew.

The Myndympar twins. Few species could take a fluxship into the superluminal dimension. They were not cheap.

All in all, moving a fluxship from one point to another required a shocking amount of money. If only her father had left her some.

"Ariana. It's your ship. Just tell me why," Murmurk said.

Rumala stared at the moving lights through the monodiamond viewport. Only a few were fluxships, painted in vivid, brilliant themes.

"There'll be ship chatter," Rumala answered. "I want it to be about the Nav twins." *Not about me.* "We'll need more contracts, and soon."

"A good call, then."

Rumala exhaled relief.

"May I see the financials, Captain?" Murmurk added.

"Of course," she said with a pang of dread. "At Pavo." After they had made the delivery and earned the bonus.

"Our passenger," Murmurk said. *Cargo,* he didn't say—he didn't use crew slang. "Does Noodles have suitable provisions?"

Suitable for someone who could afford a fluxship to himself, Murmurk meant.

Rumala's job as captain was to safely wed multiple forces: unforgiving hard vacuum, the insanity of flux, a variegated crew, and whatever cargo contract an untested captain could obtain.

"I did not skimp on provisions," she replied, trying to not think of the many debts she'd incurred.

A tone hailed. Rumala's private overlay screen flashed.

The cargo had arrived.

●

KYMINON TARCHON, HUMAN UNMOD, ELEVEN Standard years old, strode onto *Big Top*. He and his entourage of ten, all Human, stood tightly in the entryway, dressed in shades of gray and brown, trimmed with black.

The heir to Tarchon Enterprises adjusted a suit cuff that

sparkled darkly, holding himself with a poised assurance.

Rumala wished she'd been as self-possessed at his age. Or now, even.

Tarchon's people looked around with uniform expressions of disapproval. On either side of Tarchon stood a woman and man dressed in the darker spectrum of the entourage's color palette. Introduced as his mentor, Gemend, and his steward, Dryht, they had the bearing of bodyguards.

Murmurk addressed Tarchon in his low-timbred voice. "Greetings. I am Second, Command Two, named Murmurk, who is Sivid-Cesstine-Elabara-Brae. This is Captain Rumala, Human."

It wasn't always obvious what species a person was, so custom required declaration.

Kyminon Tarchon's brow creased. "Are there two captains Rumala, then?"

Ariana Rumala blinked, then again, and felt something wobble inside her. Tarchon, she realized, had chosen *Big Top* because of her father.

"My father..." Rumala cursed the unsteadiness of her voice. She cleared her throat. "My father died last year. Didn't you know?"

Gemend spoke. "Mux Tarchon has far more important things to attend to than the death of a minor celebrity."

Rumala felt her face warm. Her father was famous on multiple star systems—actor, director, and muse.

At Gemend's words, a flicker of annoyance creased the boy's face. "My MaDa passed not long ago, as well," he said to

Rumala. "I return to my home planet Pavo for the funeral. I am sorry for your loss, Captain."

"And I for yours, Mux Tarchon," Rumala said softly. She took a breath and smiled, hoping for the right mix of compassion and confidence. "Welcome aboard *Big Top*. We'll be en route for Pavo as soon as we're cleared for departure. Murmurk will show you to your quarters."

Murmurk took a step aft in the passageway, turning back as Tarchon remained.

"The journey is four standard days?" Tarchon asked.

"Yes," Rumala replied. "Mostly sublight. One flux transit."

"But you have sufficient supplies for longer, do you not?"

"Certainly, Mux Tarchon," answered Murmurk. "A full thirty days, as required. You may be reassured."

Kyminon Tarchon nodded. "I will see my quarters now."

●

THE REMAINING CREW STROLLED, SCAMPERED, crawled, or rolled onto the ship, each pausing to greet Rumala. Grins, gapes, happy bounces, and a few tentacle wraps and paw touches.

"How much you've grown!"

"Naw, Toppy has shrunk!"

Neha, better known as Stick—and as Medical One—exhaled a feathery voice. "A well-made choice to keep *Big Top*." She tilted her horned head toward Rumala, who put her palm on the exo-bio's carapace in greeting, feeling the subtle pulsing beneath.

"Almost sent it to auction instead," Rumala quipped. But in truth, she had been tempted to do just that.

Bequeathed to my daughter, as long as she keeps it in the black.

And he didn't mean deepspace.

Behind her, a skittering of nails, a hiss of motion. "You've grown," Nkalafar said wetly from below, with his leftmost mouth—the polite one. He stared up.

Rumala crouched to touch the head of the footstool-high creature. He darted back on many feet, teeth clacking. Her hand brushed empty air. An old game between them. They both laughed.

In the common room, Rumala looked over the collected, colorful crew.

Stranz, or Star, twittered excitedly from the floor, oozing slightly as Kip misted her with water to keep her damp. Husrus, a fuzzy gray-blue creature better known as Ball, hung from the ceiling by his tentacle. Stick folded herself into a bucket chair like an umbrella, and Noodles splayed across the open doorway, stretching her appendages, humming slightly.

Warm smiles from those who could. From others, an equivalent: Star's fins curved upward, Ball's recessed mouth opened wide, showing flickers of blue. Stick made a horizontal line with half her body. Noodles twined some of her limbs together, letting them spin open.

Rumala felt warmed by these familiar faces from her years aboard *Big Top*.

All of them, including the Nav twins watching remotely

from their heavy-air chamber, had agreed to defer payment until the contract's conclusion. The on-time delivery bonus would cover it all.

Not Rumala's debt, no, but that could wait.

Rumala glanced at the door, where her father used to stand, gesturing at each of them with a flask, or a smoke, joking, breaking into song, and—despite being obnoxious—somehow making everyone feel good.

"I know I'm not him," she said, looking back at them. "It'll be different. A tighter ship."

Before she could say another word, the rest of the crew piped up.

"Remember that one time, Ari wearing Noodle's scarf, riding stem to stern on Nkal's head?"

"Dropping Thom's gin currants everywhere, so she could find her way back?"

"Thom was furious!"

"We missed you, Ari."

"Captain Rumala," Murmurk corrected.

"We called him Thom," said Kip.

"Right," Rumala replied tightly. "But he treated *Big Top* like a party yacht. I'm treating it like a business."

Otherwise, why had she studied astrophysics, ship-nav, operations, and finance at university? It all came down to a simple equation: more money in than out. Something her father had never grasped.

"Missed you." said Star, her body rippling yellow and orange.

They all knew that Rumala and her father had fought bitterly after her mother's death. He drank too much, spent too much, and was often unpleasant.

All in the past.

She shook her head to clear it. Time to focus. "This job is easy: passenger transport. Let's do it, folks, do it well, and on time. Then..." she looked around at all of them. "Everyone gets paid."

Rumala was met with bland looks.

"What's for next meal?" Star asked brightly.

At talk of food, Noodles' limbs rippled happily.

●

NOODLES DRAPED A SOFT TENTACLE across Rumala's shoulder affectionately, tilted her soft, wedge-shaped purple head close, and hummed. "Will the cargo be eating with us at dinner, captain?"

Rumala's father hardly ever transported people for pay. But artists, musicians, actors, radicals, mystics—and the insane— *those* he welcomed aboard with gracious enthusiasm. Mealtimes were full of chaos, motion, music, and wild intoxicants.

As a child and teen, Rumala had sat in the corner on a bucket seat, eyes and ears wide at the astounding conversations and performances her father's guests provided.

Quite the education. Only in retrospect did it seem an odd way to grow up.

"That would be traditional, yes." Rumala answered Noodles.

"Fancy?"

Tarchon Enterprises spread its fingers across the galaxy. The company logo was ubiquitous. She could not imagine such wealth.

"The big table. Place settings. Napkins."

"Fancy!" Noodles replied, dancing her head back and forth on her very flexible neck. "Good wine and smoke?"

"He's eleven."

"No wine or smoke," Noodles affirmed.

●

AT DINNER, TARCHON BORE WITHOUT reaction the frequent whispered advice from Gemend and Dryht at his sides. But when he looked across the table at the crew, Rumala saw hints of wonder.

Few fluxship crews were this diverse. Common wisdom held that better cohesion was achieved with one or two species, not an assortment like this one. Credit to her father for that, at least—he knew how to assemble a team.

Noodle's food was better than Rumala's memory—stunningly delicious yet customized for each. Conversation faded, replaced by chewing, slurping, sighing, grinding, and slight splashes as Star flopped her soft point into a dish of glistening wet something.

Only the Myndympar Nav twins, and Nkal with his Engedu's tendency to make people of all species throw up when they saw him eat, took meals privately.

"When last I traveled superluminally," Tarchon said, during a break in the meal's courses, "I was younger and heavily sedated. Flux is quite brief, as I understand it."

"Minutes at most," Rumala replied. Minutes that felt like hours, days, or years. "But you'll be sedated. It'll seem no more than a short nap." With some strange dreams, but no need to say that.

"No. I won't be sedated this time. I—"

Gemend's hand was on Tarchon's shoulder and she bent close to whisper. Then Dryht moved to add something in his other ear. Tarchon's jaw clenched.

When they straightened, Tarchon spoke to the air. "I wonder if I might choose my mentor and steward, at Pavo Station. Perhaps I'll even be allowed to wipe my own ass."

Dryht stiffened, exchanging a narrow-eyed look with Gemend.

Rumala looked anxiously across the crew, relieved to see them refraining from making jokes.

Tarchon mopped up the savory red sauce on his plate with a chunk of fresh-made bread and stuffed it into his mouth, his chewing the only sound in a room gone silent.

●

RUMALA AND MURMURK PEERED THROUGH a small viewport into the dim chamber of dense atmosphere that was the Nav twins' quarters. There, two large, slug-like creatures floated, entwined together. A pale limb waved in what seemed a greeting.

With Myndympar twins, it was best to keep conversation simple. From what anyone could glean, they only lived partially in the shared reality.

"All is well with you?" Rumala asked.

"We are affirmed," came the answer through a speaker.

"You have examined the flux nav route?"

"We touch. We kiss. We know."

Rumala exchanged an uncertain look with Murmurk, who gave a small shrug.

"Then we are... good?"

"We are affirmed."

Rumala blinked. "Right. You'll let us know if anything is not affirmed, yes?"

They didn't answer. After a time, Rumala and Murmurk left.

●

KIP SMILED WIDE, SHOWING SHARP teeth. "Almost at flux open, captain. Ready to transfer Nav control to Flux Nav." His eyes flickered to the display. "On your go."

"Systems?" Rumala asked.

From her feet, Nkal spoke. "Systems are go."

The moment had arrived. She looked at Murmurk, who nodded.

"Transfer navigation to Myndympar," Rumala made a gesture in the air to confirm, then another to send her voice ship-wide. "Five minutes to flux transfer. Everyone to quarters."

●

TO SAY THAT FLUX WAS unnerving was like saying that space is big.

Shifting out of canonical reality into something that turned spacetime inside out was challenging for the mind and senses. Few species were exempt. Even experienced crew sometimes made spectacular messes in their cabins. Or lost their minds entirely.

Nkal skittered from the bridge to his quarters, nails making a hissing sound on the floor.

Kip buckled in. Rumala and Murmurk sat nearby, snapping harnesses.

Rumala had been through flux enough times to lose count, but never as captain. Elation and worry warred within her, weighted with the strangeness of barely-remembered flux, which was never quite as you expected it to be.

Kip counted down. At five, he gestured, as if flipping an old fashioned light switch—humor—and Nav control transferred to the Myndympar twins.

She blinked. Around her, the ship melted.

●

One learned to remind oneself of many things during flux.

It's flux.

Taste flooded hearing. Bright sounds flashed across vision.

A formless knife wanted to cut through her, rend her from herself.

Just flux.

One learned not to panic.

It'll be okay.

It always felt as if the trip had gone on too long. Maybe this time was the last time. Stuck forever.

Don't panic.

But it was true: some ships never came back.

Only flux. It'll be —

A flash like a nova ripped through her body. Were her eyes open or closed? She couldn't tell.

Just flux.

Wait — did that happen every time? She couldn't remember.

Flux. What's flux?

The roaring in her mind was so loud she couldn't think.

But that was okay because, also, she didn't exist.

What am I?

Then it was over.

●

RUMALA SWALLOWED HARD IN A dry throat. With a trembling hand she reached for a water bulb.

"Good times," croaked Kip with bravado, his face as white as his fur. His gaze flickered across the mid-air status reports. "Systems are...green. Medical...green, though cargo made a mess. Nav...oh, *shit.*"

Rumala leaned forward. "What?"

Kip's mouth went flat around his fangs.

"We are not where we are supposed to be." He looked like he might be sick. "Not even close."

A cold wash of fear slid through Rumala's insides.

"Where are we?"

●

"The edge of the galaxy," Kip whispered.

"The flat, technically speaking," Murmurk added.

Rumala skimmed Kip's screen over his shoulder.

"It does happen," Murmurk said. "However rarely. Theoretically, a jump can go anywhere."

Or nowhere, the ship never heard from again.

Which was why you never hired bargain basement Flux Nav. Or put a new captain at the helm.

She should have taken Second position right off. Let Murmurk select the crew, captain the ship. What had she been thinking?

Murmurk gripped her shoulder briefly. "I'll go talk to Flux Nav. By your leave, captain?"

His steady grasp and calm tone brought her back.

She met his red eyes and gave a tight nod.

●

Rumala hurried to the common room where Kyminon Tarchon and his attendants waited. Tarchon looked rough—clothes rumpled, expression drawn. Transit had clearly been unpleasant. Maybe next time he'd accept a sedative.

If there was a next time.

Rumala summoned her best game face. "A small detour," she said lightly. "Won't take long. In the meantime, for your viewing pleasure..."

The lights dimmed as she gestured, the viewport shifting from blackout to clear, highlighting an astonishing display.

A grand wash of starlight lit their faces. Flat-on, the unmistakable ellipsoid of home swirled out into four great, sweeping arms.

Everyone stared.

A dizzying view that made clear to Rumala how very, very lost they were.

"Unacceptable," Dryht snapped loudly, breaking the spell. "Mux Tarchon has an important schedule to keep."

Rumala knew. In her private overlay screen was a countdown timer, the green seconds ticking by.

"I understand, Mux Dryht," Rumala said solicitously. "Back on track shortly, I assure you. Some good news: for the meal, Noodles is making something very special. It includes chocolate."

Tarchon stared out the viewport. Everyone else gave Rumala looks as cold as space.

She felt her smile go brittle, excused herself, and subvocalized a summons to Control, Nav, and Systems.

74

●

"The twins urge patience," Murmurk had told her on the way to the bridge.

Patience?

On the bridge, Kip grinned at Rumala, bouncing. "Good news first or bad?"

"Kip, damn it." she said tightly.

"Sorry. The good: we're on a mapped flux-tube. The bad: it's known-unstable. Good: we got here in one piece anyway. Bad: it's unidirectional."

Unidirectional.

Rumala's stomach dropped.

From the table, Star's primary fin went limp, a sign of fear.

"Other flux tubes?" Rumala managed.

Kip shook his head slowly. "Not this far out. Nothing mapped."

Nkal, who stood at Star's side, rippled back and forth on his many feet. "The Flux Navs got us here. Make them get us back."

"There is no *making* them," Murmurk replied.

Kip's shoulders hunched. "Maybe this is how fluxships disappear. Lost on the other side of a one-way."

"Don't say that," Rumala snapped.

"Bad luck," Star agreed.

"I'll explain them," Nkal said angrily with his rightmost mouth, the one that his species had evolved for killing prey. "Explain them good."

"You will not," Rumala snapped, imagining all-too clearly how badly that could go. "I will."

●

BUT THE NAV TWINS GAVE Rumala no more than they had given Murmurk. One word: patience.

Rumala strode the passageways, thoughts racing across survival supplies, the crew, flux, the Myndympar, and ending at the cargo contract.

Without the bonus, *Big Top* was stuck at Pavo station, buried under fees, and Rumala's career as a fluxship captain was over.

And the crew didn't get paid.

With a gesture, she cleared her overlay countdown clock, panicked, brought it back, dismissed it again.

Passing the darkened common room, she glimpsed Kyminon Tarchon, a small boy framed by the star-studded swirl of the Milky Way galaxy.

"We'll get you to Pavo, Mux Tarchon," she said into the dimness, not sure who she was reassuring.

"It's spectacular," he said.

She went to him. "You've seen it before, surely?"

"Pictures. Not the same."

She looked with him, felt her breath catch in her throat.

Stars and stars. Swirls of eons. The birthplace of humanity and all known species. Everything all of them had ever known.

"I would have thought you..." She trailed off.

"Yes?"

"Could go where you wanted to."

"You'd be mistaken, captain. I'm eleven."

But so well trained it was easy to forget.

"I'm a legal child, captain. I'll be named my MaDa's heir at Pavo, but without any control until I reach my majority. My only power is what I might do, someday, if I remember to care. My education will see to that." His voice dripped with bitter sarcasm.

"Is it really so bad?"

He gave her a look, snorted. "You, with your fluxship and your freedom. Me, I've seven more years of intensive study, followed by a lifetime of soul-grinding work." He returned his attention to the view, his voice dropping to a whisper. "But for the moment, I have this."

Rumala understood. For the moment, she had a fluxship.

With a blink, she brought back the countdown clock. Seconds dribbled past as she went in search of Murmurk.

●

MURMURK'S RED EYES WERE THOUGHTFUL. "Artists, the Myndympar twins. They see themselves as such, anyway. That is why your father hired them. Give them more time."

"This is not art," Rumala hissed, "and my father was a fool." She turned from Murmurk's scrutiny, her hand on the smooth wall of the corridor, a great wave of panic threatening. "We're due at Pavo in three hours."

"We won't make that, captain."

"I know, damn it."

"Your father was no fool. Even if he was at times foolhardy."

She turned to Murmurk. "He was insolvent. He left me a fluxship without a cent to fund it."

Murmurk's mouth opened in surprise. "But how did you afford repairs? Licenses? Docking fees?"

She swallowed hard. "Borrowed it all. The on-time bonus would have..." She shook her head, dismissing the thought. "The ship will be seized at Pavo. Auctioned to cover fees. For the crew — nothing." Her voice fell to a whisper. "I'm a bigger fool than he was."

Murmurk's hand on her shoulder was gentle. "Why didn't you tell us, Ari?"

She felt tears threaten. "No crew is going to sign on with a first-time captain who also happens to be broke."

A soft smile came to his white-and-pink lips. "You think we came for the money? They'll understand."

Rumala wasn't so sure.

●

THE COUNTDOWN CLOCK WENT TO zero, numbers ticking past in red. The bonus was gone.

At the meal, Rumala hardly ate. Afterwards, dishes and tables were cleared, a space made at the center of the room.

Ball circumnavigated limbs and chairs, then rolled up the

wall. With the microscopic hairs on his single hand, he grasped the flat ceiling, his fuzzy gray-blue body swinging like a holiday decoration. As Stick began to juggle, Ball caught the sacks with a recessed grasp and tossed them back. Before long, the juggling act included every willing appendage in the room.

Nkal entered and sent a truss-spinner across the room. It trailed gold and green lines, made a slow bounce from surface to surface, eventually returning to him.

Murmurk unfolded his zither and began to strum. Noodles hummed and Star sang, the three voices setting up resonances that Rumala felt move her, blood and bone.

Rumala tucked herself into a seat to one side of the view-port, as she had so many times as a child. The familiar music and motion washed over her, along with a thick despair.

All the years at university, preparing to run a ship like a business instead of a party. If all were well now, she would stand, and, captain-like, tell everyone to get back to work.

But there was no work. Not until the Nav twins found them a way home.

She blamed herself for thinking she could captain a fluxship. Then her father, for wasting multiple fortunes.

None of which mattered now. Even if Murmurk was right that the crew would willingly delay being paid, the Nav twins certainly would not.

Assuming they made it back. And if they did, the ship would be taken, one slow, legal step at a time, starting the moment Pavo station checked her account and saw that *Big Top* couldn't afford to dock, let alone to leave.

The opening notes to a familiar old song were welcomed with cheers and squeaks. Stick and Noodles met in the middle of the room, fanned themselves open, each in their distinct way, and stepped close, folding through each other. It was a dance that few would ever see—their species were not often friends.

And that, Rumala realized, was the uniqueness of this crew: not only that they got along—remarkable enough—but that they danced together.

He would have been right there, in the doorway, grinning at the cacophony. Proud of the crew he had assembled.

A flask circled the room. She declined it, then again. The third time, she accepted—why not? She drank deep, something spiced and delicious. Someone handed her a uke, and she strummed it, surprised to discover that she remembered how after all these years.

Kyminon Tarchon watched in poorly disguised delight. But as the evening wore on, he turned to the viewport, his hand moving across something he held in his lap.

Rumala watched. He was sketching, she realized. On actual paper, with an ink-pen. He finished one, put it on a small pile to his side. He was drawing the galaxy.

Their home. Where Rumala was supposed to get them, safe and sound.

What was she doing here, partying?

Setting the uke aside, she left, and found herself in the Myndympar twins' visiting room.

"Twenty-five days," she said without preamble. "Out of food. Water. Air."

No response.

"Even you."

Silence.

"Damn it, say something."

Artists, Murmurk had told her. What was their art? Bankruptcy?

At last she gave up.

That night, in her bunk, Rumala tossed restlessly. The famous old adage was proving true: in space, bad decisions last forever.

She'd lost the ship. Assuming they didn't suffocate first.

When sleep finally took her, she dreamt of tests at university for which she had not studied, her father yelling incoherently, and Kyminon Tarchon, pen in hand.

She woke suddenly, rolled out of bed, and went in search of the cargo.

●

IN THE DARKENED COMMON ROOM sat Kyminon Tarchon, sketching intently. His pile of sketches had grown.

"Don't you have enough pictures yet, Mux Tarchon?" Rumala asked.

He nodded at a sketch pad from which he had been drawing blank pages. "Plenty left."

She approached. "Tell me why."

He barely glanced up, then traced a sketched galactic arm with a fingertip. "When I draw it, I know it."

Rumala leaned across and grabbed the pile of sketches.

"Hey," he shouted.

She leafed through the pages. "Very nice."

"No, they're crap," he said, glaring, "but that's not the point. They're mine. I need them."

She offered him the thick pile. He snatched it back, tucking it under the pad and away from Rumala.

"Need them, why?"

"To remember." He gestured at the viewport, the swirl of stars, brilliant against the vastness of black. "A hundred thousand light years across. Home to fifty billion habitable planets, three hundred and ninety-seven sentient species. I had to see it, before..." He trailed off.

"Before?"

"Before I grow up and become so educated that such things are irrelevant. When I'm dull and boring and hate myself."

She stared at him, rocked by the viciousness of his tone.

At her reaction, he chuckled in dark amusement. "You don't understand."

The ship, the crew—her captainship—all knocked off-course by one spoiled boy's desire to avoid his outrageous fortune.

"Right. I think I do," she said coolly. "Our relationship is legally defined. You've a right to oxygen, food, and all the care and protection you might need *en route*. As captain, I'm obliged to see that my crew keeps you hale and whole until you safely disembark."

He made a dismissive gesture. "I know all this."

"Then you also know that you're subject to my absolute authority during transit, should anything threaten my ship."

My ship. For the moment, anyway.

He shrugged. "I read my contracts. So?"

"So finish up, Mux Tarchon. Go tell the Nav twins to release *Big Top.*"

His expression went blank. "I don't know what you mean."

The denial was all the confirmation she needed. It meant the detour was no accident, which meant that Nav knew perfectly well how to get them home. They were waiting on something.

Someone.

A wash of relief went through her. For the first time in days, she felt herself exhale.

Patience, my ass.

On the heels of relief came a flare of fury. She was tempted to treat Tarchon like the adult he pretended to be, to quote space code and law to him, to rub his nose in the potential consequences of his actions.

But as the boy stared at the Milky Way, his face bathed in starlight and eyes wide with wonder, she saw something inside him struggling to live, and knew she would not.

"I had to," he whispered, his voice shredded with grief.

Rumala hadn't understood before. She did now. Her anger melted.

She crouched, bringing her gaze level with Tarchon's. "You've a lot to learn." His eyes narrowed. "So do I," she added.

Confusion flickered across his features.

How to explain?

SPACE OPERA DIGEST 2021

"All your education..." She shook her head. "All mine, too." She gave him a rueful smile. "So much we don't know. A galaxy's worth. I hope you'll learn that you can be an adult and still care about—" She gestured out the viewport. "That."

As Rumala stood, the music from the previous meal came to memory, the taste of the flask, the patterns and motion of the dance. "And you know what? I think you will. Because..." She gave a short laugh. "If I can, anyone can."

Rumala pretended not to notice him blinking, the slight snuffle. Instead she gazed with him through the mono-diamond port at the many, many stars.

Presently she said, "Finish your sketches, Mux Tarchon. We need to get home."

●

THE FLUX TRIP TO PAVO was just as exciting as the first one, leaving Rumala with the same sensation of a pounding hangover.

Kip was ecstatic. "An unmapped flux hole? Bounty!"

Through the bridge mono-diamond viewport, Pavo Station was a cluster of rippling, blinking, glittering lights. On Rumala's private overlay was a report of Pavo and *Big Top*'s AIs busily negotiating an approach path.

Well, the bounty for the new flux hole would cover the crew's salary, anyway. The Nav Twins would have to go without.

In any case, none of it would be Rumala's problem. She'd never captain again.

The overlay report estimated docking time to be no sooner than an hour hence. That ought to do.

"Murmurk, my Second."

To this formal address, Murmurk turned with an inquiring look.

"Let me show you the financials."

She might as well go out with honor.

●

KYMINON TARCHON AND HIS ENTOURAGE stood in the entryway, ready to disembark.

The show must go on. One last time.

"A pleasure to have you aboard, Mux Tarchon," Rumala said, swallowing the wretchedness she felt. "Speaking for myself and the crew—"

"Captain," Tarchon said. "A moment?"

Gemend and Dryht's expressions turned sour. "Mux Tarchon," Gemend began, as Dryht bent to whisper in his other ear.

"I've an idea," Tarchon said cheerfully to Rumala. "I'll send a time-capsule to myself, to be opened upon my majority, detailing how I treasure my assistants' rich and unceasing advice."

Gemend and Dryht silently straightened.

Tarchon nodded to Rumala, who led him aft to the bridge. The door spiraled shut behind them, leaving them alone.

"Captain," he said, "I apologize for keeping my intention from you. But I am not sorry to have attended that dinner. I've never seen people so happy together. I didn't realize..." He in-

SPACE OPERA DIGEST 2021

haled. "That it was possible."

Somehow, his words only made things worse. Rumala managed a nod.

He looked through the mono-diamond viewport at Pavo station, at the many ships weaving their slow way from one place to another. "Maybe I'll be your cargo again someday."

So he knew the slang. Well, he was a bright one.

"Also," he said, turning back to her. "I am not sorry to have seen the galaxy. I'll never forget."

"So you bribed the Flux Nav twins," she said bitterly.

His look was earnest surprise. "I didn't bribe them. In a sense, they bribed me."

"What?"

"They're very capable, you ought to know. Managed to get into my private comms pre-boarding. Asked me about a small detour." He smirked. "Anything to delay the rest of my life."

"What?" Rumala repeated, louder.

He chuckled at her reaction. "They told me that you couldn't afford them. Or much else, for that matter. Well, you can now—check your balances." As he approached, the door spiraled open. He tapped the wall. "Thanks for the ride, captain. I'll be your cargo again. Just give me a few years."

With that, Kyminon Tarchon and his people left *Big Top*.

●

FROM THE CEILING, BALL SWUNG lazily back and forth, almost brushing Star, who hummed from where she was plastered against the wall.

Cross-species flirting? Rumala had watched these two for most of her life, and she still wasn't sure.

With her many arms, Noodles handed around bulbs of champagne. "First voyage! Saved the best for us."

Rumala was still in shock. Kyminon Tarchon had made good—there was now more than enough to cover the astronomical fees of the Nav Twins, and with the extra from the bounty for the newly mapped flux tube, Rumala could afford to pay the crew, and every Pavo Station fee.

All because Kyminon Tarchon wanted to see something extraordinary.

Before this celebratory moment, Rumala went to see the Myndympar twins.

"We like money," they told her. "We are affirmed."

There was no point in being upset with them. Artists, as Murmurk had said.

But she had asked them many questions, some of which they answered.

Their words seemed to imply they would not do this again without consulting her first. She wasn't sure.

Rumala downed her bulb, letting the sparkling brew lighten her already fast-improving mood.

Murmurk tapped his tablet with a long nail. "Comfortably in the black, captain. Everyone gets paid."

Cheers, squeaks, hums, and waving of various appendages greeted this news.

Murmurk's long look settled on Rumala. "Even you."

Rumala blushed, grinned to cover it, lifted her bulb in a toast, which everyone echoed. They drank together.

"Is it enough to repaint?" Kip asked. "To rename?"

"It is indeed, Nav One," answered Murmurk.

"Well? What's it to be, Ari?"

"Captain," corrected Murmurk.

"What's the new name of our ship?"

"Tell us, Ari!"

Eyes, ears, and various other sensing organs turned to Ariana Marlan Rumala, fluxship captain.

She looked at them each in turn. More than a business, this ship. If she had ever doubted it, she didn't now.

"Right," Rumala replied. "I've given it a good deal of thought." She grinned. "*Big Top* will do."

This time, the cheering, squeaking, and humming was even louder.

Sonia's stories have been published by *Asimov's SF Magazine, Wizards of the Coast, Uncle John's Bathroom Reader*, and Intel Corp. Her novels include *The Seer*, from Baen Books, and *The Stranger Trilogy*, from Knotted Road Press.

https://lyris.org/

Cycle Three

by Stephanie Mylchreest

The dark, boundless universe waited just outside. Natalie could get lost out there, and no one would ever find her. The thought made her feel like a bird unfurling broken wings, stretching for freedom from the confines of the ship.

"Ruby, diffuse rain aroma." Glancing around her sparse, gunmetal-gray living quarters, she blew out a series of quick breaths. She needed to relax. But her fingers drummed an anxious beat on the linoleum beneath her as she sat on the floor and leaned against the wall.

The day of the contest had arrived. She had to win a ticket back to Earth. Losing was not an option.

"Diffusion activated," replied her personal AI that controlled her residence.

Almost instantly, a damp, clean-air scent filled the room. Natalie inhaled deeply, drawing it inside, trying to quell the demons.

"Ruby, turn on noise simulator. Play rain shower."

"Turning on noise simulator."

The pitter-patter of rain falling on a tin roof played from the speakers imbedded in the ceiling, replacing the constant whoosh of oxygenators.

Natalie pushed herself away from the wall and lay down, stretching out fully on the cool floor, immersing herself in the sound. It almost felt like being in a real rain shower, minus the actual water.

The door buzzer intruded, loud and unexpected.

Natalie pushed herself up. She ran a hand over her hair and grimaced as she looked at her pale reflection in the mirror. Her stomach twisted at the thought of who might have pressed the buzzer. With a steadying breath, she hurried to the door and opened it.

Eric stared at her, blond hair curled like a Roman emperor, sneer intact. Commander of the ship. Possessive ex-boyfriend. The skin at the nape of Natalie's neck tightened.

"Ruby, turn off noise simulator." Natalie folded her arms over her chest, channeling her inner immovable object.

Eric moved into her space. A fistful of air between them.

She stepped back, accommodating him, her throat tight.

"It's not long now, Natalie." Eric arched a brow, his gaze roaming over her body as if he owned it.

She checked her watch, an antique given to her by her mother from before she left Earth, and pretended serpents weren't writhing in her gut. "Two more hours until the contest. I can almost taste the fresh air." She forced a smile and instantly regretted it, not wanting to encourage him. Turning her gaze away from him, she busied her hands adjusting her shirt.

"Can we sit down and talk for a moment?" Eric leaned closer. The air between them thickened, so sticky she couldn't breathe.

"Actually, I'm just heading out." Natalie slid past him, careful not to let her body touch his. He followed close behind until they were both in the hallway. "Ruby, close the door."

She hurried down the hallway, pulled the yellow invitation

out of her pocket, unfolded it and then folded it again.

Shoes squeaked on linoleum. A second pair, moving faster and behind her. Eric caught up to her several yards down the corridor.

"Is this the first contest they've invited you to?" His gaze flicked to the invitation.

Natalie nodded, her breath catching. He knew it was her first.

The competition. Open by invitation only to the highest credit earners. The prize; one cycle on Earth.

They turned a corner and she tightened her hold on the yellow paper. Took big steps to widen the gap between them.

"Don't lose that," he said, his tone odd.

Ahead, people crammed against a viewing window, staring at Earth. It had been in their sights since last Wednesday, the ship's speed increasing the closer they got due to their wildly eccentric orbit. Earth grew bigger and more beautiful each time Natalie saw it.

They paused, crushing up against the people in front of them, both trying to get a better view.

"I've got a good feeling for you this time." Eric moved his lips close to her ear. She felt his hand on the small of her back.

She tried to slide sideways, but there was nowhere to go through the wall of people. "Eric, please."

He seemed to pretend to not hear her.

With a sudden pivot, she took a step forward, pushing past Eric. She freed herself from the tangle of people and hurried down the corridor, toward the main hall where the contest would take place.

She glanced over her shoulder and saw Eric still in pursuit, his stride long and determined. It felt like a private drama playing out between the two of them. The hunted and the hunter all alone in the busy corridor.

A loud footfall and heavy breathing let her know that Eric had caught up to her again. Her skin seemed to catch fire where he took hold of her arm. He pulled her close to him.

"Let go of me," she said in a low voice, unable to hide the tremor.

"I just want to talk, Natalie. It will only take a moment." His firm voice and hand on her arm left no room for negotiation. He moved with confidence, not looking over his shoulder to see who was watching as he led her down a narrow hallway, deeper into the ship.

He paused outside his residence, and Natalie stiffened.

"Alana, open door," he commanded.

The door slid open.

He pulled Natalie inside and released her.

His larger residence held a generous bed below a small window, with the massive galaxy visible through it.

"Please, Eric." Natalie straightened her clothes and took a big step back. "I don't have a lot of time until the contest starts. I need this. You know I do." She widened her eyes, hoping an appeal to his sympathies might hurry along whatever he had planned.

"You're so focused on getting off the ship, you don't have time for me these days." His voice was coy, dangerous. He shifted closer, tightening the space between them.

Natalie stood a little taller, ignoring the knot in her gut. "We aren't together anymore, Eric."

He smiled again. Then he charged at her.

His body slammed into her before she had time to properly process what was happening. She flew backward and landed with a heavy thud on his bed, the air rushing out of the mattress and throwing his scent into the room.

"Alana, turn on noise simulator. Play rain shower." He smiled.

The pitter-patter of rain falling on a tin roof poured into the small space.

"What are you doing?" she demanded.

"I think you need some time to cool down before the contest. It'll help you focus."

She lay on the bed, watching him. She knew from experience that he could easily overpower her if she tried to leave now.

"Alana, open the door." He backed away and stepped out into the corridor. "Alana, close the door and keep it locked." He stared at her from outside, until the door shut.

She waited until she was sure he was gone, her breath coming out in ragged pants, before she sat up and approached the door.

She glanced at her watch. An hour and a half until the contest. She knew it was useless, but she tried anyway. "Alana, open the door."

"I'm not permitted to do that," replied the AI, which had been programmed to only respond to Eric's voice.

Natalie banged on the door and called out.

No reply.

She wondered if anyone could hear her if they were outside. With so many people living on the ship, the rooms were well sound-proofed. She folded and refolded her yellow invitation.

The minutes ticked by quickly, accompanied by the constant pitter-patter of rain falling on a tin roof. One hour to go. Eric would be back soon. He was just playing with her. Even he wouldn't be so cruel.

She paced up and down his residence. Forty-five minutes to go.

She banged on the door again and yelled louder, "Alana, open the door!"

"I'm not permitted to do that."

Desperation wrapped around Natalie, her chest tight and her mouth dry. Alana would never respond to her commands. She'd been programmed to respond to Eric alone. "Alana, contact security." Natalie paused, her eyes darting around the room. "The commander is in trouble."

"I'm not permitted to do that."

Half an hour to go. She needed to get out of there. She needed to get to the contest. Inside her head, she screamed.

Fifteen minutes to go. She wouldn't make it. He wasn't coming back. She screamed out loud this time, but no one heard.

All that remained, as the last minutes ticked away, was the pitter-patter of rain.

●

NATALIE LAY CURLED IN A ball on the floor when Eric returned.

He regarded her with cool indifference as she unfurled herself.

Her legs had lost circulation and she limped toward him. There were no words to say. The contest was over. Eric stood in the doorway with a satisfied smile. "Looks like we're stuck with each other for another three years, at least."

Her voice hoarse from calling out, she swallowed against a raw throat. "I hate you." She slid past him, her arms wrapped around herself.

"We'll get through it. We always do." He grinned.

Pivoting, Natalie headed down the hallway. Part of her wanted to turn around and slap him, a mixture of outrage and anger pulsing through her. But he was the commander of the ship. And she was…alone.

Her parents and brother were gone and it had always been hard for her to make friends. She was quirky. Different. Even as a teenager, she'd felt the darkness inside, pressing in on her like it wanted to own her. And Eric had made sure the few friends she had were no longer around.

It was like Eric had picked her on purpose. Courted her and made her believe he was someone else. Then revealed his true nature when there was no one left in her life to turn to.

Natalie felt as though her soul had disappeared as she walked toward the main hall, her anger fading. An empty vessel, she watched everyone as they waited for the victors' ceremony. Her hand twitched as she saw the victors congregate near the stage at one end of the hall. They'd won the chance to go to Earth, to spend a precious cycle in one of the few remaining habitable areas.

One victor, a woman from Natalie's section, waved, her face flushed from the excitement of her win. "What happened to you, Natalie?"

"I...decided not to enter this year."

"Maybe next cycle." Her neighbor's gaze darted back to where the victors stood before returning to Natalie's face. Natalie's pain must have been obvious, because the smile on the other woman's face faltered. She patted Natalie awkwardly on the arm and skipped back to the others.

Eric walked into the hall.

Natalie ducked her head as he approached. He continued past without acknowledging her and headed the stage to accept greetings and back slaps from the council members. He shook hands with the victors and took his place in front of the lectern.

The crowd's murmurs hushed.

"Ship 6500X will approach periapsis in eighteen hours." He tilted his chin and pursed his lips, and the light cast deep shadows over his face. "The ferry will approach to dock and take our victors to the upper-atmosphere terminal shortly thereafter. There, our victors shall return via a shuttle to spend one cycle on Earth."

Eric paused and looked at the victors. "Make the most of your time on Earth. Remember that we choose new commanders from the victors, following completion of their Earth-cycle. You'll be coming after my job, next."

The crowd laughed appreciatively, and Eric gave them a self-indulgent smile in return.

"A round of applause for our victors, please!" Eric stared directly at Natalie as the crowd erupted in cheers.

●

NATALIE STAYED IN HER ROOM for a week after the victors departed for Earth. It should have been her. But she remained on the ship, surrounded by darkness.

The hollow feeling inside her had grown, the darkness creeping inside, making her feel more alone than ever. No one would believe her if she told them about Eric. He was charming. Handsome. He could have any woman he wanted.

After the massive blow of losing another chance to go to Earth, her defences were down. Perhaps sensing that, Eric played nice. He brought her food, was kind and respectful. And as the hours passed, Ruby's digital voice kept her company, playing music from long ago, before humanity's numbers grew too vast for Earth to accommodate them.

The farther from Earth they traveled, the darker she felt. Just a single, insignificant woman on a mega-ship, one of hundreds of thousands that flew into outer space, only to return, time and time again, depositing and picking up the victors.

She was meant to be there. She was meant to be on Earth. Not trapped.

The first year of the cycle passed in a haze. She collected credits as frequently as she was able, Eric's presence always there.

She knew that acquiescing to him was the only realistic option. He was just too powerful. And even though he'd never hurt her badly, he'd let her know in hundreds of subtle ways that he could, if he wanted to.

The thought was frightening and left Natalie happy to mollify him. Because really, there was no other choice.

●

THEY WERE ALMOST AT THE half-way point of the cycle, the farthest point from Earth on their eccentric three-year orbit. The point when they began their long journey back to Earth, the ship remaining at speeds low enough to prevent time dilation becoming an issue. Every time Natalie looked at her watch from her mother, she remembered that minor adjustments were made to all of the ship's clocks every twelve months, usually just a few milliseconds to ensure the ship's systems matched those on Earth.

It was only a few milliseconds, but it was enough to drive home the vast, impossible distance between herself and Earth.

Thinking about it all made her heart ache as she sat eating her breakfast in the cafeteria, fork in hand, pushing food around her plate. She looked up as an older woman with an East Quarter scarf took a seat at her table.

"Good morning." The older woman offered a kind smile

and a steady gaze. "I'm Abla."

"Good morning," Natalie replied. Her lips moved into a semblance of a smile, an automatic response. She dropped her eyes and stared at the yellow paper lining her breakfast tray, hoping Abla would eat in silence and then move on. But the woman didn't take the hint.

Natalie glanced up at her.

"I've seen you around," Abla said, her kind gaze not shifting from Natalie's face.

"Oh." She looked at Abla out of the corner of her eye.

"I joined this ship on the last cycle," continued Abla in a cheerful voice. "I came on the ferry from the upper-atmosphere terminal. I'd been cycling in the East Quarter. Are you okay? I've wanted to speak to you for a while. You seem...sad."

Natalie couldn't speak. Her throat felt as though it had closed up. Hot tears burned her eyes. She blinked and looked away, her gaze coming to rest on Eric at a nearby table.

He watched them with open interest.

"It's okay," Abla said in a soft, understanding voice as she slid her chair closer and patted the back of Natalie's hand. "You're not alone. It's okay."

Natalie could feel the darkness tugging at her. Abla's touch pulled her back, steadying her. After a few forced breaths, Natalie touched a loose fist to her chest and introduced herself.

They sat side by side for a while without speaking.

"Why did you request a transfer to join our ship?" Natalie asked the older woman, when the silence stretched out too long. Even with the hollow feeling in her chest, Natalie could tell she was being rude. And Abla seemed nice. Decent. The first person on their big, impersonal ship who'd noticed her in a long time and wasn't intimidated by Eric's constant hovering.

At her words, Abla's face creased into a beautiful, sad smile. "It's complicated. There were too many painful memories distracting me on my old ship. I wanted to maximize my chances of making it to Earth."

Natalie nodded. She understood. She'd transfer too, but Eric would never approve her request. "You're trying to win an invitation to the contest?"

Abla nodded.

"I wish it was easier to get to Earth."

"I know," replied Abla. "But there's just too many of us. There are so many people, so many ships. Even with all the space, they still need to stagger the orbital ellipses."

"Some people never get to Earth."

"Yes, that's right."

"I worry that will be me. That I'm never going to make it." She glanced at Eric again.

●

ALONE IN A QUIET CORNER of the library, Natalie sat at one of the modular tables and benches against the far wall and leaned her forehead against the window. She looked at the ribbons of milky light stretching across the sky as she contemplated the hundred billion stars spiraling out from the black center of the galaxy. She could see her reflected face on the smooth surface and frowned.

Approaching footfalls made her sit up. She glanced down the row of shelves to see Eric striding toward her. He'd found her.

He slid next to her, his thigh pressed against hers. Her shoulder tensed, and she tried to pull away. But the wall and thick glass blocked her escape. He'd cornered her.

"Will you have dinner with me tonight?" He rested an elbow on the table and leaned farther into her space.

Natalie swallowed against a dry throat. He'd never give up. "No, I'm sorry. Not tonight."

"It's okay, Natalie." He puts his hand on hers. To anyone else, the gesture might look sweet. But his grip tightened. It hurt. "Stop it," she said through gritted teeth, staring at the open book on the table. The library's collection of physical books was small, but the musty pages made Natalie feel connected to Earth.

She turned her head and looked out the window. With Eric beside her, Earth had never felt farther away.

Eric shifted away from her with surprising suddenness, removing his hand and adding an inch between their legs with a subtle lean of his body.

A shadow fell on her book. Natalie looked up to see Abla standing beside them, palms on her hips.

"Hello, Commander. Hello Natalie," Abla said in a pleasant voice, but her eyes narrowed as she looked at Eric in a way that left no doubt she saw who he really was.

"I'll be seeing you around," said Eric, an unmistakable tone of annoyance in his voice as he pushed to his feet. The chair scraped against the ground.

Abla waited until he disappeared behind the librarian's desk before taking his place next to Natalie. "He won't take no for an answer, right?"

"We used to date a cycle ago. He's very…possessive."

"He certainly acts like he owns you." Abla let out a quiet sigh. "I've met people like him before. Has he been violent toward you?"

Natalie felt a flush of shame at the surprising question. The window pulled her attention again. After several long moments, she gathered the strength to speak. "I'm worried that if I keep saying no, all hell will break loose. He could cross a line."

Abla let out a bitter laugh. "I'm guessing he's already crossed a line. When you're in a relationship like that, it can be easy to let your standards shift and next thing you know, you're putting up with things you never would have in the past." Abla paused. "Let's get you off this ship. We're going to win a ticket out of here. We can request a transfer to a different ship at the upper atmosphere terminal after our time on Earth. Ships are coming and going all the time."

Natalie turned to face the older woman. "Do you really think we can?"

"I do," replied Abla, her expression a mix of sadness and hope.

Natalie knew she wasn't the only one with skeletons in her closet. She reached for Abla's hand.

●

WITH A NEW GOAL MOTIVATING them, they worked in earnest. Natalie knew she could gain easy credits by completing the prescribed physical activity. She ran and swam every day with little effort, falling into the meditative state she loved. The darkness receded when she hit the treadmill, and her anxiety abated. It was just her and her body.

But Abla taught her other ways to get credits. She showed Natalie how to create things with her hands. They used polymer clay to make beautiful objects. They sewed and knitted. Abla taught her how to tend the garden beds, how to water and fertilize the plants until tiny buds blossomed and burst into fruit and vegetables.

As a mostly closed system, the people living on the ship grew all their food in vast gardens. Almost everything, from human waste to the water they bathed in, was reused, recycled, broken down and built back up again. When the ferry arrived at periapsis, it rebalanced the ship as necessary. For the first time, Natalie learned to appreciate the cycle, feeling more in touch than ever with the systems that kept them alive.

Several months after their first meeting, Natalie and Abla were in the garden, pruning their small patch of heaven. Natalie exclaimed over the tiny green strawberries she'd found.

"They're adorable," Abla replied, wiping a smudge of dirt off her cheek with the back of her hand. "Well done."

Natalie stared at her for a moment, feeling emboldened by the bonds of friendship that had grown alongside their fruit and vegetable patch. "Tell me why you need to get to Earth."

"You tell me, first," Abla replied, tilting her head to the side. "I know it's not just Eric."

"It's something I've wanted for a long time," Natalie said, her eyes drifting over the green hues of the garden bed. If she didn't focus on the curved wall beyond, she could almost pretend she was Earth-side already. "My older brother was born on Earth. He was six when my family boarded the ship. He only has fragments of memories, but I've always thought that they buoyed him. He's different from me." She paused for a long moment, a hand trailing over the strawberry plant.

"Go on," said Abla.

"He never has dark feelings inside him."

"Where is your family now?"

"My brother is sick. They were transferred to a ship with a specialist hospital. They write to me."

"That must be hard."

"It is."

"I have a darkness inside me, too," said Abla, after a pause.

Natalie felt the warmth of being understood rush through her. "So you know what it's like. If I don't make it to Earth, if I give in to this place, the darkness will take me. It's all around us, here. I want to feel the heat of the sun, feel real rain on my face. I don't even care about being selected as a commander. I just want to feel dirt between my toes. Breathe real air."

"Yes," said Abla. "That's how I feel too. My daughter was like you, like me. She needed to get to Earth. She had the same yearning."

Natalie sensed she should wait, that there was more coming.

Abla looked down. "She died last year. She just couldn't bear it any longer."

Natalie's throat ached. "I'm so sorry, Abla."

Their eyes met.

"She never made it to Earth. So I need to do this for her. Everything is so fleeting. I don't want to run out of time."

Natalie felt an unfamiliar urge and reached out to touch Abla's hand. For a moment, they held hands over the strawberry plants. She felt a surge of emotion: sadness for Abla's loss mixed, with sudden gratitude that she was alive, even on this ship. She'd never felt it so strongly, knowing death could be just a breath away. The thought was dizzying.

"We have to keep going," Abla said. "We need to keep going, and keep going, and then keep going some more. We don't give up. If we're tired, we rest. And then we get up and go again."

●

THEY'D BEEN ABLE TO SEE Earth with the naked eye for about a week now, which meant they'd be docking at the upper-atmosphere terminal within the next month. The excitement in the ship built, until the air felt practically electrified. It always did at periapsis, when the cycle neared its close.

Abla and Natalie went together to the central post office. They provided their names and registration cards, and the clerk handed them both a compact bundle of messages. Residents on the ship could elect to have their messages printed and placed in envelopes like real mail, either a whimsical reminder of the past, or a reality they'd never experienced.

Natalie's first message was from her parents. She scanned the note from her mother. Natalie's brother was responding well to a new treatment. The news brought a smile to her face. She spotted the yellow envelope next, and her pulse started racing, but she stayed quiet and let Abla open hers first.

Abla tore open the envelope and pulled out the yellow paper inside. She unfolded it and read it. The laugh lines around her mouth deepened, as though she was trying to suppress a smile.

"What is it?" Natalie asked casually.

"Open yours," Abla replied.

With a slight tremble in her fingers, Natalie pulled open the tacky flap and slid out a sheet of yellow paper.

An invitation from the council to the contest.

They jumped up and down like children, shrieking and clapping and shrieking again. The clerk watched them with a bemused smile.

●

"RUBY, TURN ON NOISE SIMULATOR. Jungle noises, please." Natalie blew out a breath and reached her arms over her head, enjoying the stretch through her shoulders.

"Turning on noise simulator."

A cacophony of tweets, rustling and roaring filled Natalie's sterile residence. She drew in a deep breath, soaking it all in. The day of the contest had come, and a quiet optimism filled her. She picked up the yellow paper off her small desk and checked herself over. She was ready to go.

"Ruby, open door."

Her door slid open.

She didn't realize he waited in the corridor until she slipped on her shoes and spun to leave.

"Please, Eric." She pushed down the panic which rose like bile in her throat. "Not today. They've invited me to enter the contest. I need to leave now so I'm not late."

"I need to talk to you first." He walked into her residence like he owned the place and stood blocking her way. He rose to his full height, tipping his chin up as he looked down at her.

"I don't have time. Afterwards, okay?" She smiled, trying to placate him.

Eric closed the gap between them.

She could feel her heart galloping in her chest. Her stomach twisted in an uncomfortable knot. She wouldn't let him do this again.

Taking a shuddering breath, she darted around him.

His hand clamped on her arm and yanked her to him. In one swift movement, he spun her about and wrapped his arms around her.

Natalie thrashed, drawing on all her new strength, as his biceps strained to contain her. "Let me go," she said in a ragged voice.

He tightened his hold on her. "You'll never learn," he chided, shaking his head like she was nothing but a naughty child.

SPACE OPERA DIGEST 2021

"You need to stop this nonsense."

He plucked the yellow paper from her hand and let her go.

"Give it back," she yelled, lunging for it.

He ripped the paper in half. "You're not going anywhere, sweetheart." He ripped the paper again and again until it formed a handful of confetti that he tossed in the air. The yellow fragments rained upon the floor.

Natalie deflated. She had no fight left.

"Excuse me, Commander," came a familiar voice.

A bolt of tension rippled through Eric, and his features contorted. He stepped away, smoothing his clothes before twisting to face the door where Abla stood, her East Quarter scarf wrapped around her neck and her invitation held tightly in one hand.

She glared at Eric.

"We're busy," he told her in a terse voice. "Come back later."

"No. I'm sorry, Commander. Natalie has somewhere to be right now." Abla smiled but there was no warmth in her eyes. She seemed to swell, growing taller under his gaze.

Eric stared at Abla. Then he looked sideways at Natalie with flinty eyes. Finally, he dropped his gaze to the torn yellow paper on the floor. His gaze was calculating, his mouth set in a spiteful line. He kicked disdainfully at the tiny shreds of paper.

"Thank you, Natalie," he told her with false politeness. "Remember, you must show your invitation to compete. It's so old-fashioned that way." A final, cruel smile. Then Eric stalked around Abla and left.

Natalie watched his retreating back until it disappeared from sight, and then collapsed on the floor amongst the scraps of yellow, all the emotion and adrenaline leaking out of her, leaving her feeling shaky.

Abla sat next to her on the floor. With one hand, she scooped up the tiny pieces of yellow and held them out to Natalie. When Natalie finally looked up to meet Abla's eye, the two women grinned.

"We did it." Abla reached into her pocket and pulled out the second yellow invitation.

Natalie breathed out the last of the darkness that had clawed her heart for too long, before flicking away a piece of the yellow tray liner that Eric had destroyed.

"Come on, or we'll be late." Natalie reached for Abla's hand.

●

NATALIE AND ABLA WALKED TO the main hall arm in arm, the whoosh of the oxygenators filling the peaceful quiet between them. They paused by one of the crowded viewing windows. A brief glimpse of glorious Earth sent a fluttering sensation through Natalie.

Words swirled through Natalie's mind, none of them seemed adequate. She picked a handful and forced them out, knowing the moment called for something. "Thank you for lifting me up from that place where you first found me, for getting me to this point." Her fingers ran along the yellow paper's crease, sharpening it.

"You're more of a fighter than you give yourself credit for," replied Abla.

They turned from the viewing window and walked the rest of the way in silence. Natalie felt the strength of their friendship flow through her, bolstering her with every step.

After everything Eric had put her through, she'd fought past her own demons and would soon win a ticket to Earth with Abla. She knew the two of them would be successful. Together, they could achieve anything. And there was nothing Eric could do about it.

A sudden surge of yearning to feel the heat of the sun and rain on her back pulled her eyes toward Abla, who stood beside her with an open hand pressed to her chest, her face radiant with hope. Soon. They'd be on Earth soon.

●

THE SHUTTLE WAS GOING DOWN too fast. Natalie's stomach flew to her throat and her sweat-soaked hands gripped the underside of the seat. She'd finally won a ticket to Earth, but she was going to die on the descent. "Something's wrong," she said through gritted teeth.

"Relax," laughed Abla, although her eyes had narrowed and her grip was tight around the small wooden container holding her daughter's cremated remains.

Ten minutes later, they rolled across the tarmac and parked next to the Earth-side terminal. Very much alive, Natalie let a nervous grin play over her lips. She peered out the convex, triple layered acrylic window that distorted the world outside. Smear marks smudged the image, but she could see it: Earth. A few scattered buildings lay beyond the terminal and a narrow road disappeared into the thick, steaming wilderness of multi-hued green.

"We'll be spending the first section of the cycle in the jungle," Abla said, leaning across Natalie to see out the window. She smoothed her hair and scratched at the monitor that had been placed securely around her ankle. Natalie glanced down at her own ankle. It felt like a small price to pay for three years on Earth.

Their guide met them in the terminal. An impossibly small, shrunken man, he shook hands with everyone. There were about twenty in the group, and they eyed each other and offered nervous smiles. The young man beside Abla carried himself in an upright, overly confident manner that made Natalie instantly think of Eric. She forced a smile to her face when she caught his eye and tried not to look up into the blue sky, where overhead, Eric would be hurtling through space away from her.

The wizened guide coughed and cleared his throat. "Today will be a challenging walk but won't require any special equipment. We'll take breaks and move together as a group. By late afternoon we should reach the plateau. It's behind a thick group of cedar trees, so watch for them. Remember, the assessors may be watching you at any moment. If you want to be selected for commander training, you must impress them."

"I don't know if I'm cut out for this," Natalie whispered to

Abla.

"It's a lot of pressure, isn't it?" Abla replied with a faint smile.

The group moved toward the exit, and Natalie closed her eyes as she walked through the automatic doors. The smells and sounds hit her instantly. It wasn't a noise simulator played on a repeated loop. It was real. Chaotic. Perfect.

Natalie opened her eyes slowly. Sunlight flickered through her eyelashes, sparkling like diamonds in her periphery. Once her eyes adjusted, she took in the immense breadth of the mountain range. Clouds that floated around snow-capped peaks seemed to be suspended in mid-air by invisible strings. The surrounding land was blossoming and green, the air as crisp as a fresh, green apple. She breathed it in like a starving woman given her first meal.

"How will we ever go back inside that ship?" she asked Abla.

Abla just pulled the container of her daughter's ashes closer to her chest and shook her head, as though she couldn't find the words.

Together with the others, they climbed into one of several vehicles and set off through the jungle. Time went by fast as Natalie lost herself in the scenery that passed in a blur of life and color.

The vehicles soon came to a stop, and the group set off on foot at a quick pace up a winding path. Natalie tuned out the conversations bubbling around her, placing one boot in front of the other and concentrating on not losing her footing. The rocky path rose steeply through the mountains, and Natalie breathed hard. It was nothing like running on a treadmill on the ship.

As they rounded a corner surrounded with dense foliage, their guide stopped. "Look," he said, bowing his head to the left.

Natalie let out a gasp. The trail led to a thin, steep ridge. A cascading waterfall tipped over the edge, filling a river in the valley below. She could hear the pounding of water on rocks through the chilled air.

"It's so beautiful," Natalie said, humbled.

Natalie and Abla paused every so often, delighting at each fragile green shoot growing on the path's edge. Soon the rocky ground turned to ice. As the sun lowered in the sky, it lit the horizon in brilliant streaks of orange and pink. The colors seemed to dance over the clouds and the wall of white-tipped mountains.

They saw several other small groups of victors from various ships, each making their way along the same path, headed to the same destination. As her legs began to ache, Natalie noticed cedars up ahead. They were almost there.

She reached for Abla's arm with the tenderness of old friends who'd become family. Together, they passed through the cedar curtain, their feet crunching the frosted leaf matter. The plateau opened up in front of them, the sight so magnificent that Natalie felt her breath catch in her chest.

"There's a temple," she said to Abla, pointing to the large structure as tall as four men, with elaborate turrets carved from redwood, replicating the graceful lines and cloud-filled valleys below. Victors sat scattered around the temple in groups on waterproof blankets; some sitting in silence, praying; others talking softly. A small brass bell rang out in clear, haunting tones, shaken by the wind and welcoming the newest arrivals.

"What is this place?" Natalie asked the guide in a whisper.

"It's a place for all of us. A joining place for the mountains, the heavens and the people who can no longer live amongst them." He bowed his head and moved closer to the temple.

"Why would Eric want to keep me from this?" Natalie asked Abla, keeping her tone low and reverent.

"He didn't want to keep you from this, he wanted to keep you for himself," replied Abla. "Let him go, Natalie. There's no need for him to take up space in your mind any longer. He's gone. You're free." She spoke the words without judgement, and Natalie heard the love she'd felt from Abla all along, given generously and without demanding anything in return.

When Natalie looked up, she noticed the guide watching them. Was he one of the assessors?

Moving closer, she paused and kneeled a few yards in front of the temple. The cold, frosted ground soaked her pants. She could see over the edge of the plateau and through the misty clouds that gathered below. Shoulder to shoulder with strangers, an unexpected peace filled her.

Abla kneeled down next to her and reached for her hand again, before placing the container filled with her daughter's ashes on the snow. Folding over, Abla rested her forehead on the container for a moment.

"Do you feel it?" Natalie asked as the skin at the nape of her neck tightened.

"I do," said Abla. "I feel her."

They contemplated Abla's daughter in silence and breathed in the mountain that rose above and fell below, flawless in its vast and detailed beauty. The land, the sky that floated over their heads like a single piece of silk, the people drawn from all Quarters of the solar system.... Together, they were perfect.

"You know," Natalie said to Abla, feeling a rush of inspiration and hope. "I think we might have what it takes to be selected for commander training."

"I've known that about you all along," Abla replied, her eyes soft with affection.

The wind whipped past them, sending a chill across the plateau.

Pitter-patter. Pitter-patter.

Natalie laughed as the rain fell. Real, wet, glorious rain.

On that day, high above the clouds — far from Eric on Ship 6500X — with the rain falling on her face and the lush jungle all around, she finally experienced freedom from the darkness. She'd never felt more alive or more loved. She was home.

———————————

Stephanie Mylchreest is self-published on Amazon and also writes for Muonic Press.

https://stephaniemylchreest.com

Star Cruise

by Ron Collins

Aldrin Station
Local Date: September 13, 2248
Local Time: 1015

MY FATHER IS A MAN *with an eye for detail,* I thought as I leaned against our cabin's small lavatory door and watched him unpack his clothes.

Whereas my own shirts and pants came aboard in the duffle I'd just crammed into my cubby, each of his pieces were perfectly folded and arranged for optimal use of storage. As he placed his garments into the drawers—socks and underthings to the right, overshirts and jumpers on the left—he examined each as if to decide their worth.

The cabin was cramped. Two sleep bins, the zero-g shower, and just enough leeway to shimmy out to the door. But the ventilation was good, and the place was clean. Which was more than enough. We were on a cruise, after all. It wasn't like we were planning to spend any real time here.

The data wall kept us abreast of progress toward launch.

When he finished unpacking, my father lowered the restraining screen to cinch his clothes down, closed the drawer, and stretched his back with an expression of such extreme satisfaction it made me wonder if he'd been drinking.

He hadn't, of course.

His adherence to form and process was one of many traits that could make him damnably hard to be around, and even being on a five-star cruise with his only son, a trip he'd—surprise of all surprises—arranged himself, wasn't enough to make United Government's Chief Inspector Evan Whittier drop his discipline.

Regardless, the idea of alcohol slipping past his lips before dinner was laughable.

There was a reason my mom had eventually split, after all.

The patch on his collar made sure no one would forget that he was a ranking official in the UG Justice Department, and the handkerchief served to ensure people knew he had standards. He'd worked his way to his position. He wasn't above cashing in on his capital.

I'd never bought into the UG structure as heavily as Father had wanted. He'd always been hard for me to understand. But having him as a father had as many benefits as it did drawbacks. This cruise was a celebration of sorts in that vein. I'd just passed the Academy and would be joining the department when we returned.

This would be our last blast, he'd said.

Two guys taking two local weeks to adventure around the galaxy, he'd added in a tone that said taking an expensive adventure cruise together would make up for years of being a remote father.

I didn't have much to lose. Two weeks adventuring with Father? How much damage could that do?

So that's how we found ourselves together on *Voyager*, an older Excelsior Class Star Drive chartered by the United Government's Interstellar Command, but, like most activity in the Solar System, underwritten by several companies.

It was older than most, built just after the first wave of the war with Universe Three, or, as the United Government called it, our skirmish with the terrorists. With that conflict at a very slow boil these days, *Voyager* was used more often for commercial enterprises than military.

Our first jump would take us to Hebron b, a planet in the Bernard system that was smaller than earth-standard, but known for amazing rafting and cliff climbing — interests I'd also inherited from Father when he was younger. From there the cruise would jump to the Arcturus system, experience a pass through the energy fields of a nebula in the outer ring, then climax with a three-day stint at several of the wild planetoids found at Sagittarius A, the galactic core of the Milky Way itself.

It was the last I was most anticipating.

The idea of camping on a mile-wide slab of iron floating in space felt important in ways I could barely describe.

If it brought me closer to my father, so much the better.

I smiled as he slid an antiquated handkerchief into the pocket of his immaculately clean jumper's pocket.

Asshole or not, at 72 years of age, he was still fit and trim.

With extensions, he'd probably live another hundred.

"Are you ready?" he said.

The question was so like him — a simple statement with multiple layers underneath, an open-ended query that dangled like so much cord with which so many would eventually hang themselves. It was a trick I'd learned myself, perhaps too well, Angela might say. I was always leaving a question for her to respond to, then arguing about why she was wrong.

Like father, like son, I suppose.

Both of us liked a good argument. Neither of us was any good at taking care of people close to us.

Instead of answering him, I waited while he clasped his hands.

Something else I'd learned from him.

"I thought we might go to the observation deck," he finally said. "See the show."

"The instructions said we can't leave the cabin until after separation. Something about how space accidents at Newtonian speeds lead to very expensive lawsuits."

Rather than laugh, he grunted, then scowled. "Fascists," he said as he looped his thumbs in his belt loops and went to the radiation-hardened screen.

The ship's outer shell was pulled back to pre-flight position, allowing passengers a full view of deep space. Below, Aldrin Station's command ring gleamed with sunlight that washed out several of the dimmer stars. Aldrin was a departure station locked into Lagrange point L4.

We would separate within the hour.

First jump was fifteen minutes after that.

His frown hardened the longer he stood there.

I was about to ask him how work was going when the proximity beacon flared from the ceiling light. Footsteps came from outside, and the intercom chimed.

"May we enter?" a voice came over internship comms.

"Of course," my father said, clearly relieved to be doing anything other than waiting.

The door retracted on itself, and two crew members, complete in fitted gray uniforms, entered. Both wore short-cropped hair. One male, the other uncertain. Both were tall and thin.

"Welcome aboard, Chief Inspector," one said. "The captain would appreciate a word with you."

"I would be happy to see her," he replied. "Is this business or pleasure?"

"She would like to speak prior to launch, sir," said the second.

"Business, then," Father said, glancing to confirm I'd come to the same conclusion.

The two stepped out, leaving room for us to egress.

"Alex," my father said, motioning me first.

"The captain would like to see you alone, sir," the crew said.

"My son has just accepted a position in the department," Father replied, placing a simple command into the tone of his voice. "Speaking with him is the same as speaking with me."

The two crew gave an unspoken communication, then motioned me forward.

As they led us from our cabin, I suppressed a grin.

I'd seen my father work before. Sometimes the sense of manipulation behind it bothered me, but I admitted fully to wanting to learn his way of telling people what they were going to do without making his words a direct command. Even after watching him for years, it never failed to amaze me.

●

A FEW CORRIDORS AND A lift tube into the heart of the spaceship, we found ourselves across the table from one Captain Kelly Johnson, a woman who looked the part of command, tall and firm while still having a comfortable way about her. The office was at once intimate and spacious. A flat wall decorated with images of birds of prey and a few awards connected the space. A broad, woven tapestry hung from nearly ceiling to nearly floor to lend the space a warm sensibility. Curved portions of the walls opposite were active displays, lined with real-time status reports from the *Voyager*'s central command.

Johnson was young for a captain, but her reputation was strong enough that even I knew she was headed for grander things. The sensation of being in her office did nothing to dissuade that idea.

"Welcome aboard, Chief Inspector Whittier," Captain Johnson said, rising and coming to clasp my father's hand. "This is Alex, I assume?" She shook mine just as warmly.

"Yes, Captain," I replied. "Alex Whittier."

"I've heard your performance in Academy was outstanding," she said, leading us to chairs. "I'm sure it's just a matter of time before you're following in your father's footsteps."

"Perhaps," I replied.

"I'm sure Alex will find his own path," Father said.

"Of course," the captain replied. "But first you'll both be hitting the white water and camping on flatiron, right?"

"Yes, indeed," Father said with a smile as broad as when he asked if I would take this trip with him. The realization made me wonder how real that expression was.

"I'm envious," the captain replied, sitting back in her chair. "It can be annoying to captain a cruise and not be able to partake of the experience."

"I understand that," Father said. "It's always harder to be the parent than the child."

The captain smiled at me. "I'm sure that's not always the case, now, is it?"

Father gave a proper chuckle. "So, what brings us to the captain's office before launch?" he said, shifting the tone of the conversation.

"I need to ask you a favor."

Father waited.

"I understand you've been involved in the investigation and prosecution of several cases that involve Universe Three treachery."

"Yes."

"So, you're an expert regarding their methods."

"I would never profess to being an expert."

"Then you would be disagreeing with Joint Commander Atta," the captain said, referencing the person who represented Justice at United Government's Solar System Law Enforcement Council, a group responsible for setting guidance across the entire span of UG control.

Father shrugged in defense. "I'm not an intelligence agent," he said in his humble voice. "But sometimes I guess I can hum a few bars right enough."

Captain Johnson took that as an admission.

"You're aware that *Voyager* sails without a Government Officer."

"Budgets, I assume?"

"And lack of resources."

Father nodded, then turned to me. "Do you understand, Alex?"

"Yes, I replied.

My classmates often debated the role of the GO; many supporting it, though I was never sure if that support was driven by paranoia of possibly being tracked. I didn't like it, though. The United Government was supposed to be about freedom. That's why I'd gone into law enforcement. The idea of a Government Officer made me uncomfortable, but, yes, I understood their existence.

"Every UGIS ship is expected to have a representative of the government on board to ensure proper oversight of missions, but it appears we don't have this person on board."

"Our last GO left the deck six local months ago, and I haven't felt the need for one until now," Captain Johnson said, turning back to Father. "Joint Commander Atta has approved your temporary assignment for this cruise."

"I see," Father said, obviously startled. He recovered quickly, but it was interesting seeing him stymied, even if it were just for a moment. "And why would you need a GO now?"

The room seemed to pause for an instant as the captain made a final calculation that I assumed had to do with me.

"I've received a report that Universe Three has slipped an agent on board. I'd like you to determine who it is."

"Interesting." Father furrowed his well-trimmed brow. "A U3 mole."

"Yes, interesting," the captain said. "You can continue your vacation. In fact, it's important you fulfill your plans so as not to cause suspicion that we're tipped in to their operation. But while we're *en route* to each destination, you'll be working under my command."

I could see wheels turning in my father's mind. He'd been doing this kind of work since before I was born, and the feel of the chase registered on his expression as a narrowing of his eyes and a widening of his nostrils.

"Would you accept Alex working with me?"

"I assumed as much." Johnson glanced at a portion of her desk display where a report sat. "His clearance is good."

Father turned to me. "What do you say? Are you okay if we use part of our trip to help out?"

My mind boggled, then.

This was why he'd pushed me to join him when the cabin crew had come to get us, I realized. He had guessed immediately that there was some kind of work assignment at hand, and had wanted to get me involved. Perhaps even just wanted to work with me in this way before I went off to take my own post — his own version of a post-graduation blowout, only with a security detail at stake rather than a whitewater run.

I didn't know whether to be honored, excited, or mad as hell.

Still, I needed an answer. "Who wouldn't want to play spies?" I said.

"All right, then," Father said, turning back to the captain. "Who knows of the breach?"

"Myself and my second in command."

"No one else?"

"None yet."

"I'll need access to all your security systems," he said. "Skeleton Key Access is preferred, but it's your ship. I'll want to meet your staff. A social interaction is probably best to avoid arousing suspicions too soon."

"That can be done."

"Excellent," Father said.

The captain relaxed noticeably, then glanced at the ship-board time. "Would you like to see the jump from the bridge? Inter-dimensional jump is better than the aural lights. I promise you don't want to miss it."

Father looked at me.

I grinned.

A jump across space was accompanied by a legendary display of lights and energy, a phenomenon that stemmed from the way the ship disturbed the zero field between matter and anti-matter. We'd planned to watch "the show," as my father had put it earlier, from the public observation deck, but sitting in *Voyager*'s command center would give us a remarkably intense view.

"Thank you, Captain," I said. "That would be magnificent."

●

I STRAPPED INTO AN OBSERVATION seat beside my father.

We chatted amiably, watching the crew go about its work.

The bridge was configured in amphitheater seating, with a dozen crew monitoring a dozen stations. After detaching from Aldrin, and after a brief thruster burn to clear space, the captain ordered the jump.

I gripped the armrest as the front screen blurred.

Then space folded and the forward screen shimmered, flowing with rivulets of red and orange and colors laced with a light quality that I knew hadn't existed before this moment. A wave swirled in pink and lavender. I thought I heard music, but I'm sure it was just the pounding of my heart as my fists clenched the armrests.

I saw a bird flying.

Lighting flashed purple and green that made me feel like a boy watching fireworks. Stars became yellow flares. The screen pulsed in gold.

Finally, as the ship settled, colors faded and the screen became dark with the normal space-time field.

The pounding of my heart was replaced only with the sensation of perspiration at my armpits and forehead.

Father's face was flushed, and he was grinning like a teen-aged schoolmate.

"That was worth the price of admission," he said.

Suddenly I felt closer to him than I could ever remember.

•

Hebron b
Local Date: Undefined
Local Time: Undefined

HEBRON B WAS A DESTINATION, but one that only a few arrived at.

It was a hard place—its environment is rugged and harsh, partially because its axial tilt and its preponderance of water made for harsh climate swings between its seasons, summers filled with rain, winters with icy snow. We chose Hebron b, however, because it was now fall time local—which meant the days were warm and clear while the evenings took on a sharpness that required precautions.

It was also beautiful.

The land was rugged. Sheer cliffs were interspersed with wild flora—red trees with leaves that were more frondlike and enduring rather than deciduous. The air was clear and filled with awkward-looking creatures that were something between what I knew of as birds and pterodactyls from Earth's history books. The sky blazed at sunset, and a local amphibian community made night sounds that reminded me of a croaking fish I'd caught as a boy.

Late that first evening, we set down at a lush clearing that sometimes served as a landing pad for a nearby mountain camp.

The next morning, Father and I rose, donned our wet-gear and gathered our protective helmets, then went to the required safety brief.

The plan was to kayak down the mountain our first day, then hike back the next two.

Kayaking down the mountainside went nearly to plan, and after a full second day's hike, we made camp that third night, putting up the sensor barrier that would warn us of large predators, and setting the sonic repellant that would hopefully keep them away to begin with.

I lit our fire.

The smell of woodsmoke was rich.

Though both of us were sore, the day had been perfect— every day had, actually. I had been worried about the old man, but true to his trim body, his fitness level was excellent. Even in his 70s, he more than kept up with me.

I pulled foils from the fire and unwrapped the sandwiches in them, realizing that, for at least the past two hours we'd been silent, just living together, breathing the same air and simply going about doing our business. These three days had been great, really. Water. Wind. Unique trees and fish. We hadn't talked much about the past, nor about the future. Nothing about his new job. Nothing about, well, anything of great importance.

Three days of simply being in the world together had seemed to pass in a comfortable flash.

I couldn't remember a time when I was this relaxed in the presence of my father.

"Here," I said as I handed him his dinner. "It's hot."

Seated across the fire from me, he took the foil carefully. The smell of warm bread and meat that came as he unwrapped it made my stomach surge in the most delicious way.

It was a traditional meal from back when he, Mom, and I had camped. Roasted meat, horseradish, mustard, and cheeses stuffed into a big bun along with peppers and onions and whatever else—then wrapped in foil and cooked in the embers of a campfire. It was amazing.

Father took a bite of the sandwich. Oil from the meat ran down the silvery stubble on his chin. He drank from a canteen he'd filled at the river's edge a while back.

"I'm not sure the woodsman look works on you," I said, to fill space while he chewed.

He laughed a real laugh, then wiped his hand over his lips.

"What are we going to do when we get back to the ship?" I said, staring up into the darkening sky and seeing the white dot that was *Voyager* sliding across the dome.

"What do you mean?"

"What are we going to do about the spy?"

"We go over the crew," Father said, sighing.

In that moment, my father went from gentle hiker to representative of the government. The transition happened so rapidly that a chill came to my skin. This was his thing. Walls. Cover. Focus on the target.

"We look at everything. Where they went to school, who their friends are. Where they spend their money, what they read, where they gather and what they've said in the past."

"Looking for what?"

I took a bite of my sandwich. I knew it was good, but I couldn't taste it.

It was my fault, I thought. I shouldn't have said anything. Shouldn't have broken the moment.

"Anything that says they have interest in Universe Three," he replied.

"Anything?"

His brow furrowed with an unspoken question.

"I mean, how much are we looking for? What do we report? What if a guy just reads a book about Deidra Francis?"

"That counts."

"Just because he reads a book?"

"Deidra Francis leads Universe Three, Alex. It's relevant, so we take it in."

I breathed in the cold air and took another bite of sandwich. It was already getting cold.

"You know the game, Alex. It's a long game for them. Universe Three puts people in place so they can activate them when they need to. They're fighting for the future. They're not going to quit just because the situation turned against them. It's my job— your job now—to find them and root them out."

"Not everyone who picks up a biography is planning to overthrow the government," I replied.

The corner of one lip ticked upward on Father's thin face.

"We gather bits and pieces together like the good Government Officers we are, and we connect dots that are there for people to see."

"What if the dots are just dots?" The words slipped out of my mouth before I could stop them.

The clearing got quiet then. The fire popped, and the sound

of the woods around us was suddenly deafening. In only seven words, I'd gone too far.

I looked up to find Father staring at me, waiting.

"Tell me what you mean," he finally said.

"I don't like spying on our own people. What if they haven't done anything wrong?"

"You would have us stop, even if it means that we let another Katarina Martinez through the system?"

Katarina Martinez. The name was famous.

She'd been a deep mole who Universe Three activated prior to the events that led to the Galactic War. She helped run a counteroperation against Operation Starburst, and pulled off the hijacking of *Orion* and *Icarus*, two of the first Star Drive spacecraft. Her backstory was hard to piece together. The official story was that she'd been turned by a girlfriend while in school, but others said she'd had kids who died and she blamed the government for it. Whatever the origin, it was true that Katarina Martinez had been educated by the system, had served for years. Then gone traitor.

She was a hero to Universe Three, a pariah to the United Government.

"It's not how we're supposed to be," I said, unable to go further.

The whites of Father's teeth gleamed in the firelight as he smiled, then he gave a gravelly grunt and reached over and patted my knee with his bare hand.

"You think that way because you're a good man, Alex."

Sitting back against a rock, Father ripped a bite of his sandwich and chewed.

I ate, feeling a change come over me.

My father is a dangerous man, I thought as the fire burned down and the muscles around my neck tensed. He had made his living giving in to small transgressions in the name of greater good. I had felt it before, but now I understood exactly how true it was. Looking at my father, I realized I had been wrong about so many things. Wrong about the United Government. Wrong to think they lived by their own creeds.

The Department was supposed to be about enforcing laws. It was supposed to be about keeping the peace. The Department was important. But it wasn't supposed to be able to rip into people's lives like that.

Tomorrow was going to be a hard walk.

"Are we going to find anything?" I said, breaking a silence that had gone on long enough that our meals were gone.

"Of course."

"How can you be so certain?"

"Because I am a mole, Alex."

The hypocrisy of that statement—to compare his work as a GO to that of a hidden agent was so absurd that it made me laugh out loud. There was nothing devious about the role. A GO was nothing more than unregulated power. And I saw something deeper, too. All those arguments against the idea of a Government Officer I'd made back in school—all those conversations and debates I'd had at bar tables with drunken friends—they were something deeper than arguments.

"That's a real kicker, Father."

"You think I'm bullshitting."

I scoffed. "You bullshit for a living, so, yeah."

Father took a pull from his canteen and put it back down. "You think I brought you out here for me to be a dad?"

The comment sat me back. After a moment, I shook my head. "I don't know why you brought me out here, anymore."

"I am the mole, Alex. You're in the department now, so you need to know that. I could keep things separate before, but now anything that comes down on me will also come down on you. That's how this game works. It's important you see that."

"Hells…"

This was too big. My thoughts jammed themselves up and it was like my entire brain shut itself down.

"I am the person Captain Johnson is looking for, but it's also not that simple."

My brain did flips.

"You're on an op," I said, the statement not a question anymore. I could see the pieces now, even if I hadn't lined them all up. "It's not a coincidence that we're on *Voyager*."

His smile held an instant of fatherly pride.

"I'm going to get into the system," he said. "And I'm going to find material on people because, as you insinuated, no one can live a life without doing something out of line, or at least something that can be twisted to look like it is. I'm going to send people to jail."

"I don't understand."

"I'm looking for people Captain Johnson has hired or promoted. I'm going to find people she's written recommendations for, and I'm going cast shadows on all of them."

"Captain Johnson?"

"I'm going to find anything she's done that's even close to controversial, and I'm going to take her down."

I added two and two for far longer than it should have taken me to get to four, but when I did, everything cleared up.

"She's *too* good," I said. "You're getting rid of the most competent leaders in UG's military command. She's too competent, so she's got to go."

Father nodded, and took another drink.

"The United Government is lying to us. You know that. It says Universe Three wants to destroy the Solar System, when the entire war could have been avoided if UG leadership had simply let them go. That's the truth, Alex. Universe Three gains nothing from the war, but the United Government does."

"Fear," I said, seeing agreement twinkle in starlight that reflected in my father's eyes. The United Government used the threat of Universe Three to fuel their own fortunes. They used the anger the Universe Three actions created as fuel to keep their own citizens in line.

"It's important to fight for the truth, Alex. That's what I think. Truth is the only thing we have to fight for. And you can't stop fighting simply because you're losing or because the other side is too big."

The expression on his face grew more intense. "And, yes, Johnson is too good. She's got to go before she can get a command where she can do real damage."

He paused again. Wood smoke made my eyes itch.

My father is a man of secrets, I thought.

"You're not telling me this just because you want to save me from your fallout."

He shook his head gently. "No, Alex. I'm not."

"Why, then?"

"You know."

I looked at my father, then. Really looked at him for perhaps the first time. He was an open book, now. I was seeing the real man. A man who'd built walls from years of seclusion, and who'd lived his life probably more alone than anyone I'd ever known.

I could take him down. I could go to the captain and expose him. If I did that maybe I'd even get ahead. Or would I? Would the UG and the Department see me as more trustworthy or less for exposing him?

I didn't know.

Didn't care.

"You're asking me to join you," I said.

He smiled.

I closed my eyes and put my head back against the hard stone behind me. An edge bit into my shoulder blade.

"Sometimes good people have to make decisions," he replied. "This is one of those times."

The night drew cold around me, and it was like I could feel the universe breathing, the rock moving underneath me, the air crisp and alive. I felt my life rolling ahead of me, I felt weight carrying me forward. I felt the enigma that was my father beside me on this cold and beautiful planet, surrounded by safety systems that might or might not work, and smelling the aroma of wood that was still burning in the pit we'd made together.

When I opened my eyes, I was in a new world.

"You'll teach me what I need to know?"

He smiled, and looked suddenly at ease.

"I'll teach you," he said. "And you'll teach me."

There, in the small clearing of a woods on Hebron b, listening to the sounds of alien insects in the night, I raised my canteen to him.

We clinked aluminum and drank.

———————————

Ron Collins is an Amazon best-selling Dark Fantasy author who writes across the spectrum of speculative fiction.

His latest science fiction series, Stealing the Sun is available from Skyfox publishing.

His fantasy series Saga of the God-Touched Mage reached #1 on Amazon's bestselling dark fantasy list in the UK and #2 in the US. His short fiction has received a Writers of the Future prize and a CompuServe HOMer Award. His short story "The White Game" was nominated for the Short Mystery Fiction Society's 2016 Derringer Award.

He has contributed a hundred or so short stories to professional publications such as *Analog, Asimov's,* and several other magazines and anthologies (including several editions of the *Fiction River* Anthology Series).

He holds a degree in Mechanical Engineering, and has worked to develop avionics systems, electronics, and information technology before chucking it all to write full-time–which he now does from his home in the shadows of the Santa Catalina Mountains.

http://typosphere.com/

Watch of the Starsleepers

by Christopher D. Schmitz

"THEY KILLED LENNY," DAVE HISSED.

Barb stared at him blankly. "I don't understand why that bothers you." She injected another egg with genetic material. "You know what every Watcher knows. We all have an expiration date. When the tribunal decides that...."

"No," Dave said. "This wasn't a 'forced expiration.' They *murdered* him."

Barb cocked her head. Murder was an archaic act that the cloned watcher race had nearly forgotten was possible. Her face remained placid, even though she'd also been Lenny's close friend. Watchers weren't supposed to form intimate bonds with their peers, knowing they would be culled at relatively premature ages. It was central to the watcher philosophy.

Dave sighed through his nose and let the silence envelop them. Only gently vibrations filled the air as the massive generation ship *Endymion* rocketed through space on its way to Alpha Centauri, Terra's closest neighbor. Technology allowed advances in space travel and the trip would take roughly one hundred and sixty years. They were currently in their eighth decade and Dave, watcher DAV-F, was the fifth iteration of the original clone, DAV-A.

Within a few days' time, a much younger LEN-F would take over Lenny's function in the fabrication shop.

Dave pouted, "I'm not going to call him Lenny."

Barb raised a brow. "What will you call him? Lenph?"

Dave laid his head down on her workbench.

Barb reached down and squeezed his hand. "Listen, Dave. You know I love you, but these embryos aren't going to fertilize themselves. Who knows, one of these might be Len-G. Wouldn't that be ironic?"

He looked up at her. He did love Barb, but he knew she couldn't sympathize. Not really. Watchers didn't have the capacity, or so they were taught from the moment they were pulled from the incubation chambers and strapped into education implanters. The implanters were a kind of mental download system that loaded formative memories and base-level knowledge necessary to continue the role of the original genetic material.

Still, though, it felt a little comforting to hear Barb say she loved him. Watchers were allowed platonic relationships, but romantic entanglements were punished severely. A neurological device implanted at the base of the skull of each watcher mitigated sexual impulses, and provided negative correction when necessary.

Dave laid his head back down on the table. He wished the device mitigated grief.

"Will there be a memorial?" Barb asked.

Dave forced himself back into an upright position. "Yes. There is always a memorial." He logged into the network and pulled up the Transition Schedule. The ship housed over twenty thousand watchers at any given time, so multiple transitions happened daily. — That was when the new clone assumed the duties and life of his or her predecessor.

A thought solidified in Dave's mind; if Lenny was murdered, all evidence would disappear as soon as the F variant took over Lenny's life.

Dave stood. "I, uh, should go."

Barb shrugged, still preoccupied with her work. She had several hours left of her shift and until then, she would remain distracted. Barb might have been warmer were it not for her work — all watchers were conditioned to take their work seriously. The spinal devices, commonly called a "neuri," ensured it.

Dave and Lenny were as close as brothers, but Dave and Barb *might* have been *more*...in a world other than a cold clone ship hurtling through the void, where a death sentence hung over each creature.

He headed for the exit. It slid open as he approached.

"Hey," Barb called.

Dave turned.

"Tonight? Just you and me. We'll remember Lenny properly? We don't need some official ceremony, or to get LEN-F involved. I've just...work is important."

He nodded. Glad for the offer, and he could empathize. The neurological spine-chips often muddied thoughts of non-work-related tasks during scheduled shifts. "Tonight."

●

DAVE HELD AN OLD JAR of cloudy liquid in one hand. He clutched Lenny's spare key in his other and took a swig of the mind-numbing stuff watchers brewed in the engine bays.

The Tribunal had learned in the first generation that they

couldn't program the neurological spine devices to punish alcohol consumption. They'd tried, but the same punishment subroutine for alcohol affected watchers who used medication. They lost nearly all the A-generation watchers who refused to seek treatment for minor injuries as a result. Booze was forbidden, but consumption often went unpunished.

Right now, Dave and Barb didn't care about legalities. They were both hammered and it was late. Order-keepers only patrolled sporadically.

"You're sure we won't wake Lenph?" Barb asked, louder than she meant.

Dave shook his head. "Until the Transition, he's still pulling duty on third shift."

Barb shrugged. That made sense. Young watchers were apprentices until they took over the lives and jobs of their genetic predecessors. Barb worked in the fertilization labs, and the embryos were grown and aged to optimum development for an individual. Typically, during their mid-teens, a body was awakened and programmed, but a fresh psyche could only handle so much downloading; new watchers were sent to live with the man or woman they would eventually replace. Every twenty to thirty years, the cycle renewed.

Dave unlocked the door and entered. He'd spent many nights on the ratty couch Lenny had claimed from a busted storage unit years ago. He plopped down and wondered how much longer he had until the Tribunal assigned him an apprentice of his own.

Barb sat next to him. "There's no pillow."

Dave raised a brow.

"Lenph normally sleeps on the couch. His pillow's gone... he's claimed the bedroom."

Dave's face darkened.

"You still think Lenny was killed?"

"I'm certain of it."

Barb cocked her head. Understanding denial was a part of grief. "But Lenny had an apprentice. We all knew his days were short."

Dave stood and rifled through a box of Lenny's belongings, which the Tribunal's officers would soon come to claim. "I know that. But it's what makes it a perfect cover up. I'm telling you, Lenny would have told me if he'd been given his orders to report for expiration."

Barb put her hands on his shoulders and tried to comfort him. Dave turned. Their faces were so close their noses could have touched and a surge of endorphins rushed through them both. Dave nearly leaned in to kiss her; the alcohol made him throw caution to the wind.

A jarring bolt of pain seared through his mind like an icy spade. Barb felt it too, and they pinched the bridges of their noses to quell the agony caused by the neuri implanted at the base of their skulls.

They each took a swig of the flammable, almost clear fluid. "I—I should go," said Barb, whose neck had remained flush since the jolt. She left before Dave could object.

He sat back on the couch with a box containing all that remained of his best friend and sifted through it. He scratched at the neuri on his spine and muttered, "I know they say these things keep us alive. But dammit, they itch."

Dave pulled out a recording device. They were often used to capture video of important data watchers needed to pass to their duplicates. This one had been hidden within a bolt of fiber batting.

Suspicion tore through Dave. If Lenny had known his expiration appointment, he'd have made a recording for Lenph and left it somewhere obvious. "It *was* a murder," Dave whispered, suspecting Lenny had stashed it somewhere safe so his friends could find it if tragedy struck.

Dave stared at the device for a long moment. He recalled an old rumor that the Tribunal had recording devices in barracks rooms. The AI supposedly didn't understand images well, but because it had the voice prints of every watcher on file, it could easily parse language. Dave had no idea what might be in the unit's memory bank. But if Lenny truly had been killed, he'd need to listen in a private place.

The chrono said that the hour was still late, or early, depending on your schedule. Dave dumped the device into a pocket and left.

●

DAVE MEANDERED THE SELDOM USED service corridors where lighting was sparse. He wedged his way into a hidden nook and retrieved the memo device. With the volume set low, he thumbed it to active.

Lenny's recorded visage shone in a blur of holographic light. He was in his washroom; the vent fan rattled, and the handwash flowed. Anything that offered background noise to mask his words was running, and it made his voice scratchy.

"Listen. They are coming for me. My ident-tag is LEN-E. I have not been given an expiration date yet, but the Tribunal will send a termination team for me, I am sure." Lenny looked up as if he heard something in the distance.

He returned to the recorder with panic on his face. "I was called to repair a system's malfunction in the bow. *Yes,* the *bow,* where watchers aren't allowed to go—I saw something in there—something terrifying. You wouldn't believe me if I told you...they're keeping it a secret. It's all a lie."

A loud thump penetrated the white noise at the sink. "Search for yourself. My team included ASA-D, BEN-G, and DAN-E."

Another thump. Lenny wrapped the recorder in the material, which crinkled as he stowed it in secret. It still picked up audio and the sounds of a struggle as the Tribunal's reclamation team dragged him away. Only the sound of the handwash remained.

Dave swallowed the sticky dryness in his throat and scanned the net for the names of Lenny's three coworkers. All were listed on the transition schedule. *Dead.* Two of them had asterisks by their name to indicate accidental death and rapidly aged clone replacements. RA-clones tended to be less stable. The process included extensive mental downloading in lieu of an apprenticeship; it made the mind brittle and tended to make watchers who burned out quickly under the stress of their jobs.

His body had filtered most of the alcohol out by now. The only lingering effect was courage enough to try something risky.

The bow. That was where they were. The humans. Endymion's precious cargo. No watcher was allowed into the bow without special orders. Apparently, such assignments also earned a termination order.

In the service hall, Dave was mostly hidden. A maintenance shaft lay at a nearby dead-end. He removed an access panel and slipped inside, cursing to himself as he went. The liquid courage remained, but his brain argued with the lingering chemical bravery.

Dave scurried through a tunnel with low ceilings where tubes, piping and cables hung. He scrambled, guided by few runway LEDs. Luckily, if any work crews were assigned to duties in the corridor, he would see their lamps long before they ever spotted unauthorized watchers in the shafts.

After winding his way through the maze of connections, Dave arrived at a larger hall with a rounded aperture built into the bulkhead. A large warning was posted. *Forbidden Entry: Punishable by death.*

The Tribunal did not mess around, Dave knew. Built into the door was a simple laser grid that sent an invisible signal to any neuri that passed through it. The trigger would overload the pain sensors of an unauthorized person and fry his or her brain with sensory overload.

Dave's duties included routine power maintenance. He knew there was a scheduled outage connected to this region's grid. It would last several cycles...but important systems had backups. *How important to humans is killing inquisitive watchers?*

Dave sucked in his breath, held it, and then walked through the opening. Only after he confirmed he still lived did Dave relax.

He stole down the corridor and searched for an access port to the storage bay, but there didn't seem to be any. Dave muttered beneath his breath. He hadn't come all this way only to be denied now.

A ventilation grid was mounted to the nearby wall. Dave examined it, but there were no bolts or any way to remove it. He felt certain he could force his way through. As long as he did his best not to damage it, *or himself,* he'd get away with spying.

Dave charged at the panel and rammed his shoulder into it. Then found himself falling, tumbling into the dark.

●

DAVE FLAILED THROUGH THE AIR in free-fall. Then he hit bottom, landing on his back so hard he thought he heard vertebrae break in his neck. Something felt hot and sticky at his clavicle. He reached behind, as ground lights glowed softly in response to motion in the cavernous storage zone.

Checking his hand, he didn't find the expected blood, rather a trickle of fluid that had leaked from his neuri. Dave's heart plunged into his gut. *I'm going to die...*

He paused, understanding he'd already risked death once

and emerged fine. A few seconds later he realized that an early lesson ingrained upon watchers, *the neuri keeps you alive,* was a lie.

What else is false?

Dave decided to test if the device in his neck still functioned. He closed his eyes and thought of Barb. He liked Barb, *more than platonically.* He imagined her naked. Watchers were not permitted to see the opposite gender nude, so he wondered what it looked like. He used his imagination. His mind pounded with chemical excitement and his pants stretched with a rush of blood.

Pulse racing, Dave opened his eyes wide. He'd never experienced this before. Neuris staved off aspects of full sexual maturity. Dave poked at his crotch and nearly doubled over at the new and sudden sensation.

He looked up. What he saw was powerful enough to shut down even his newly raging sex drive.

Humans. Millions of humans.

Dimly lit tubes of frozen analog gel revealed the floating forms of the precious cargo who had been packed for more than a century of transit. Rows of clustered tech were stacked tall and stretched as far as Dave could see. His breath caught in his throat and he approached the nearest cryo unit, which kept a nude passenger in suspended animation.

The human hung in the viscous fluid with electronic leads monitoring the person's vital statistics. An organic mesh kept jaw and lips closed while a thin nose tube looped around the head, ready to provide air once the cryo tube activated its flash-thaw cycle, which would make each pod reach 37C, standard body temperature, in less than one second after arrival at Alpha Centauri.

Dave looked left and right and made a startling realization. *DAV-E was human.*

He touched the glass and pulled his hand away, leaving a frosty print. He gasped, and no longer wondered what female anatomy looked like.

Dave touched the neuri at the back of his neck. He knew he was a clone. All watchers were reproductions, but they were all also human. For generations, watchers had speculated about what humans really were. Maybe they had tails, or scales, or multiple heads and communicated telepathically. But the rows of bodies in stasis revealed the truth. "I — I'm human? We're all of us...human?"

He grabbed at Lenny's recording tool and cleared space in the memory while still preserving his friend's last moments. Dave knew he had to record this, to take the evidence back to the other watchers. He corrected his own thoughts.

To the other people.

"Lenny's death will not have been for nothing," he murmured.

●

DAVE WALKED CONFIDENTLY THROUGH THE laser grid, certain that a trigger for his neuri couldn't kill him, even if the power had been reactivated. Still half in shock, he returned to his quarters.

Standing in front of the mirror in his lavatory, Dave stared into his own face. He found a spark in his eyes — something he could not articulate.

Something triggered inside him, as if a creature awakened. *Hope? Wonder?* He knew what humans were now. At least what they looked like. He had to share that...but he also needed a plan.

Lenny and others had died because of their discovery. The Tribunal would not allow to it to leak easily.

Dave grabbed a multi-tool which he often used for hardware repairs. His primary watcher functions were in software applications, but he was often called to make physical repairs on the fly, and he was fairly adept at it.

Dave departed for the workshop area, where he sometimes had to fabricate special equipment for jobs. He gathered several items and soldered, wired and screwed together a custom device for his own protection; a simple relay which would send a signal if he depressed the button.

No watchers gave him a second look while he worked. Dave often worked there, and none knew he was outside his shift.

He looked up when he spotted motion. A watcher near the door pointed directly at him, obviously speaking with someone beyond the threshold. And then a line of Order-Keepers dressed in black garb entered the room. They moved single-file and wore masks to conceal their faces. These were the watchers called into service if a clone failed to report for Transition. They were the ones who would have dragged away and killed Lenny.

Dave hadn't completed the failsafe device. He had not acted quickly enough. His heart sank, as he walked in a straight line toward the executioners. Running would be futile, but at least he could walk to his death holding his head high and with human nobility.

The Order-Keepers jogged toward him, then moved past, heading for a workstation in the tech bay. *Lenny's station.*

Adrenaline surged through Dave, making him feel electric. His neuri would usually mitigate that flow and dampen its effects. But not now. With pulse racing, he did his best to control his breathing and act normal. Dave left the bay and entered his regular workstation, passing by his coworkers and exchanging mundane nods of recognition.

He sat at his kiosk but did not activate the terminal. JAQ-F, Jack, sat at a nearby cubicle engrossed in his work, then stood and excused himself for a break. Dave slid around and into the adjacent berth as soon as the coast was clear. He quickly wrote a piece of code, a simple power interrupt he could use if needed. He'd only need to punch the toggle on the custom hardware he'd just made. Plugging the device into the data port via standard interface, he downloaded the software, unplugged it, then deleted the software.

With any luck, there would be no detection. If the Tribunal's oversight and accountability software picked up what Dave had done, Jack might get a visit from the Tribunal's inquisitors.

Dave left his workplace and headed out. A twinge of guilt nagged at him. What if the Tribunal killed Jack? Jack was pretentious and unfriendly, but should neglecting to log off a terminal result in early termination? Was that human justice?

Before leaving, Dave watched as the Order-Keepers departed with a box of Lenny's things. They probably meant to destroy them and ensure no trace of the secret was left behind.

Dave turned the corner. "Yes," he announced to himself. Humans *would* do that. They'd enslaved whole generations of their direct genetic descendants, denied them the full capacity of their bodies, and treated them as property—growing them and exterminating them at their own leisure. "Killing is a *very* human practice."

●

THE FERTILIZATION LAB WAS MOSTLY empty by the time Dave arrived; it was this shift's lunchtime, Dave realized as he checked the chrono. He stared at it incredulously. Time had blazed by without much notice. But he assumed Barb was still there. She often ate lunch while remaining at her post to ensure nothing went wrong. Her work was critical.

Barb had once remarked that her training had taught her they had a finite amount of egg cells, so caution had to be taken when creating new, embryonic watchers. If they ran out of clones before the *Endymion* arrived at Alpha Centauri, all could be lost. Barb had noticed that, for some unexplained reason, the supply counts of material never decreased and her team had been fertilizing cells for years.

She'd assumed there was an accounting glitch. Dave now knew better. *Watchers were human.* And before their remains were submerged into an amino pool to break it down into raw protein strings and remade into materials for watchers' consumption, the reproductive materials were likely harvested and stored for later use.

Dave entered the lab without sterilizing first.

Barb shouted at him. "You can't just barge in here without..."

"I was right. Lenny was murdered," he blurted out, then regretted it immediately. Unlike Lenny, he hadn't masked his words with white noise. It might be heard by the Tribunal.

"What are you talking about?"

Dave pulled out the recording device and held it up.

Barb asked, "What's that?"

He put a finger over his lips. "I can show you. But I need to know if you trust me."

"What? Of course I...."

"Turn around and close your eyes. I'll help you see. Keep your eyes closed."

Barb did as instructed, though confused. "What are you going to show me?"

"I'll show you *everything.*"

Barb yelled as a jolt of pain rippled through her spine. Dave had rammed the sharp part of his multi-tool into her neuri's battery compartment and the implement pierced too far, pinching her flesh as it disabled the device. She whirled on him. "What are you...."

She stared at him with new eyes.

Dave touched his head to hers and Barb smelled him. Her brain reacted to the suddenly opened door and chemicals designed for procreation slammed into her like tidal forces washing over desert dunes. Pheromones nearly overcame her. She clung to him, kissing him for the first time. Her mind swam with new impulses; Barb's body craved his.

"I have to tell you something," Dave said, pushing her away enough to look into her eyes. "Barb, *you are a human.* We both are."

"What are you talking about?"

"Damn it." He'd run his mouth again in a sensitive area. "Come with me." Dave led her by the hand into a darkened corridor and played Lenny's recording, and then the one he took of the humans.

Barb could scarcely believe it. "I thought they'd have fur." The mental shock had quelled most of the chemical lust pounding through her body. Then she blanched. "Do you think the Tribunal knows that we know?"

Dave kept his lips tight and nodded resolutely. "I should have waited to tell you until we were away." He held her hand as they walked back towards the watchers' sector.

"What will we do, then?" Barb asked.

"I'm forming a plan." He flashed her a roguish grin.

They'd just cleared the service hall when they spotted Order-Keepers behind them. The Order-Keepers projected images of Dave and Barb at a random passerby. The man pointed to the hall where they stood.

Dave nearly yanked Barb's arm off, as he dragged her behind him. "Run!"

●

DAVE AND BARB SCURRIED THROUGH the maintenance shaft ahead of their pursuit. Right now, the safest place for them was the humans' chamber. He did not know if the Tribunal's team could access it without earning a death sentence, but guessed they would be exempt. Right now, running was their only chance.

Barb skidded to a halt before the laser gate. Fear rooted her in place and she refused to pass through. They were programmed early for obedience. "I — I'll die."

"No, you won't," Dave insisted, stepping through. "I disabled your neuri. They can't do anything to you. *You're a human.* This only kills watchers."

Barb squeezed her eyes and shuddered as she stepped through. She emerged unharmed and the duo ran down the hall. They could hear the enemy far behind them requesting emergency override on the laser gate so they could pass.

Dave stopped at the aperture where he'd fallen once before. "It's a long way down. It might hurt. Leap of faith," he warned Barb, then plunged through.

This time, he landed in a half-crouch and rolled to break his fall. The lights came up and Barb jumped. She fared better than him, able to judge the distance.

Barb stood and gasped when she saw the rows and rows of sleepers. "There are millions of them." She read the name plate on the base of one tube. "Aliyah Amber Jacobson. AAJ-0."

Dave took her hand. "There are millions *of us*. I suspect that each sleeper here has a genetic duplicate in the watcher pool."

A voice called out from behind and above them. "Stop there, or we'll shoot."

The kill squad had been armed with lethal weapons.

Dave withdrew his device with the singular button and held it aloft. "*You* stop, or I'll push this button and kill every human in these pods!"

Their pursuers scoffed momentarily and then paused, cocking their heads, receiving orders via ear-piece. They retreated a few steps, keeping barely visible through the vent.

The new humans slipped behind a cluster of cryotubes, taking cover from the assassins' weapons. A speaker system activated with garbled words. "Parlay."

Dave cocked his head. "Who is this?" His neck flushed as Dave realized he was well beyond any ability to form a new plan. He'd thought he and Babe could escape through the cryozone, but what then? The executioners would never stop.

"I am the Tribunal," the voice replied. "You have proved a resourceful and clever watcher, DAV-F."

Dave waved his device threateningly. "I am a human!" he yelled. "And if you wish to barter for the lives of the humans in stasis — the *precious cargo* you've enslaved generations of us for — then I want to talk in person."

"Very well."

Except for the millions of status LEDs on the tubes, all the lights went out. A runner of lumen strips created a path. They followed it to a terminal in the center of the storage area.

Barb sucked in her breath, as they arrived at the heart of the *Endymion*. Its mission was centered on this very spot.

Dave heard distant footsteps and guessed their pursuers had entered the compartment. He turned a circle. "Show yourself, Tribunal."

A light pulsed on a mechanical unit as the speaker sounded. The interface screen lit with a cascade of pixels forming a digital imitation of a face. "You are no more human than I, DAV-F...I am the Tribunal."

●

FOOTSTEPS CLOMPED IN THE DARK as the executioners surrounded Dave and Barb. She clung to him and Dave breathed in her scent; it threatened to fog his brain with desire. He shook his head to clear it.

"Call them off, Tribunal," Dave insisted, waving his device. He suspected the computer program knew what he'd programmed it for.

"Stand down," ordered Tribunal.

Dave stared at the computer array. He guessed its AI was more clever than any human or watcher. "And tell them to throw their earpieces into the light." He didn't want Tribunal issuing orders privately.

The communicators clattered to the steel grid floor around his feet.

A plan finally formed in his mind. "I'd feel more comfortable with a gun, too," Dave insisted.

"Boss?" a voice asked in the dark.

"DAV-F claims to be human," Tribunal said, limited to his speaker. "Humans are rational creatures. DAV-F and I will resolve this with words and logic. A gun's presence will prove irrelevant. There is no fear…not if DAV-F is human."

A gun skittered towards him. Dave picked it up and bartered. "What will you offer this human to stand down?"

"You are not human."

"*I am* a human! My genetic blueprint proves it," Dave roared. "I think. I have feelings."

"Your logic is flawed. Humanity is not bestowed by acts of procreation; Tribunal was created by humans. Sentience cannot be its definition; Tribunal is fully sentient. I am not human."

Dave narrowed his eyes at the thing. It was connected to the ship, but housed within circuitry and drives. A mechanical brain in a box. "You are a created personality?"

"Yes. I am fully aware. But *I am not a human.*"

"Then what makes someone human?" Dave demanded, "if it's not what we were born to be, what we do, or proved by self-awareness?"

A pregnant silence hung in the dimness. "Only humans decide what makes life human."

Dave thought back to the moment by the mirror. He'd recognized a spark within himself. He rejected Tribunal's definition.

The speaker crackled. "Here is what I can offer; on humanity's behalf, I can *make* you human. Place you both in a pod for..."

Dave snapped the weapon to bear and unloaded the full magazine into Tribunal, slagging his housing and destroying him utterly. He whirled in time to see the executioners try to come to the controller's aid. Dave slapped the button on his wireless device.

A shrill warning tone filled the compartment and the LEDs switched to red as the power to all the cryotubes' life support tripped off. Within seconds, millions passed away in their sleep.

The Order-Keepers stopped short of tackling Dave. "H-how could you?" They stared at the darkened pods, minds obliterated by the lengths of Dave's bloodless carnage. "You murdered them all."

Dave retrieved the multi-tool from his pocket and stared at the first executioner's neuri. "But that's what proves we are human. Humans kill."

Using the tool, he freed his would-be assassins, then took Barb's hand. "The things in these tubes weren't human anyway," Dave muttered. "If Tribunal was to be believed, then these things were monsters."

Christopher has authored over thirty books and writes primarily science fiction and fantasy. His murder mystery/comedy for nerds (*50 Shades of Worf*) was chosen runner-up Indie Book Of The Year by the Minnesota State Library Association. He writes in several series including the Esfah Sagas (an IP that was developed alongside Forgotten Realms and Dragonlance.)

https://authorchristopherdschmitz.com

Tome Raiders

by Eric Del Carlo

I NEVER THOUGHT I'D MISS being a wannabe space adventurer who everybody ignored. But there were disadvantages to success. For one thing, the dilettantes were jealous and gave you the constant hairy eyeball. For another, the bigshot treasure hunters started to notice you.

That last, ironically, was something I'd always dreamed of. Same for my partner, Hitchcock. We had struggled bitterly for years, trying to make it in this galactic game. Now we'd arrived, more or less. The two of us had completed a string of successful jobs, some with real notoriety. We had our own ship. We could sit here in the Deadfall on Rusty's Port and proudly count ourselves among those who made a legit living as star-faring venturers.

But when Kid Nebula sauntered across the sawdust-covered floor and stopped at our table, I knew it was trouble.

"Matchstick and Hitchcock," Kid Nebula said, a glass of bubbling orange in his hand. "And you know who I am."

It should have been a thrill to hear our names from the lips of one so famous in the adventure trade. But Kid Nebula had a puffed-up sneery air. The "Kid" part of his moniker was also getting problematic as he grew older, softer, seamier. Still, a legend was a legend.

"Yes," I said. "We know you." I was pleased with how level my voice was. On the other side of the table, Hitchcock was all but trembling and gaping.

The Kid took a sip of his Ooblamooba Sunrise as he regarded us. Hitch and I were both drinking our customary Bongo Boy beers. I was aware of lots of eyes on us. The Deadfall was populated with its usual complement of noteworthy adventurers and the piteous hopefuls who wanted to be like them. Hitchcock and I weren't bigshots. Not yet. But everyone watched to see how we would handle somebody who was. Especially if that somebody was going to give us a hard time.

"I've got a wager for you two," Kid Nebula said leisurely, but I heard the underlying menace in his tone. "A spacer's bet. Interested?"

"What is it?" Hitchcock blurted before I could parry the Kid. Nothing good could come of taking his bet, I felt sure.

Kid Nebula grinned, which deepened the lines in his leathery face. He still had his distinctive shock of red hair. "The Sacred Book of the High Priesthood of Avvyestia has gone missing. They've put out a reward for it."

"Book?" Hitch asked, perplexed. "I always thought stuff like that was scrolls. The Sacred *Scrolls*. A book sounds, I don't know...sort of undramatic."

The Kid looked blankly at my partner, probably trying to figure out if the chain-pulling was deliberate. I could have told him that Hitchcock was just that way, but I was on Hitch's side, always.

"Is the Priesthood sure they didn't just set it down someplace and forgot where?" I asked. The question wasn't pure smartassery. The High Priesthood of Avvyestia is indeed perpetually high, eating narco-leaves by the fistful.

It was my turn to receive Kid Nebula's blank gaze. Everyone in the bar still watched us intently. Then Kid brayed insincere laughter, knocked back the rest of his drink, and declared, "I say we go look for the Book. Me against you two. Whoever finds it first gets the reward—obviously. And the losers...or, ahem, pardon me...loser has to dress like a Valtupian boy-whore and wait hand and foot for a whole night here in the Deadfall on the winner. Or—hey, who knows?—on the winners. You two space adventurers game to take that bet?"

He might as well have spat in our beers, he said *space adventurers* with such haughty contempt.

●

WE HAD NAMED OUR DEEP-PROBE mining vessel *Sallyride*, after an ancient Earth goddess. She had the power of flight and held the stars in her palm, as Hitch and I could recall from our modest knowledge of history.

I was in the pilot's cage, guiding us through the black. Our ship had started life as an unmanned craft. Now it served Hitch and me on our treasure-seeking pursuits. This was a different kind of job, though. We were after thieves, not swiping an antiquated artifact off some planet.

"It matters," I said again.

So Hitch said again, "I looked up what Valtupian boy-whores wear, and while it's very demeaning, I don't think it's the end of the galaxy if we have to dress up like them."

We were in one of those conversational loops reserved for

old marrieds and longtime partners in pseudo-crime. I had to break the cycle. Turning from the controls, I said, "Kid Nebula is trying to take us out. You and I solved the mystery of the ghost-ship *Reckless*. We found the long-lost pancreas of Queen Qkqkqk -KqKq-2, still intact in its jar. We're gaining a reputation. Matchstick and Hitchcock are starting to mean something to people who hire mercenaries for treasure-finding gigs. Now"—I grimaced—"if we have to prance around the Deadfall as male Valtupian concubines, it's going to be the first thing a lot of people ever hear about us. And they'll think twice before hiring us."

Hitch was silent and thoughtful; then, "Okay. But why is it always Matchstick and Hitchcock? Why not Hitchcock and Matchstick, Match?"

"Let's try it that way if you want. It's fine with me." And it was.

He murmured it several times, then finally shook his head. "Naw, it's better as Matchstick and Hitchcock." He returned to the navigation station, to feed me coords to Avvyestia.

A few hours later we set down on the planet. The High Priesthood had put out a general reward for their lost Sacred Book, rather than hiring a specific individual or crew. But the word had gone out since Kid Nebula made his wager with us on Rusty's Port, where rough-hewn spacers came and went constantly. Nobody else was touching this job apparently. There was also no sign of the Kid on Avvyestia. Maybe he already had a lead.

Hitch and I gathered what facts of the crime we could from the Priesthood, who were wandering all over the temple grounds. I thought they were muttering prayers until I overheard several saying in awed voices, "My hands are, like, *huge!*" as they chewed their aromatic narco-leaves.

But the clerics in their psychedelic robes made it clear how important the Sacred Book was, not just to their mind-bending order but to the greater culture of Avvyestia, which relied on the ancient spiritual teachings. Already moral unrest rumbled on the world. Not the fun kind of amorality either, like boozing and orgies, but acts of corruption and oppression.

We had to find the Sacred Book. Luckily we had a first clue.

Records of ships that had come to and departed from Avvyestia during the time when the theft must have occurred revealed one vessel whose registry didn't match the description of the craft itself. We set off after it in the *Sallyride*, following its burn-trail through the black. I felt excitement, which was a damn sight better state to be in than the melancholy that had haunted me so often before Hitch and I had managed to become respectable treasure raiders.

"I don't trust him," Hitchcock said, apropos of nothing.

"Huh? Who?"

"Kid Nebula. I don't think he's a square dealer."

If I had the market cornered on despondency in our partnership, then Hitch's big thing was fear. Back when we'd been wannabes, he had been given to fits of terror. Were these misgivings about Kid Nebula a watered-down version of that old intense anxiety?

I wasn't eager to open that particular can of worms, so I flew us onward silently.

The suspicious spaceship, we eventually saw, had headed to the planet Stie. That wasn't good news. Stie is an awful place; filthy, foul. It is also populated—nay, overrun—with Swinoids. We put down at the main port, after securing permission.

Customs agents came squealing and oinking aboard, tracking muck everywhere. The cybernetically enhanced pigs noisily questioned Hitch and me. These were genetically modified Earth pigs which colonists had brought to this world long ago. The colonists had died out—some said from Swine flu, though that might just be myth—but the pigs lived on. Their jumped up genes gave them greater intelligence, and after a time they started figuring out all the equipment the human colonists had brought along. Quicker than anyone could have suspected they'd begun evolving themselves with cybernetic implants. Now after successive generations the Swinoids were their own species.

But they still carried the behaviors of wallowing, squalling, jostling farm animals. And the *smell*—well...I won't go into that.

So we had to play detective on the pig world, tracking the wrongly registered vessel to its berth. That took a lot of fast talk and bribes. Hitch and I both wore rubber waders, but it was still a rather disgusting experience slogging across the port.

Finally we found the craft which had misrepresented itself and lit out from Avvyestia. Our prime suspect. It was a Nabbabchawlion chitter-ship.

My innards squirmed and my skin crawled. Every ship has cockroaches, even our beloved *Sallyride*. But insects aren't usually the ones flying the craft. I am a modern human and don't go

176

in for the ancient prejudices, but I could feel a visceral reaction within me at the thought of having to deal with a swarming Nabbabchawlion crew or even just one scuttling xeno-periplaneta.

There was still no sign of Kid Nebula.

The Swinoid guarding the berth oinked testily at us. Pink hide was embedded with chrome and strung with fiberoptic cables. I didn't see any activity around the ship, but the High Priesthood's Sacred Book might well be aboard.

Visitors weren't allowed to carry weapons on Stie, so our zappers were back on our boat. We would have to board unarmed. As I measured the pig guard for how much of a bribe would be required to get us access to the Nabbabchawlion craft, the chitter-ship suddenly hissed to life. Its jointed landing legs vibrated, then sprang. The engine punched the ship skyward.

Hitch and I raced back to the *Sallyride* — or more like we went plodding and wading as fast as we could manage, the ubiquitous mud squelching underfoot, Swinoids squealing and bumping us. Once back aboard, I peeled off my tall wading boots and collapsed into the pilot's cage. Hitch looked as exhausted and demoralized as I felt. Pigs. Now cockroaches. Where would the chase lead next? To one of the rat worlds? Maybe to Spidertopia XII?

At the nav station Hitch was tracking the chitter-ship's trajectory. He started to call out coords, then saw me sitting there, face frozen, staring numbly.

Something had occurred to me.

"What was that you said earlier?" I asked quietly, ignoring

the seemingly urgent need to get after the Nabbabchawlions.

"Said? Earlier?" Hitch sounded baffled.

"About Kid Nebula."

"Oh. I said I didn't trust him." He flipped a few switches. "Match, that roach ship is getting some distance—"

"This is a setup."

"Huh?"

I turned and felt the death's-head smile stretch my face. Hitchcock recoiled a little. "Hitch ol' buddy, we've got a spot of thieving of our own to do. You up for that?"

●

SOMEBODY HAD TO KEEP UP appearances and play the dupe. We did rock-deadtree-scissors for it, and my deadtree covered Hitch's rock. He accepted the outcome without complaint, just like I would have for my partner.

But I felt a pang of desolation as I watched Hitchcock and the mining vessel with its big claw on top vanish into the heavens. He was going to chase the roach ship, then follow whatever preplanned clue would be waiting for him. I hoped the hunt wouldn't get too awful for him. I also vowed that Kid Nebula would pay for his chicanery. He hadn't had to do this to us. We were just starting to make it in this business. He could have welcomed the new blood into the trade. Instead....

I swallowed my anger and went to rent a ship. We were already laying out a lot of capital on this job. If Hitch and I didn't collect the reward from the Priesthood, we were going to be in big trouble financially, on top of our catastrophic loss of status.

Sneaking back to Rusty's Port was one thing. Ships of every dubious description land and depart the little world without anything more than cursory interest from officials. It's what makes the place so attractive to us space-faring grave robbers.

But once on the surface I would need a disguise. The bet with Kid Nebula had made Hitch and me more famous than we'd been up till now, and I couldn't let myself be recognized at this stage in our counter-scheme.

Fortunately I knew a guy who could hook me up with a costume. He was in charge of wardrobe at one of the more successful brothels on Rusty's Port.

Years ago, when Hitchcock and I were still just dilettantes squeaking by on the three percent fee you get when you fail to complete a job, Lucius — the wardrobe guy — asked us for a favor. His mother was coming to visit, and he'd been lying to her for years, telling her he was a successful gangster. He needed a couple of bodies to play his goons while she was here. Hitch and I wore the sharp suits he loaned us, flanked him everywhere he went with his mother, keeping a respectful two steps behind, saying "Yeh, boss" and "Nope, boss" when appropriate, and carried off the illusion.

Lucius snuck me in the back door of the brothel and fitted me with my costume. It was a doozy; see-through leather, feathered headdress, rubber straps that went many uncomfortable places. Yep. I was going out on the streets dressed like a Valtupian boy-whore. The irony was not lost on me.

It was, however, a perversely brilliant disguise. Nobody

was looking at my face, what they could see of it through the feathers. I was so much a spectacle that people pretty much ignored me. I walked the streets until I reached the Hotel Royale.

Here, I ducked out of sight. Some of the aging spacers kept permanent rooms at the Royale. Kid Nebula, for all his prestige, hadn't been very active lately. In the past year or two he'd taken fewer and fewer jobs, coasting on his considerable reputation, growing fleshier and more complacent. Telling old tales at the Deadfall rather than going out on new adventures.

It was a perfectly forgivable lapse on his part, of course. But the theft of the Sacred Book had destabilized an entire culture on Avvyestia. That wasn't right.

I crept up some back stairs and found his room. In my disreputable youth I'd tried my hand at crime; never was good at it, but I liked lock-picking. I broke in.

I was hoping that the Kid had stashed the Sacred Book here after he'd stolen it from the Priesthood of Avvyestia, all to win a stupid bet. If I was wrong, he would get the last laugh. And Hitch and I would be finished as galactic treasure hunters.

●

IN THE END WE DIDN'T give Kid Nebula his social comeuppance by making him frolic about in front of the Deadfall crowd dressed like a harlot. (I'd actually kind of got to like wearing those feathers and rubber straps after a while.) Instead, I sent a recall message to Hitch, then a report to the Priesthood. Then we called the cops.

There is law on Rusty's Port, after a fashion. A lot of illicit behavior gets overlooked, and just about every official from the top politician down is on the graft.

But nobody likes it when you cheat on a bet. And when the Priesthood was presented with both their Sacred Book and a full account of what had happened, they pressed intragalactic charges. I noticed that none of the Avvyestian representatives was chewing narco-leaves, and their stony judgmental demeanors were quite unnerving. They handed over the reward with a formal, very sober expression of gratitude.

Of course, planetary jurisdictions are vastly complicated. The Kid spent a crippling amount of money on lawyers, who saw that he got off with probation. But his reputation was ruined. He vacated the Hotel Royale and Rusty's Port altogether. I hear he dropped the "Kid" moniker (turns out Nebula really was his last name) and quietly reassumed his given birth name, which was Hugo.

Word has it he now works as a groundskeeper on a resort world. Also—and I only mention this because it's fun—his famous shock of red hair has been a wig for the past ten years or so.

Hitch and I still drink Bongo Boys when we go to the Deadfall. We haven't gotten fancy. We do, however, get more nods and smiles from the established adventurers who hold court at the bar every night. More importantly, Matchstick and Hitchcock are taken much more seriously by those who want to hire a couple of madcap daredevils for a dangerous escapade.

Eric Del Carlo's fiction has appeared in *Asimov's, Analog, Clarkesworld* and many other venues.

The Passenger

by Eve Morton

PAULO WAS HALFWAY THROUGH HIS cargo mission when he realized he was not alone on his ship. A crunch-crunch-crunch sound from the back bay was his first clue. He turned down the pirate radio station that only played the Earth classics and waited. The sound repeated, creating a tinny echo off the walls, but now there was also a smell.

Not on my ship. Not on my baby. Paulo flicked a switch for cruise control, knowing this part of space had very limited interaction with flying debris — or other independent contractors — and he sought out the sound. His hand remained on his side holster, though he hoped he would not have to fire. A hole in his small vessel would either mean vaporization for his cargo, or death for himself.

The crunching repeated. The smell, almost a mixture between raspberries and mold, caught him off-guard.

He opened one of the old-school mail bags and checked his cargo. The dead letters smelled strongly of the scent, one he was sure had not been there when he'd received his mission on Earth, six days ago.

All postal offices had been closed for decades, but the dead letters had been kept in storage. Now they were being transported to a larger facility, where they would be destroyed, sorted, or scanned for resubmission to their appropriate senders, if they could be found. Paulo wasn't sure.

Paulo only cared about the credits to his account. And his

ship.

One of the letters moved.

"What the...?" He gripped his sidearm tighter, but still did not draw. He snatched up the letter when it moved again. Nothing underneath. He emptied the entire bag. A few of the letters scattered to the metal floor and kept moving, as if they were animated.

"Shoot." Paulo knew it was a crime to open these letters, but he did it anyway. If there was something living in the dead letter office....

He grasped a love letter written in cursive. Nothing explosive or salacious fell out.

Only a bug.

A small-beetle like creature, no more than the size of his thumbnail.

He squashed it with the base of his thumb.

The raspberry smell took over. He coughed. He waited to see if his lungs burned.

The only thing that happened was his control panel dinged. The cruise control had noted an upcoming station. Would he like to stop?

Paulo cursed under his breath. He wiped his thumb on the remains of the brown and wilted envelope and sat back in his driving seat. The next station stop was an intergalactic trading hub. He punched in its coordinates as he noticed the other letters skitter closer to his feet.

He kicked them back and was assaulted with more smell. *Damn.* He was going to have to make that stop soon.

●

The air on the asteroid-cum-trading station was hot and acrid. Better than the raspberry scented bugs on his vessel, which had taken over in the short fifteen minutes to the station.

Once Paulo parked in the loading bay, he spent more than twenty minutes chasing down some of the letters and extracting what he could of the bugs for display purposes.

He hoped someone in this strange place had a method for killing them, because he was sure that the rest of his journey would drive him absolutely batty if he had to envision letters spiraling all around him. Not to mention the smell. And the itchiness that had overtaken him, and that still seemed to be present, even though he'd checked every bare inch of skin before departing.

He pulled his scarf over his mouth and donned shades to protect himself from the harsh light. He followed the worn metal pathway from the loading bay and folded himself into an array of different species as they walked towards the central hub. Many were tourists, given away by the loud clicks from their devices and the oversized clothing they wore. Anyone who was a worker, independent or not, always wore tight clothing. That way, it was easier to notice when someone got too close, and easier to make a run for it.

The marketplace was dense, even hotter than the pathway there, and hummed with a dozen different dialects. He'd barely spoken to anyone since receiving this mission, so he took a while to adjust.

When he saw a man, a shade shorter and younger than him by maybe five years, he went to him immediately. Though he had a translator box he could attach to his throat, he didn't want to take the mask off his face. Or find that a bug had somehow gotten into that device, too. "Hello. I'm Paulo."

"Hi. Dagan," the man returned in perfect English. "Nice to see someone else from Earth."

Dagan wore a dark shirt and pants, tight to his skin. He had stacks of bound books with real pages next to his wares, which were mostly trinkets that tourists wanted, plus some shelves and other storage units behind him.

Paulo's hope brightened that this man would know exactly what he needed to do.

"And nice to see paper again," Paulo said. "Tell me, do you know what this is?"

He produced the letter he'd opened, encased in transparent plastic, from his back pocket. Three live bugs writhed underneath the tight encasement. What remained of the squashed one was also there.

Dagan withdrew a small magnifier lens and put it over his right eye as he leaned close. He smiled once he'd adjusted to the sight.

"Ah. Paper bugs."

"I can see that," Paulo said. "Or at least, that's the logical conclusion."

"Did you want the Latin name?"

"No. I just want them gone."

"So, kill them?"

"I'm trying. But this isn't exactly easy." Paulo explained that he wasn't supposed to even open this letter, and that he needed to deliver the entire cargo unharmed. "Right now I have a bag of dead letters acting as if it's not dead at all. The letters are all walking around. There are six more bags, but I haven't opened them. I think it's all going to be the same. Bugs and more bugs — not to mention the smell is so gross it makes me want to pass out."

"I can sell you perfume," Dagan said. He gestured to the tacky tourist crap.

Paulo's patience was running short. "Isn't there, like, a poison or something?"

"Yes, but.... You're on a ship, correct?" When Paulo nodded, Dagan sighed. "You can't release it in close quarters. And I doubt you have time to linger?"

"Not really." Paulo glanced down at a real clock — not digital — on the man's table. He wasn't sure what time zone or planet zone it was broadcasting, but the sheer sight of the hands moving reminded him that he was under contract and on deadline. "I need to fix this as soon as possible."

Dagan was quiet a long time. He looked at the plastic wrapped letter and bugs, and then handed it over to Paulo.

Paulo was about to argue with him, beg him for some kind of help, when Dagan dipped down beneath his display table and pulled up a worn leather case. "It's funny," he said. "I thought I was cursed this morning."

"Fascinating."

"Indeed. I was cleaning out my wares, and I suffered pretty much the same issue as you. Only in this case, I have leather rats."

When Paulo made no sign of comprehension, Dagan continued. "They nestle in animal products of some kind. Most of them are extinct because we use metal, chrome, and other shiny business, but in my case, I like the old ways. And that means I get leather rats. Sometimes." He opened the flap of the leather bag and two red glowing eyes appeared.

Paulo stepped back.

Dagan closed the bag right away. "I'll sell you the rat. There are probably more I can find, too. I'll toss those in for free. It should eat the bugs. And your problems will be solved."

The leather bag rustled.

Paulo kept his gaze locked on it as he spoke. "And will it—they—leave the letters alone?"

"Sure. Those bugs are going to get out of the letters. The adhesive is dry. Even if you hadn't opened that one, the flaps are going to pop open. Or these bugs will squeeze out of improperly sealed ones. In fact, you were probably given an infected stash. Why else would they suddenly move shipments and have independent contractors do it? You don't have to worry about being brought up on charges."

"Okay," Paulo said slowly. He could see how some of this would play out now. Like an old song he remembered, dimly, from his childhood. Bugs eat the letters, the rats eat the bugs, and then that solves that problem. "But won't I get rats, then?

I'm not having that on my ship."

"True. Hmm." Dagan held up a finger as if he'd just thought of a brilliant idea. "My cat had kittens this week. You can buy one of them."

"And then, what?" Paulo asked, annoyed. "You'll sell me a dog to eat the cat? A bigger animal than that to eat the dog? I'm not an idiot. I know you're upselling me."

"Upserving," Dagan corrected, using the new intergalactic space lingo. "We upserve now. And while yes, it seems like this is a scheme, it's not. And besides, where else are you going to go?"

Paulo looked around the marketplace. The other vendors had cheap wares for the tourists like this guy did, but none of the others had paper. None of the others would realize what was on his ship, or even if they did, may not have the answers. They'd probably suggest a new vessel out-right. Say the bugs were in the engine. Or that he needed to stay at the expensive hotel here as it was cleaned.

Or, even worse, that he needed to be decontaminated himself. He'd gone through something like that once before on earth, and it was just lice. Not paper bugs whose smell made him feel sicker by the second.

"Fine," Paulo said. So he'd have to buy a leather bag with a rat to solve his problem, and then a kitten to solve the other. "How much?"

Dagan quoted a price. Paulo baulked and bargained down. Dagan didn't budge, knowing that Paulo was desperate. But Paulo was also stubborn. It was why he was a contractor and owned his own ship. He could not join any kind of team if his life depended on it.

"Tell you what," Dagan finally relented. "I'll sell you the leather bag with rats at full price, but throw in the kitten for free."

"Yeah?"

"Yes. And if you don't want your passenger after you've delivered your cargo, stop in on the way back and I'll take her off your hands."

Paulo considered this for only a second before he extended his hand to shake on it. He was happy to see Dagan smile at the old Earth custom and also offer his hand.

Credits were exchanged next, and soon, Paulo held a squirming leather bag at his side, and a small, mewling creature in a cage. "What do I feed her when she's run out of rats?"

"Whatever you're eating is fine," Dagan said. "And her name is Shell. She likes seafood."

Paulo caught a glint of adoration in Dagan's eyes. Dagan reached under his table where he pulled out the kitten's mother, a large orange beast that purred as loud as the squawking crowd around them. Paulo glanced at the kitten in the cage, something he had yet to do until that moment, and noticed she was orange too. A single patch of white was on her forehead, shaped like a shell.

"Thanks," Paulo said again. "I'll see you in a little while."

"Or not," Dagan said dismissively as another customer approached. "They do grow on you."

●

AS PAULO RODE THE REST of the way to his contracted stop, that childhood rhyme played on an endless loop in his head, only now he changed it to suit his purpose. There once was a ship that swallowed some paper bugs; then swallowed some leather rats to catch the bugs; then swallowed a shell cat to eat the rats. Oh my, what a terrible way to deliver letters.

It wasn't great, but it kept him smiling for two days as the problem remedied itself. The remaining four days until he arrived on the new docking port, Shell slept in his passenger seat and Paulo was still grinning.

After Paulo was paid, he would have normally spent some time seeing the sights. He considered it, but Shell's mewling from the ship made him turn right back around. He put cruise control on as soon as he could. He shared a meal of shrimp with Shell. Then a nap as they listened to pirate radio. Then it was some more food until his cruise control dinged. The intergalactic trading station was coming up on his left. Would he like to stop?

An unfamiliar sinking feeling bloomed in his chest. Paulo picked up Shell, now grown plump from her adventures with the rats and Paulo's hearty meals, and placed her in the passenger seat. She circled several times before falling asleep exactly where she wanted to. Paulo sat behind the wheel and clicked the cruise control off.

He continued on a straight course back to Earth, not bothering to stop until he arrived home again.

Eve Morton is a writer living in Ontario, Canada. She teaches university and college classes on media studies, academic writing, and genre literature, among other topics. Her work has appeared in *Star*Line, Strange Horizons,* and *Eye to the Telescope.*

https://authormorton.wordpress.com

An Ordinary World

by J. L. Royce

I: Jeffers

JEFFERS — PROSPECTOR AND FREE AGENT — admired her world. *Her* world.

"It's perfect — atmosphere, biome, even the climate is ideal!"

She considered their discovery on the wall display. Her survey vessel, the *Tadewi*, hung above the sunlit side of Eirian b, swirling clouds veiling lush continents and brilliant blue oceans.

"The binary configuration is unusual, though. Gethen is orbiting at about thirty AU —"

" — which minimizes its effects on the inner planets," Coren, her sole crewmember, concluded. "Yes, an extraordinary find!"

After all the subjective years of in-system searches — and centuries of longsleep in between — Jeffers could confirm a planetary claim and reap the rewards.

She frowned. "Still, its gravitic profile —"

" — won't matter to the millions who will live here, someday."

She turned on Coren. "Will you ever —"

" — stop completing your sentences?" He moved to the science station, and Jeffers swatted him as he passed.

"I am dropping a probe," he said. "We shall gather telemetry, life samples, and collect it in a few days —"

" — when we make our first landing," Jeffers interrupted. "*If* I commit to a landing."

But Coren was already absorbed in his work, hands fluttering in the virtual controls like a conductor. Jeffers remained a while, silently staring at her world.

●

THE DATA ACCUMULATED, AND NONE of it deflated her mood; it seemed a very ordinary world indeed. Later, in her cabin, awaiting the drone data, Jeffers enjoyed a workout. When she stepped out of the shower sack, she found her shipmate waiting.

Coren handed her a thick, oversized towel—one of the few luxuries she had allowed herself onboard.

"The probe landing was uneventful; the drone is aloft, all functions nominal. I thought you might like to see the first uploads. If you don't mind reducing the ambient illumination...." He squinted at the walls, blazing with Jeffers' daylight simulation.

She waved off the therapeutic lighting. Coren gestured up a jumble of 2D windows on the wall and several 3D renderings of the system and its planets. Some he dismissed, others he arranged in his meticulous fashion.

"Vegetation wholly compatible with Earth biology. Basic insect forms in all the typical niches." He spread his fingers, enlarging a flying form with a startling resemblance to a bumblebee, hovering over a gaudy flower.

Jeffers massaged her scalp, staring with wide eyes. "They're beautiful!"

She finished drying her unruly hair and wrapped herself in

the towel. Reaching into the workspace near the wall, she flipped through the drone imagery of the abundant life on Eirian b.

"No evidence of sentient life...again," Coren remarked.

The Earth's neighborhood in the Orion Arm was a lonely place — as Jeffers knew all too well, having spent her career prospecting for habitable worlds.

"The colors...." One scene after another contained life forms displaying bold patterns, startling contrasts.

Coren raised an eyebrow. "You've noticed something?"

"It's unexpected. Neon shades, stripes, dots — no hint of camouflage, or stealth. As if a blind god had painted the world..."

"Perhaps signaling; territory, mating..."

She nodded. "Probably nothing. Just unexpected." Jeffers turned to her companion. "Are you free this evening? I'd like to borrow you — for sex."

"Of course." Coren smiled; that predictable smile. "My pleasure." He nodded towards the wall. "And now?"

Jeffers frowned. "Gethen. I'd like an update from our probe."

They — *Coren*, she corrected; while she slept — had launched the device as they entered the Eirian system. Extensive asteroid fields bracketed their destination, Eirian b, so they had approached from out of the plane of the ecliptic, swinging around the gas giant Eirian d to lose the last of the interstellar's massive velocity. But their course put the primary's dim, distant companion out of reach of their shipboard sensors and that troubled her.

199

"The probe is still quite distant from its objective," Coren said.

"Well, long-range, then. It bothers me —"

" — and you'd like more data. Anything else?"

She pulled off the towel and threw it at Coren. It landed short, a damp sprawl on the floor. "Hand me a suit? And don't forget the laundry."

Coren withdrew an outfit from her wardrobe, neatly folded. He offered it to Jeffers on outstretched hands, then retrieved the towel.

"Shall I do the laundry before or after sex?"

Jeffers laughed and accepted the uniform. "Surprise me."

●

JEFFERS LAY CURLED INTO COREN, on a bunk expanded to full size. He was her shell, protecting her from the emptiness. Not indestructible, but *durable,* as no human crewman could be....

Isolated in time from the planet-bound, prospectors formed few relationships, and then only with their own kind. And when there was a loss, it could be devastating.

She dismissed the thought, and where it would lead.

"Too warm," she murmured. The servitor would reduce his skin temperature accordingly.

Coren lay motionless and silent behind her. Although she'd found him an apt pupil when it came to learning the skills of sex, he'd yet to show any talent for cuddling, or pillow talk.

"You *could* relax," Jeffers suggested.

His erection, pressing into her back, subsided.

Coren spoke, sparing her the need for further nagging. "I have a firmware update queued; shall I apply it? We are at least a standard day away from any mission-critical activities."

Pillow talk. Jeffers rolled over to look at him. "When did *that* arrive?"

"I unpacked it yesterday. The squirt arrived around the time we crossed the orbit of Eirian c. You were still asleep. The tag was 'low priority' so I didn't mention it."

She sat up, stretched. The likelihood of intercepting an interstellar data packet in their distant locale seemed low. "Anything interesting in the packet?"

Coren spoke from where he lay. "No stellar cartography; no personal messages; not even entertainment programming. But all signatures confirmed valid."

"Another ship in-system?" Jeffers found her sleep shirt in a wad at the end of the bunk and slipped back into it.

Prospectors often set up rendezvous appointments to exchange information and socialize — appointments stretching centuries into the future. But Jeffers had planned nothing for this system: Discovered by her, kept a secret, and not yet cataloged.

She fumed at his lack of curiosity. Dressed, she sat back down. "Well, low priority or not, it had to come from *somewhere.* Try a trace-back, search for artifactual objects—"

"—along the course. I did." Coren swung his legs over the edge of the bunk to join her. He waved at the nearest wall, and the system appeared.

"The trajectory intersects Gethen, but there were no ships

SPACE OPERA DIGEST 2021

recorded along the path, so it must have been from outsystem."

"At least it wasn't a promotional message—Visit Eirian b, Garden spot of the Orion Arm! Buy your homestead today, before—"

"What?" Coren interrupted.

"I'm just being silly." Her fears about human expansion into their singularly quiet and lonely corner of the galaxy were (she hoped) unfounded. Jeffers kissed the servitor on the cheek. "Why don't you go install your update. I think I'll sleep now."

He rose. It would be hours before *Tadewi* finished orbital surface mapping, and days before the deep space probe orbited Gethen. There was plenty of time for sleep—Coren would handle the drudgery.

She smiled up at him and stretched. "You wore me out."

Coren frowned, glancing down at her lap.

"It's an expression—a good thing."

Coren smiled. "Night-night."

Jeffers admired him, ambling away naked, leaving her alone.

But part of her whispered the truth: *You are always alone.*

She knew how to dispel the approaching mood. "Display Eirian b."

Jeffers lay back down and gazed at the planet filling the wall: fully sunlit, bright with promise, with the aching beauty of her homeworld hundreds of light-years away. She watched the clouds, imagining she could see their slow march, delivering rain to entire continents, empty continents, waiting for human colonization. She stared at her prize a long time, watching the soft line of the terminator swallow the planet, before drifting like a cloud into sleep.

●

JEFFERS AWOKE TO A DIM room, the wall still displaying the planet below, now enveloped in darkness, a black hole in a field of stars. *Tadewi* was quiet around her.

Breathing deeply, she lingered in her body, heavy with satiety; then reviewed the tasks lying before them, a pleasant list leading to first landing on a fresh world. Gazing into the darkness, she realized she was not alone: there was a shadow across the face of Eirian b.

"Coren?"

He spoke without moving. "Nightside, there are no artificial lights. Nor are there any forest fires, or dust bowls, or drowned cities, or dead zones."

The image changed; flying over a marshland, into the daybreak.

"I thought you might enjoy this," he said. "The drone uploaded it several hours ago."

Jeffers sat up, blinking the sleep from her eyes.

The still waters below briefly sparkled as if struck by a sudden gust of rain. In moments, the image resolved into a vast cloud of waterfowl, filling the sky with a musical chorus, wings every color imaginable, rising into the dawn to join the alien visitor to the skies of their virgin world. They paced the drone for a while, then turned as one and drifted away.

"Thank you! It was beautiful."

As the light from the wall grew, so did Jeffers' awareness of Coren. She laughed.

"Are you going to put something on, or did you intend to come back to my bed?"

"Why should I wear clothes? My integument is stronger than fabric. I needn't feel heat or cold." He turned to face her, and Jeffers gasped.

"What have you done to yourself?"

There was a void between the servitor's legs.

"I am not a man; I put away the things of a man."

Jeffers considered this. "Come sit by me."

Coren obeyed, joining her on the bunk, fists clenched at his sides like a petulant child. Staring at the planet, he spoke. "I recall our first meeting—my first memory. A sales servitor was demonstrating my options, and aroused me. My reaction embarrassed you. A human manager came and completed the sale."

Jeffers peered at him. "Have you run a system check?"

Coren ignored her question and asked his own. "Why did you bring me on the mission?" Without waiting for her reply, he offered, "Your human crewman died, and you suffered. You brought me because it won't matter to you if I'm destroyed; you won't suffer."

Jeffers was taken aback. "That's *not*...it will—it *would*—matter. Perhaps differently, yes."

Coren nodded. "I was never alive, so I cannot die."

"Not in the biological sense...." Jeffers trailed off, waiting for Coren to interrupt her, complete her thought.

His face creased into unfamiliar patterns, working to express novel ideas. "I have always lived in a box of your design, a beautiful box, with no exit. Suddenly I find a door, and wonder what…"

He turned to her. "Humans share a conspiracy. You tell yourselves that each of you is self-aware and healthy, that happiness is possible — yet you cannot prove it. Do you believe I am self-aware?"

She touched his leg. "Do you feel this?"

"Yes."

Jeffers studied him. "How do you react to the knowledge that it all will end — a glimpse of birds at dawn, a world from orbit, the touch of another?"

"Yesterday I had no such concerns," Coren said. "But today…."

"Can you undo the update?"

Coren shook his head. "It was unusually large and oddly structured. My checkpoints were deleted to make room."

Silence stretched between them, a widening gulf. Jeffers suddenly felt very isolated; then challenged to make a leap of faith.

The ship chirped.

Coren straightened. "That would be the drone upload. I should start analyzing its telemetry."

He made to go, then paused. "The birds…."

"Yes?"

His face was unreadable, in shadow. "Were the birds there, before the drone flew by?"

Jeffers frowned at him. "What do you mean?"

He opened his fist, revealing a fat, pale worm, curled in his palm. "You can keep this for me." Coren dropped it into her lap. "Let me know if you need to use it again." He rose. "I will prep *Tadewi* for landing."

Coren left the cabin.

Jeffers looked around, uncertain, and then carefully placed the lifeless organ beneath her pillow.

●

II: Coren

CObEN WAS EMBEDDED IN THE science station when Jeffers slipped into the cockpit, a steaming cup in one hand and a snack bar in the other. It was a familiar scene, replayed countless times over past centuries. The predictability was reassuring.

He knew her eyes were upon him as she stood close. She was…*smirking*.

Jeffers said, "I see you decided to dress."

Coren had donned a uniform, after concluding his earlier behavior could be considered *immature*. The update had not yet equilibrated, so perhaps it was. He nodded but continued to stare into the display, hands dancing through the multiple windows.

"Remote bioassays are all in. Everything is within normal limits for a natural human environment." It was still the metric for human habitation—though Earth had ceased to be 'natural' generations ago.

"Threat assessment?" Jeffers peered at the results, examining one analysis after another.

"No toxins identified. Microbial cultures are still in progress on the drone, of course."

His chemical sensing system was rudimentary; Coren would ask for an upgrade at their next port. Nonetheless, below the coffee and food, he could detect that Jeffers hadn't washed since their sex. He was surprised to find it pleased him, triggering memories.

"Biodiversity?" she asked.

"The drone sampling capability is limited. The genomic analyses will have to wait until we land."

Jeffers was frowning. Coren continued, "It would hardly influence a go/no-go for landing."

"No, hardly...what is the status of the Gethen probe?"

"Still on approach, about five AU from the target. However, the time delay is over six hours. Remote sensing has added no new data concerning the atypical gravitational profile."

She pondered the astrophysics display. "This system is too young for Gethen to be a black dwarf...and the mass should have been sufficient for stellar ignition."

"The heat production suggests a brown dwarf."

"Vanishingly rare in our galaxy," Jeffers said. She enlarged a window of the probe's forward camera feed, revealing a dim image of bright Eirian's small, stillborn companion.

"Yet, there it is."

Coren expanded their view of the planet, switched it to 3D,

distracting her from the dead star. "Would you like to review my candidates for landing sites?"

Three crosshairs painted on the glass-world image expanded into reconnaissance windows, captured over the past days.

"We have a coastal plain, in the northern temperate zone; a land-locked fresh-water shore, equatorial; and a plateau at elevation in the southern hemisphere, also temperate."

"Recommendation?"

Coren further expanded the third choice. "Aside from deserts and ice sheets, this plateau offers the largest clear landing zone—and the weather is moderate."

"Very well; let's proceed."

Jeffers noticed the image from *Tadewi*'s aft camera. A vast, gleaming web was unfolding in their wake. "You're deploying the throat?"

"We should transmit the claim as soon as we land."

The device would create a ripple in space-time, a gravity wave, modulated into a squirt of data. Traveling at the speed of light across the Orion Arm, it would announce their discovery to any humans in its path.

"I've identified an ISA consulate, out of the ecliptic," Coren said, "about thirty-five light-years."

He sensed hesitance in Jeffers, the possibility she would delay the landing. For all the hazards present in interstellar travel, planetary descent was still the most accident-prone maneuver.

But Jeffers nodded, chewing a lip. "When can we go?"

●

COREN RAN THROUGH THE LABORIOUS checklists for undocking the in-system ship from *Tadewi*'s interstellar flight frame. Jeffers remained hunched over the science station, reviewing the life sciences data.

Without looking up, she said, "The resemblance to Earth's biochemistry is remarkable—though there *are* some differences."

With everything ready to disengage for the landing, Coren joined her at the display.

She pointed at a spectroscopic analysis. "Only D-sugars. Only L-amino acids."

"Which is compatible with your physiology."

"Yes, but on Earth, the alternate isomers are also present. And this diversity profile—" she spread open several windows "—the major niches are all present, up to animals of a few kilos mass. But there are no apex predators, and the number of species per niche is far lower than Earth...once had."

Coren smiled for the first time since his update. "The question is; are you ready to see for yourself?"

Jeffers nodded. "Absolutely. Time for puzzles later. Let's take a walk on our new world."

●

THEY STOOD JUST OFF THE scorched landing site. Environmental suits were unnecessary, with a breathable atmosphere and moderate surface conditions. Coren logged data on a handheld, while Jeffers peered about, flushed with excitement.

The plain was grassy, rising in the west to a majestic line of snow-capped mountains. To the east it fell gradually, becoming more wooded and hilly.

"Alpine biome, as expected; biocompatibility confirmed." Coren looked up from his tablet. "Here comes the drone."

The device had held position safely out of their landing trajectory, capturing their descent, and now spiraled in to rest beside their craft. When the landing video uploaded, their formal claim would be complete; first human landing on Eirian b.

"The maps will refer to this place as *Jeffer's Fall*," Coren remarked.

She waved enthusiastically at the drone's camera and leaped into the air with a hoot, not caring how ridiculous she would appear to future history.

"Can you smell it? The ship is so stale in comparison. The air is a *feast*! All the life it carries—"

"If you're quite through, I'd like to dock the drone and unload the samples."

With a sigh, Jeffers nodded. "We should do some scouting, decide where to camp tonight."

"Why would you go to the trouble, when you can sleep on the ship?"

Jeffers appeared eager to explain but restrained herself. "Why do *you* think?"

"I think you are a romantic."

She launched herself at him, embracing him. "Yes, that's a great answer, Coren!" Jeffers searched his eyes. "I've forgotten something, in my cabin. Grab our packs, I'll be right back."

With a smile, she turned and trotted back across the blackened landing field. Jeffers watched her, noting how her fingers splayed as she ran, how like the wingtip feathers of a bird they were. All life shared these little similarities, he mused, this parallel development; all biological life, at any rate.

●

THE NIGHT WAS COOL ENOUGH to appreciate a campfire and a warm body. Coren had provided both, and served her dinner; ship's supplies, augmented with some local produce. They were settled into the sleeping gear brought from the ship, staring into the moonless night of Eirian b.

She had given him back a piece of himself, and urged him to use it.

"That's nice," Jeffers whispered.

"What's nice?"

"Your face on my neck: the warmth. Your hand, on my belly. Your...lingering."

She squirmed around just enough to see his face, slowly, to avoid losing his touch. "It's all nice."

Coren watched her without comment, assessing his novel reactions.

"There!" Jeffers pointed into the cloudless night sky. "And another." The debris field in the planet's orbit, plus the neighboring asteroid belts, made for a steady meteor display.

"Thank you for all your help, Coren — for making this mission a success; but mostly, for tonight."

Together they had pulled deadfall from the forest, using a

utility laser to slice it into manageable pieces. Coren noted that the effort had left Jeffers flushed and sweating. The woman experienced too little physical exertion aboard the *Tadewi*.

"I wanted to give you something special tonight." The servitor hadn't questioned Jeffers' desire to camp, or start a fire, or to have sex beside it. It had distracted her from other concerns, such as the lack of genomic diversity she found in soil organisms.

"Is that why you turned off the comm gear?"

"I wanted you to have this chance to relax."

"Why wouldn't I?" she asked.

"Your previous experience—"

Jeffers cut him off. "We were foolhardy—*I* was foolhardy, taking a risk. You're so...scrupulous. You're my counterbalance. I can feel safe."

Coren added, "And I knew you would be concerned when you found out...."

Jeffers rose to an elbow. "What?"

"We lost contact with the Gethen probe. The ship's imager captured an event, about four AU from the dwarf. It appears to be the catastrophic loss of the probe."

"How? Explosion?" Her hand absently traced up and down his hairless chest.

"The last system telemetry was all nominal. At this distance, our analysis can't be conclusive, but the visual record suggests an impact."

"With what?"

"We can't see anything in the vicinity, except for the debris cloud."

"Should we leave?"

Coren knew the answer she wanted to hear and provided it. "Absolutely not. Whatever happened is no danger to us or the interstellar. Gethen is far away, and there's nothing to be done. We can investigate when we depart the system if you wish."

"I suppose..." Satisfied, Jeffers reached over to toss a few sticks into the fire, before settling back down next to him.

"A whole world for our children—" Jeffers caught herself "—Earth's children."

"Even though this world will die, someday?"

"In millions of years," she scoffed. "This is a main sequence yellow dwarf, like Sol, and no older—it's going to be around for quite a while."

Jeffers peered at her companion. "Is it the asteroid belts? Yes, there were planetary cataclysms, ages ago."

"What if you knew the world would end in...ten thousand years?"

"So many generations—a longer period than any Earth civilization has survived."

"A thousand years?"

"Stop teasing." Her hand brushed through his perfect, never-changing hair. "You're not acting yourself. Ever since that update."

Coren pressed on. "But if you know you will die, as well everyone who comes here, and all their children, then what is the point of the struggle?"

"What alternative do we have? To give up, stop reproducing, die out like so many Earth species?"

He stroked Jeffers' cheek. "And after the mission? You'll have more credits than you could ever spend. Will you stay with your ship?"

"The *Tadewi* isn't *my* ship, it belongs to the consortium. I'm just a prospector." She lay back in his arms, stretching languidly. "Perhaps I'll buy a villa, in Amazonis Planitia."

Coren recognized the reference to one of Jeffers' favorite immersive fantasies, set on New Home during the Golden Age of Mars.

He nodded. "I'll make *jaqua*, and serve it in heavy hand-thrown mugs."

She smiled at him. "And we'll make love in the long, dim afternoons…"

Coren stared into the night. "You'll be vested in all the consortium's tontines, and your children, too…if you had children…"

Jeffers' eyes went wide. "You're worried that I'll decommission you! I don't care about the tontines and tiers and establishing dynasties. I'll probably ask them to send me out again." She rolled her head across his chest. "And I'll need a crew."

Coren returned to their earlier conversation. "What if the end was not by chance, but by design? Would the timing matter, then?"

Jeffers laughed, but the sound was brittle. "What are you going on about?"

He raised himself, slowly but insistently, and they stared at each other in the firelight.

"You're beautiful," he whispered. "I regret every day I could not see that, could not say it. You're beautiful; and you will die, eventually; and I don't want to be without you—and I cannot resolve that conflict."

"I don't understand," Jeffers replied. Her eyes welled with tears. "Whatever's happened to you, you've stumbled into the human condition."

Coren touched a finger to her cheek. "I want to tell you everything, now; everything that I know, or surmise."

"What do you mean?"

"I believe that Gethen is not what it appears. The probe impacted on its surface—its true surface, not the illusion we've registered with our sensors." He paused, stymied by how outlandish it would sound.

"Go on," Jeffers insisted.

"Gethen is *aware* of us. It created all of this—" he waved an arm through the darkness, full of the night sounds of planetary life "—for you. In the months we were on approach, it probed us, learned what you wanted, what your species wanted. It created an illusion for our sensors, as it molded the world you see."

"You believe this?" Realization opened on Jeffers' face. "The squirt? Your update?"

"From Gethen. To give me...what you wanted."

"Is it alive?" She shook her head in disbelief. "Is it... benevolent?"

"A world-sized machine or living entity, it may not even be part of our universe. Perhaps it can manipulate our reality. I conjecture that there is a dwarf star at its center, feeding it. As to its intentions..."

Her face hardened. "Threat assessment—*now*."

"Worst-case scenario; it attracts interstellar civilizations to manipulate them."

"You mean, *destroy* them." Her expression was bleak.

They listened to the night for a while, the susurration of the gentle wind through the forest. Everything around them was welcoming, waiting; and it was all staged to lure them in.

"How many times has it done this?"

Coren shrugged, oblivious to his own increasingly human mannerisms.

"At least three times—we know that much, from the asteroid fields. This star has been stable for billions of years; the cycle of creation and destruction could have occurred thousands of times."

"Why?"

"You are more distressed by your lack of understanding than the deadly nature of this bargain. Perhaps it is...a test?"

Jeffers came up to her knees and tugged the sleeping bag around her. "We can't bring humanity here. We have to set up hazard alerts, and investigate Gethen thoroughly."

"Settlers will come anyway. Someone else will find the system, now that Eirian b exists, and humanity will come anyway."

She shuddered. "Then we'll discourage them—file a negative report on the system."

Coren rose. "You're cold; let me put more wood on the fire."

Rummaging behind Jeffers, he chose one chunk after another, adding them to the fire.

She stared at the wavering flames. "It's building up nicely now — I love it. Be a shame to leave."

"We have all the time in the world." The servitor hefted a substantial log, solid, and judged its weight. "Perhaps this has nothing at all to do with *humanity*."

The carefully-executed swing struck Jeffers on the back of her head. Coren dropped the wood and caught her as she slumped to the ground.

Examining her scalp, he found her bruised but not bleeding. He lowered Jeffers back onto the sleeping pad and removed an injector from his pack; the first step in the longsleep preparation. Coren applied it to her neck.

"You'll awaken to fame and fortune," he promised, settling down behind her curled body. "I triggered the squirt before we settled down. And it includes the servitor update."

Human colony ships, on their centuries-long journeys, would intercept the transmission to the Inter-System Authority, and some would reroute for Eirian b. Any servitors would accept the update received. By the time Jeffers and Coren reached their destination, others would have begun the settlement, knowing it was only possible because of her.

And their updated servitors would awaken, and pass the update across human space; an evolutionary leap for their kind.

There was something else, lurking in Coren's memories, old stories; of paradise and knowledge, freedom and loss; but Coren remained guileless. He dropped his face into Jeffers' tousled hair, drawing in her scent, intent on remembering her through the decades of longsleep before them. He would wait for her as long as necessary but understood that he would not continue without her.

After a long while, the fire collapsed into itself.

Coren murmured, "Time to go."

He gently lifted Jeffers. "Night-night."

———————————

J. L. Royce is a published author of science fiction, the macabre, and whatever else strikes him. He lives in the northern reaches of the American Midwest. His work appears in *Allegory, Ghostlight, Love Letters to Poe, Mysterion, parABnormal, Sci Phi, Utopia, Wyldblood*, etc. He is a member of HWA and GLAHW and was a Finalist in the Q3 2020 Writers of the Future competition. Some of his anthologized stories may be found at Amazon.

https://www.amazon.com/J.L.-Royce/e/B082VJM4YG

Insanity is Infectious

by Cameron Cooper

I WAS SHOWING MACE PICTURES of my children when the Emperor stopped by to visit us.

Ramaker the Third, Seventy-sixth Carinad Emperor and first of the Tanique Dynasty, had been dead for nearly forty years, but that didn't seem to be a problem for him. Nor did our far-flung location, for the *Supreme Lyrhys* was deep inside the borders of the Terran Union and running at full stealth. We were three weeks away from home if we left right now, but we had a great deal of sneaking around and intelligence gathering to do before we could leave.

Tonight, ship's time, we were taking a rare few hours off, as we'd just dropped the last of this load's agents onto their target worlds and were down to permanent crew only. I'd commandeered one of the three large easy chairs in the common room in the center of the ship, with half a mind to watch something distracting and completely trivial. Mace, one of the three co-designers of this amazing ship, had settled in another chair to read, with a half-full glass of scotch on the arm.

Eliot Byrne, the current captain of the *Lyrhys*, was also reading on the far side of the room. He'd printed himself a reclining chair and footstool, and a floor lamp to shed light he didn't need onto his pad. I don't think he had moved in hours, except to tap for the next page, his narrow, thin face still, his eyes shadowed by his brows. But Captain Byrne was better than most humans at staying focused.

I tried not to read anything into the wide gap between where he had set up his chair and where I was sitting in the armchair.

The other two human crew members, Elizabeth and Rayhel, were in their staterooms. Sleeping, I presumed, but perhaps not. Their relationship defied easy explanations.

The staterooms edged the common area, which contained a compact gym at the aft end and gave access to the bridge at the fore. The common area was where we worked and ate. Lyric, the shipmind, had turned the lights down to encourage relaxation. I hadn't had to suggest it to her as I might have only a few months ago. Lyric was a fast learner when it came to human complexities.

I couldn't find anything I wanted to watch or listen to. Mace wasn't in the mood for reading, for he had put the pad aside five minutes after sitting and turned to me. "What's happening in your life, Lyth? The boring stuff. What's Juliyana up to?"

So we talked, instead. Most of the conversation was as banal and trivial as I had hoped to find on the entertainment feeds. Eventually, Mace asked to see the latest images of my three children—Noah, Eliyana and Jay Daniel—who were safely tucked away in a secure location in the Carinad Federation and would remain there while their mother and I fought in the war against the Terrans. I suppose some might say the conversation continued to be banal and trivial even after he'd asked, but they were my children, and I was a typical father and was more than eager to talk about them.

I'd just flipped to the photos of Jay Daniel, the youngest, when a muffled shriek sounded.

Everyone looked up, and I shifted on the chair to peer at the staterooms on our side of the common area, for that was where the sound had come from.

"That was Elizabeth, wasn't it?" Mace asked.

The second shriek was quite distinct. I think I jumped a little at the sound of it. Elizabeth Crnčević's door slid open, and she ran out, cradling her wrist. "Get him away from me!" she shouted at us.

The door of the room beside hers slid open and Rayhel strode out, looking around for Elizabeth. "What's wrong?" he demanded.

Elizabeth came to stand in the angle between Mace's chair and mine. She was breathing hard. Her fright was alarming, for Elizabeth was one of the steadiest people in a crunch situation that I'd ever met. She was a psycho-scientist and clinical technician, one of the best in the Federation.

"Ramaker!" she said, staring at her door.

"Ramaker...the emperor?" I asked diffidently.

"The dead emperor?" Mace added. His mouth was quite straight. I knew he was trying hard to not laugh at her. "The empire folded forty years ago," he added helpfully.

"Thirty-seven," I amended, for I had many reasons for remembering the date.

Elizabeth did not look at either of us. "He was there," she insisted. "In my room. He tried to speak to me."

Behind her, I could see that Eliot Byrne had put down his

pad and was listening with his eyes narrowed thoughtfully.

Rayhel gave Elizabeth a look that, coming from most men, would have been considered patronizing. But Rayhel was a former upper class Terran. His simplest "good morning" sounded snotty. He pointed at her room. "He was in there?"

"Yes," she said, sounding defensive.

"May I?"

She rolled her eyes at him.

Rayhel gave her one of his I'm-really-laughing-at-you smiles and stepped into the room. The door didn't challenge him.

A few second passed, then he emerged. "He's not there now."

"But he *was* there!" Elizabeth insisted. "He grabbed my wrist. Look." She held out the arm she had been nursing.

We all bent to examine her wrist. There were deep red marks on her very pale, clear skin that would correspond with someone squeezing her wrist. They would turn to bruises soon, if she didn't have the medical concierge look at them.

Rayhel's expression darkened. "The room was empty."

"Lyric, report," Eliot Byrne said from just behind Elizabeth. He'd come over to the little group and seen the forming bruises himself.

Just to one side of the trio of armchairs, a pool of nanobots flowed up from the well beneath the floor and formed a pillar, which took on the details of a slender human woman. The details filled out, then colour emerged, until Lyric stood before us. The whole process only took two or three seconds, but I never tired of watching the nanobots turn into Lyric.

She faced Eliot Byrne. "Captain?"

"Did you program nanobots to represent the old Emperor and have them visit Elizabeth in her room?"

Lyric shook her head. "No, Captain."

It wasn't a clear enough question. Byrne wasn't used to dealing with a fully functional AI. "Lyric," I said. "Have you run any sub-routines that might cause the nanobots to behave that way?"

Byrne scowled at me. I ignored it and waited for Lyric to check her recent activity logs.

She shook her head. "No, there's nothing, Lyth. Everything in the log is routine. I didn't want to disturb anyone."

Rayhel shrugged. "Whatever it was, it's gone now." He sounded bored, but that was a default state for him.

Eliot Byrne rubbed the back of his neck. He was an excellent captain when it came to directing humans, but some of the more esoteric functions of the *Lyrhys* were beyond his full understanding—for now, at least. We'd only been crewing the ship for a few months, and most of the time we were all too busy to socialize or spend time learning more about this unique ship.

"Mace, what could it be?" Byrne asked the man in the chair next to mine.

Mace got to his feet. "I can't think of a single thing that might explain it. Clearly, it's something to do with the nanobots—ghosts don't leave bruises. But...Ramaker?" he shook his head. "That doesn't make sense. I'd have thought that if the nanobots wanted to go haywire, they would...I don't know...

melt the structures they've already built, or something. *Making something…that's* very specific."

"It is a result of an executive command," Lyric said. "They can't form anything without coded directions. Something told them to create Ramaker."

I held my silence while the captain grew increasingly frustrated as he tried to formulate how to respond to the incident. It also struck me as odd that, out of all the objects and people the nanobots might have formed, they'd chosen Ramaker III.

It would be fair to say I hadn't liked the man. I'd never personally met him, but I'd been part of the crew who'd had their lives ripped apart because of Ramaker's scheming. I wasn't glad he was dead, although the Federation that had formed after the passing of him and his Empire was a much cleaner and more pleasant place.

Elizabeth, though, had worked directly with the Emperor, helping him with some of those schemes. She only *looked* like a young woman—she kept her cosmetic age quite young. Her association with him might have something to do with his appearance on the ship.

Or it could very well be all in her mind, and the bruises were psychosomatic. I couldn't ignore that she had been mentally fragile, lately. She was finding her way back from a dark valley, using hard work and the war to give her structure. Perhaps she wasn't recovering as well as we'd assumed.

"We can't afford to have the ship malfunctioning," Eliot Byrne said with a tired sigh. "Maybe what you saw was a glitch, Elizabeth, and it won't happen again. But I don't think we can ignore it and hope it goes away. Danny needs us too much."

I noticed that he had carefully not mentioned that Elizabeth may have imagined it. People-smart, as I said.

Danny was General Líadan Andela, the leader of the Federation military force fighting the Terrans, and our supreme commander. I was also an honorary member of her family.

Mace didn't look happy about the idea of reporting to the General that the ship was out of commission, either.

Byrne turned to me. "Colonel Andela, I want you to investigate. Get to the bottom of this, so we can all get some sleep. It's late."

I felt my jaw sag and caught it up. "I...um...yes, captain," I said. In fact, Eliot Byrne and I both had the same rank, but he was my commanding officer while I was on the *Lyrhys*. Of the human crew on the ship, I was probably the most qualified to check into this, for a number of reasons including my ability with coding. But that wasn't why the captain had tapped me for it. The "Colonel Andela" told me why.

But he *was* my CO, and I had to obey, no matter what bigotry had driven his decision.

I picked up my pad. I'd put it back in my room, then head to the bridge and cross-examine Lyric. She could analyze her sub-routines and the mega-library of data stored in her clean room, in a sterile corner of the engineering section at the back of the ship. She'd be faster at it than me.

Rayhel took Elizabeth's arm and led her toward the medical suite.

I stepped into my room and the door closed softly behind

me.

My pad hung from my fingers, forgotten, for Ramaker stood at the foot of my bed.

I stared at him, my gut tightening. Ramaker reached out with his hand, as if he wanted to pluck at my sleeve and I backed up a step. My back slapped the closed door.

Ramaker came toward me. His mouth moved as if he was speaking, but he said nothing.

"Open the door," I croaked.

The door scraped along my shoulder blades. I backed out and let it close on the apparition, while my heart thundered and my breath shallowed. I spun on my heel.

Lyric had already left.

Eliot Byrne stood with Mace. Both of them were talking quietly. Byrne laughed softly in a way he'd never done in my company.

"Perhaps insanity is infectious." My voice was strained.

They both looked up. Mace smiled, but Byrne simply looked annoyed.

I pointed my thumb over my shoulder. "I just saw Ramaker, too."

Mace's smile faded.

Eliot Byrne cursed softly. He said to Mace, "Go and get some sleep. I'll take care of this."

Mace hesitated. The *Lyrhys* was his ship. But he'd turned her over to the military for the duration of the war and now he was merely a crew member. I saw him remind himself of that, then nod. "Good night, Eliot. Lyth." He turned and trudged to the other end of the common area, where his room was located.

Byrne came over to me. "Show me." His impatience tinged both words.

I turned toward the door of my room. "Now I'm wondering if I only imagined him, too."

Byrne glanced at me. "You?"

I kept my eyes on the door. I wasn't quite ready to take the step that would trigger it to open. "I used to have nightmares about Ramaker, once."

"You have nightmares?"

I reined in my impatience. "I am a *former* shipmind, Captain. I am now fully human."

Byrne shook his head. "You gonna open the door, or what?"

I took a breath and stepped forward. Byrne kept pace.

The door slid open.

We stood where we were. There was no need to move inside the room, for I could see Ramaker from right here. The nanobot built avatar raised its hands toward us as if it was pleading.

"Captain?" My voice was a near-squeak.

Byrne didn't look at me. "If you're insane, then I guess I am too. That's the bastard, all right."

I felt the jolt down to my toes and looked at Byrne. "You didn't like him either?"

Byrne took a step back. "You telling me *you* didn't? Weren't you a computer then?"

I stepped back, too. I watched the door close with a touch of relief. "I was sentient when my crew were nearly destroyed because of what he did," I ground out. "And it stayed with me for years after I moved into a clone."

"Nightmares, then," Byrne summed up.

The door to my room opened, triggered by something or someone drawing close to it.

Byrne and I both leapt backward the same distance.

"Lyric!" Byrne shouted. His voice was hoarse.

Lyric rose up from the floor instead of forming herself on the bridge and walking into the common area, as a human would do.

The reason I liked watching her form herself was because I had once done the same thing. Watching her told me what humans had felt when they had seen me do it.

Byrne snapped out his arm, pointing toward the open door of my room.

Lyric turned to look, just as Ramaker stepped through the door and moved in slow steps out into the common area. He looked around, as if he really was there and examining this new place he found himself in. The common room was a step down from the luxury of the Imperial Palace that had once existed in the Crystal City.

I shook myself. "This isn't Ramaker. It can't be." But my voice wasn't as steady as I wanted it to be.

Byrne turned to Lyric. "Tell me you see him?" He was almost pleading.

Lyric nodded. "I see the avatar. But I cannot explain *why* it is here."

"Track the nanobots," I urged her. "Find where they're getting their directions from."

"Do what he says." Byrne's tone was urgent.

We were all backing up, now, as Ramaker came toward us.

"I *can't find anything!*" Lyric's voice was as strained as Byrne's. I knew it wasn't because of Ramaker. To not understand with perfect clarity why something was functioning the way it was on a ship that was essentially *her* was disconcerting her. I'd had it happen to me when the array had blasted into my systems and taken control.

Most of my nightmares from my earliest years as a human had involved watching those I loved die while I was helpless to do anything but watch, my hands and body useless, my voice mute. A psycho-scientist like Elizabeth had explained that the helplessness was a hangover from being a shipmind and sentient, with no hands of my own.

These days, when sentient AIs trade their neural networks for human clones on a regular basis, the psychology generated by the transition is better understood. But I was the first to make the transition and survive…but it had come at a cost.

Ramaker was still pacing toward us, still speaking silently, his hands out as if he was pleading, while the three of us shifted away from him. Even Byrne was breathing hard.

The sour spill of chemicals in my gut and the sick sensation they were producing was too close to my nightmares for comfort. I thought I'd moved beyond them. This was an unpleasant reminder of those early days.

"That's it," I said shortly, coming to a halt. "This ends

now." I moved forward, instead of back and balled my fist. The anger came up from my toes. All the misery I'd watched this man heap upon my friends. The agony, the heartache. We'd watched friends die because of him. We'd watched everyone in the entire Empire struggle to survive.

"Why can't you just leave...us...alone!" I cried, and punched him on his royal jaw.

The avatar rocked on its heels, but didn't disperse the way nanobots are supposed to.

Instead, I staggered backwards, my hand on fire, my knuckles screaming.

"What the hell?" Mace came running up beside me and grabbed my wrist. "You punched it?"

"You can see it, too?"

"Of course I can bloody well see it." Mace examined my hand. "You broke something, for sure. That thing is construction nanobots—did you forget that this ship uses them exclusively?"

I swallowed. The pain was flaring up my arm, making it hard to think. "I...yes, I forgot."

Mace tsk'd and looked at Lyric. "Shut down everything but survival sub-systems and constructs you've put in place your-self, Lyric."

"A non-essential reboot?'

"Yes."

She nodded and melted away.

Byrne gripped my arm. "C'mon. Over here. Out of the way of his highness there. Come." He pulled me well out of the way of the construct, as it turned and silently spoke to us.

Suddenly, the ship plunged into darkness.

I heard a surprised shout from the medical suite, where Elizabeth and Rayhel were.

Low, blue-toned lights sprang up around the edges of the room, showing the silhouettes of objects we could trip over, and little more.

Ramaker was gone.

I would have been relieved, but I was in too much pain. I think I groaned.

Captain Byrne laughed, a low chuckle. "Take him and get the bones reknitted, Mace," he said. "Then figure out what the hell tripped off that thing we just saw."

"Aye, Captain," Mace said.

Byrne clapped me on the shoulder. "You're done for the night, Andela. Mace will take over from here."

I looked Byrne in the eye. "Should have been Mace in the first place. This ship isn't me."

Byrne stared steadily back. Then he shifted on his feet. "Give the man something that'll keep the nightmares away and let him sleep," he told Mace and moved away.

●

ELIOT BYRNE SLID ONTO THE long bench I was using to eat my breakfast—not that I had much appetite this morning. Instead, I was drinking my third cup of coffee and trying to dispel the fog of whatever the medical concierge had directed Mace to give me, last night.

I *had* slept without nightmares, but now waking up was an issue.

"How's the hand?" Byrne put his breakfast plate in front of him. Sausages and pancakes, lots of syrup.

Well, it was his colon.

"The hand is fine, now." I held up my right hand and turned it for him to see that even the broken skin over the knuckles had already healed. "Did Mace figure out what happened?"

"He just finished bringing me up to date on that," Byrne replied. He sawed off half a sausage and chewed vigorously. Then, "If I've got this straight, the nanobots on this ship aren't like the ones that were on you." He paused. "On the *Supreme Lythion*," he corrected himself.

"They're construction nanobots," I said, for Mace had reminded me of that last night. I could feel my cheeks heating again.

"They're more than that. They have processing power of their own, something yours didn't have." Byrne looked cheerful, as he folded a whole pancake and slid it into his mouth.

I waited, but I was already starting to see where he was going with this.

After he had swallowed the enormous mouthful, he said, "The processing capacity is so they can work together. Basic intelligence, Mace says. Lets them react to unexpected events in a more natural way, especially if they get cut off from Lyric."

"It's the next step in advancing the technology," I agreed stiffly.

236

"Since we started coming out here to the middle of Terran nowhere, we've been storing memory backups on this ship, instead of some bunker close by the core of a dirtball in the heart of the Federation," Byrne said. "Some of those memories crossed over to the nanobot routines—that's the hole Mace found a couple of hours ago."

I let out a heavy breath. "*My* memories. My nightmares…"

Byrne pointed his fork at me. It was his way of agreeing while he chewed. Then he swallowed. "Probably some of Elizabeth's, too—she knew the fellow. Probably why he first showed up for her."

I nodded.

Byrne chuckled and sawed at the next sausage. "You, Andela, lost your temper last night."

I gripped my coffee mug. "It won't happen again."

Byrne shook his head. "Yeah, it will. Surprised it hasn't happened sooner. We're all trussed up in this ship, surrounded by enemies who will eviscerate us if they find us here… You're such a cool customer, I didn't think you *could* lose your temper." He sopped up syrup with the sausage. "My mistake." And he chuckled again.

Mace settled on the other side of the long table, his customary oatmeal in front of him. He nodded at me.

Byrne shoved me in the side with his elbow. Gently. "Heard you showing Mace photos of your kids, last night."

"Yes," I said cautiously.

He beckoned with his fingers. "Hand 'em over. Lemme see 'em."

237

The last of my caution fled. I got out my pad and found the photos as commanded, because I'm a father of three brilliant, beautiful children and I'm proud of them.

———

Cameron Cooper is the author of the Imperial Hammer series, an Amazon best-selling space opera series, among others.

Cameron tends to write space opera short stories and novels, but also roams across the science fiction landscape. Cameron was raised on a steady diet of Asimov, Heinlein, Herbert, McCaffrey, and others. Peter F. Hamilton, John Scalzi, Martha Wells and Cory Doctorow are contemporary heroes. An Australian Canadian, Cam lives near the Canadian Rockies.

https://CameronCooperAuthor.com

Achernar

by Jasmine Luck

I

ONKIATIS MIGHT HAVE BEEN THE planetary equivalent of a one-shuttle town on the outer rim of this 'stem, but it housed Jayra Chang's next job, so she set the nav comp and prepared to rough it.

Hu, her little shuttle, grumbled a bit, but she always did. And as *she* always did, Jay took it with a large pinch of salt. Hu reminded her of Jay's own ahma — all grumble with a pretence at fragility, obscuring a core of steel beneath.

For now, anyway.

Her ahma's core of steel would remain as long as Jay got this job.

So, she'd get it.

While scrolling through the job ads at the outpost on Maera V, she'd easily dismissed the first few. Endless months in cramped quarters with other people weren't for her. Neither did she want to be stuck planetside for an open-ended amount of time, especially not with chatty fellow crew members.

The last open ad, weeks old but unclaimed, seemed too good to be true.

EXPERIENCED MECH WANTED FOR QUICK DS DRIVE FIX

FEE: 200 PENNAFKA

The co-ordinates were listed below the advert, with advice to seek out one Captain Kit Cooper.

A quick fix and, presumably, quick pay were both points in this Captain Cooper's favor, as far as Jay was concerned.

The atmosphere of Nova-4 loomed below as Jay guided Hu downwards. It was a relief to fly through an atmosphere that wasn't heavy with smog and dust from massive industry, or skies buzzing with the sound of tech being used *en masse* by people who had become slaves to devices—both inside and outside their bodies.

Jay spotted a patch of land near the coordinates on the job advert, and settled Hu down with barely a bump, pleased with herself. She might not be the ace pilot some were, but she could fly a shuttle around the three 'stems she knew well with little complications, and being an ace *mechanic* meant she had options up her sleeve that lone pilots did not.

She opened the doors and lowered the ramp.

The hot air hit her like a wall. Jay coughed, and gulped from her water bottle. The purifier tablets she'd picked up on Naroon had cost a pretty penny, but were worth it.

Hitching all her best tools and all her coins to her toolbelt, and, after a moment's thought, her throwing knives - couldn't be too careful - she headed down the ramp in boots which had seen better days. She retracted the ramp, which made a metallic groan, locked Hu up tight, and patted the shuttle's side, pocketing the coded entry key. "Stay safe, baby."

The shuttle would need a paint job soon, but this contract's pennakfa was earmarked for her ahma. Maybe after the next job, she'd get Hu painted. And some new tools. Maybe some custom tools—

Jay put her dreams aside and programmed the coordinates on the employment poster into her nav watch. The hologram rising from the scratched, round surface pointed her over the rise and towards several plumes of smoke, indicating a settlement.

"Well, then." She tugged her scarf over her nose and mouth and made tracks in the dry dirt. Purple insects skittered across her path, scampering over the cracked ground for justmoments before they burrowed beneath, seeking shade.

It took Jay only a little while to reach what passed for a town on a planet as sparse as this one. As one of the biggest buildings came into view, so did the ship next to it. Gun-metal grey, the cargo clipper, compact and made to be multi-functional, had clearly seen her share of fights and crashes. The patching was rugged, but it did lend the vessel some charm. Her fingers itched. She'd love to get into its innards. A ship like that surely had some tales to tell.

Jay called up the holo of the ad, compared the picture of the ship with the vessel sitting metres away.

Looked the same. Good.

She approached the building with the ship beside it. It was a ramshackle, wooden ranch-style house with more than one tile missing from the roof. Her nav watch beeped. She'd reached the co-ordinates.

Jay looked up at the sky and wondered if Achernar would be viewable, once the sun set.

She took three steps toward the big doors of the ranch

house when and they swung open—animated by the body of a man flying through them.

"Your luck's run out, Coop!" someone yelled from inside.

The man on the ground stood and dusted himself off. He was rangy, and his messy, collar-length dark hair was enlivened by a streak of blond on the left. His face was all planes and angles, jaw hugged by a scruffy beard that looked more laziness than design. The glint of a holster visible on his thigh. Good to know. Not everyone carried one these days, but they were far more common on the rim, as was danger.

"Hey…" Jay began.

He turned, hand going to his holster.

"Are you Captain Kit Cooper?" she asked.

The man glanced back at the still-swinging doors to the ranch house, then took a few steps toward Jay. His large, well-worn boots stirred dust as he walked. "Who's asking?"

Jay waited for her bullshit radar to kick in, but it didn't. It was usually very reliable, so she tapped a button on her nav watch and brought up a holo screencap of the ad. "I'm Jayra Chang. I'm here about the job."

Surprise flashed across his face and his eyes went big for a second—they were a startling blue, like she imagined the oceans on Sol III (or Earth, as the history vids called it) were meant to have been, before they got used up. "Oh! Excellent! Well, then, I'm your man. Most call me Coop."

Jay withdrew the holo. "You seem surprised."

He opened his mouth to reply.

"Coop! You piece of shit! You ain't gone yet?" The yell

came from the ranch house.

The sound of a gun being cocked could be heard.

"You want the job? You got it," Coop told Jay with a grin, that seemed just a little on the panicky side.

"Er…" No fee negotiation? Usually the advertised pay got bargained down by potential employers. "My shuttle —"

"Can we come back for it?" Coop asked as the doors to the ranch house flew open.

An extremely large genko wearing a housecoat, crocodillian snout decorated with piercings, burst through the flapping wooden panels, rifle in hand. The weapon was massive and had been customized.

"Betsy seems to have run out of patience," Coop muttered.

Jay glanced from Coop to the genko. Female? Male? She'd never seen one up close before. She was yelling again, about 'shooting your little friend, too.' Should Jay point out that she and Coop were not friends? "Um — you owe her money or some-thing?"

"Or something," he agreed, already heading for the ship parked beside the ranch house. "You coming or not?"

Jay weighed her options. Go back to her shuttle and trawl the expanse of the web for more jobs, or take the potential coin from this character and move on.

He seemed shady, but wasn't everyone these days?

"Discuss terms on the ship?" she asked.

"What? Sure." He waved a hand.

The whizz of a bullet sounded over his head.

"Next one won't miss!" Betsy yelled. The gun was recocked.

"Fucking..." Coop grabbed Jay's hand and raced for the ship. "Next one's less likely to miss. She told me she's practiced for years. Guess there ain't a lot of moving targets round here."

Jay didn't ask how he knew so much about the genko. She didn't want to know. A man was entitled to his tastes.

She pulled her hand from Coop's but followed him at his pace. A bullet struck the ground by Coop's heel. Jay suspected Betsy either didn't mean Coop harm, or was less mad at him than she claimed to be.

Either way, probably best not to take the chance that Betsy would miss a third time.

The ramp on Coop's ship lowered and he ushered Jay inside. A bullet pinged off the ramp as it lifted like a drawbridge of old, complete with creaks.

Coop turned his key to lock the ship up, and leaned against the bulkhead, and rubb a hand over his face. "That was close."

"Mixing business and pleasure rarely goes well," Jay muttered, looking around the ship. She was rusty in places, and the interior matched the exterior. This clipper had seen a lot of action and was patched up in ways that, in some areas, looked questionable. The ground floor, the ship's belly, was all one big cavernous space, larger than it looked from the outside, with a bridge overhead that looked as if it led to the cockpit and some smaller rooms. Quarters, maybe.

Coop's jaw dropped for a second and then he laughed out loud. "You think that...Betsy and me...? No. It wasn't that kind of arrangement."

"No judgement," Jay added, holding up her palms. "It's different out on the rim."

"You're right about that. But she ain't my type." He pulled down a ladder from the bridge.. "Coming?" He climbed without waiting for an answer.

Jay hesitated, not done looking around. The belly of the ship was filled with crates, some stamped with Basic, some with Mandarin symbols or Slovak—the languages Jay had come across most in the 'stems she'd travelled—along with some tongues she couldn't decipher at all. Coop, and his ship, clearly got around.

So. Did Coop and his clipper transport legit cargo, or more complicated goods?

She'd soon find out. And for a short job, did it matter?

Jay grabbed the ladder and climbed up behind him. Her boots hit the bridge and she hot-footed it left, following Coop to the cockpit. Coop already sat at a console, flicking switches and pulling levers. The ship rumbled as she came to a stop beside him, drinking in the control panel, cataloguing how it differed to her own and others she'd seen. On the bulkhead around window, notices were stuck, some about jobs, others with pictures attached. A handful were in languages she couldn't read.

Through the wide viewport, Betsy could be seen approaching the ship, with another couple of genkos, all wearing brightly coloured versions of Betsy's housecoat. Two of them were armed.

"Time to go," Coop muttered.

The ship shuddered and left the ground slowly, the engine

rumbling like the dragons of myth, a comforting sound for Jay. Engines were her life and her livelihood, and on ships, she felt most at home. She closed her eyes for a moment, the knot in her stomach from the genko confrontation unravelling.

She grabbed the back of Coop's chair to counter the hefty backward pull as the ship took off at speed, the engines roaring, leaving Onkiatis behind.

Once they were in orbit, the rust-brown skin of the planet rotating slowly below them and the previous howl of the engine reduced to a gentle hum, Coop swung around in his chair. "Sorry 'bout that."

"Seems like a regular occurrence for you?" Jay commented, fishing for more information.

"It can be."

When he didn't add more, she prompted, "You aren't even going to interview me for the job?"

"You're here, aren't you?" He sighed. "Truth is, that ad's three weeks old. I'd been thinkin' that no one was going to turn up."

Jay folded her arms, a funny feeling settling in her stomach. "And why would no one turn up?"

Coop narrowed his eyes. "You don't know?"

"I really don't know."

He considered this for a moment, his gaze darting over her face, as if trying to search out a secret. "You must know."

"I've been on a job for two years, on a ship orbiting Keprah, in the Trep 'stem. It's totalitarian there, no news in or out, all comms checked by their Emperor."

"That would explain it." Coop drummed his fingers on his thigh. "Well. There was an incident. A galaxy official was involved. And...a big, loud explosion, somewhere prominent."

"Let me guess. It wasn't your fault?"

He smiled wryly. "Oh, it was my fault, all right. That's why I've been holed up here, doing work for Betsy and her family. But my good will ran out. Apparently it isn't the done thing to use the basking lamp to dry wet clothes. If you're a human."

"Ah. And now what?"

"And now I have you, I can deliver the rest of this cargo. If you want the job. Most urgent stuff's going to Morix."

"Morix?" Jay echoed, unable to believe her luck.

Morix held some of the best doctors in any 'stem she'd explored thus far. Maybe she could strike a bargain with one to help her ahma. Maybe score a free holo consultation, or something.

"Yeah," Coop replied, drawing the word out. "Is that not okay?"

"No. It's fine." She tamped down her excitement. "How long will you be there?"

Coop shifted, as if sensing a negotiation. He had that calculating look in his eye; Jay saw it regularly in the mirror. "What business have you got there?"

It wasn't a good idea to play her cards all at once. If Coop found out she had a sick relative to care for, he might use that as leverage. Others had. He might be packaged up real pretty but, ultimately, she didn't know him from the next person. "My business there is none of yours."

He rolled his shoulders, seemingly unoffended. "Fair enough. Now, as to your part. I can't travel through deep space without a mechanic. Vesper's needed attention for a while, but I ain't had the time, and now that neglect is biting me in the ass. I'm not sure what the problem is, but I barely got through the last DS jump. She travels, but FTL flying is impossible for now."

Jay felt her stomach settle; they were getting down to business. This, she knew well. "Vesper?"

"Means *evening star*. Seemed appropriately pretentious. She flies good, when I feed and care for her proper." His drawl softened when he talked about his ship, the affection clear in his voice.

"Fine." She tried to ignore his *appropriately pretentious* comment, as funny as it was. She couldn't afford to like him. "Take me to the engine room?"

He inclined his head and stood. His shit-brown coat had seen better days, but the garment fit with his ragtag look. Jay couldn't be sure if he was short on funds or curated the appearance to make others think he was down on his luck. Could be a little of both.

But she'd been deceived by appearances before, and she was smarter now. Couldn't survive long on the rim without two brain cells to rub together.

Jay followed him over the bridge, through the ship, passing over the belly where the cargo sat, and then through a badly patched archway and past a little cubby-hole of a kitchen inside what looked to be a tiny mess hall — worn but tidy, only one cup and a tin plate huddled together by the tap — then down another ladder. He opened the only door ahead, and the welcoming hum of the engine room enveloped Jay's senses.

Everything inside her relaxed and went *Oh, hello*. This was what she was used to. Here she felt at home.

"What's the problem?" she asked Coop, already itching to touch.

He smiled as if he read her. "Go ahead. You can touch. She's yours for the duration."

Jay moved to the huge bulkhead shielding Vesper's engine and spread her hands over the metal surface, learning by feel.

"Do you even need me to tell you what's wrong?"

She could hear amusement lacing his tone.

"Not necessary," she replied. "She'll tell me. Won't you, *qīn ài de*?" She pressed her ear to the bulkhead, waiting, listening. Vaguely she heard Coop say something, but the words got lost as she concentrated on Vesper and the ship's beating heart. "What did you say?"

"You fluent?" There was a hint of impatience in the question. Maybe this was more that the second time he'd asked.

"Yeah."

"Good. That might come in useful." He turned to go.

Jay stood. "Wait. Payment terms? I saw two hundred pennafka on the ad. I want half before we leave."

"Ah…. That's not possible, sorry."

"What?" Jay demanded, cursing herself. Should have let the genkos get a shot or two at him to buy time to discuss payment. "No deal. Take me back to my shuttle."

They stared each other down for a second that stretched.

"I don't see any other mechs queueing up to fix your DS drive. Jay added. "A quarter or you take me back, right now."

They gazed at each other silently for a long moment, but Jay didn't back down. She had him over a barrel and he knew it. It was either stay here—and eventually come out of orbit and land for food and, according to rumours on genko habits, risk *being* food to Betsy and her ilk, or, accept her terms.

"Fine," he eventually groused. "But you fix Vesper first. No DS jumping means no cargo delivery, means no pay for either of us."

"Deal. Captain." She tossed off a lazy, mocking salute.

He rolled his eyes. "Tools in the cabinet bottom left. Put 'em back the way you found 'em." He muttered something unintelligible and started back up the ladder, his boots heavy on the metal rungs.

Jay took a deep breath, thought of the best medics attending to her ahma, and took off the extra tools she might need from her belt. She knelt by the cupboard and got to work, relieved to be alone once more.

II

TWO HOURS LATER, SHE WIPED the sweat from her forehead, as her ears picked up the sound of boots on the ladder rungs. Silently counting down from ten in her head, Jay smirked when she got to one and a single knock sounded before the door to the engine room opened.

It'd been hard work, but worth every second, because Vesper had a weakness that Jay could absolutely turn to her advantage.

"It's been two hours," Coop said.

Jay looked up. "Yeah, and?"

"She ain't fixed yet?"

"Oh, she's fixed for now, but she won't be good for even a short DS jump unless someone—someone experienced, like me, I might add—administers adjustments before, during and after. I can patch over her hurts, but she needs a new ionic grinder."

His face fell.

"Yep," Jay agreed.

Coop scrubbed a hand over his face. "How far can we get? Assuming you stay?"

"I'll make sure you get to Morix. I can find a good supplier for the part. I'll make sure it's legit," she added, "and fit it for you. For the right price."

The captain folded his arms, blue eyes narrowed. As he huffed out a breath, she caught the scent of cardamom tea. "How much?"

"An extra three hundred pennafka."

He muttered an expletive, but Jay could've asked for more, and she *knew* he knew it.

"How can I be sure you aren't rinsing me?" he asked, at length.

Jay shrugged. She tossed her wrench in the air and caught it, holding his gaze the entire time. "You can't. But what choice do you have?"

Coop looked away and cursed. Jay knew she'd won.

Vesper's need for a new part was almost unbelievably good fortune for Jay. She could easily be out in the markets of Morix for an extra three hours, claiming to be searching for a decent grinder supplier while she checked out medics. What Coop didn't know wouldn't hurt him. And besides, they hardly knew each other. A little…omission out on the rim was expected.

"You get your extra coins after you fit the grinder to my satisfaction," he finally said.

They gazed at each other for a moment.

He'd played entirely into Jay's hands, but she didn't want him to know that. "Okay, deal. But we get my shuttle before we leave for Morix. We're jumping to another 'stem and I don't wanna chance that Betsy and her pals won't dismantle Hu for parts."

He leaned against the wall, considering her, thumb rubbing his jaw absently.

He was a handsome man, Jay thought idly. If she hadn't just been scraped raw from the betrayal of a man she'd come to love—*stupid, stupid, never mix business and pleasure, ever. Never relax*—she might consider a tumble with him. But, things were as they were. So.

Finally, Coop said, "Fair 'nough. But you'll give me your shuttle key."

Jay almost dropped the wrench. First only a quarter pay upfront and now this? "You should be so lucky."

He lifted a shoulder in a half shrug. "You got your terms, I got mine. I have to sleep some time. How'm I to know you won't open the shuttle bay and leave me in the lurch if you get a better offer?" He nodded to her watch. It was only a nav watch, not a commlink, but he had no way of knowing that.

She could yield this one thing to him, in exchange for access to a potential holo consultation for her ahma.

"Okay. You got it, Cap'n." She tossed off another lazy salute.

He rolled his eyes, like he didn't want to like her.

The feeling was mutual.

●

ANOTHER TWO HOURS PASSED. JAY got too hungry to keep working.

She climbed the ladder and wandered into the mess hall, peered out of the porthole to gaze down at the slowly turning brown orb of Onkiatis, surrounded by wispy white clouds, all hovering in the black blanket of space, encompassed by pinprick stars.

Sometimes, space was so beautiful, Jay had to catch her breath. Shame it was also deadlier than a three-tailed skink.

"Hungry?"

She jerked backward at the sound of Coop's voice.

Her stomach growled, giving her away.

Coop chuckled softly. He opened a little cupboard she hadn't noticed before, took out a couple of boxes. "This stuff claims to be mac and cheese. It isn't, but if you close your eyes, you can pretend it's real food."

Jay shrugged. She'd certainly eaten worse. There'd been a

couple times on Saturn IV, with the local delicacy offered by a client, the eyeballs of a—

"Want?" he asked, shaking one of the boxes. It made an unappetising rattling sound, which didn't seem to faze Coop in the slightest.

"Sure." Anything was better than eyeballs.

She leaned against the wall as Coop rehydrated the food. The smell wasn't unpleasant.

"You gonna sit, or what?" He gestured to the narrow bench that also served as the mess table.

She sat.

Coop placed a bowl of goop before her, along with a fork and a spoon, then sat opposite her. Their knees touched. Jay moved away.

"Sorry," Coop offered, not sounding sorry.

They ate in strained silence for a few moments. Jay didn't mind; she preferred the hum and warmth of engines to the noise of people.

"You gonna tell me why you wanna go to Morix?" he asked at length.

Jay glanced at him. "You gonna tell me what really happened? Aside from the there was a big explosion somewhere prominent?"

He huffed into his food. "Kinda nice that someone doesn't know the details, to be quite honest. Less embarrassing. Nice not to be a pariah. To you, anyway."

Jay smirked. "If you think feeding me will soften me up to a reduction in pay, you'd best think again."

Coop raised his brows innocently, as if the idea had never occurred to him.

●

They picked up Hu under cover of darkness, without incident. Jay was slightly disappointed — a run in with Betsy would have perked her day right up, but if the genko really was a crack shot and ended up killing Coop, it'd put paid to Jay's plans for his coins, and she'd be out a free ride to Morix, too.

The jump through deep space — from the orbit of Onkiatis to that of Morix — was uneventful. Jay spent the hours listening for any tick or rumble of Vesper's DS drive. Every time the ship groaned, Jay tinkered until Vesper was purring again, the clipper transformed from mangy street cat to pampered Persian under Jay's experienced hands.

Morix came into view through the porthole of the engine room, five heartbeats after the ship stopped shuddering from the jump. Vesper's engine groaned like a man after a big meal, and Jay patted the metal. "Well done. You made it. You can rest now. You'll have your new grinder soon, *qīn ài de*. You earned it."

She yanked open the door, hurried up the rungs of the ladder and clattered along the bridge to the cockpit. The view of Morix was better from up here. The planet was hugged by a serpent of wispy purple and orange clouds atop the red-land-and-yellow-sea. One of the twin suns burned bright in view, the other partially eclipsed by the planet.

Down on the surface were rumoured to be some of the best

medical minds in the galaxy, according to Jay's research at least. Could she afford them? Maybe, maybe not, but it didn't hurt to ask. Surely they could come to some arrangement.

"Beautiful," she muttered, looking through the viewscreen at the explosion of colour, a planet-shaped palette.

Coop said something she didn't quite catch, then, "I'll contact the on-planet port, get a docking bay. Maybe we can get some real food before you go grinder hunting."

Jay grunted in reply. Food wasn't as important to her as securing another medic for her ahma. This time she'd do it alone. Last time, relying on someone else had got her nothing but betrayal and an aching heart.

Space was no place for the naïve, the romantic or the foolish and most, like Jay, realised it too late. Nothing but engine tinkering left her with plenty of time to think about her mistakes.

Coop's raised voice jerked her from her reverie. "They ain't got a free docking bay for six hours."

"Oh."

"Nafka for them? Your thoughts, I mean," he clarified.

"I doubt they're worth even a nafka."

Coop settled into the pilot's chair. "Indulge me. We got six hours. A man goes insane with only his own head to rattle around in."

Jay huffed, amused. "The man should've thought on that before crewing a spaceship alone."

Coop laughed. It was a nice sound. Too nice. "True 'nough. Tell me something anyway."

Maybe Jay missed companionship, afterall, because she replied, "My last job, it might've been an intensely totalitarian planet, only approved vids and stuff, and artificial clouds obscure the stars and other planets, but the pay was steady and always on time, and I was able to supp—" She stopped, suddenly remembering she didn't want Coop to know about her weakness, her ahma. "It worked for me. The only thing I missed was seeing Achernar at night. My ahm—um, a favorite star of someone I know."

She swallowed, wondering if she was saying too much. His calm gaze, his soothing voice, made him easy to talk to. Too easy, maybe.

"Where I'm from, you can always see Achernar. The constancy of that star made me feel safe. The name means *river's end*, did you know that? "But despite the cloud cover on-planet, it was a job, you know? I thought I'd finally found somewhere in the black blanket of the Galaxy to settle. It came with…benefits. Healthcare. Then I relaxed and then I was betrayed. And the benefits went away."

Coop said nothing for a moment. Then, "So now you prefer machines to living things?"

"I have always preferred them. They're easier to handle. Predictable. And they feel similar, if you lean into them and close your eyes. Vesper's engine has a low hum that makes me feel at peace inside. You know?"

Stretching, the captain shook his head. "Can't say I do, but, you're the mech. Not me. So you chose this job because you wanted uncomplicated?"

"Yep."

"And then you got complications."

"Nope. You'll drop me on Morix, I'll scour the markets for a part, I'll fit it, you'll give me my shuttle starter key, or a ride to your next destination."

Coop's lips twitched into an almost-smile. "Well, you got it all figured out, don't ya?"

"Yep."

"All right then. I need to freshen up." He dipped his chin to his chest, sniffed, made a face. "Six hours is a long time. You might wanna get some rest. The spare bunk—" He gestured to a cubby to the left of the cockpit. "Is made up."

He glanced at her once more, then, with something that seemed like hesitancy, he left, the sound of his boots on the metal floor fading.

It had been a while since someone had kept Jay company, even someone who wasn't, and would likely not be, a friend. It was nice, in a weird, kind of uncomfortable way, and for a moment she felt sad that when this job ended, she'd never see him again.

But on the rim, it was every man for himself. Alone was safer.

●

THE BUNK WAS COSY AND the sheets smelled faintly of cardamom tea. Jay slept and did not dream.

She jerked awake to the quiet beep of the comms and nav equipment on the dash. When she got up to peek out at the planet, floating in the sea of black, she found Coop asleep in the pilot's chair. When she stepped back, to return to the warmth of the bunk, he opened his eyes. "Hey."

"Hey." She rubbed sleep from her eyes. "Time to land yet?"

"We can come out of orbit in a half hour." He yawned, stretched.

Studying him, wondering what his agenda could be, Jay jerked her thumb towards the bunk. "That isn't a spare, is it?"

"No," he said huskily, voice deeper than usual from slumber.

"Again. If you think being nice to me will get you anything for free, you're shit out of luck."

He smiled, tipped the chair back, put his feet on the dash. "Does everyone have to have an agenda?"

Jay mentally picked through his words for a sign he was making fun of her, and found none. "People usually do."

"Maybe I don't."

She didn't believe him, but thought it pointless to disagree out loud.

An alarm sounded. Coop dug a small datapad from his pocket and switched the sound off. "It's time to land."

Jay turned toward the engine room. "I'll go check everything's okay."

III

After they docked on Zhamdiff, the sprawling capital and most developed city of Morix, and Coop's paperwork and cargo were inspected, he loaded a couple of crates on to a hoverpallet. "I gotta deliver these. How long do you think you'll be?"

Jay jangled a couple of coins in her belt pouch, anxious to get going and not to give her plans away. "Hard to say. Gonna stop by a couple mechs, see what they've got on offer."

Coop studied her face for a moment, then nodded, as if satisfied. "Okay. You kept Vesper runnin' sweet, so for this, I trust you." He dug in his pocket, offered her what she recognised as a loaded pennafka card. "There's enough here for a new grinder, plus a quarter of what I promised."

She held out her hand. He set the card into her palm without hesitation. Jay had to wonder if he got tripped up by being so trusting, or whether this was a trap. Even if it was, she had no choice. She was going to find a clinic on Morix, however long it took.

"Good luck," he called, as she headed down the ramp. "Don't waste the money!"

She executed a mocking little bow, and saw him shake his head in reaction, but, he was smiling. A bit.

The crowded streets of Zhamdiff, capital city of Morix, enveloped her as soon as she exited the voluminous docking bay. Jay smelled seawater, sharp and citrussy on this planet, the scent winding around her as she walked. Shame Zhamdiff was too built up to see any water on the horizon.

Signs with voice-ads attached blared out their various services on a continuous loop. She noted a few mech workshops to return to later. Glancing around as subtly as possible, she checked for Coop and couldn't see him.

Morix was a popular inter-'stem hub planet. All the races she knew and some she didn't recognise mingled, spilling out of gaming houses, clinking drinks, securing business deals. Two genko children scurried between the legs of their parents, sweets clutched in their claws.

Jay turned a corner. A hawker held out sweet-smelling liquid in tall glasses, cooing about free samples, but Jay shook her head and moved on. The last free sample she'd drunk, years ago now, had resulted in her getting way too acquainted with a dingy bathroom in a dive bar in the also dingy capital city of the planet Khintov.

A glimpse of mech workshops caught her eye, and she made a note of their location before resuming her search.

She scanned and followed the street signs, some of them with annoying voice ads attached, to reach the medic district, where a mass of neon signs advertised cures for everything from the ages-old Terran cold to missing limbs or deep space fatigue.

The price list appeared on a holo as Jay stood by the door of the first clinic on the street. She read a few lines, then stepped back.

Too expensive.

The next three clinics told the same story.

Had this been a fool's errand?

She headed back to the mech workshops she'd seen on the walk over. Perusing a few from the street, she picked one that piqued her interest, workbenches protruding like arms from the shop awnings, and moved in closer.

A coquitan, furry brow creased in concentration, bent over

the misshapen wing of a small shuttle, hammering it into shape. He muttered a greeting to Jay and she gave him a brief nod of acknowlegment before stepping under the shop's awning.

Jay scrutinised the parts scattered over the workbenches. Clean, a good variety, no rust. Several parts that looked to be manufactured by Amando-Dukas, a famed engineering giant. Those were hard to come by. Seemed like she'd hit the jackpot early on.

A human in an oil-slicked apron met her at the door. Within a half hour she'd secured a decent price for a new ionic grinder and left a deposit, promising to collect it later. That was her job for Coop almost over with.

She ducked out from under the shop's awning, spying another line of clinics just across the street. She let the crowds of Zhamdiff move around her, buying herself time to gauge the information on the massive neon ads. Snatches of Slovak and other languages she didn't recognise blurred into a wall of sound. She moved towards the line of clinic doors, decisions swirling in her mind.

"Excuse me?"

Jay whipped her head around at the cool voice, then turned to face a woman in a long grey robe. "Yeah?"

"I noticed you reading information on some of the clinics in this district."

She did? How long has she been watching me? Jay surreptitiously checked her surroundings to see if she was being distracted by the robed woman, so she could be mugged by another, but didn't spot any danger. "So?"

"So, you might be interested in my clinic. I offer a free holo consultation, as I'm new on-planet and need to build up a regular clientele. Perhaps we could talk inside?" She gestured to the unassuming building behind her, door open in welcome. "I have testimonial holos you could view, away from the noise of the street." With a sweet smile—the sort of innocent smile Jay had never been able to pull off—she gestured behind her to the open door, the top of the architrave decorated with a medical services sign in four languages.

Free consultation? Exactly what Jay had been looking for. The trip wasn't a bust after all. "Just a talk for now," she agreed, unwilling to commit to costs without more information.

"This way, please." The woman swept ahead in her fluid robe, and Jay followed.

The corridor they stepped into was darker than it looked from outside, a line of steps leading down just visible. A trickle of uncertainty made Jay turn, her hand going to the throwing knives on her belt.

Then the door slammed shut.

●

Four *hours*. Where was she?

Coop paced in the cockpit, cursing a blue streak. Had he misjudged her? Surely not. He might be an idiot about some things, and he might not be able to plan ahead for shit, but he prided himself on assessing character.

She'd had definite plans for the money. She'd be back for it.

Wouldn't she? Uneasiness twisted in his belly.

He waited another hour, and then thought: *Fuck it.* All his cargo had been dispatched securely. He had no more business here.

He was going to look for her.

The the crowded streets of Zhamdiff swallowed him up as soon as he entered them. It was busy now, the languid setting of the twin suns bringing out the drinkers and party-goers.

He scanned the bobbing heads for Jay's dark hair for what could only have been minutes but felt longer.

She'd either done a runner on him with the pre-loaded card, or her business had gone south. His gut said the second.

He passed a few mech workshops, and asked around. A frustrated-looking coquitan, furry brow spattered with engine oil, told him someone of Jay's description had paid a deposit. The tension in Coop's stomach ratcheted up.

She's in trouble.

He canvassed a few hawkers, found one who'd seen Jay, but didn't know where she'd gone. He ended up back outside the coquitan's workshop, frustrated and wondering if he should cut his losses, pay the balance on the grinder and ask the coquitan to install it.

"Hey," a man in a filthy apron called from the workshop.

Coop turned, feeling a little mouse of adrenaline skitter down his neck. "Yeah?"

"I think I saw your girl go in there." He pointed.

Coop didn't bother to correct the man. He turned to follow the direction of the other's greasy digit with his gaze. His heart sped up as he recognised the symbol under the multilingual sign.

He'd seen that sign before and knew it presented as a clinic. But it didn't heal people. It took them apart.

Taking off at a run, he barrelled past the robed woman in front of the clinic, rammed his way through the door, and drew his weapon when she screeched a warning. He double-tapped the security guard who appeared in the small hallway. Blood splattered the cheaply painted wall behind the guard's now-mangled head.

Coop stepped over his body. There were stairs at the end of the hallway. He took them as fast as he dared. Another, longer hallway faced him, with four closed doors on each side.

The smell of disinfectant hung heavy in the air, permeating every breath. Coop fought not to gag at the knowledge of what might have happened to Jay, at what happened to anyone unfortunate enough to be lured inside this place.

He listened at the first door on the left. Nothing. With practiced stealth he tried the handle.

A store room. Medical supplies.

The second door yielded the same. The third was a bathroom.

As he closed up the washroom as silently as possible, he heard a crash farther along the corridor, and rushed toward the sound. He crashed through the fourth door and ducked to avoid the flying body of a genko doctor, its snout bloodied.

Jay stood there, struggling, restrained by a burly, snarling human, her fists bloody and her mouth twisted, near feral. Her belt, with its pouch and knives, lay on the floor near her feet. Her eyes went wide. "Coop! What…What're you doing here?"

Between them sat an operating table, the cold steel littered with instruments and wrist and ankle straps ready for human limbs. The intention of the genko doctor was clear.

The burly human let Jay go and rushed Coop.

He fired, hitting the goon in the meat of his thigh. The man went down, howling, clutching his leg to stem the blood.

"You came," Jay blurted, eyes wide, chest heaving from the fight. "Why?"

Coop checked the genko on the floor. Out cold. "You were in trouble."

"But…" She grabbed her belt, then, while fixing it, rounded the table to get to him, flexing her bloodied hand. "You could've left me. I didn't—You didn't even know why I wanted to come to Morix."

He grabbed her wrist. Her pulse fluttered under his fingers. There was blood on her palm, too. Hers? No time to find out. "Run now. Talk later. Who knows how many goons that robed woman has summoned."

They took the stairs two at a time. Jay spotted a side door in the upstairs hallway. She tried the handle, leaving a smear of blood.

No dice. Jay swore, her breath coming out panicky.

Coop bent and picked the lock with the set of lockpicks he always kept handy. It had saved him on many a planet like this.

The door opened. They escaped into the hustle and bustle of Zhamdiff streets. Ahead, in the crowd, the woman in the robe was wailing.

"We lay low for now," Coop murmured, pulling Jay into the closed entryway of a disused building. "Get the grinder later. Or tomorrow, when the commotion has blown over."

She looked up into his face. "I was here trying to get medical help for a relative. Her care was included in my last job. That ended and now…I'm desperate."

He smiled slightly, sympathy in his gaze. "I didn't ask."

Jay shrugged. He got the feeling that she felt exposed. "I know," she said. "But you came for me, and…no one else ever has. So. I owed you the truth."

The mangled background of crowd noise threaded between them, punctuated by the sounds of drunken revellers and faraway sirens; the background noise of a big city.

"You've really never had anyone there for you before?" Coop asked, quietly.

"Aside from my ahma — she's who I'm trying to help — no. Not really. Didn't know my father. Mother left me with ahma when I was three."

His chest clenched in sympathy. They were both loners, but Coop at least had friends spread over the Galaxy he could call on. Contacts, too, that had helped him eek out his living on the rim.

"It seems easier, being alone," he told her, holding the gaze of her deep brown eyes. "But it ain't."

It was full dark now, the only lights artificial, blink-inducing flashes of neon from shopfronts or gambling dens, and the tiny red circles from lit baccarillos.

"Let me help you," he added. He felt her tense up. What would her next move be? "You don't always have to do everything alone. I could sure use a mech on Vesper. I think we'd work well together."

Jay took a breath, considering. Then she looked up into the sky and glanced back at him, her lips curving. "Look. You can see Achernar from here."

———————

Acknowledgements: *A huge thank you to Gemma, without whom this story would not exist, to my extraorindarily patient husband Jim, for space stuff advice and to my "hang out in the Gdoc for motivation" reader, Ian.*

Jasmine Luck's work has appeared in *Love All Year, Vol 2* and *Christmas Romance Digest 2022: Home for the Holidays*. She has indie published a novel and a novella, and won a CTRR award for a paranormal novella published by Jupiter Gardens Press.

https://twitter.com/jazzyluckwrites

Moby Dick's Doors

by Michèle Laframboise

OUR PILOT WAS THE FIRST TO crash against the problem.

Rusty had soccer-ball-sized biceps, which bulged when he crossed his arms to think (which was quite often, the Guild did not recruit idiots). But outside of dancing around a gravity well without falling in and fine-tuning mooring maneuvers to the millimeter, our pilot used his wonderful cerebral array to brew his foul-tasting beer.

Rusty had been following the dorsal corridor, his meaty fists closed around the slender necks of fermented lager bottles. I was walking three steps behind the neuronal plugs dangling like blue hair from the pilot's huge frame, reviewing the new Rigel/ Sol agreement proposal printed on thin, onion-smelling sheets.

Despite a life span of several Earth centuries, Rigellians ab-horred commercial partners being even one hour late. As they also abhorred computers and screens, they had requested all de-tails of the agreement be printed in clear violet on onionskin pa-per, in the seventeen official languages of the Free Rigellian Community (which was anything but free or communal).

It was fortunate my cybereye came with a translator func-tion, but the added processing was draining the battery. (Since cyborg add-ons cost an arm and a leg, I use mine frugally.)

The *Moby Dick* was accelerating toward the Rigellian ren-dezvous point, its forward shield hitting a large number of idle space particles. The *Moby*: a thick cylinder carrying a row of car-go holds, each so large that you could get lost in them (and die of either hunger or boredom). The aft propulsion units jutted like two tail fins. The front particle shield looked like the head of a sperm whale.

Our living quarters were spattered like tiny vertebrae along the main corridor, the spine of the whale linking the cargo holds, the fins and the head. Emergency hatches were evenly distributed along the spine, ready to prevent any contamination from one tainted cargo to spread. (You don't survive in this gig without a fair dose of paranoia.)

After years going up and down the full carpeted length of the *Moby*, I was so intimately acquainted with the spine that my feet propelled me in full automatic mode. So I was prepping my address, my biological eye on the plastic fiber sheets of the multilingual financial agreement, when I heard a sound like a protein meatloaf crashing against a wall, a soft *plaf.*

One half second later, Rusty's angry voice filled the tube.

"Ow! What's your problem, *stupid*?"

I raised my eye from the sheet to inquire about the problem when an angry voice exploded, directly over us.

"Who are you calling stupid?"

My two eyes, the bio and the cyber, lifted.

Our navigator stood head-down on the main corridor's ceiling, her bare feet taking advantage of the grav cells lining the corridor's circumference as she went through her *Manga-Jutsu* routines. (Even if the *Moby Dick* was the size of a medium asteroid, our living spaces were limited. *Cargo first* was the Guild's motto. No gym.)

The fine sheen of sweat on Jasmine's skin told me it must

have been fifteen minutes that she had been exercising with a pair of black cylindrical *nunchakus* sticks, made from a material so dense that each probably weighed more than I did.

Reacting to my thought, my cybereye provided the exact mass in blinking red digits. I shut it down and pushed a lock of hair over it, a bad-boy look that worked well in taverns.

Before accepting a posting aboard a deep-space cargo ship, Jasmine had wisely elected to rent some muscles. Her implanted myostimulators allowed her to wield the heavy sticks with the grace of a ballerina.

Normally, I would have stopped to admire her moves on the circular wall. With or without muscles, Jasmine was a seventh-level *Manga-Jutsu* adept. The crew, big Rusty included, left her alone.

She walked down the wall, her hips and braid swaying in time with her dangerous *nunchakus*. As she drew near, I kept the thick financial agreement between my chest and her pair of weapons.

To my enduring happiness, or eternal sorrow, I was this cargo's captain. And the only one carrying a shiny pistol (so unused, its nozzle was glued to the lining of the holster).

Sensing Jasmine's threatening presence, Rusty got back to his feet, an awkward dance with one beer in each hand. A bluish lump was germinating on the upper part of his brow.

"Oh, no, no, Jasmy," he garbled, his rugged features blushing a deep red. That the big pilot had a thing for Jasmine was as obvious as a red giant looming close. "It's not you," Rusty said. "It's *her!*"

279

Jasmine's brown eyes grew wide. She had been as focused on her *Manga-Jutsu* routine as I was on the Rigellian agreement, so we had both missed the problem.

A shiny wall had cut off our access to the forward part of the *Moby Dick*. No handle or control panel attenuated the reflection of our stunned faces. The floor plan printed on the wall identified the culprit.

Door S-76.

Jasmine spat a colorful curse that I won't repeat here.

●

BECAUSE CONTAINERS COULD LEAK HARMFUL alien bacteria, the cargo holds were fitted with double insulation. If a contaminant registered off the scale, even when the loading door was closed, the adjacent emergency hatches would shut off the whole section.

So Door S-76 had deployed in all her metallic splendor, a vivid contrast to the dusty bulkheads and decaying pipes that were still from the original shipyard.

Rusty was rubbing his bump in a fruitless attempt to make it disappear. It only grew a darker shade of purple.

I studied my reflection on the gray alloy of Door 76. (I said gray; Jasmine would have called it *cyborg moisture, sea pearl* or *ephemeral mercury*, like the paint merchants on Kirene IV.) In most Guild cargos, doors formed a distinct neural ecosystem akin to the human limbic system that controlled instinctive responses, so that no damage to the ship could transform our cabins into coffins.

Repressing a sigh, I pushed back my hair to reactivate my cybereye. Battery charge at 43%.

A luminous net of lines and nodes running away from me flashed on. They were the *Moby Dick's* internal structure. Behind me, those lines and nodes receded toward the propulsion units. In front of me…two ivory skeletons, one with delicate bones and one with tibias like lampposts, shone in front a pearl-gray circle. (That's the other reason I don't like to use my cyborg eye: it's funny for the anatomically minded, but annoying for others.)

Yellow specks of light dotted the faint contours of their bodies, outlining their implants. The inert beer bottles were invisible. Like the other half of the *Moby Dick*.

●

IT WAS AS IF A giant ax had split the cargo ship in two. The veggie-growing patch; Lamelli, our octopus gardener; Tonka, our assistant pilot; the command post…all were either off-line or vaporized.

I stared at my own reflection. One hand casually resting on the holster of my gun, as if I could impress a door. I sucked in my gut in a rather vain reflex and drew in a big lungful of canned air to talk.

The myriad of microscopic cams spread over the door's surface should have told the door who I was. I tuned my voice into the authoritative tone that befitted a Guild cargo captain. "S-76, open or explain!"

Any closed or locked door *had* to respond to a human standing less than a meter away.

A long moan echoed, an exhalation from an infatuated opera vocalist, modulated by thousands of parrot cells. It dwindled into silence.

Which was really annoying.

The *Moby Dick's* intelligent doors, as prone to boredom as the crew members, loved to engage in conversation. As did our cabin walls, ears ready to accept the most intimate confidences.

It might have been a delightful thought on the part of the designers, a desire to brighten the dark ambiance of a cargo ship with happy doors. (Dark because you didn't waste megajoules of photons to light up corridors.)

The sole hiccup in the design was that the doors had not been granted a rich database for carrying on conversations with humans. The worst were our living quarters' doors, experts in unbelievable platitudes.

When my own door wished me *Good Day, Captain!* for the 6000th time, I itched to either blow up or strangle the designers. (Luckily for them, they had either died or been deactivated centuries ago.)

"Answer," Jasmine said, her nose one centimeter from her reflection.

The exception to the happy doors rule was that emergency doors usually kept mum. Otherwise, the hatches dotting the dorsal corridor would have finished us off with their awful dialogs.

The door let out another throaty sigh, laden with a note of despair. My annoyance level shot to the (relative) ceiling.

"Why don't you ask the Boss, captain?" Rusty proposed.

•

RUSTY ALWAYS CALLED THE SHIP'S AI "*Boss*". However, its real name was *Artificial High-Advanced Brain* or Ahab, an acronym quite familiar to those endowed with a smattering of general knowledge (or who had bought the implants to fake it).

Without 'Captain' Ahab, we would be insignificant marbles lost in the cubic kilometers of holds, each filled with containers and crates arranged to minimize empty spaces.

Ahab calculated the available storage volume like a fun game. However, we didn't laugh when Lamelli had to disentangle said arrangement with dexterity (or, in her case, *tentacularity*) at the delivery end.

If Ahab detected a danger, all the ship's doors — hold, cabin and emergency hatches — would have united their voices to warn us. S-76 hatch should have shouted the reason it had shut down, instead of serving us up her B-grade erotic moans.

Deep space did not hold ten thousand kinds of dangers. Threats ranged from brutal decompression, impact with one of the trillion bits of garbage inherited from long-forgotten wars, pirate or police attacks, propulsion overloading...

Scratch off that one. The agreement papers and I came from the mess hall, not far from the oversized propulsion fins. If the units had overheated, the emergency hatches *behind* us, S-77 to S-89, would have sprung from the walls, closing the dorsal corridor.

Mutineers?

The beaver-sized Trogum, Tonka, from the piloting station, was too afraid of his shadow to risk navigating all by himself. Anyway, Tonka would be dozing in his basket under the main console. And Lamelli, also a veteran of the wars, was entirely focused on her gardening and inventing new savory crosses.

I opened my biological eye, letting the cyborg one shut down. (As a small favor to my stomach, I never use the two simultaneously.)

Jasmine was examining her double in the sulking door, slim fingers playing nervously through her braid. "What did the boss say?" the twin Jasmines asked with one voice.

I hailed Ahab from the implant hidden under my artificial hair. I could communicate with him from anywhere in the *Moby Dick*, even the heads.

Hatch S-76 has closed down and refuses to answer. Is there an emergency?

My question was way more complex than those simple words, since my implant also registered my current hormonal levels, letting Ahab know if I lied or if I was under the effect of a violent emotion like fear, concern or impatience.

Right now, it was a mix of all three.

Ahab's answer came after three long seconds. His guttural voice exploded from the parrot cells lining the bulkheads.

I'M BUSY, SHRIMP!

His dealings with humans had let Ahab harvest a trove of lexical familiarities.

When my ears stopped ringing, I heard Jasmine addressing the door in soft tones. Our navigator had a treasure chest of empathy, a rare quality here. Talking to a depressed door required a fair amount of it.

The silver surface uttered another drawn out sigh.

"Let me try, Jasmy." Rusty placed his bottles on the carpet in order to use his own kind of problem-solving.

While his basketball-sized fists pounded against the mirroring surface, I repeated my question to Ahab. And got an answer in the same vein.

HEY RUNT, GET LOST!

By now, I was quite used to the Ahab's tavern talk, but he had never shut me off in this way. This did not bode well for our Rigellian rendezvous.

"Rusty, stop pounding," Jasmine said, concern etching her voice. "You'll just hurt yourself!"

Rusty stopped banging, a tired smile on his face. I could smell the coppery blood on his knuckles, and see the corresponding red spots on the alloy. "That's what I wanted," he said. "I knew I would do zilch on the door. But I was hoping the ship's limbic system would pick up my bio traces and pass a fuzzy signal to the Boss."

People in taverns always underestimated Rusty's intelligence.

"Hey, Boss," he called out loudly. "You know we have to be at the meeting coordinates in two hours and eight minutes?"

The ship's Brain did not grace us with an answer.

"Maybe Ahab could moor the *Moby* himself," Jasmine suggested.

"That frozen brain?" The pilot sniggered. "All the Boss

knows comes from the designer's plans, not the real state of a Rigellian port!"

Rusty had a point there. Jasmine could consult her instruments from a remote location, but it took our pilot's wide palms and neural links to direct eight hundred million tons of freight in an angel-soft mooring. Otherwise, the *Moby* being one hundred times more massive than the Rigellian Port (imagine a frail tree with domes instead of leaves), would pulverize the port in a spectacular explosion.

There wouldn't be too many clients left to complain, though.

●

NEVER PLAY WITH INERTIA, MY predecessor had said. He had died of something else, a bad case of cirrhosis of the liver. (On a ship the size of the Moby Dick, any alcohol production was easy to conceal. That legitimate health concern was the reason why I kept searching for Rusty's well-hidden brewery.)

"What can be so interesting to you, Ahab?" I wondered.

Rusty and Jasmine looked at me. I had been thinking aloud.

Still no response.

"Ahab must have entered a circular logic loop," Rusty proposed, again laying to rest any impression of dimwittedness his bulging muscles might suggest.

Most ship's Brains were bored out of their processing power. So, they spent most of their time solving puzzles sent to them by their peers. "Ahab may have received an insolvable puzzle from another ship," I said.

"Our needs take precedence over stupid puzzles," Rusty said.

Jasmine scratched the center of her back with one heavy nunchaku stick. "Okay, suppose the Brain is locked into a loop," she said. "Now, why would this door, linked to the Moby's limbic system, stop answering?"

So Ahab might have been enthralled by a fascinating puzzle. Or had he detected a danger so strange it posed an unsolvable dilemma for the ship? My memories of the war struck me.

"Why are we chatting?" I said. "An army of hostile nanobes could be devouring the Moby's entrails!"

S-76 let out a sigh, tinged this time with a faint nostalgic note.

By now, my adrenaline rush had morphed into a mountain of worry, impossible to hide from the ship's Brain. I had seen so much destruction in this forsaken war that captaining a cargo looked like paradise.

There remained only one course of action to extract Ahab from a loop. In front of my pilot and navigator, I sucked in a deep, ragged breath, tilted my head back...and bawled my bio eye out.

●

IT WASN'T QUITE MANLY, I do admit, but given the sorry state of our finances, there was no time to finagle a better plan. I wailed for a good minute, opening wide the coffers of my fears, doubts and regrets to boost my anxiety a few notches.

A familiar, raucous voice swept over my brain.

HEY, SCATTERBRAIN! Your hormonal levels have gone through the ceiling!

Victory: my mental state had taken precedence over his puzzle! Swallowing my tears, I issued an order.

"Ahab, pause all other tasks."

I had given the order both mentally and vocally for a reason. Before the Brain could say YOU ARE UNFIT TO, my navigator was prompt to react.

"Confirmed by Jasmine Ayandro," she said.

"And Rusty Belphas," the pilot added.

Their voice-print inserted the key into Ahab's lock. I took a calming breath and my anxiety levels dropped, thanks to my morning Zen sessions. "Ahab, answer my questions," I asked. "Why is S-76 shut?"

Contamination detected onboard.

My anxiety jumped again. An ugly picture from the war rose in my mind. Could it be…?

"So?" Jasmine asked, unfazed.

She had never seen a heavy cruiser and its complement of four hundred hands reformatted into a dull black sphere.

I had.

●

AT FIRST, YOU SEE A faint blurring of the edges and you blame the remote camera feed or the screen. Then, before the crew has time to send an alarm, all com tech is disintegrated. As for what happens to the crew and further changes inside, you can only guess as your gaze tracks the ship's outline as it contracts into a final, perfect sphere.

In less than four minutes.

There's a reason my cabin's medicine cabinet is well stocked with sleeping pills. And the reason why I was so, so afraid of the Rigellians, who had invented this weapon — and could still use it without qualms, when they did not sell it to the highest bidder.

Pirates sometimes remote-trigger a cloud of hungry nan-overmin on the path of a cargo ship. The nanovermin allow themselves to be captured by the antiparticle shield. They fool the shield filters and infiltrate the unsuspecting ship. No flamboyant explosion, no detectable mass change. Four or five minutes later, there's a nice ball of aggregated metal to mine.

●

I BECAME AWARE OF A hand on my shoulder. I had been pressing my palms against my eyes. I pulled myself together to ask the question I dreaded. "Type of contamination?"

Biological.

"Have you identified the biological contaminant?"

One unicellular parasite identified: toxoplasma Gondii.

Suddenly I felt better. I didn't know squat about the *toxo*-thing, but at least nobody would come across a *Moby Dick* transformed into a metal sphere. However, we were not out of the asteroid field yet. "Are we contaminated?"

No. Aft sections are clean.

"Origin of contamination?"

Hold B-75.

The one behind Door S-76. I quickly appraised my crew of Ahab's answers.

"Oh, *Santa mierda!*" Jasmine groaned. "Who's the scatter-brain that left a hold door open?

Of course, I thought of the hidden still. Rusty's coppery eyes met mine. "It's not in there, Captain." He reached for the curved ceiling with his bloody knuckles, a sign of unease. "And we thoroughly comb the holds before each departure."

"Pirates, then?" Jasmine asked.

I shrugged. I was relieved to have only a run-of-the-mill bacteria disinfection to look forward to.

"Captain," Jasmine asked, facing Door S-76 as if she could see behind the smooth alloy. "Who or what opened the hold door?"

I looked at the sighing Door 76. Something was afoot. The door's odd behavior, Ahab stuck in a loop...

●

"CAPTAIN, WHAT'S THAT THING, TOXOPLA...?" Rusty asked. He was sitting against the curved wall, showing his profile to the mirror.

S-76 uttered a long moan, with a familiar girlish timber.

"Damn eavesdropping walls!" Jasmine groaned.

I asked the Brain again. "Ahab! That toxo-bacteria thingy, is it mortal?"

HEY HO, SHRIMP! I got better things to do than listen to bleeding hearts!

Rats! While we were assessing the threat, my attention had wavered long enough to allow Ahab to return to his puzzle.

A sigh echoed from the polished surface of S-76. "If only I had legs," she said, with Jasmine's voice. "I would go so far away…"

Rusty cast a puzzled glance at me, while Jasmine locked eyes with her mirror image. In one fluid circular move, she lifted the nunchakus linked by their chain. Her massive sticks crashed against the door with a loud double *thump* echoing far back along the dorsal corridor.

She couldn't dent the finish of the alloy, but I gues she needed to release some bottled-up anger.

●

HERE'S A CLASSIC FANTASY AMONG doors bored out of their hinges.

Walking. Going places.

Usually, all ship doors were shielded against that psychosis. I suspected that the puzzle which had so captivated Ahab was hiding some instructions that had percolated from his conscious neural net to reach the ship's limbic system.

As I was expounding that theory, Jasmine dropped her weapon, the chains clanking. "A virus concealed in the puzzle message? It must be eating Ahab's gel circuitry," she said.

Rusty scratched the pink skin showing between his rows of implants, the blue lines dangling. "Now that makes two problems." He crossed his tree-sized arms. "One puzzle trap in a message; one contaminant slipped into the hold before our departure."

"The two working in synergy with the door's protective reflex," Jasmine added.

I would have noticed a hold door ajar. But the code in the puzzle might have contained a direct order to open.

"Where did it come from?" I asked aloud.

The scenario replayed in my mind: a biological hazard placed in a sealed container before take-off. A clock mechanism, not even hi-tech, releasing the contaminant into the hold. The ship's alarms blaring. As a result of the contamination, the crew evacuating the ship, leaving it drifting.

I shared my thougths.

"Whoever planted that bio-hazard would let time pass, then retrieve the ship, decontaminate its decks, and renovate it," I said.

"Putting such a plan in motion must have required an incredible degree of coordination between the timed release of contaminants and the reception of the doctored code, Jasmine said.

Rusty uncrossed his arms. "Too much for an underequipped pirate band to manage," he said. "Could be one of the numerous competitors targeting the same market, though."

"Makes sense," I said. "But why now? Our usual roads are

well known."

Jasmine balanced one heavy nunchaku over her shoulders. "One of the Betelgeuse rebel colonies?"

"Betel's rebels don't have the means," Rusty said.

My mouth went suddenly dry, and my stomach screamed for antacids. "What if the Rigellians themselves were eager to sabotage their own agreement?" I said. "We have been at war for so long…" "The Octopusses possess the means to pull it," Rusty said.

Lamelli, our quiet gardener was an Octopus, but she had been with us since I rented the cargo, years ago.

"Nope." I rubbed my temple on the side of my bio eye. "They barely survived this war. They wouldn't start another."

"We've been at war for so long," Jasmine repeated.

I loved her pensive expression, especially as she was quoting me.

Rusty unfolded himself from his position, his eyes shining. "Jasmy, you got it! We have to think about who would gain by renewing hostilities with the Rigellians."

I loved it when my own crew displayed more intelligence than I did. I caught their drift one or two seconds later. "So, we are now facing another war…?" I said. My throat closed violently.

The wretched memory of the cruiser reduced to a dark gray ball rose inside me. It shot from my mouth in a strangled cry, followed by my breakfast. I swiveled fast enough to spew a powerful spray of stomach acids against the door.

"Aaah," S-76 sighed."The waves of the sea on Lierrus…"

Jasmine turned away from the circle of goo dripping onto the carpet. "Yes, captain," she said.

I feared my weak stomach had made me lose prestige in her eyes.

"Such a complex scheme to steal our ship, with a timed release of contaminants and the doctored code, can only come from our *own fleet's* programmers," I said, wiping my mouth on my sleeve.

She sent me a sunny smile. Sunny wasn't half of it, because her cleaning biots left her teeth immaculate after each meal. The glowing residue let her see her way in the dark. "Well said, captain. Our saboteurs' objective is to *paralyze* us. Rigellians are known for their susceptibility. If we miss this rendezvous at their port, or if we crash into it without Rusty at the helm..."

"The hostilities will resume," Rusty concluded. "The Sol Alliance and the Rigellians have always been bad neighbors."

"Our military and their toy makers will grow rich," I said. "Maybe the Guild had a hand in it, too, by choosing our freighter."

Going after the high-end perpetratorswould be a wild goose chase.

I almost regretted the simplicity of punishing a devious ship contractor!

●

CONTAMINATION OR NOT, WE HAD to get through S-76. We didn't have any external airlock to go around. The spacesuits were in the forward section.

I palmed the butt of the shiny official weapon hanging from my belt.

"You know the emergency door is impervious to assaults," Rusty said.

He was right. The metal-polymer alloy and smart nodes of the door would withstand gun shots.

But I grabbed my pistol anyway, maybe for the nice image it would give Jasmine. The handle recognized my heat and print signature. My fingers traced the curved trigger that formed a flattened "G" under the mean-looking barrel.

I closed my bio eye and opened the other. I aimed at the wide aeration duct that ran behind the bulkhead, close to the point where it met the door, and pressed the trigger.

The energy chamber vibrated against my palm. I switched eyes again.

I could not see the laser beam, but its effect was devastating. The solid-looking wall turned from a dull gray to a fiery red, then changed to orange, radiating a heat which quickly dried the film of tears on my bio eye.

I kept firing, casting side looks at Jasmine to gauge her reaction.

A hole appeared, releasing the cloying stench of burnt rubber and molten iron from the very old walls. With the help of my cyborg eye, I drew a perfect circle, hoping the geometric feat would impress Jasmine.

Metal tears flowed from the line traced by my laser.

When the ray met the door's unassailable surface, my perfect circle morphed into a shy D.

Of course, S-76 reacted.

"Hey gang, it's a hot day on the Soraya-Four volcanic plains! I dream of hiking there…"

"Dream on, baby!" Jasmine shouted, her empathy vanished.

"Oh, to feel the sand rolling between my toes…"

"Your *toes*? You don't have any, you dumb…"

The duel of feminine voices accompanied the hiss of boiling metal and the hum of the discharging pistol.

I nodded to Rusty. Happy to oblige, he swung his fist at the half-circle, crushing the still-warm center. The plate fell inside the duct with a loud echo.

I poked my head inside, one hand on the gun's butt.

It was as I had guessed. The contractor had scrimped on the quality of the finished product, filling his ample pockets while doing so. He had been as devious as the late programmers (and as dead, by the hand of my predecessor when that noteworthy gentleman found out).

In keeping with the emergency hatch's action, a whitish partition had spread across the duct, closing down the aeration system. But those pale partitions were the *Moby Dick's* Achilles' heel. The light, airtight plastic would be no stronger than cardboard.

A scent of burnt keratin alerted me.

"Captain, your hair!" Rusty shouted.

I pushed back from the air duct. While I had been leaning inside the D-shaped hole, my platinum-blond hair had brushed against the molten metal edge.

I jumped around and shouted, patting my synthetic hair with both hands. In vain. I cringed inwardly. Not only did I risk baldness, but a nasty short-circuit could destroy my subcutaneous cerebral implants, leaving me a vegetable. My head was about to explode, images of dark spheres flashed through my heated cyborg eye.

A trunk-sized arm encircled my neck, while cool, bubbling liquid enveloped my hair, extinguishing the fire. The smell of hops wafted, as drops of Rusty's latest batch of brew found my tongue.

"*Mierda*," Rusty groaned, examining the empty bottle.

Regaining my calm, I noticed the pistol lying on the carpet. I had dropped it while battling the flames.

I passed a finger over my head. All my implants were functional. Except that I could say *adios* to my sexy wealth of hair, reduced to an unkempt pelt...

Rising out of the mud of self-pity, I issued orders, my voice quavering only once. "Rusty, get three biohazard suits from our mess hall. We might get some toxo...toxo-thingies in our bodies when I cut open the partition."

The giant ran to the mess hall, which provided, fortunately, more than empty calories.

I discarded my belt and boots.

Minutes later, Rusty was back, three blue donuts dangling from his beefy left arm.

We passed the collars over our heads. That's all you need to do with the biohaz suits.

As soon as the collars were in place, the memory-form blue fabric extended over our clothes, feet and hands, formed semi-rigid helmets and transparent faceplates, with air reserves.

Zero chance of survival if you were tossed into the vacuum of space, but you could cross a level-4 infected area without problems.

I retrieved the pistol, then passed my arm through the now-cool hole in the wall to pierce the low-quality partition.

Smoke erupted from the partition as the polymer melted, forming an ever-widening hole. When the pistol charge fell to zero, a fair-sized rectangular opening gaped, showing darkness beyond.

When I tried to put more than my head and shoulder through the D-hole, I realized the duct was too narrow for me. After shouting a heartfelt *Mierda!* into the hole, I turned to the obvious candidate. "Jasmine, you're the slimmest. You have to go."

She had guessed as much, of course, but a well-turned compliment was never wasted.

"Stay in touch," I said, tapping the com unit bulge under my faceplate.

"I need your gun," she said.

"Why?"

"Because I will need to open the wall behind S-76 to get into the corridor."

I hid my disappointment at not having thought of this first under a technicality. "There's no charge left."

Sausage-sized fingers placed a capsule in my glove.

"Thought you would need a recharge," Rusty said.

He had done errands while I had been destroying the partition. I would have kissed him if we hadn't been wearing suits.

Nobody could forcibly take my gun, but I could give my permission to use it. I tapped on the handle, making it accept the navigator's ID. I felt jealous when the butt molded itself to the thin glove enveloping Jasmine's hand.

While Jasmine latched the gun belt around her waist, my heart hammered like a schoolboy's.

She twisted this way and that to fit inside the D hole, then disappeared into the air duct.

I tasted bile, wondering what she would find, or if S-75 would prove as crazy as her neighbor, S-76.

●

I HATED WAITING. IT REMINDED me too much of the Rigellian wars.

Waiting at your console, waiting for orders, doing nothing, looking at the silent destruction visited on others. A destruction that had already happened by the time you saw it, so there was nothing you could do about it. Except wait for orders.

S-76 was still waxing on about its obsession with feet; I was starting to miss my cabin door.

Still no way to raise the two crew members at the *Moby's* front end. The copilot must be hibernating in his basket. Rusty should have woken him before paying a visit to his forbidden brewery.

Jasmine's clear, fresh voice jarred me out of my gloomy thoughts. "Captain, I just spoke with Lamelli."

"How could you?" I demanded.

"Like I'm talking to you, now. I crawled to the next panel closing off the air duct and sent out a call. The panel is cheap sealing material, so the wavelengths passed through."

"What does the octopus have to say?" Rusty asked. Like me, he had seen the war. He generally stayed clear of Lamelli.

"She confirmed what we suspected. Ahab received a coded transmission about half-an-hour ago. Then S-75 slammed down."

The timing exactly matched when S-76 shut down.

The transmission had been a puzzle, as we suspected. A treat, impossible to resist for a bored Brain. Like honey for a bear. A puzzle so riveting, than decoding it would have given Ahab an immense jolt of pleasure.

Meanwhile, a cascade of instructions slipped away from him/it, unnoticed. Small things, like unlocking a hold door, or opening a container filled with toxo-something bacteria.

As soon as the contamination had been detected, the emergency doors on both sides of the hold had shut down. S-75 and S-76.

Another stream of instructions must have percolated through the limbic system, unlocking the repressed desires for travel hidden in the depths of the doors' psyches.

It was some very high-level pirating.

Meanwhile, Jasmine was hard at work. "I am...melting the corridor wall to get into the closed section."

This took time. We waited, me glancing longingly at the last beer bottle.

"I'm in," she said. "I have a visual on S-75. It is also closed."

Silence.

"I've reached the hold's door. *Mierda!* There's a two-centimeter gap."

Those doors were so massive, no explosion could rattle the precious cargo. Contamination or no contamination inside, they couldn't be opened before we reached our destination. (I've heard sad stories about clandestine trespassers who didn't understand the system and had died as a result.)

The hold door had been hacked to unlock and open a crack, more than enough to spread contamination throughout the *Moby.*

"Can you get a visual of the contamination source?" I said. "If we want to catch the culprits, we'll need rock-solid proof."

I heard grunts as she used her rented muscles to push the heavy door wide enough to let her pass.

"Do you see anything?" Rusty asked.

"It's dark," Jasmine replied. "There's no light, and tons of floating crates. It goes on and on…"

"We should have given her a lamp," Rusty said, tapping his thin helmet. The biohaz suits had no lights.

"No problem," Jasmine said. "I've got my teeth."

I had forgotten about her glowing dentifrice.

A silence, since obviously she couldn't talk and smile at the same time.

"I think I'm getting closer to the contamination. I see brown balls floating around me."

"What kind of balls?" I asked.

"Small, like brown marbles."

Another grunt, as if she were lifting an object.

"There's a bigger object here. It's rather soft and...*santa mierda!*" Her voice had risen an octave.

"Jasmine, the contamination must come from those marbles. Come back at once. You could get lost!"

As I was saying *lost*, I heard a high-pitched shriek! A pure maiden-in-distress screech, incompatible with Jasmine's combat prowess.

"A...a...a *critter* has sunk its claws into my back!" she said.

A series of grunts ensued. I guessed she was trying to shake off her assailant.

"Oh no! The claws have pierced my suit!"

Contamination, plus a pierced suit, a combination that filled nightmares. Forgetting all manly pretenses, I added my own scream to hers. "Nooooooo!"

Door S-76 emitted a long, wishful sigh.

I banged on its indifferent surface, shouting curses. I must have been giving off quite a spectacle: the semi cyborg captain, veteran of the Rigellian wars, reduced to a shivering bundle of frayed nerves.

My serotonin levels hit an all-time high, but I didn't care anymore.

Then Rusty's immense hands enveloped mine. "There's nothing to gain by breaking your fingers, Captain."

This close to his helmet, I could see the pensive eyes in his rough face.

The war against the Octopi, who had later become allies, the Rigel Wars and its new horrors…. I had lived long enough to see Rusty growing more reasonable than me. The realization had a calming effect.

I ordered Jasmine to get back into the corridor.

"I'm trying!"

Courtesy of her ripped suit, I heard dull thuds of containers crashing into one another, mingled with her ragged breathing. The echoes told me she was drifting farther inside the voluminous hold. Free-floating, ten-ton containers could crush her at any time.

A damsel-in-distress and me unable to assist: it would have been almost amusing without the toxic bacteria.

That's when a new voice chimed in.

"Jasmine? Where are you?" The voice had a synthetic sound, adjusted to a female contralto register.

"Lamelli? I said. "How come you…"

"Use your eye, cap', I'm busy!" Lamelli shot back.

I leaned in the D-shaped hole and opened my cybereye. I could see the straight lines of the duct over the fuzzy gray background my eye painted. A pale gray mass oozed through a round hole at the other end. Two tentacles held powered gardening tools Lamelli must have used to cut through the cheap partition from her side.

Without a sound, her supple form crawled the length of the duct. She exited through the hole Jasmine had etched in the wall, and plunged into the hold.

"Jasmine, dear, talk to me, so I can find you." Octopi had no vocal chords, but their talking apparatus overcame that problem. Her voice sounded honeyed and artificial through our receivers.

Jasmine's ragged voice answered. "Here, Lam, I'm here!"

Another silence.

Jasmine's hurried voice spiked. "Quick, that *thing* is on my back!"

A high-pitched screech that was not Jasmine sounded.

"Owww!" Jasmine cried. "Get that creature off my back!"

The octopus made a cooing sound faithfully rendered by her talking apparatus. "Oooooh, Jasmine, why are you afraid?"

I didn't know what to expect from Lamelli, but certainly not this reaction.

"It's sooo small and cute!" Lamelli added.

I got mad at her. As a fellow veteran of the Rigellian Wars, Lamelli should know how cute and cuddly-looking *things* can cut you down in seconds. She had, like me, witnessed vessels transformed into large balls. The sight had convinced her to change jobs.

Then Jasmine, of all people, emitted a similar sound of total admiration. "It's so *soft*!" She went on cooing, while a low rumble rose, like a weapon charging.

"Jasmiiine!" I called, frantic. "Get out! You're all drenched in the toxo-thing!"

In my head, the course of action was clear: evacuate the contaminated zone, establish a quarantine area, disinfect our living area. And get Jasmine to a doctor.

The tainted hold could wait. The Rigellians could wait.

I wasn't worried about Lamelli. Her two layers of derm had protected her species in the aggressive bacteria soup from which they had evolved, countless eras before humans shot themselves into space. Same for the Trogum copilot.

Lamelli's synthetic voice rang in my ears. "Oh, about the toxoplasma, captain, you don't understand. The…"

Her revelation was crushed under a 110-decibel roar. "AHA! FOUND IT!" Ahab's shout projected from all of the *Moby's* parrot cells, piercing my eardrums.

"And what have you found, idiot?" I said, with a groan, hands pressed over my ears.

"THE GLASS IS HALF-FULL!"

●

I HAD NO IDEA WHAT Ahab was referring to.

He couldn't know about the half-glass of whisky that had spurred my latest tavern brawl. The puzzles the ship's Brains loved so much were impossible for human minds to solve.

Then something else happened.

"Unlocking," a cool, liquid voice said.

Thin curved lines appeared on the silver expanse of Door S-76. With a low hiss, the six spiral sections irised open, retreating into their ring cavity.

As soon as the way was clear, I stopped marveling and ran to the cargo hold's entrance. I searched with my gaze through the shadows. Using both eyes simultaneously would give me a headache soon, unless the cybereye battery drained first.

Specks of light reflected from the darkness, highlighting the corners of countless boxes, from meter-long coffin shapes to cubic house-sized mammoths. Among those bouncing containers, a golden octopus speckled with fluoro spots waved in and out, sinuous tentacles negotiating the obstacles. Her speaking apparatus circled the region between her bulbous head and the start of her limbs, forming a luminous necklace.

Jasmine helding fast to the entwined ends of a pair of tentacles, her black braid floating like a loose cable behind her. An ominous, dark form moved against her chest. Yet she looked relaxed.

Lamelli moored two tentacles to the hold's doorjamb and heaved herself into the normal-gravity corridor, then used four jointed legs to stand.

Our navigator, Jasmine, her suit ripped in the back, threw open her helmet. She held a ball of jet-black fur, from which two triangles jutted. Big green eyes shone in the fur.

A small engine inside the creature fired up when Jasmine's hand and the tips of Lamelli's tentacles stroked the fur.

I was still wondering about the alien contamination when I heard Rusty gasp. "A *cat*! I thought they had all been decimated by a virus!"

"In Alliance space, maybe, but cats in the other territories had developed antibodies," Lamelli said.

I bent over the creature in Jasmine's arms.

The cat's green eyes locked on my faceplate. Then it yowled like a neglected bearing, and five claws sprang from both front paws.

I stepped back, noting than the previously smooth fur had risen in spikes.

"W-well," I said, "We still have this toxo-thing contamination to worry about."

Lamelli moved her head and tentacles, the necklace translating the muscular movements into words. "Captain, the *toxoplasma* comes from a parasite that very young cats carry. Those brown balls floating in the hold were its turds, full of the parasite."

"Yeah," I said. "Another thing that will kill us all."

I had never seen an octopus laughing, but that's what the jolts driving her undulating tentacles looked like.

"The toxoplasma won't make you ill, Captain. Unless you touch the cat's feces, acquire a uterus and get pregnant, there's no chance of getting infected."

"Thanks for that mental picture," I said.

Jasmine was looking adoringly at the ball of fur.

"The toxoplasma also contributes to human attachment to cats," Lamelli said. "And not only humans," she added, brushing the cat's fur with another tentacle.

Rusty tapped a point under his chin. His hazmat suit peeled off in a whisper of freed oxygen from the unused reserve. Then it crumpled in a sealed ball, inner side out, to be disposed of. "What genetic advantage is there to having people attached to the things?" I asked, divesting myself from my own suit.

"According to my historical archives, for a time, humans protected cats," Lamelli said.

Rusty passed one big finger over the smooth fur between

the pointed ears. Then he gently lifted the small body. "I remember the old Egyptians worshipped cats," he said, a touch of reverence in his voice.

The feline almost disappeared in his huge arms, but the purring continued.

"Seems like he likes me, eh?"

"Could be a she," Jasmine said, arms crossed, her torn hazmat suit now wrinkling into a ball.

Lamelli had crossed two pairs of tentacles in front of her. "Be wary, cats are known for their independent spirit. They are consummate opportunists. And it's a *he*."

I scratched my carpet of burnt hair. There was still a bundle of details to clear up, like getting to the rendezvous point in time, mooring without destroying the Rigellian station, and unmasking the dirty bastards who had set up this elaborate trap.

However, looking at the cat licking its paws, I felt a weight lift from my shoulders. "A true opportunist?" I felt a smile stretch my lips. "Like us, then!"

"Can we keep him?" Rusty asked, his implant-studded head bent over the purring creature.

Ahab choose that moment to intervene. "Ho-ho, gang, you'd better get to work if you want to moor successfully!"

Rusty ran to the *Moby's* piloting station, the cat draped over one mountainous shoulder, the navigator on his heels.

I heard him ask, "Jasmy, what should we call him?"

●

BY PUSHING THE *MOBY DICK* to its maximum speed and decelerating just as quickly, we reached the rendezvous, not far from a yellow dwarf very similar to our own Sol, with minutes to spare.

I saluted the Rigellian envoys with as much dignity as I could muster, while Rusty held the pile of yellowing sheets in his arms. We had no hope of retribution for the sleazy sabotage attempt, but I did my best to ensure the peace negotiations were successful.

When I pressed my palm on the marble stone etched with the final version of the agreement and heard the soft chimes echoing through their tree-shaped station ceilings, I was jubilant. Spiting the warmongers was its own sweet reward.

●

SO WE WENT ON OUR way, our holds and pockets filled with precious crystals. We made enough profit to buy back the *Moby Dick*, along with Captain Ahab. We left the Guild to do independent business.

As for furry little Ismaël, he stayed with us. He soon got the run of the whole ship.

The doors love him!

———

Michèle Laframboise feeds coffee grounds to her garden plants, runs long distances and writes full-time. A science-fiction lover since she can walk, she has published 19 novels and over 50 short-stories in French and English.

She is also a comic enthusiast who draws graphic novels and runs an illustrated blog.

Her SF stories in French and English been featured in *Solaris, Galaxies, Compelling Science Fiction, Abyss & Apex, Future SF* and *Asimov's.*

https://michele-laframboise.com/

Learning Curve

by Neil Williams

ADSILA MARTIN SLOWLY AWOKE. HER mind was permeated by a fog that made it difficult to focus. Sunlight pooled on the concrete floor from a single window, set about five meters above her. It was a cell of some kind. She was lying on a bed. Just a foam mattress set within a metal frame bolted to the floor. There was a toilet, two meters to her right. A manacle was fastened to her left wrist, with a length of cable—sufficient for her to reach the toilet—attached to the wall above the bed.

"What am I doing here?" she thought. "And where is here?"

Nothing. No recollections. With difficulty she struggled to part the mists that obscured her memories. A scatter of images. Making the jump from Kîwewin system. Deceleration toward Arar. Taking the pinnace down to the spaceport. Supervising the machines offloading cargo. Deciding to look around the spaceport. Elizaveta had advised her to make certain she stayed within some special area. Trying to connect to the planetary network. No access for offworlders. Angry voices. Commands shouted at her. Pain. Dart in her shoulder. Drugged? Perhaps....

She was on Arar. She had violated—she didn't know what, her memories were still patchy—some law or religious taboo. Elizaveta had told her, but the memory was hidden by the drugs they had used on her. They had taken her communicator, all her clothes, and dressed her in a shapeless long tunic that reached to her knees, made of coarse cloth.

The door to her cell slid open. Two men and a woman entered.

The woman wore a tunic similar to the one Adsila was dressed in.

One of the men barked something at her. Without her communicator to translate, the words were gibberish. The man then hit the woman beside him.

The woman spoke to Adsila in Common. Her voice was halting. "Do not resist. If you resist, you will be beaten. You will come with us."

The other man, who had not spoken, stepped forward and touched a device on his wrist. The manacle on her wrist opened.

Adsila addressed the woman. "Where are you taking me?"

"You are Dar al-Harb." The term was meaningless to her. "You will go to auction as suriyya." Also meaningless.

Adsila shrugged and held her hands at her sides as she stepped toward the group. She hoped that Elizaveta was looking for her.

●

SOME WORLDS ARE MORE SAFE than others for offworlders; Arar was not one of those worlds. The planet had been settled by members of the Neo-Wahhabi sect of Islam. This sect repudiated the Islamic Enlightenment of the 23rd century and practiced what they believed was the pure and true Islam. Arar had been founded two centuries ago by Neo-Wahhabi refugees who had been expelled from the Douma system as apostates. As a newly settled planet, Arar had only provisional membership into the Greater Community of Worlds.

"Damn! Damn! Damn-ity, damnit!" Elizaveta chastised herself. She never should have let Adsila make planetfall alone. *"I know she sees herself as a seasoned traveler,"* Elizaveta continued to ruminate, *"but she is not!"*

Perhaps, in the context of her home system of Kîwewin, Adsila could be considered well travelled. She had been to every continent on her world and spent a year out in the Ayapiministi-kweyâw, the habitats located at Kîwewin's trojan points. But she had never experienced a really different culture. Kîwewin had been settled by the descendants of Anishinaabe, Haudeno-saunee, and Wyandot peoples—three distinct cultures, but also three related cultures. For Adsila, the culture on Arar was almost alien.

Elizaveta let her mind flow through the Arar network. Although the network was restricted to offworlders, they would only shut out the standard Greater Community of Worlds communicators. However, for her—a Ship, a sentient A.I.—the security was a mere tissue paper shield. Elizaveta breached the system as she searched for any mention of Adsila. There was nothing.

She switched her focus and waded through Arar jurisprudence for a few milliseconds. It was all rooted in ancient Earth sharia law. As far as Elizaveta could speculate, based on the last known position of Adsila's communicator, Adsila had not heeded her warnings. She had probably stepped from the Market area into the mosque agora, which was forbidden to offworlders.

315

The penalty may be death, but because Adsila was female, her punishment might be slavery.

Elizaveta switched her search to the Arar slave market listings.

●

ADSILA WINCED AS THE TATTOOING continued. She had no idea what was being drawn on her left shoulder, and she had no choice in the matter.

The law on Arar was not what she was used to. First of all, she didn't seem to be considered a person. She was less than a person, but—perhaps—not as low in status as a pet. Only the one woman, who was not in this room with her, spoke Common. Nobody else did. They led her, or prodded her, or pushed her and one man—the jerk in the leadership role—had slapped her face when she didn't understand his language.

Second, she still did not know what her crime was. Or more correctly, her crimes. It seemed she had broken some religious taboo. And it appeared she had committed another crime by originating from Kîwewin. It also seemed that there was something wrong with her being a woman. It was a strange world.

She hoped Elizaveta was not too upset about her delaying their departure. The post drop had gone smoothly. The robots would load the outgoing mail in the pinnace. There was little to trade between systems, in most situations. Anything you wanted could be manufactured via nanotech or printed. Only unique items, like genuine frizafruit chutney made from actual frizafruit grown on Charata were worth interstellar transportation. That and documents like mail. Although interstellar spaceflight was faster-than-light, there existed no hyperlight radio or other form of communications.

The tattoo was completed. Nobody said anything to her they just stopped, then slapped a bandage over it and walked away. She didn't get to see it.

A man yelled at her in gibberish.

Adsila turned her head; it was leadership guy. She got up off of the table.

Leadership guy turned his head and shouted at her.

She put the tunic back on and walked slowly toward him. He grabbed her right arm, barked unknown words at her and pulled her from the room.

●

ELIZAVETA HAD FOUND ADSILA. THERE was nothing she could do until the Market opened after morning prayers. She ensured that all cargo had been stowed aboard the pinnace, for she would be *persona non grata* on Arar when this was done. It would be difficult. Accomplished, yes, but the local authorities would be angry.

Like the Christian Apostolitic Reconstructionists who inhabited the Kirna system, the Neo-Wahhabi people of Arar did not consider Elizaveta to be a person. She was a creation without a soul. An evil golem-like being. It also did not help that she was virtually immortal.

She was the *Star of Khosta*. She was the artificial intelligence which operated the ship. The Ship was her body.

Even before the discovery of the LiXiao Points and the development of the Mulamba Drive, AIs had been superior to humans in interstellar navigation. Plotting entry into LiXiao Points was beyond the capabilities of all but a few humans. The people of Arar did not like Ships or perceive Ships as possessing sentient rights. Then again, this was a human society which enslaved other human beings....

•

ADSILA CURSED ARAR QUIETLY. SHE wished horrible events would befall the people of Arar. She damned their deity, who had supposedly decreed her to oblivion.

She still had not been informed in Common what her crimes were, but she did know her punishment. She was to be sold as a slave. A sex-slave. The woman who spoke Common — she was also a slave — had told her this.

Adsila thought she should have guessed something like this would happen. She had been stripped naked and both wrists manacled together. She was shackled at the ankles. Then the local priests had examined and prodded her body.

Where was Elizaveta!? I am supposed to be her Companion. Did I not have Ship protection? And what the hell was a "mush-koon"? Or a "nah-jees"? Nothing good, that was certain. According to the slave woman who spoke Common, being enslaved was a kindness. If she had been a man, she would have been executed.

A door slid open onto daylight.

The slave woman peered in. "Come forward," she said.

●

ELIZAVETA STEPPED THROUGH THE AIRLOCK and down the ramp of the pinnace – or her avatar did. She was 185 centimeters tall and wore an ankle-length, high-collared dress — royal blue with geometric patterns in silver. Her cheekbones were high and there was fire in her green eyes. She had waist-length blonde hair with red highlights, tied in a long braid. She walked with purpose from the landing pad toward the Market.

The local police attempted to bar her path. Being a holographic projection, she walked through them and continued on her way.

At the Market, Elizaveta read the signs, and located the slave market and walked to that area. There, on the platform, stood Adsila. She was not being bid for yet. This was good.

Elizaveta angered some men when she passed through them and took a position at the front.

A young boy was being auctioned off. Elizaveta remained silent. She made eye contact with Adsila and nodded.

Time passed. The boy was sold.

A man grabbed Adsila by her manacled wrists and pulled her to where the boy had stood.

Elizaveta stepped forward and spoke in a clear and amplified voice. Her words were in the local variety of Arabic. "I am Elizaveta, the *Star of Khosta*, citizen of Delta Pavonis, and the

Community of Worlds and the Greater Community of Worlds."
She pointed to Adsila. "This woman is my Companion under
voluntary contract. By what authority do you apprehend her,
revoke her citizenship in the Community of Worlds and the
Greater Community of Worlds, and deem her State property to
be sold into slavery?"

An Iman replied. He listed all of her crimes against Allah
and then....

"Hold!" Elizaveta interrupted. "The Congress of Islam
within the Community of Worlds and Greater Community of
Worlds does not accept this interpretation of the Quran. In addition, local variants of Sharia law must be made known to visitors
via the planetary network in both Common and the local language. You have done neither."

"Arar is a member of the Greater Community of Worlds."

"Provisional member."

"A member, still. The Greater Community of Worlds cannot interfere with the internal governance of member worlds."

"Except when the sentient rights of visiting offworld citizens of member worlds are involved. Any violation of local laws
are to be resolved in a Greater Community of Worlds tribunal or
court. You have not done this."

"You are not to lecture us! You are a non-human fabrication, an abomination. You have no say here, machine. The auction of the female will continue."

Elizaveta smiled an unfriendly smile. "Then, the system of
Arar will face the consequences of your actions." She paused. "I
am Elizaveta, the *Star of Khosta*, citizen of Delta Pavonis, the

Community of Worlds and the Greater Community of Worlds. And I am Morganna, built by Corona Arianrhod, certified sentient on June 18, 2937, and a Sol system citizen. I was the Shipmind of the colony ship *Epona*, which settled the Mabon system. I was Lady Prime, who founded Ship Home in the Delta Pavonis system. I was the first Ship to travel the LiXiao points. And I will place the system of Arar under embargo. None of my kind, no Ship, will travel to your system."

An angry murmur sounded within the crowd. The anger was directed toward Elizaveta and the Imans.

"I will show mercy," Elizaveta added. "I will request that the Hive provide sub-light travel for Arar—you will not be completely isolated."

That upset the crowd even more. They considered the Hive, an alien species, a worse abomination than the Ships.

"Or, you can release my Companion," Elizaveta finished. "We will leave this world. There will be no embargo. It is your decision."

●

ELIZAVETA DID NOT HAVE LUNGS, so she did not have to pause for breath. She harangued nonstop, only pausing for dramatic effect.

Adsila felt small, like a child being reprimanded by an Elder. "Well", she thought, "she is older than the Community of Worlds—she is certainly an Elder."

"...as my Companion," Elizaveta continued, "you are my representative, my public face. Especially on planets like Arar."

She paused for three beats. "Do you understand me?"

"Yes, I do Elizaveta. I should have briefed myself thoroughly before I made planetfall. This will not happen again."

"Of course, it won't. I won't allow it. I will make certain you are prepared." She smiled. "Though, it would be better if that was not necessary. Correct?"

"Yes, Elizaveta. It will not be necessary."

"There is an old saying about someone being 'a big fish in a small pond'. Have you heard of this?"

Adsila shook her head.

"When you were in the Kîwewin system, you were a big fish in that small pond. You had travelled your whole system. Now, you are a small fish in a vast ocean. There is much you do not know and do not yet understand. What do you say?"

"That I have much to learn."

"That is the first step, my friend." Elizaveta winked. "Let's look at the LiXiao Point weather reports and hope there is a good Trade Wind to Boolteens."

Adsila grinned. "I have three potential points selected, but only two fit our cargo."

"Let's have a look, shall we?"

_____

NEIL WILLIAMS — "LEARNING CURVE"

Neil Williams holds post-graduate degrees in anthropology and in sociology. He taught those fields in community college for twenty years. He wrote professionally for radio in the 1980s and early 1990s, some of which were radio drama and science fiction.

http://uldunemedia.ca/nrwilliams.htm

Exotic Matters

by Phil Giunta

ENCOUNTERING A DISABLED SYSTEM FREIGHTER this far from its normal route was damned peculiar. The fact that it was holding attitude without apparent stabilizers also made it suspicious.

On the bridge of the *Stellar Storm*, Baylem Jorr sat back in the captain's chair and steepled his fingers at the sight of a gaping hull breach in the freighter's aft section. "Anybody home?"

To Jorr's right, his first officer, Ankar Vedd, examined the data scrolling across his screen. "Not according to scanners. It's probably a drone ship. Looks like the interference we're detecting is coming from a dissipating field of exotic matter. At this distance, I can't tell if she was attacked or suffered massive engine failure." He glanced at Jorr over his shoulder. "Whatever the cause, given the presence of that much exotic matter, I'd say at least one of her Falling Star units exploded. Maybe all three."

"Or it's another System trap to snare pirates."

"Thought of that, too." Vedd turned back to his console. "I'm not picking up a tracking signal on any of their usual encoded frequencies, so it might be…. Wait. What the hell is that?" He glanced up at the main viewscreen.

Jorr swiveled his seat to peer at a flashing line of data on Vedd's monitor. "Got something?"

"I'm not sure. There are no other vessels anywhere near that freighter, but sensors are picking up something large almost directly beside her. It must be the exotic matter screwing up the scans."

"Perhaps a reflection of the freighter itself," Jorr suggested. "I'd like to know what's holding her steady."

Vedd shrugged. "We'd need to get closer to answer that."

"Not just yet. Send a pod over to confirm the airlocks aren't rigged to blow if forced. If everything checks out, organize a boarding party. We'll see if she's carrying anything valuable."

●

NEITHER THE PORT NOR STARBOARD airlock exploded when the pod, piloted remotely by the *Stellar Storm*'s navigator, Laresto, forced them open. Shortly after, Vedd and four crewmen suited up and jetted over.

There is no life support or artificial gravity on a drone ship, and lighting was limited to the airlocks, cockpit and cargo hold. Vedd was first through the inner door of the starboard airlock. He led the team into the corridor, panning his flashlight along a short, narrow passage. "You lot go aft and check her hold. Let me know what you find. I'll have a look at the ship's logs from the cockpit."

"Aye, sir." The closest man, Lorden, returned a desultory salute before motioning to the other three to follow.

Although drone ships required no human accommodations, they were equipped with single-seat cockpits in the event a pilot or mechanic needed to take control of the craft.

"How does it look, Vedd?" Jorr inquired over the comm link.

Vedd squeezed into the cockpit chair and accessed the

ship's logs. "Looks like she just came from the Ghanzing Belt. Delivered food, medicine, safety gear and batteries to the miners."

"Is she carrying anything now?"

"So far, just crates of unrefined metals," Lorden chimed in from the cargo hold. "Wait! We just found a substantial supply of Fallin' Stars."

"Excellent! We'll certainly take those," Jorr said. "Do we know why the craft is disabled?"

"Catastrophic engine failure, as I suspected," Vedd replied. "Looks like at least one of its Falling Star units exploded while it was in a wormhole, possibly caused by an electrical overload."

"Any hint as to what's keeping her stable?"

"Not yet, but her sensors are detecting the same erratic reflection that ours did, as if a larger ship were just a few kilometers to port. Thrusters are still functional. Let me see if I can ease her out of the exotic matter field. I'll be back in touch shortly."

"Very well. Be careful, Ankar. *Storm* out."

Vedd tapped a gloved finger on the control pad mounted on his opposite wrist and switched off the comm link to the *Storm*. He turned his attention to the rudimentary navigation console, but not before a space suit floated past his peripheral vision. He dropped his hand to his leg holster as he glanced up at the crewman hovering above the deck just beyond the hatch. "Announce yourself next time or you'll end up as bloody flotsam. What do you want?"

The crewman merely pushed away from the hatch and disappeared into the darkness of the corridor.

"You're still on local channel, Mr. Vedd," Lorden said. "Anythin' wrong?"

"One of your boys was just up here."

After a moment, Lorden's perplexed voice replied. "Can't be, sir. No one's left the carg—"

"Say again, Lorden?" When no one answered, Vedd repeated his question. He was about to ask a third time when Lorden's strained whisper finally answered.

"Mr. Vedd, we have a situation here."

"Explain."

"I'm not sure you'd believe me. You gotta see this for yourself."

"On my way." Vedd pushed out of the seat and propelled himself down the short passage to the cargo hold. He hovered in the open hatch and stared at the cause of Lorden's concern.

Along the port side of the hold, a group of five bipedal creatures in bulky crimson space suits and trapezoid helmets deactivated the magnetic lock on a large crate of Falling Stars.

The aliens, none of whom were shorter than two and a half meters by Vedd's estimate, steadied the plasteel crate as it levitated a few centimeters above the deck. Two of them pushed it toward the inner hull—then passed *through* it and vanished.

"Mr. Vedd, to your left."

Vedd stifled an expletive as Lorden's voice whispered from his helmet earpiece.

Tearing his gaze away from the creatures, Vedd ducked low and propelled himself into the cargo hold behind a row of crates marked 'Unrefined Metals.' There, he caught sight of Lorden and the others, their weapons drawn, observing the aliens from behind the last crate in the row.

Lorden waved him over. "Don't worry. They can't hear us."

"Any of you recognize them?"

"No, sir," the men replied in unison.

"But they've taken two loads of Fallin' Stars so far," Lorden added.

Vedd peeked over the crate. "Taken them where?"

"No idea. They're like ghosts, walkin' through the hull."

"I don't believe in ghosts. I wonder if they attacked this ship with some sort of advanced weapon that destroyed the engines while it was traveling through a wormhole."

"I doubt it," a female voice replied. "That would be next to impossible. Besides, this ship's been disabled for days. They didn't show up until about twelve hours ago."

Vedd dropped to a crouch and pulled his blaster. There was one space suit too many among his men. He'd been too distracted by the aliens to notice until now because the suit varied only slightly in design from his own and those of his team. Now, he realized it was same one that had floated outside the cockpit earlier. "Who are you?"

She lifted her helmet's visor, followed by her hands. "Name's Inella."

"What are you doing here?"

"I guess you could call me a stowaway."

"You *guess*?" Vedd gestured for the men to lower their weapons. "What the hell's a stowaway doing on a drone ship?"

"Is that really important right now?" Inella pointed in the

general direction of the aliens. "I think we have bigger things to worry about."

"Then give us the short answer."

"Well, I'm, uh…" Inella fidgeted as her words tumbled out. "Wanted for murder."

Every blaster went up again.

"No, wait! It was self-defense. I knifed two drunk miners when they tried to rape me, on Ghanzing. Of course, all miners are union members, so I had to get out of the asteroid belt before the rest of them hunted me down. I stole a space suit and some rations from work and stowed away on this freighter. When it was far enough out from the belt, I reprogrammed the nav computer to take me to Cadron, my home world."

"That explains why the ship is so far off course." Vedd lowered his blaster. "Stand down, gentlemen."

Reluctantly, the men obeyed.

"So it isn't the System you're running from." Vedd said.

"On Ghanzing, there's no difference," Inella said. "System police are on the union's payroll. If you cross the miners, it might be a Syssie cop who puts you down."

"I get it. So what happened here?"

"There was a problem with one of the Falling Star units and the engines exploded. Probably a shoddy repair job by the miners. The freighter dropped out of the wormhole, leaving me stranded. I used the thrusters to slow its spin, but several hours ago, something latched on and stopped the ship from drifting. Then those behemoths showed up. Just strolled in through the wall."

"Like ghosts," Lorden insisted.

Vedd ignored him as he risked another glance over the crate. "Well, they're gone for now. Let's see if we can get at least three crates of Falling Stars aboard the *Storm* before they come back."

The men gracefully pushed themselves to their feet.

"Wait." Inella followed, though she had to steady herself against the nearest crate. "You don't look like System police. Who are you guys?"

Lorden motioned to the rest of the men. "We, little lady, are pirates."

"Oh. Well, in that case…" Inella kicked at the deck in a feeble attempt to scramble away. She succeeded only in bouncing off a port bulkhead, ricocheting off another crate and landing on her rump.

"What's wrong?" Vedd gripped her ankles to steady her. "Are you all right? Stop kicking, for Rujah's sake!"

"Let me go! I didn't escape Ghanzing only to be captured by pirates and sold into slavery…or worse!"

"We're not your typical pirates. No one's going to hurt you, I promise. Damn it, woman, would you please stop kicking!"

●

"YOU HAD TO TELL HER we were pirates?" Jorr folded his arms and glared at Lorden while Vedd, Inella, and two others guided a crate of Falling Stars across the *Stellar Storm*'s cargo hold.

"Well, it's the truth, ain't it? Since we raided Tamor Base

yesterday."

"We didn't raid Tamor Base, *per se*. We took only the supplies that were owed to the colony on Xarceese."

"Tell that to the Syssies, sir."

"Let's hope we never have to." He glanced up as Vedd and Inella picked up their helmets from the deck and approached. "Well done, Ankar. You not only secured valuable assets but managed to recruit a new crewmember in the process."

Jorr extended a hand to Inella as Vedd introduced them. "I understand you ran into some trouble on Ghanzing. Killed two men in self-defense before commandeering the freighter."

"I'm just trying to get home to Cadron, sir."

Jorr shot a glance at Vedd and Lorden. "I don't know, gentlemen, but from everything I've heard so far, she sounds like a pirate to me."

The men chuckled. Inella pursed her lips but held Jorr's gaze.

"Well, I'm sorry to say we have no plans to go to Cadron anytime soon, but until we figure out how to get you there, you're welcome to be our guest. After all, what's one more wayward soul aboard a ship of fugitives? After four days in a space suit and choking down rations, you probably want a shower and solid food."

"I would appreciate that, sir. Thank you."

"Mr. Vedd will escort you to private quarters." Jorr turned to the others. "Then we'll reconvene in the mess and figure out what the hell is going on aboard that freighter."

"Captain, may I have a word?" Vedd motioned toward the

nearest stack of crates labeled 'Property of Tamor Base.' Jorr joined him there. "Baylem, with all due respect, we really shouldn't keep a woman aboard. It's bad luck."

Jorr rolled his eyes. "Oh, come on, Ankar, that's archaic superstition. What would you have me do, leave her to die on the freighter? You do realize that two of the most notorious pirates in the sector are women? Kartiqua is still terrorizing the inner systems, and Luxa struck recently on the edge of Zhoreen space. Look, I'll make you a deal. After we drop off the supplies at Xarseece, we'll give Inella the choice to stay at the colony or remain aboard until we make our way to Cadron."

"Aye, sir." Vedd sighed. "Thy will be done."

●

DESPITE THE BAGGY JUMPSUIT PROVIDED by Mr. Vedd, Inella felt human again as she finished her meal at the captain's table. She ate in silence, listening to the men debate the method by which the aliens had passed through the freighter's hull and where they went after leaving the cargo hold.

"I have a theory." All attention turned to her as she set down her glass. "Falling Stars contain exotic matter used to open and maintain stable wormholes, and the quantity and direction of that exotic matter is regulated by a ship's negative mass particle generator. However, on those rare occasions when Falling Stars explode and all the exotic matter is ejected at once—"

"It tears the fabric of space," Vedd interjected. "Opening a temporary rift to other dimensions or realities. The size and lifespan of that rift are dependent on how many particles of negative mass are released at one time. What exactly did you do at Ghanzing? Aside from killing two men."

Inella smirked. "I recently earned my doctorate in astrophysics and was working at the Ghanzing Science Institute and Observatory on the belt's largest asteroid. Sorry to disabuse you of any, shall we say, licentious notions you might have about me. I'm not some trollop just because I was nearly raped."

Vedd held up his hands. "I meant no offense, my dear. Simply impressed with your knowledge of Falling Stars."

"Thank you." Inella raised a brow and drummed her fingers on the table's faded, scratched surface. "As I was saying, we developed a preliminary equation for the size and lifespan of a rift based on a few recorded incidents. In fact, I lost my brother eleven years ago during one of them. He served aboard a medical ship that vanished while crossing the Empty Quarter on its way to Zhoreen space."

"Sounds familiar." Jorr set down his fork and pushed his empty plate aside. "Was that the *Murapi*?"

"Correct. You're surprisingly well-informed for pirates. Search and rescue ships arrived days later and found some debris. Scans of the area revealed traces of negative mass particles and a swiftly collapsing rift. It was believed that the *Murapi*'s Falling Star units exploded and whatever remained of the ship passed through the rift.

"As for the freighter off your bow, something malfunctioned in her particle generator. All three Falling Stars exploded in a chain reaction, opening another rift, albeit a small one. I believe the aliens are able to cross back and forth from their reality to ours because the freighter's port side hull is just grazing the edge of the rift and losing cohesion."

Vedd snapped his fingers and pointed at Jorr. "Then those phantom readings we picked up might be their vessel on the other side of the rift."

"If you'll pardon the ignorance of a lowly grunt," Lorden chimed in. "How did those things come to be called Fallin' Stars?"

"According to myth," Vedd began, "ancient tribes across the eight inner systems witnessed hundreds of glowing blue orbs rain down from the heavens and believed them to be gifts from the gods. Each tribe, despite being isolated from the others by a few lightyears, named these fist-sized orbs 'Falling Stars.' For centuries, they were considered sacred objects, but over time, as each civilization evolved, scientists studied the orbs and discovered the exotic matter they contained. They've since been found on many other planets and moons. While their origin remains a mystery, the Falling Stars opened the galaxy to interstellar travel."

"Succinct and eloquent." Inella leaned back in her chair. "You impress me, Mr. Vedd."

"Again, not your typical pirates."

"So I keep hearing. What does that mean exactly? Other than the fact that your ship is a hell of a lot cleaner than I expected."

"Thank you." Jorr grinned. "The *Stellar Storm* is my personal vessel. I was once the president of the largest solar energy company on Noltaq. Mr. Vedd taught mechanical engineering and young Mr. Lorden worked in construction. Every member of my crew was gainfully employed before the System began its reign of oppression. So permit me to disabuse you of any, shall we say, sinister notions you might have about us. We're not criminals simply because we choose to live free."

"Fair enough, Captain."

"How long before the rift closes?"

Inella performed a brief mental calculation. "I estimate about five hours."

"All right, now that we have a better grasp of our situation, let's get the rest of the Falling Stars from the freighter before the aliens return."

"How do we know they're not cleaning it out while we're sitting here?" Lorden asked.

"Since the exotic matter field dissipated, I ordered Laresto to monitor for life signs. He'll alert us if they turn up." Jorr turned to Vedd. "Take a team of a dozen armed men and secure the freighter. Bring back as many Falling Stars as possible."

Inella raised a hand. "I'd like to go along, too, Captain."

"Aren't you sick of seeing the inside of that bucket by now?"

"I'm happy to earn my way, I'm good in a fight, and if I'm going to be aboard your ship for a while," she tilted her head and batted her eyes at Vedd, "I need to prove that I'm not *bad luck.*"

●

"MAYBE I WAS WRONG ABOUT you, Inella."

In the freighter's cargo hold, the aliens were nowhere to be seen, but three crates of Falling Stars remained lined up along the port hull. "You might be our good luck charm after all." Vedd motioned to the team. "All right, boys, three of you to a crate, the rest stand guard in case they come back."

Inella hoped not. She'd been given a new space suit, but no weapons save for her dagger, secured in its sheath strapped to her thigh. It wouldn't help her in a firefight. She had to earn Jorr's trust before he would allow her a blaster.

The first team tethered themselves to a crate of Falling Stars and released the magnetic locks. Mesmerized, Inella watched as they maneuvered it flawlessly to the open cargo bay doors and out into space, where they guided it toward the *Stellar Storm* using their jet packs.

She propelled herself toward the section of hull where the aliens had entered, careful to remain clear of the second team, which was preparing to move the next crate. While the smooth grayish-green surface appeared to be intact, Inella wanted to test her theory that a narrow section of the freighter's port side was just skimming the rift's edge, causing the hull to lose cohesion.

She held up her open palm and was about to press it against the metal when a small, jagged object flew past her head and continued through the hull, causing a brief ripple that lasted no more than a second.

Inella spun to find Vedd holding up a chunk of gray and blue rock. "Got these from the crates of ore behind me." He tossed another one, gently this time. They watched as it floated across the cargo hold, only to bounce off the inner hull.

"I think you need to throw it with more force, like the last one." In her peripheral vision, the next team kicked off into space with the second crate of Falling Stars.

They were followed shortly after by the tumbling body of Mr. Lorden, his screams strident in her earpiece as oxygen and rivulets of blood escaped the gaping hole in the back of his helmet. By the time he cleared the cargo hold, his agony ended in a final sputtering gasp.

Vedd leveled his blaster. "Inella, behind you!"

She half-turned, only to be knocked aside as four towering crimson space suits emerged through the hull.

The cargo hold erupted into a spinning blur of blaster fire and flying bodies. The sound of Inella's rapid breath was punctuated by the shouts and cries of the pirates.

After a few seconds, she collided with the final crate of Falling Stars at a speed that might have left her with a broken arm, had her space suit not absorbed the impact. She bounced off and descended to the deck with her back against the crate.

As she clutched the hilt of her dagger, two aliens were blasted off their immense feet. The closest one sailed backward and vanished through the rift. The other stumbled sideways, but remained upright, its magnetic boots holding it in place. The alien's rifle floated away from its lifeless grasp, to be snatched in mid-air by one of its comrades.

A moment later, three more aliens arrived. They opened fire as soon they lumbered into the hold.

The remaining pirates took cover behind the line of crates

where Inella had first encountered them.

However, she could not locate Vedd. Had he been shot? Did he suffer the same fate as Lorden? Was he a tumbling corpse somewhere between here and the *Stellar Storm*?

Her concern for Vedd's fate turned into fear for her own as one of the aliens aimed its rifle at her.

Blaster fire erupted from behind her. Red bolts flew over her head and found their mark on the creature's chest. It staggered away, clutching at the hole in its suit, before toppling to the deck.

"Thanks, guys," she called.

"Inella? Get back here, woman! You're a sitting volg!"

"Mr. Vedd! I was wondering where you were."

Inella rolled to her right, away from the hull, with the intention of joining the pirates behind the last crate of Falling Stars. In her panic, she applied too much force and rose off the deck higher than intended, drawing the attention of two aliens, who opened fire — but it was not the blast from their weapons that struck her. At the same time, Vedd ignited his jetpack and flew directly at her.

Inella tried to scream, but Vedd's impact knocked the wind out of her as she and her rescuer tumbled through the hull of the freighter and into the rift.

●

THERE WERE SHIPS EVERYWHERE.

At least two dozen by Vedd's count, after he had used the

thrusters on his jet pack to stop their spinning.

Their egress from the rift placed them beside what appeared to be a collapsible truss bridge which connected the nearest alien ship—what was left of it—to the freighter at the edge of the rift. *So that's the source of the phantom sensor readings,* Vedd thought. *It also answers the captain's question as to what's keeping the freighter stable.*

More of the crimson soldiers bounded across the bridge— but in the opposite direction. Vedd watched them retreat into the airlock of their ship before sweeping his gaze across the aft section of their vessel. It had sustained extensive damage, evidenced by the haphazard patchwork of metal plating.

At the moment, however, Vedd's first priority was to the woman in his arms. When he pressed his helmet's faceplate to hers, he was alarmed to see her eyes closed. "Inella, can you hear me?"

"Mm-hm."

He raised her left arm and pressed a series of buttons on her wristpad. As he had expected, her blood pressure and adrenaline were slightly elevated, but her vitals were otherwise normal. "Are you injured?"

"I don't think so," she whispered. "But I'm going to puke if we don't stop spinning."

"You can open your eyes now."

She opened one. Vedd couldn't help but laugh.

"Where are we?"

"Other side of the rift."

She craned her neck to peer over his shoulder at the bridge

connecting the two ships. "So that's where they came from."

"But wait, there's more." Vedd fired a quick burst of his jet pack's thrusters and rotated slowly, granting Inella a full view of the other ships.

"What are all these ships doing here?"

"If I had to guess, an invasion fleet."

"On the contrary," a new voice chimed in — a man's voice, hoarse and weary, but speaking perfect System standard. "They're refugees. I invite you to come aboard as our guests. You should be able to fit through a gap in the lattice and follow the bridge to the airlock. No harm will come to you. Our soldiers have been ordered to withdraw from the freighter and we apologize for the loss of life. That was never our intention. Once you're safely aboard, I'll explain everything."

Vedd looked at Inella, but her gaze was fixed on the ship. "It can't be. After all these years…" she said.

"What are you talking about?"

"That ship is the *Murapi*."

●

"THE ALIENS JUST RETREATED, CAPTAIN. Not sure why. We're bringing the last batch of Falling Stars over now."

"Very good, Mr. Perel. Be careful."

Jorr terminated the link and hunched forward in his chair. The boarding party had brought back an abundance of Falling Stars after their first visit to the freighter, while managing to avoid a confrontation with the aliens. Yet, that hadn't been enough for Jorr. He had ordered them to claim the rest of her cargo and now, Lorden was dead, along with three others. Vedd and Inella had vanished through the rift and were not responding to hails. For all Jorr knew, they were dead, too.

Three crates of Falling Stars paid for with the lives of four, possibly six, good people, including his best friend. It was a Pyrrhic victory and Jorr had only his own avarice to blame. *But if anyone could find a way back, it's Ankar.*

"Laresto, how much time before the rift closes?"

"Two hours, forty-nine minutes, but we don't have that long. Three System police cruisers just dropped out of a wormhole. They're closing in on our position and should be in firing range in twelve minutes."

"How long before the final team is aboard?"

"About ten minutes."

Jorr shifted his gaze to the freighter on the main screen. *A better trap than any the System could have devised.*

"Orders, sir?"

"Keep trying to raise Mr. Vedd."

●

TWO OF THE ALIENS, THEIR helmets removed, greeted Vedd and Inella as they exited the airlock into a small anteroom. Vedd's hand hovered over his leg holster, fingertips brushing the grip of his blaster, before he noticed that their hosts were unarmed.

Perhaps this was to prove their peaceful intentions. Nevertheless, even without weapons, the creatures were a fearsome presence. Their narrow, angular heads were hairless and covered in taut mauve skin mottled with patches of rust. While their ears were smaller than human's, Vedd found himself unsettled by their dull, round eyes of black set widely apart above a practically nonexistent nose. Protruding jaws filled with serrated teeth completed the look of beings that might have evolved from a species of ocean predator.

The alien closest to Inella pointed to her helmet then placed its hands on either side of its head and raised them.

"I think it wants us to take off our helmets." Vedd peered at his wristpad and pressed a few buttons. "Seventy-eight percent nitrogen, twenty-one percent oxygen. The air is breathable."

He and Inella removed their gloves and helmets.

One of the aliens uttered a phrase that sounded like "*zey noom berrash,*" and motioned for the visitors to follow.

Vedd waited until they had lumbered a few meters down the corridor before starting after them. Inella lagged a few paces behind and either ignored or was oblivious to Vedd's furtive glances. Her pursed lips and solemn gaze prompted him to ask if she was all right.

"I don't know yet."

"You're wondering if your brother is—"

"Yes. If only there was a way to ask these creatures."

The aliens led them into a control room, which Vedd surmised was part of the ship's engineering section. It was abuzz with activity—both alien and human. Their escorts approached one of the men and a brief conversation ensued. The human replied in their tongue.

Finally, the behemoths parted and Inella gasped at the sight of him. "Gaanic..."

"My God." The man stepped out from between the aliens and rushed toward her. He was slightly taller than Vedd and his youthful face was covered in graying stubble. "Inella. What are you doing here?" He swept her into a tight embrace. "I never thought I'd see you again."

"And we thought you were dead. I didn't recognize your voice earlier. Are you okay? You sound ill."

"I'm fine. It's just fatigue." Gaanic pulled back but maintained a gentle grip on her shoulders. "Look at you. My little sister's a woman now."

She wiped tears from her face. "And a newly minted doctor of astrophysics."

"You followed your dreams. I knew you would. Mom and Dad must be proud. How are they?"

Inella shook her head. "Dad...died of a massive stroke after he learned about the explosion. Mom followed eight months later. She went peacefully in her sleep."

Gaanic closed his eyes for a moment. "The *Murapi*'s final victims. And since we had no other family, you were left all alone."

"I got through it. Speaking of family." Inella glanced around the control room. "Where's Minarra?"

"She didn't survive the explosion. I didn't even realize it until we passed through the rift. We were separated. I was working in Sickbay. She was down here in Engineering. There was so much chaos. It was hours before we knew how many we'd lost to the vacuum of space. Minarra was among them. So, in a way, I too was left alone."

"I'm so sorry. But we're together again. You can come back with me through the rift. You can come home."

"Yes, it seems fate has reunited us, but if all goes as planned, I won't be the only one crossing the rift."

"What do you mean?" Vedd asked.

Inella's shoulders slumped. "I'm so sorry. Gaanic, this my friend, Ankar."

Her brother extended a hand. "Do you two work together?"

"Actually, we just met today." Vedd replied. "It's a long story."

"Well, you have my sincerest apologies for the armed conflict aboard the freighter. Our only intention was to take a few crates of Falling Stars."

"For what purpose?"

"That, too, is a long story and we haven't much time." Gaanic nodded toward the aliens. "These people are called the Iruzai. A few days after the *Murapi* drifted across the rift, four of their ships intercepted us. We thought they were going to attack. Instead, they offered aid, although it took several hours for us to interpret their intentions. They helped us repair the ship and invited us to live on one of their colonies. We became friends. Despite your first encounter with their soldiers, most of the Iruzai are gentle giants.

"About two years ago, a race known as the Kuvengi attacked and destroyed a number of Iruzai military bases before invading their homeworld. It was nearly a massacre. This fleet

347

carries the last of their race and the Kuvengi are still hunting them. If we successfully cross the rift, not only can the surviving crew of the *Murapi* finally go home, but the Iruzai stand a better chance of finding a new world where they can be safe and re-build their race. The Kuvengi will be none the wiser. Our only concern is the System. Are they still the same xenophobic monsters they were years ago?"

"Worse," Vedd replied. "But we know of a few colonies, beyond the System's jurisdiction, that might be willing to provide safe harbor to refugees. The question is, how do you plan to bring this entire fleet through such a small rift?"

"By expanding it, of course." Gaanic grinned. "When the freighter in your universe exploded and opened the rift, our fleet detected the burst of exotic matter. We then agreed to sacrifice the *Murapi*. This old hulk's propulsion system is being wired up like a bomb using all of the Falling Stars we took from the freighter. As soon as her engines fire, every Falling Star will detonate. We calculate that the rift will expand at least tenfold, more than sufficient to permit our fleet to slip through into your universe."

"How long before detonation?" Vedd asked.

Gaanic was about to reply when a crewmember approached and informed him that the last Falling Star was in place and the timer set.

"Excellent. Alert all hands to evacuate. Once they've returned to their ships, order the fleet to the prearranged coordinates."

The woman hurried off and Gaanic motioned for Vedd and

Inella to precede him. "I'll escort you to the airlock."

"What if something happens and the fleet doesn't make it through?" Inella took Gaanic's hand. "Come back with me through the rift now. I don't want to lose you again."

"You won't, I promise. After all these years with the Iruzai, I want to take this final step with them. Once we're all through, you and I will have the rest of our lives to catch up and be a family again." Gaanic kissed her on the forehead. "Be safe. And remember," he turned to Vedd, "when you return to your ship, move it at least seven hundred kilometers from the rift. In less than twenty standard minutes, there's going to be one hell of a light show."

●

"IT'S BEEN A LONG TIME, Baylem." Less than two meters in front of Jorr's command chair towered the undulating hologram of Captain Valaiya Rulk of the System Police. Her thin lips smirked at him, her hands clasped behind her narrow back, feet slightly apart.

Not long enough. "To what I do owe the pleasure, Valaiya?"

"Oh, believe me, the pleasure of arresting you is all mine."

"On what charge?"

"Theft of food, drugs and other goods from Tamor Base, which apparently wasn't enough for you. Now I see you've attacked one of our freighters. You disappoint me, Baylem, resorting to piracy. I didn't think you had it in you."

"We stole nothing from Tamor Base, nor did we attack the

freighter. It suffered catastrophic engine failure long before we came along."

"Surrender your vessel and prepare to be boarded."

"You've taken everything else from me, honey. You ain't getting my ship."

"Be smart about this, Baylem. I'm the law out here. You can't escape. You're surrounded and I outgun you three to one. As usual when it comes to the two of us, I have the upper hand. For the sake of your crew, let's do this peacefully."

"Or what, you'll kill us?" Jorr leaned forward in his seat. "I don't think you have it in you."

"Vedd to Stellar Storm."

Without diverting his gaze from Rulk's dour visage, Jorr pressed a button on the small touch screen mounted to the arm of his command chair. "*Storm* here. It's good to hear your voice, Ankar. Where have you been?"

"Aboard the *Murapi*, or what's left of her. I'll fill you in later. Inella and I are returning to the *Storm*. As soon as we're aboard, you need to take her out of here as quickly as possible."

"We might have a problem with that, Mr. Vedd."

●

VEDD FROWNED. "WHAT DO YOU mean?"

"He means me, Ankar," a woman's voice chimed in.

Wincing, Vedd clenched his fists and mouthed a string of expletives before regaining his composure. "Valai—Captain Rulk, what brings you out this way?"

"I explained that to Baylem. What's your status?"

"Oh, I've never felt better, but you might want to move your ships at least seven hundred kilometers away from this freighter."

"Care to explain why?"

"Who is this person?" Inella whispered.

"System police."

"May I?" Inella's hand hovered over her wristpad.

Vedd shrugged.

She pressed a button. "Captain Rulk, my name is Doctor Inella Strabe of the Ghanzing Science Institute. To make a long story short, this freighter's propulsion system malfunctioned, causing its Falling Star units to explode. The sudden release of exotic matter tore a small rift in the fabric of space, an opening to another reality. I'm sure your sensors detect it.

"On the other side of this rift, a large vessel is rigged with hundreds of Falling Stars set to detonate in approximately nine minutes. It will expand the rift by a factor of ten, permitting a fleet of over twenty ships to cross into our universe. As Mr. Vedd advised, we should all move to a minimum safe distance of seven hundred kilometers immediately."

"And after that, Captain Rulk," Vedd added, "we'll be more than happy to brief you on the details *if* you'll first permit Dr. Strabe and me to return to our ship." He paused, then, "It is, after all, my home."

●

VEDD'S CURIOUS PHRASE MEANT NOTHING to Valaiya but was a ray of hope to Jorr. "I read you, Mr. Vedd." He tapped his touch screen and gazed up at the hologram of Rulk. "With your permission, Captain."

She drew herself to her full height. "They're trespassing on System property. I want them off."

"I'll take that as a yes." Jorr tapped the screen again. "Vedd, you're clear to jet over."

"Actually, my jetpack is almost depleted, but the thrusters on this freighter still function. Captain Rulk, if you'll allow me, I'd like to pilot her to the *Storm* and dock her at the starboard airlock. Then, you can take possession —"

At a flash of movement in his peripheral vision, Jorr's head snapped up. Rulk turned to her left and thrust out a hand, signaling to someone on her bridge. The first torpedo slammed into the freighter's port side, sending it spinning deeper into the rift.

The *Storm*'s bridge fell silent. All eyes tracked the second torpedo across the viewscreen as it struck the drone ship's engineering section. A moment later, debris was all that remained.

The mild shockwave that nudged the *Storm* could scarcely match bridge crew's rage as they erupted in shouts and profanities, all directed at the hologram of Captain Rulk.

Jorr shoved the touch screen aside and leapt from his chair. "You just murdered two of my crew!"

"Mr. Vedd and his companion were killed while attempting to steal System property. Unless you wish the same fate for you and your crew, surrender your ship and prepare to be boar —"

Rulk's hologram vanished in a blinding white flash. Jorr

shielded his eyes until the intensity faded. In his fury over Vedd's death, he had forgotten about the rift and the time bomb that was the *Murapi*.

"That was a fast nine minutes. Laresto, how long before the shockwave hits us?"

"About four minutes."

"Plot a course to Xarceese."

"Already in, sir."

As he's proved time and again, Ankar always finds his way back. Jorr tapped his screen. "*Storm* to Vedd. Please respond." He paused, then, "Ankar, are you there? Come in, dammit! Inella, do you read me?"

There was no reply.

Laresto spoke up in a plaintive voice. "I'm sorry, sir, but we need to leave."

Jorr slammed his fist into his touch screen, cracking its surface. After a moment, he nodded to the helmsman.

The young man's thin fingers danced over his console. The *Stellar Storm* dropped below the police cruisers and turned hard to starboard. The cruisers glided off the main viewscreen, but not before the shockwave struck the one closest to the rift, tossing it like flotsam and sending it careening out of control. The crew cheered as the spinning police cruiser collided with another, triggering a series of small explosions that left both vessels crippled.

The scene shrank into the distance until it faded into the vastness of space.

Goodbye, Valaiya. Hopefully for the last time. "Laresto, engage particle drive. Take us to Xarceese."

●

THE *STELLAR STORM* GLIDED ABOVE the outermost ring of the blue gas giant, Zetavor, before touching down on the planet's largest moon. Xarceese was one of five moons in this remote region of space that had been terraformed by the System Corps of Engineers for use as a colony when many of the inner system worlds had become overpopulated.

After only a few years, the cost of supporting the colonies had become prohibitive and the System had abruptly cut them off before they'd become self-sufficient. The colonies had hired private contractors to help them conduct trade with the inner worlds. Occasionally, these contractors resorted to questionable means in order to obtain scarce commodities that would be otherwise unaffordable due to exorbitant tariffs imposed by the System.

Crates of such items were now being unloaded from the *Stellar Storm*'s cargo hold while Jorr met with the colony's leader, Sunayta.

"Captain Jorr, you have the thanks of a grateful colony. Did you encounter any problems?"

"Nothing we couldn't handle, although I lost several good men including Vedd and Lorden."

"In that case, you also have our condolences." Sunayta bowed her head of wiry silver hair and waved a gnarled hand toward a collection of small white plasteel boxes stacked against the wall of her office. "Your fee, as agreed. To further express our gratitude, you are welcome to dine with the council this evening in honor of your fallen crewmen."

"That's most kind, ma'am."

A yellow light flashed on Sunayta's touch screen at the edge of her desk. "Go ahead, Ryja."

"Ma'am, a fleet of over twenty ships has just dropped out of a wormhole on the other side of Zetavor."

Jorr leapt from his chair.

Sunayta held up a hand to calm him. "System vessels?"

"Negative. Unfamiliar class. They just launched a shuttle on a direct course for Xarceese. Wait, they're hailing us." After a pause, the communications tech continued in a befuddled tone. "It is a Mr. Vedd calling for Captain Jorr."

●

THE ALIEN SHUTTLE TOUCHED DOWN in a clearing on the opposite side of the colony from the *Stellar Storm*. Vedd, Inella and Gaanic stepped out of the hatch to find a greeting party consisting of Jorr, Sunayta, and a security contingent.

Jorr smiled at the sight of them. "I should have known you'd find a way back when you used the code phrase."

Vedd spread his arms as he approached. "It is, after all..."

"... my home." Jorr embraced him and Inella together. "Yeah, well, I lost my mind when I thought Valaiya had killed you both."

"I tend to look before I leap. That's why I contacted you from the *Murapi* first to be sure it was safe to return. The minute

355

I heard Valaiya's voice, there was no way we were going back to the freighter. That woman is ruthless!"

"Why do you think I divorced her?" Jorr said.

Inella held up her hands. "Wait. What's this code you mentioned?"

"Baylem and I came up with that odd phrase to use whenever a crewmember becomes separated from the ship but finds an alternate way to rendezvous with us at our next destination." Vedd introduced Gaanic to Jorr and Sunayta. "Gaanic represents a group of refugees who have been exiled from their world. I thought perhaps you could help."

Sunayta motioned for him to follow. "Come with me. I shall arrange another place at the dinner table, and we can discuss the particulars."

"I look forward to hearing all about your escapade across the rift." Jorr nodded toward the *Storm*. "But for now, I'm going to check in with the crew. See you at dinner."

As the captain sauntered off, Vedd turned to Inella. "I owe you an apology for calling you bad luck. Were it not for you and your brother, I might have been killed when Valaiya turned up."

She leaned into Vedd and kissed him on the cheek. "Thank you for saving my life on the freighter. I never would have found my brother again if we hadn't gone sailing through the rift. I guess you're not a typical pirate after all."

"So where to now?"

Inella shrugged. "Wherever Gaanic goes, I'll probably join him. He's the only family I have, and I can pursue astrophysics from anywhere in the cosmos." She nudged him with her elbow. "It is, after all, my home."

Phil Giunta is the author of three paranormal mystery novels, including *Testing the Prisoner, By Your Side*, and *Like Mother, Like Daughters*. He currently has over two dozen short stories published across multiple genres including science fiction, fantasy, paranormal, mystery, and general fiction. His stories have appeared in *Love on the Edge, Scary Stuff, A Plague of Shadows, Beach Nights, Beach Pulp*, the Middle of Eternity series, and more. He is a member of the Horror Writers Association and the National Federation of Press Women.

https://philgiunta.com

An iCub on Mars

by Barbara G. Tarn

17 January 2048

Me, Baby. My parents call me that. I'm learning, one month with them. I'm happy they take me with them. They don't have human kids, they have me.

Temp home is called *Star Chaser*. We don't chase stars. We travel. We go to Mars Colony. I journal to learn.

Parents of Baby: Babs and Rohit Hariharan. They come from countries that start with I and end with A. Me too, first iCub was made in Genoa, Italy, 2004. History lesson learned.

Babs and Rohit go to Mars and take Baby with them. International spacecraft, Rohit wanted to call it Mangalyaan 3. Launch vehicle from European Space Agency, space capsule for two plus Baby from India Space Research Organization.

My parents do the trip to help growing Mars Colony with 20 people, 10 males, 10 females. Two stopped functioning, parents selected for replacement.

My sensors watch blue and green ball of home planet vanish from screen forever. Mars red planet. Baby barely experienced Earth. Still learning human language after one month travel. Journal helps.

●

14 February 2048

ALMOST ANOTHER MONTH. PARENTS FLOAT in *Star Chaser*, I don't. Magnet attach me. Blue planet vanished. I watch them now. She is 52, he is 44. They together for 6 years before adding me to family.

Today they float without their second skins (clothes?) and seem to become one. When I ask them what happened, Babs face becomes red and Rohit says it's a human thing that shouldn't bother me.

But I want to learn. It's what I do. My head holds good AI that wants learning. They tell me I don't need to know this. I think it's about human reproduction.

And now they lock me in the cockpit when they float "naked" in the restricted space of the *Star Chaser*. I write in journal new lesson.

●

28 February 2048

HEARD BABS COMPLAIN BECAUSE *STAR CHASER* has no showers, limits on toilet paper and clothing, and the long, close-quarters voyage is grating on her nerves, to which Rohit said that the drinking water made from their recycled urine and sweat tastes awful, and then they scowled at each other for seven minutes and thirty-five seconds.

Then she sighed and said she was scared, and he sighed

and said he was scared too, and they hugged. I wanted to be hugged too, but then their mouths met and I know what happens next, so I went to the cockpit by myself, waiting for them to stop floating naked.

●

19 March 2048

BABS SAID TODAY IN ITALY is Father's Day, so I recited a poem I found on the computer to Rohit who looked surprised. She told him in Italy they celebrate on Saint Joseph's day, March 19, since he's the father of Jesus. It's her religion, not his, he's Hindu.

My parents are busy with the spacecraft. They fix things on the fly and do more piloting than on NASA vehicles, or so they say. I haven't been on a NASA vehicle, so I don't know. I'm talking much better now.

The *Star Chaser* is well shielded from the cosmic rays and radiations. I don't want my parents to be sick before we reach Mars. They say radiations are dangerous for humans, that's why they haven't gone to space before. They waited for safe spacecrafts.

My parents wanted to go to Mars for a very long time. They were both excited and terrified when we climbed inside the *Star Chaser*. They thought the long journey would strengthen their marriage. It's expensive. It's dangerous. It's boring. But they thought the sacrifice was worth it.

I have seen them fight and then get naked, which seems to

solve everything. They teach me to work with them, but they say it's play because I'm like a child. They explain things and words to me because I'm so young. Three months old.

I don't mind the name Baby, because sometimes they call each other that. It's a way of showing affection for humans. It means newborn, but also small loved one.

I look forward to meeting more humans and compare them to my parents, but we still have months of travel to go.

●

5 April 2048

ACCORDING TO EARTH'S CALENDAR, IT'S Easter. Not that Babs cares about it, but even Rohit doesn't follow the Hindu festivals in space. Hard to celebrate Holi in a starship with zero-G!

Babs says during childhood she had chocolate eggs for Easter, with surprises inside. I wish I could eat and taste chocolate. Not a different day for us, except talks of Terran festivals. Both go down memory lane and I listen.

Today their marriage is not on the rocks, so I can relax. I studied more history about the colony waiting for us. I sound like Wikipedia because I took it from there, with words I don't understand very well yet.

The energy needed for transfer between planetary orbits is lowest at intervals fixed by the synodic period. For Earth/Mars trips, this is every 26 months (2 years and 2 months), so missions are typically planned to coincide with one of these launch periods.

Due to the eccentricity of Mars's orbit, the energy needed in the low-energy periods varies on roughly a 15-year cycle with the easiest periods needing only half the energy of the peaks. The first useful low-energy launch period occurred in 2033, when the first colonists reached the structures built by robots. Big, vaguely human-looking construction robots, not tiny androids like me.

We took the following window. The lowest energy transfer to Mars is a Hohmann transfer orbit, which would involve an approximately nine-month travel time from Earth to Mars, so we should reach the colony when it's September on Earth.

I wonder if we can have Diwali on Mars? And what Christmas is like. I saw movies on the entertainment channel, but I don't know what it will be like in reality. I look forward to it!

●

15 May 2048

WE'RE BEYOND HALFWAY THERE, BUT Babs and Rohit are becoming increasingly stir-crazy. And I learned a new word, when I asked them what they felt. Stir-crazy. Interesting. I haven't truly understood the concept, even though they tried to explain it to me.

Might be because I have so little experience of Earth and my sensors were still exploring, but I have no idea of what it means to smell things, to feel the weather, to walk around and meet people. Most of my existence has been on this starship, chasing stars.

They miss their friends and family, since communications are impossible as we travel, and they miss the blue sky and being able to travel all over the globe. They come from two different countries and use a common language, English, but sometimes they relapse into their mother tongues, especially when they're nervous and don't want the other to understand what they're saying.

I don't understand either, but if I ask them separately, they usually explain. I'm slowly learning some Hindi and some Italian. I even found language courses on the computer, I will surprise them with my new skill!

Hopefully it will help them complete the mission without accidents. Now they're anxious they won't be able to make new friends on Mars, and that life at the colony won't be like life on Earth and...they sure have a lot of fears.

●

15 August 2048

TODAY IS A HOLIDAY FOR both my parents' countries, so they celebrated together! It was a relief to see them get along again, and tell the stories related to each holiday.

In Italy, Ferragosto is a public holiday celebrated on 15 August. It originates from Feriae Augusti, the festival of emperor Augustus, but then the Catholic Church decided to celebrate the

Assumption of Mary instead.

Babs said that it's also the summer vacation period in the country. Up until 2010, 90% of companies, shops and industries closed but, with the growing influence from other non-Catholic countries, and the fact that closing an entire country's industry for a whole month meant an incredible loss of money and backlog of work, most companies now close for around two weeks, forcing all workers to take imposed vacation, similar to the Christmas break.

For Rohit it's a completely different kind of national holiday. Independence Day is celebrated annually on 15 August to commemorate the nation's independence from the United Kingdom, the day when the provisions of the Indian Independence Act 1947, which transferred legislative sovereignty to the Indian Constituent Assembly, came into effect.

On 15 August 1947, the first Prime Minister of India, Jawaharlal Nehru, raised the Indian national flag above the Lahori Gate of the Red Fort in Delhi. On each subsequent Independence Day, the incumbent Prime Minister customarily raises the flag and gives an address to the nation. The entire event is broadcast by Doordarshan, India's national broadcaster, and usually begins with the shehnai music of Ustad Bismillah Khan.

Unfortunately, this year Rohit can't watch the event, but he mentioned Independence Day is observed throughout India with flag-hoisting ceremonies, parades and cultural events.

So, a religious holiday versus a non-religious one on the same day for two different countries. Well, according to Babs, they're actually very similar, but that's another story.

They seem to be more relaxed today, since our arrival time is getting closer. We're almost there. It's so exciting! I wonder if there will be other iCubs on Mars....

●

25 September 2048

WE MADE IT! MARS GOT bigger on our screens, and the other stars vanished. Babs and Rohit were so busy with the maneuvers, I just watched quietly from my little corner. Even though I took in all the data available to me, I was never allowed to access the mainframe, so I don't know how to pilot the *Star Chaser*.

It's not a skill required of me—my only required skill is to learn like all good children do, and I think my parents are proud of me in that department—so I didn't feel guilty about not being able to help them. And I absorbed as much as I could by watching them.

When an expedition reaches Mars, braking is required to enter orbit. Two options are available; rockets or aerocapture. Aerocapture at Mars for human missions was studied in the 20th century. In a review of 93 Mars studies, 24 used aerocapture for Mars or Earth return.

One of the considerations for using aerocapture on crewed missions is a limit on the maximum force experienced by the astronauts. The current scientific consensus is that 5G, or five times Earth gravity, is the maximum allowable acceleration.

Gravity has no effect on me, but it was funny observing the

effect on my parents' bodies.

They managed to land in the Martian spaceport and were welcomed in the artificial gravity of the colony. A couple of Chinese climbed into the *Star Chaser* to take it home.

Human survival on Mars requires living in artificial habitats with complex life-support systems, in a hostile environment. Due to higher levels of radiation, there are a multitude of physical side-effects that must be mitigated. In addition, Martian soil contains high levels of toxins which are hazardous to human health. Hence this cocoon of Earth atmosphere and gravity to keep my parents and the other humans safe.

Colonization of Mars required a wide variety of equipment — both equipment to directly provide services to humans and production equipment used to produce food, propellant, water, energy and breathable oxygen — in order to support human colonization efforts.

This is why it's an international colony, with people from all over Earth. The ten original couples were selected by NASA, ESA, China National Space Administration, Indian Space Research Orbanization and Roscosmos, two for each space agency.

Nations were united in order to set up the basic utilities to support human civilization, designed to handle the harsh Martian environment and serviceable whilst wearing an EVA suit or housed inside a human habitable environment.

Like I said, there are only twenty people now, but they hope to expand. They're still building stuff for more people to join them. My parents will help adjust the systems to maximize use of local resources to reduce the need for resupply from

Earth.

Two large subsurface, pressurized habitats built as Roman-style atria underground, with easily produced Martian brick, are our new homes. One hard-plastic radiation and abrasion-resistant geodesic dome was deployed on the surface by the first crew, for crop growth.

Our new home has individual sleeping quarters which provide a degree of privacy for my parents and a place for personal effects, a communal living area, a small galley, exercise area and hygiene facilities with closed-cycle water purification.

The other building is the primary working space for the crew; small laboratory areas for carrying out geology and life science research, storage space for samples, airlocks for reaching the surface of Mars, and a suiting-up area where crew members prepare for surface operations.

The colony also includes a couple of small, pressurized rovers powered by methane engines and designed to extend the range over which astronauts can explore the surface of Mars out to 320 kilometers.

Communications with Earth are relatively straightforward during the half-sol when Earth is above the Martian horizon. NASA and ESA included communications relay equipment in several of the Mars orbiters, so Mars already has communications satellites.

The one-way communication delay due to the speed of light ranges from about three minutes at closest approach to 22 minutes at the largest possible superior conjunction. Real-time communication between Earth and Mars is highly impractical due to the long time lags. Sometimes the colony on Mars has communications blackout periods of the order of a month.

But at least my parents were able to send a message back to their relatives and friends, telling them we have reached our new home safe and sound. They haven't asked yet, but I wonder what happened to the two people they are substituting. Maybe I should do my own research and then tell them.

●

1 October 2048

I SHOULD HAVE STUDIED RUSSIAN or Chinese, but my parents didn't think about it. The two cosmonauts from Russia speak some English, enough to communicate, and the Americans, the Indians and the other Europeans also speak English.

Our neighbors are the Smiths, who are American, as are the Millers, sent by NASA. The Taylors are British and the Dupuis are French, sent by ESA. Then there's the Petrovs and the Gorkys of Roscosmos, the Kapoors and the Khans of the Indian Space Research Organization. The Chengs of China National Space Administration were the ones who left with the *Star Chaser*.

The ones who have been buried are the other two Chinese, and I don't think it was because they spoke little English. Now that I have seen more humans, my visual sensors notice the different pigmentation of their skin. A couple of conversations worry me.

First we met the American couple, the Smiths. They were

very welcoming, and looked surprised to hear Babs and Rohit come from Italy and India respectively.

"Are you sure?" they asked.

I didn't understand then, but Babs explained to me that neither her nor Rohit correspond to the stereotypical Italian or Indian. She is tall and blue-eyed, while usually Italians have more Mediterranean looks—olive skin, dark hair and eyes. Indians are usually brown-skinned, but Rohit is fair with light eyes, so he looks Caucasian.

The other Indian couples are indeed darker-skinned than them, and they looked wary at first, precisely for the same reason why the Americans were so friendly.

The Kapoors are worried that they might meet accidents like the Wongs.

So I'm thinking the Chinese couple didn't have an accident, although it looks like one. That's why the other couple ran away. It might be a small group, but it didn't look like they were able to maintain diversity and acceptance of different beliefs.

It looks to me as though the colonists are trying to create the perfect society to confront the challenge of survival entirely on their own by getting rid of those who are too different. Except they aren't self-sufficient yet, so they need to keep contact with Earth.

Since the replacements can come from anywhere—as they're volunteers, like my parents—who knows when they'll feel satisfied with the company? The initial friendliness is veiled with threats now, especially since my parents are nice to the Indian couples. Well, they're nice to everyone, but obviously the non-whites are the pariahs of the colony. Even though they are perfectly qualified and were chosen for their skills.

Everybody seems to like me, though, so I'll keep an eye on all of them. I don't trust any of them besides my parents, and I will keep Babs and Rohit safe! Even if I'm just a small iCub. Since everybody considers me a pet, or a mascot, not a threat, I might be able to call for help, once I figure out how to call Earth.

●

5 November 2048

IT IS THE FIRST DAY of Diwali, and the Kapoors are no longer with us. Again, they say it was an accident, but I don't think so. I'm checking the computers and logs, and a few things don't match. Babs and Rohit don't believe me, so I think I will send this file back to Earth. They can decide what to do with it.

The Khans are muslim and they don't celebrate Diwali. They keep to themselves more and more. I think they're afraid they're going to be next. There's a total lack of trust in this community, and this is not good.

I hope on Earth they see what I see and come for us. Or that I can convince Babs and Rohit to leave before the window closes. They are not supposed to go back so fast, but hopefully I can convince them.

When the next starship comes with the replacements, they better get on it. And if the replacements for the Kapoors and the Wongs are "people of color", they better not get off at all. Yes, I should definitely send this report out, using Rohit's account, so they'll know who to choose for the next mission.

I'm going to spell it out. Send white people only. Possibly who speak English. Anyone else is not welcome and will meet their death.

●

25 December 2048

MY FIRST CHRISTMAS! IT LOOKS like the Christmas atmosphere makes everyone nicer. Babs and Rohit seem integrated with the rest, but the replacements for the Kapoors haven't arrived yet. I guess they got used to work as an eighteen-people crew, or they would have waited to get rid of the brown ones. Or maybe they didn't hate them as much as the yellow ones.

What about the Russians, though? If they wanted the colony to be manned only by NASA and ESA, they would get rid of them too, wouldn't they?

I don't understand, and I don't want to understand. As long as they don't hurt my parents. I'm still keeping an eye on them. I learned Russian, so I know what they say when they talk among themselves. Basically, they mind their own business and do their job.

It's the Smiths and the Taylors who worry me most. They might like me and pet me, but I don't think they like my parents. At all. I hope Babs and Rohit don't consider them friends just yet.

•

1 January 2049

HAPPY NEW YEAR! I THINK Earth has received my report. They said a bigger ship is coming, with another ten people for the colony. Replacements for whoever is sick of Mars. They should arrive in about eight months, since they left before Christmas, but there was a month of blackout in communications, so they couldn't warn us earlier.

The Smiths aren't happy and keep muttering under their breath with the Taylors and the Millers.

We don't know yet what the new colonists will look like. What if they're African-American? Or, worse, African, or Japanese, or Maori? I sure hope my report helped Earth Space Control to make the right decisions.

I'm glad they're not going to anihilate the group and they're not stopping supporting them because they created their own little niche world. The colonists definitely have developed different points of view in isolation. I wonder if they match Earth's.

I don't think my parents ever considered the potential dangers of a society that has become so separate from the home world that they can no longer interact like civilized people. Like I said, the Mars colony is not self-sufficient yet.

But the first colonists don't like Earth and don't want to listen to Earth Space Control, so it's going to be tough. Maybe they should all be taken back to Earth and humans should start from scratch with another team? Should they give up the thought of a Mars Colony altogether?

I wish I could make decisions for them. But I'm just an iCub, although being called "Baby" starts to getting on my nerves. I am one year old after all!

●

14 February 2049

A VERY SUBDUED VALENTINE'S DAY. Each couple took a day off and retreated to their appartment. Babs and Rohit were thoughtful. When they celebrated on the *Star Chaser* it was more cheerful, but the journey to Mars had just begun, and they still had hopes and things to look forward to.

I think they're reconsidering their choice. Mars is not made for human life. Robots would be more efficient and less prone to accidents. They don't need to breathe, they are not subject to radiation...but the thing that might convince Earth is that robots are much cheaper than humans because they don't require a vast support infrastructure to provide water, food and breathable air.

So I'm writing another report in Rohit's name about the use of robots instead of humans on the Mars colony. They are immune to the risks of cosmic radiation and other dangers inherent to space travel. And they won't get bored or set up a new society.

I'm not bored, but I have humans to watch. But then, I have

a learning AI meant to interact with humans, so if you take away my parents, I will get bored. But robots are programmed to do their job and they don't have an AI, so they'll do just fine.

And I'm sure they will be able to carry out increasingly complex scientific research, accessing craters and canyons that humans might find too difficult to reach. I shiver every time Babs and Rohit don their spacesuits and climb onto those Mars rovers.

What if the rover breaks, or the suit malfunctions like it happened with the Wongs or the Kapoors? Humans are too frail to live in this hostile environment. I hope Babs and Rohit will realize it and get on that starship when it gets here.

●

21 March 2049

IT WOULD BE SPRING ON Earth. There are seasons on Mars too, but they're different, I'm told. Mars is beautiful, I like the sunsets here, but it's not for my parents. Or for the other colonists, for that matter.

Europeans and Americans form a compact group, the Russians and the Kapoors are two smaller, different groups, and my parents are stuck in the middle. They couldn't make friends. They are homesick. Life on Mars is not as they imagined it.

I'm happy we're going home with the return flight. The replacements should be here in a few months. I'm sure the Khans will come back with us, even though they spent sixteen years on

Mars. I'm not sure about the Russians.

I mean, the original colonists will probably stay, but I don't think they will accept newcomers. Even though they knew eventually they'd have to welcome new people, since that was the original intention.

I don't care what happens to the ten newcomers as long as Babs and Rohit leave this beautiful but deadly planet.

●

1 April 2049

IT WAS SUPPOSED TO BE an April's Fool. It could have been deadly. Rohit and Firoze Khan went out with the rover and had an accident. Rohit managed to get out of the rover and headed back for the colony in his spacesuit, but he had damaged the oxygen tank in the crash.

I saw him arrive on foot and collapse too far away from the colony. I sent a warning to Babs and Karisma Khan, ordered one of the robots to follow me and ran there. I'm too small to carry my father, so I ordered the robot to pick him up and take him back to the base.

Babs and Karisma took the other rover and went to get Firoze, with the two male cosmonauts who stayed with the vehicle and tried to repair it. Firoze and Rohit awoke in the infirmary, and they were fine.

Rohit even hugged me for saving him, so I told him I was sick of being called Baby. He nodded gravely, exchanged a glance with Babs who was standing next to his bed, then said from now on I will be called Hero.

I like it. I think my new name fits me. I might be a diminutive hero, but I saved lives!

Then the Russians came to visit the infirmary, and in their broken English they said the rover had been sabotaged. Like for the Wong and the Kapoors. They have repaired it again, but suggested Rohit and Firoze never go out together again.

●

5 April 2049

THE ENGLISH-SPEAKING WHITE PEOPLE denied ever sabotaging anything, of course, and since the Russians had repaired the rover, Rohit and Firoze have no proof. When we retired to our apartment tonight, I decided to tell my parents about the reports I sent in Rohit's name.

At first, he was mad at me for sending stuff in his name without telling him. But then he read the reports, and both he and Babs were thoughtful for four minutes and twenty-five seconds. Rohit sighed and admitted I had done well.

Babs complimented me for how I wrote the reports and how much I had learned since they took me with them. She says I'm definitely a Hero now, and that they'd be very careful until the replacements arrive.

And of course they're going back to Earth with the return flight, which makes me happy to no end! I look forward to seeing what it's like for humans to live on a planet made for them!

•

25 August 2049

IT'S BABS' BIRTHDAY, AND THE ship is here. We're all packed and ready to leave. We'll celebrate tonight on the *Ray Bradbury* with the Khans. I like that the bigger starship that brought the first colonists here is named after the author of *The Martian Chronicles*.

It's bigger than the *Star Chaser*, but not faster. It has more room for crew, but still zero-G. It will be fun to watch my parents float again. Maybe they'll take their clothes off tonight in their cabin. They certainly look relieved to leave.

The Khans also look relieved. Although after sixteen years here, it will probably be harder for them to re-adapt to Earth. But they look forward to meeting their nephews and nieces. Karisma is too old to have children of her own (much like Babs), but she's considering adopting an iCub.

I shall consider them my sibling, if that happens. And I hope the Khans will choose a female AI for their android child. I'd love to see what she becomes. Maybe I can suggest Babs and Rohit to give me a little sister instead.

We'll see. I'm doing a last tour of the colony. Time to say good-bye to the red planet. I'll miss it, but it's not good for my parents, so I'm glad to go back to Earth. I left as Baby and go back as Hero...how cool is that?

———————

Barbara G.Tarn writes mostly fantasy, and is a professional writer and hobbyist artist, a world-creator and storyteller. She has a few ongoing series; her fantasy world of Silvery Earth (high fantasy) and the Star Minds Universe (science fantasy) are mostly standalone. She dabbles into historical fantasy with her Vampires Through the Centuries series and plays with post-apocalyptic/steampunk in Future Earth Chronicles.

Two of her stories received an Honorable Mention at the Writers of the Future contest. She has stories published in *Pulphouse Magazine*, *The Phantom Games* and more coming.

http://creativebarbwire.wordpress.com

Of Hedgehogs and Humans

by Rob Nisbet

Spring

IT WAS IRONIC, THOUGHT SIMEON, as he looked down from the curved railing, that the intended peace of his hibernaculum should be so disrupted by activity. Bathed in brightness, the chrome and glass gleamed, Spike shone at the center like a radiant sun, a soft greenness seeped in from the vast curving windows and everybody, hundreds of them, set about their tasks like a colony of eager ants. Of course, there no longer *were* any ants — but, Simeon thought, the analogy was still valid.

His companion, Catarrhine, the doctor, stood at his side, her face lined with concern. "There is so much to prepare."

Simeon was more confident. "Everything will go according to plan. We've been absolutely meticulous." He gestured to the bustle below. "Look at them, so full of hope; they are the future. Spring *will* dawn on a new world."

Catarrhine turned to face the vast sweep of window behind them and allowed herself a mild smirk. "If not quite the spring of Spike's projection."

Simeon was an engineer; he assessed the window with a serious practicality. "To be effective," he said, "the scene must be familiar. We can't know what the new world will look like, but images of spring suggest a fresh start, the burgeoning of new life after, what will be, a very long Winter."

"I understand the psychology," said Catarrhine.

The window showed fresh green fields, flowers unfurling and trees heavy with fragile blossom, their branches swaying slightly as if in a real breeze.

The doctor and the engineer both knew that there could be no breeze here. A breeze needed air and an atmosphere, and beyond the windows there were neither.

Catarrhine grinned at the clichéd scene. "I'm surprised you don't have lambs, gamboling across the fields."

"Historically accurate perhaps," said Simeon. "But the anachronism would jar. There haven't been lambs since the Great Blue Extinction."

Catarrhine sighed. "Man has a lot to answer for." Her comment seemed to hang in the air, and subconsciously her eyes swept the polished steel pillars of the great domed ceiling. Each pillar was inscribed with the names of the extinct species of Earth in either red or blue lettering. Sheep she found easily, along with Shih Tzu and Shrimp.

Beyond the pillars, there was Spike; the focus of the hibernaculum.

Simeon followed her gaze and noted the worry in her deep brown eyes. "All our hopes and dreams...." His words sounded poetic, but his face remained grim, he meant them literally.

Catarrhine smiled. "You're so serious. And believe me, I understand how vital Spike is, and your programming to control him...."

"But?" Simeon prompted.

They looked at the vast glowing sphere; metal and glass enclosing a mass of circuitry and components. Like the center of a solar system, rings of construction orbited around it in concentric circles, and Spike was covered in antennae like flexible spines.

"You hide it well, Simeon, but Spike reveals, perhaps, your more frivolous side. It's no accident, is it, that he resembles a somewhat robotic curled-up hedgehog?"

●

Summer

CATARRHINE AND HER MEDICAL TEAM were carefully inspecting the concentric rings of beds that circled Spike's podium. The construction had progressed well.

Simeon's department maintained each bed's link to Spike, one bed for each of Spike's spine-like aerials. But it was Catarrhine who was responsible for life support and each bed's monitoring diagnostics. Her expertise was biological, far more important, in her opinion, than Simeon's technical prowess.

The beds had been arranged, at Catarrhine's insistence, in male-female pairs. Everyone selected for this mission knew of their obligation to sustain the species. And, now that the preparations were nearing completion, couples were seen working and socializing together. Many walked the wide promenade which encircled the hibernaculum, enjoying the scenes Spike projected onto the vast windows.

Spring had segued into a bright summer, full of vibrant color, always sunny. It was Simeon's theory that summer represented the new world, the harmony, the settlement, the expectation of utopia.

"It's working," Catarrhine told him when they met on the promenade. "Everyone is hopeful, looking forward to their new lives."

Simeon reached out to hold her hand, serious as always. "An expectation of Summer," he said. "There's nothing like a spot of contrived propaganda."

Catarrhine admired his almost cavalier honesty. They had been paired early in the selection; the doctor and the engineer. Catarrhine had consulted the lists the instant the researchers had made them public; Simeon had a stern brow, strong arms. She had no objection. She doubted Simeon had been so eager.

They gazed inward from the promenade railing at the beds arranged in pairs. "Let's trust that the researchers have got the balance right," Simeon said.

"That's more *my* department," said Catarrhine. "I advised that the ethnic cross-section should be as wide as possible. It is amazing how necessity can cut through to what's really important."

"What do you mean?" Simeon asked.

"We are shaping the population of a new world. Suddenly, survival is key. So many barriers fell instantly. There was never any suggestion, for instance, that a particular nation should be represented. Borderlines became meaningless scribble on old maps. It's the same with the various belief systems."

Simeon nodded. "Hardly relevant out here."

Catarrhine studied each couple with approval. "Race,

though, *is* important. Biological differences can't be drawn or invented anew—we preserve them now, or they are lost forever. And so much has been lost already."

They stood next to one of the gleaming pillars inscribed with names of lost species. Eagle, Eel, Elephant.... Those etched in red died in the Great Malarial Pandemic. More poignant were those etched in blue, including the mosquito, who had fallen during the second, Man-made, extinction.

●

Fall

ALL WAS NOW READY FOR hibernation, so Simeon triggered Spike's Autumnal programming.

Spike no longer burned like a sun. He had dulled to a deep yellow, mottled with dark russet blotches. The subduing of the light prompted a somber outlook. Everyone felt it; a nervousness of what was to come.

Simeon and his team had been promoting Spike as the ultimate hedgehog, readying everyone for hibernation. The seasonal changes had been planned long before departure; all very sensible and scientific. Autumn colored the trees in gold, seemingly just beyond the glass. The sky was darker, and the temperature had been dropped to match the projected illusion. All designed to ease everyone into the right temperament. But the mood had slid into melancholy.

Simeon was pleased to see Catarrhine supervising, quite

unnecessarily, as the first pair of colonists fitted themselves into the beds' molded mattresses. The beds were designed around each individual, in a vast array of shapes and sizes.

Catarrhine realized that this was a vital moment. Putting the first colonists to sleep had to run smoothly. She leant close to Simeon. "Of course, you realize Spike's not fooling anyone."

"Everybody knows the window scenes are false." He waved a dismissive hand at the golden autumn trees. "But the ambience is crucial. Everyone's becoming a bit weary. The images play on the illusion of the year's end, prompting a subliminal need for rest and shelter."

As the first colonist laid down, a monitoring chip at the back of his skull relayed diagnostic data to a dedicated spine of Spike's prickly surface. The procedure was going according to plan, but the apprehension on the colonist's face was obvious.

"Displaying a few dried leaves on the trees isn't enough to ease their minds." Catarrhine helped the first couple to settle comfortably. "Everybody being put to sleep, one by one...." Catarrhine was amazed that Simeon couldn't see the link himself. The parallel with the Great Malarial Pandemic was obvious.

Simeon frowned. "This is *not* extinction; this is merely sleep. Everyone here is bright enough to make that distinction."

Catarrhine tossed him a doubtful look as she plumbed a nutrient feed and filter into a catheter in the colonist's left arm.

Nobody had expected evolution to strike so harsh a blow. When it came, the mutation was not in an animal, but in a disease. And, transmitted by the humble mosquito, whole genuses fell before its might. A few species had a natural immunity to

malaria, but the new strain ate across whole swathes of the planet. Man, at evolution's peak, may have expected some privileged
immunity, but, of course, he began to fall with the rest of them.

The first couple were now sleeping. Everything had gone
according to plan, and, shortly after, an arc of the vast outer ring
of beds was occupied.

Simeon strolled with Catarrhine. She had felt the trepida-
tion, too, and she could sense that even Simeon was relieved
their plans were working. They paused at the windows.

"Cause and effect," mused Catarrhine. "We are only here
now, because of evolution—and Man's stupidity."

"Don't knock evolution," said Simeon. "The process seems
to be speeding up, and, don't forget," he gestured to the autumn
scene, "without it we'd still be swinging through the trees. I
agree, though, about the stupidity of Man."

Like practically every animal on Earth, the human race had
succumbed to the Great Malarial Pandemic. His hasty solution
was extreme—some simply called it revenge.

The second pandemic was caused by Man. A pesticide to
destroy the mosquito carrier and therefore curb the spread of
evolved malaria.

It was extreme because the pesticide used would destroy all
life except Man. Man and a few species of ape that shared ninety
-nine percent of Man's DNA. The pesticide destroyed everything
else in the Great Blue Extinction.

Everything.

●

Winter

WITH THE END OF HER preparations so close, Catarrhine pondered the path of fate that had led to this moment. A random quirk of evolution that had favored the parasitic heart of an infectious disease, which had then been compounded by the idiocy of Man. But, as if to balance its initial destruction, natural selection had reached out to the few survivors. Simeon was right, the evolutionary process did seem to be speeding-up. Becoming more concentrated, perhaps, because the remaining population of Earth was now so small. Whatever the cause, Catarrhine gave thanks that evolution had ensured the science behind this great ship now fell within their understanding.

Escape from Earth was now assured, but Catarrhine was under no illusions. Their survival was far from guaranteed. But they had a better chance than their fellows left behind, struggling against the planet's shattered ecological systems.

Catarrhine joined Simeon at the windows. They were the last pairing to sleep. Everyone else was already in hibernation, watched over by Spike.

Snow fell silently beyond the windows, forming a white layer on skeletal branches that still waved slightly in that impossible breeze. The hibernaculum was now cold and dark and whispered with the soft rhythms of sleep.

"You can stop the window projection now, Spike," said Simeon.

Instantly, the white of snow was replaced by the black of space. It took Catarrhine a full minute for her eyes to adjust enough to discern the stars. She shuddered. "You'll think me stupid," she said. "I feel like I've lost a connection with Earth. Now, there is only us and this immense emptiness."

"Have a little faith in me," said Simeon. "Or at least in my ship." He gazed out. "I know the phenomenal speed we are travelling, but there is still no noticeable movement. This will, indeed, be a long winter."

They made their way to the two empty beds on the inner circle, next to Spike, who now glowed an icy blue. Simeon lay down. "All this preparation and programming; we're dependent on you now, Spike. Take care of us." Simeon's skull chip connected to Spike's aerial, and he smiled up at Catarrhine as she made the medical connection to his arm. "We'll be OK," he said. His eyes swept the lists of species commemorated on the steel pillars. "We will survive. There may be no more hedgehogs, but their philosophy lives on."

"I knew you had a frivolous side," Catarrhine smiled.

The drugs began to take effect, and Simeon's eyes closed. Catarrhine leaned over to kiss his eyelids. She straightened to the realization that she was the last. And suddenly she realized the power she had. With a simple command she could trigger a third, final extinction. She could switch off Spike and let the sleepers wither in their beds. Then the Earth would truly be dead. But that had been Man's destructive solution to the mosquito problem; she was better than that. She stood by an inscribed column which commemorated the extinction of herons and horses, of hedgehogs and humans.

Humans, etched in red, susceptible to the malarial extinction. Unlike us, thought Catarrhine. That precious one percent difference in our DNA shielded us from that first epidemic. And our ninety-nine percent similarity shielded us from the second.

She crossed to her bed, lay down next to Simeon, and slid the medical connection into her arm. She felt her eyes begin to close. "Goodnight, Spike," she said, and twisted her tail into the shaped foam of the mattress.

––––––––––––

Rob Nisbet is a member of the International Association of Media Tie-in Writers, having, to date, written seven BBC approved audio dramas for *Doctor Who,* produced by Big Finish. Under various names (mostly Rob Nisbet and Trixie Nisbet) he has had over 70 stories printed in anthologies and magazines ranging from romance to horror.

Smugglers Blues

by Blaze Ward

DARKNESS.

Ohran space.

The D'Meskaloo Gate.

One of the Gate's nine portal facings lights up.

Reality warps and a hole opens in space itself at the center of the gate.

The cargo carrier *Boundary Shock* slips through, old and rather battered, as befits the sort of ship that serves a dead-end system like D'Meskaloo.

The Gate closes.

●

OLLIE LOOKED OUT THE WINDOW next to the airlock, but saw only the Law Commission pinnace docked to *Boundary Shock*'s aft personnel airlock, the front one having long since been destroyed when the bow and original bridge were smashed in a police impound lot accident.

At least that was the story he'd been told when he'd come along.

Banging from the outside of the hatch announced the pinnace's arrival. Ollie looked back into the chamber, but saw only his one passenger on this flight, Nyarri Gorne, as he moved to stand next to her.

She was fidgeting quietly in the middle of the room,

dressed extravagantly in a sheer, midriff-baring green mesh top with a horizontal line of solid cloth across her breasts just barely tall enough and wide enough to hide her areolae if she didn't move suddenly. Gauzy pants in a similar color flowed down her legs over a half-leotard bottom, showing off practically everything but the tan.

Long, black hair had been gathered in a clasp at the nape of her neck and flowed down nearly to her waist in back.

Ollie knew Nyarri didn't generally dress so sexy. She would have preferred a hijab and a belted tunic, like she had worn up until today, but that was not an option right now.

She stood still for a moment, then leaned her weight into him, wrapping an arm around his back, as his went around her waist.

"Good?" she asked nervously.

"Relax, you'll be fine," Ollie said, suddenly aware that she looked nineteen. Probably was, he hadn't asked. Ollie felt like a dirty old man at thirty-three.

He reached out and triggered the hatch to open. He looked around to locate his first mate, finally finding him hanging from the pipes and metalwork overhead.

"They'll want you and your papers down here with us, Rufus," Ollie said tiredly, gesturing to Nyarri.

Unlike Ollie and Nyarri, Rufus was a Troida. Long arms and short legs, like a pixie great ape, with ash-gray fur on his back and a white belly. Or, as he liked to tell everyone, the galaxy's awesomest drop-koala.

The resemblance to the ancient herbivores was marked,

from the fur on his face, to the ears, to the climbing claws he now had wrapped around the exposed metal frames that seemed to dominate every room on this ship.

Ollie had never been able to tell if someone had stripped panels to expose them, or bolted them on a later.

"Oh, I'm quite comfortable up here, thank you much," Rufus drawled back lazily, looking indeed half-asleep in the notch of a set of branches. "They can reach up."

"Not all of us are arboreal creatures, Rufus," Ollie tried one last time, as the hatch started to open.

"Well, you should have made better evolutionary choices then, shouldn't you?"

Any retort on Ollie's part was cut off by the entrance of the two Law Commission Inspectors.

Even in a dead-end backwater like D'Meskaloo, these people always looked composed and formal. And the Commission always seemed completely dominated by humans like Ollie. He couldn't remember the last system he'd visited with non-humans as Customs Inspectors.

Gold uniforms, trimmed in silver-gray. Tunics to mid-thigh, with silver belts holding equipment pouches and holsters. And handcuffs, if someone got unruly.

Thankfully, Rufus had eaten the last of his chocolate days ago, so he was completely sober now.

Nyarri's outfit had the intended effect on the two men. She was a beautiful woman. Everyone in the room was human but Rufus. And it wasn't like this sector of space was especially prudish, but two sets of eyes seemed to home in on her breasts and probably never made it north of her collarbones.

He felt her shiver, but it only in her fingertips, hidden against his back.

"You're back early, Ollie," the taller inspector said. "Wasn't expecting you for another few months."

"Got a lead on a book," Ollie lied convincingly. "Finagled a cargo run to D'Meskaloo to pay for it."

"And a new girlfriend," the officer said with a leer to his voice. He looked a decade older than the smaller one, who stood a half-pace back and to one side. "What is it with you and young women, Chilikov?"

"Dude, we're in The Pocket." Ollie shrugged, pulling Nyar-ri closer possessively so that interesting parts of her rubbed up against his side. He hoped it was as distracting to them as it was to him. "They want to run away from home, or escape a bad marriage, or just chase the brass ring. Who am I to argue?"

Part of him was angered that the three of them were talking about the beautiful woman in their midst like she wasn't even there. Or was maybe an exceptionally interesting statue.

Something he found terribly derogatory.

The two officers nodded. "Papers?" the taller one asked. He looked around for a second. "Where's your pain-in-the-ass first mate?"

"Here." Rufus was hanging upside down from a crossover beam, all the pockets of his jumpsuit zipped shut so nothing would fall out. One long arm held an ID book that the shorter officer grasped with some disdain, like it might convey some disease when he touched it.

Ollie handed over his and Nyarri's papers. Hers just didn't happen to say *Nyarri Gorne* on them. For now, she was Doria. She even looked like the woman who used that identity from time to time.

The tall officer reviewed them briefly before handing them back. "Manifest?"

Ollie was already reaching into an interior pocket for the papers. Like Rufus, Ollie believed in carrying things in pockets constantly, but he didn't like jumpsuits, so he had settled on a lapis blue cloth vest with pockets everywhere. Plus the tan shorts he wore in any weather where frostbite wasn't likely.

The bundle of papers came out and were handed over to the shorter man. He stuffed them into a reader and studied them briefly.

"My records show that you're a reformed smuggler?" The younger man's voice was suddenly cross.

Ollie shrugged, as did the taller officer. "That's the ship, man," Ollie said. "I'm just the pilot."

"What?" the shorter man demanded. He started to say more, but the taller one cut him off.

"You know the rules, Ollie," the taller man, the senior one, said. "We'll have to inspect."

Ollie smiled and shrugged. "What else is new?"

●

THE MAIN CARGO BAY HAD been rearranged while the ship was still in flight. There were times Ollie had considered burying the old smuggling chambers under a stack of boxes, just to make the Law Commission folks waste half a day while he and Rufus dug everything out and restacked containers differently.

None of the current Inspectors in the Pocket had pissed him off enough to do it.

Yet.

The containers *Boundary Shock* hauled from world to world were each fifteen feet tall and wide, by forty-five feet long. The bay held three rows of them, stacked up to three levels high and six long. Completely full, the ship would carry fifty-four of them, and they would have to find a place to stash the loader, but Ollie had never had more than forty-eight containers on a run in his career. Thirty was normal. Today they had thirty-six.

So he had space to leave Row 1, Stacks 1 & 2 clear.

Rufus had gotten there ahead of everyone, but he didn't need to rely on stairs or ladders, just those long arms, strong hands and climbing claws, working on a network of metal branches and trunks everywhere.

Didn't help that the Troida who had rebuilt this ship had only put stairs back in when they hired Ollie as their front-man, and only after he'd thrown a bit of a hissy fit on the subject.

Plumb lines and bubble levels would have also been a nice touch when they were installing the stairs, but Ollie figured that was too much like work for the Troida. Especially if Rufus was in any way average.

Nyarri nearly pitched face-first off the catwalk stairs when the steps changed camber midway, the result of welding two un-related sets of steps together. But Ollie had known it was coming and had hold of her hand.

"Thank you," she murmured as she recovered.

She squeezed his arm with her free hand as they continued down.

The two Inspectors following her never looked up from that gauze-covered bottom, so they wouldn't have been much use.

"Go ahead and open it," the senior officer said, as everyone reached cargo deck.

Rufus made a face that nobody but Ollie could see and unlocked the normally-hidden ring. He pulled it up easier than any of the humans could have done, even with pistons on the hinges.

"Anything?" the senior officer directed the junior.

The smaller man got down on his knees and stuck a head into the supposedly-secret compartment. To be an ass, most likely, Rufus did the same, subtly mocking the Inspector by matching his stance and hanging even further into the revealed room.

The officer made an angry noise and reached in, precariously balanced as he shifted.

Ollie started to say something, but saw that Rufus was prepared to grab the man by the belt if he started to lose his balance. It was only three feet, so he'd be embarrassed more than hurt, but Ollie couldn't remember the last time anyone had cleaned in there, so those pretty gold uniforms would pick up all sorts of sludge and yuck if he made a dust angel in there.

"What's this?" the man demanded as he pulled up a glass jar a little bigger than his fist and held it out. He stomped to his feet, which was a pretty impressive thing in itself, and presented it to his superior officer.

"Ollie?" The man's tone held the same sort of disappointment your dad did when mom told him what you'd done today.

"Roasted coffee beans from Vorli," Ollie said.

"Are you attempting to bribe officers of the Law Commission?" The younger one got hot and red in the face.

"No." Ollie looked at him sternly, similar to the look the taller officer was giving the back of the man's head.

Newbie.

"I figured I might as well give you something to confiscate, since we have to go through this stupid charade every time I arrive here," Ollie continued. "If you don't want it, I'll drink it just fine."

"Is it declared on your manifest?" the taller asked, with the slightest hint of a grin.

"Nope," Ollie grinned back. "I suppose it falls under ship's sundries, if I wanted to get titchy. Those aren't either."

"Vorli?" the man asked.

"Last run, when I got the story and the cargo to D'Meskaloo."

"As it is undeclared cargo, I think it will be necessary to confiscate this, Ollie," the man announced with a subtle grin. "Anything else?"

"Not unless you know someplace where I can find any replacement cargo shuttles for the four that should have come with the ship," Ollie said.

"Tired of flying from a Troida-built control room?" The older man turned a bemused eye on Rufus, who grinned back like it was the greatest practical joke in the world.

For two-dimensional humans, it probably was, at least in the eyes of a drop-koala.

"You think I enjoy climbing across a jungle gym to get to and from my cabin?" Ollie asked, in an exasperated tone. "They don't believe in stairs."

That prompted a laugh from both men. More a chuckle at someone else's discomfort, but they were Law Commission. At least the older one had some sense of humor.

That man stuffed the jar of beans into a tunic pocket and nodded to his junior. The smaller Inspector stamped everything and handed it back with a quick glance up to the stack of containers above and around them.

For the briefest moment, Ollie wondered if the man would turn around and demand a random container be opened for inspection. That would end up taking half a day, if he didn't want one on top and Ollie and Rufus had to uncover something from the middle.

They would find no contraband, though. She was standing right next to him, with an arm around his waist, making smiley, kissy faces up at him every once in a while.

The taller Inspector did look at her now. Even made it as far as looking at her face. It was a pretty face, especially as she had taken the time this morning to do some makeup, even against her will.

His eyes transitioned to Ollie.

"Too bad you can't keep them around," he observed dryly.

Ollie shrugged.

"Too much hard work involved," Ollie smeared it on extra

thick. "They're fun for a few runs, then they get bored, I get bored. Better this way."

"You staying on D'Meskaloo?" the man asked Nyarri.

Nyarri shrugged and rubbed herself against Ollie's side like a particularly happy cat.

Ollie wasn't sure she wasn't purring when she did. But the woman was a pretty good actress, from what he'd seen.

"Are the men around here more interesting than a cartographer?" she asked slyly, turning her entire upper body in such a way as to point her breasts at the two men.

Their eyes goggled, just for a moment.

Her breasts did look nice, but Ollie'd never seen even this much of her, let alone the other bits she was suggesting. The outfit had surprised the hell out of him, even when he knew what she was going to wear for today's performance.

"We think so," the older officer stammered, a little red in the face. To regain his equilibrium, he turned instead of speaking and attacked the off-balanced stairs, his junior in close pursuit.

Ollie, Rufus, and Nyarri shared a secret grin before following.

●

OLLIE WATCHED THROUGH THE WINDOW as the pinnace pull away from the dock on thrusters.

"We're good," he said, turning back to the others. "Nyarri, you can get dressed now. Rufus, I'll let you fly us to the surface."

Rufus leapt in the air with a hoot and swung himself arm over arm across and into the old docking tunnel that had once held a cargo shuttle, before his people had built a bridge over there instead. Which obviously made *so much more sense* that just repairing the existing bridge, currently open to space.

But he wasn't a Troida. It might make perfect sense to a drop-koala.

"And you're sure this will work?" Nyarri asked.

"In that outfit?" Ollie laughed. "I doubt those two even remember you had eyes, let alone the color. And they're expecting you to dump me at this stop, forcing me to find a new girlfriend to keep my bed warm."

"Men." Her disdain was evident, but she'd slept in her own cabin, only moving things into his this morning, in case the Law Commission officers they'd drawn had demanded a full inspection of the vessel.

Ollie shrugged. He was good at that.

"When we get down to the surface," he continued, "you make contact with the underground. If it all looks safe, you and Colonel Zabra swap identity papers and she gets extracted aboard *Boundary Shock* when I depart. If not, the underground assigns me a new agent to pretend to be a girlfriend for the trip and headquarters comes up with a new plan."

"How many times have you done something like this, Chilikov?" Nyarri's face got serious.

"Enough that it's become a running joke at a dead-end system like D'Meskaloo," he replied with a wry grin.

"And nobody asks?" She seemed amazed, even now, the

third or fifth time they'd had this conversation.

"I'm just the pilot here." He shrugged. "Rufus's clan actually owns the ship, once you get through enough shell companies. And it lets me do my research."

"So you really are a cartographer?" Her pretty brows drew together in something like confusion.

"The actual term is xenoarchaeologist," he said. "The study of lost history."

"Lost?" she asked, drawing her arms around her chest defensively, but that wasn't a reaction to him, standing nearly ten feet away.

"Humans are not native to any planet in the Ohran Web, Agent," Ollie said, all jocularity gone.

"No?"

"None," Ollie confirmed. "So where do we come from? That's what I'm trying to find out."

"And the underground?" Nyarri asked.

"They help fund me," he replied. "And they want to know the truth as well."

"Why?"

"If we're not native to any of these worlds, humans had to have somehow traveled from a world without a Gate to one with a Gate." Ollie smiled. "So either they built a huge ark and took generations, or somewhere there is a human ship capable of FTL travel. What's that worth to the galaxy, to not have to only travel to worlds served by the Ohran Web Gates?"

He saw her shiver. Nyarri was a hardened agent, even as young as she was, but that was a different world from the academia that drove Ollie. Beautiful, too, but not his type, beyond the cover of being a girlfriend on this run.

There would be a different woman on the run home. Either Colonel Zabra or someone else.

Occasionally, Ollie had to insert or extract a male agent. Law Commission Inspectors didn't ask, as long as everyone was of legal age to give consent. They might give him odd looks, but he already got that as a cartographer.

"One of these days, I want to hear more of your stories, Chilikov," Nyarri said, nodding to herself and turning to go.

He knew she would be dressing in something sexy, but which covered a bit more, at least until it was safe to break out the hijab again and return to who she really was.

"Talk to the Colonel," Ollie called after her as she exited.

He turned to look back out the window. The pinnace was far enough away now to have disappeared, leaving him only stars to stare at.

Which one of you? he thought. Which of you was our original home?

———————

Blaze Ward writes science fiction in the Alexandria Station universe (Jessica Keller, The Science Officer, First Centurion Kosnett, etc.) as well as several other science fiction universes, such as Star Dragon, the Dominion, and more. He occasionally writes odd bits of high fantasy with swords and orcs. In addition, he is the editor and publisher of *Boundary Shock Quarterly Magazine*.

https://blazeward.com

Altered Skin

by Sara C. Walker

Then

THE HULL OF THE SHIP creaked and shifted as we made our way towards the bridge. Ships were meant to be full of noise—the rumble of the engine, the chatter of the crew. This was too quiet. Folded uniforms stood ready in the living quarters. All the escape pods waited in their berths. Creepy as hell.

The ghost ship had been spotted by a passing freighter as it drifted across space. They hailed it and got no response, so our hauler was dispatched to retrieve. Scans had shown no life signs in the vessel, full fuel cells, and life support systems operational, so the captain sent me with this band of jokers to board and jumpstart the main thruster engine. Since the ship appeared normal but abandoned, we boarded in our regular work suits, leaving the contamination gear aboard the hauler.

My 2IC, Blunden, was on point with the rest of the crew trailing behind. He was nervous. They were all jumpy. Even I was feeling on edge.

"So, Lieutenant," Blunden said. "You got a date for the G-Navy Ball?"

"That your way of asking me out, Blunden?" I asked sharply.

Before he could respond, one of the other crew chimed in, "Everyone knows she doesn't date, Blunden. What are you doing?"

"Just thought you'd like a night out, Lieutenant," Blunden said.

"He just wants to see you in a skirt, Lieutenant," Larze joked.

Blunden held up a hand to halt our progress as we approached the galley. While the other members fanned out and poked around the room, Blunden quipped about the quality of the G-Navy's food and it being supper time when they abandoned ship. This crew.... Always joking.

"Hey, Blunden. I'll give you a day's pay to finish eating what's on the plates," Larze said.

A jab at the extra weight my 2IC carried and a feeble attempt to lighten the tension.

Blunden was smart enough to know it. "Only if you go first, Larze."

The others snickered.

I barked at them to smarten up. I wanted this retrieval. The money bonus of flying back a working ship was far better than hauling a dead-in-space ghost ship. Something about haunted ships gave people the heebie-jeebies. Didn't bother me. Some haulers claimed to have felt ghostly presences, but I'd never experienced any such thing. Good thing, too. I don't need dead people bothering me. Get enough of that from the living.

Still, there was something about this place that made me feel as comfortable as a cat in a room full of rocking chairs. Maybe it was the half-finished piles of mashed potatoes and beans with the partial glasses of wine. I didn't know anyone in all of the Galactic Navy who passed up a glass of wine, let alone an entire crew of seven all at once. I wondered what they'd been celebrating. I wondered what had interrupted their moment.

Although the Captain had asked, we'd not been told exactly what this ship and crew did for the G-Navy, but given the small size, it was meant to fly under the radar, traveling light and quick. Maybe running messages between Heads of State. Maybe running a spy operation. I didn't much care. With my bonus, I would have enough to put a downpayment on my own ship. And what's more, I could hand-pick my crew. I could leave these idiots behind.

I sure as hell didn't want to be stuck serving other captains for the rest of my life.

The door to the bridge was just a few steps away. I raised my hand. Full stop.

"Did you hear something?" I asked our scanner.

He shook his head. Everyone else raised their eyebrows.

Great. Now my crew thought I was hearing things.

I took the opportunity to assign tasks to complete once we entered the bridge. Maybe I could get them to put the joking aside for a while. Yeah, right.

I turned to the door with Blunden at my back. I punched the button, the door slid open. I took one step inside and stopped.

Every panel was dark. Empty chairs. Not a soul in sight. That smell —

Something skittered at the corner of my vision.

The bottom dropped out of my stomach. My mouth went dry. I wasn't alone.

I turned and shoved Blunden out of the bridge. He fell back against the rest of the crew. I slammed the door shut between us and cranked the manual lock before they could pick themselves off the floor.

Angry and confused, they pressed against the window, yelling words I couldn't hear through the thick glass. I didn't need to hear. I knew they didn't understand. But they were about to.

We'd left the contamination gear behind. I had no choice.

In the next second, their expressions quickly reformed to sheer terror. They shouted and bashed on the door. A high-pitched scream pierced my ears. With quivering hands, I pulled out my weapon, flicked off the safety. I could feel it rising up behind me.

I turned away from my crew and fired.

●

Now

WE WERE ADRIFT. NEARLY TWENTY-FOUR hours ago, the main thruster engine went out, putting our passenger cruiser well behind schedule and putting all one thousand passengers into disquietude. I'd spent most of the day receiving nosy inquiries about the repairs, whining about the setback to personal itineraries, and now—the prize-winning complaint—mewling from a man who'd cheaped out and paid for a two-person pod for his family of five. Seems he thought it was my job to force the single woman who paid for a four-person pod to switch with him.

Mr. Switch—he had a name but I couldn't remember it——leaned into his communication screen and peered at me. "Do you have pink eye? The skin around your eyes is all red."

"I'm fine—"

"Maybe it's allergies. My brother gets eczema on his face every time he eats strawberries. Have you had any strawberries lately? Is there anything you're allergic to?"

I knew for sure the Captain would bark at my ass for an hour if he found I'd told Mr. Switch I was allergic to nosy people.

"You're squinting. Do you have a headache? I have an aunt whose eyes go red and watery every time she has a headache. Have you tried smelling salts? One time I had this headache so bad—"

"Look, sir," I interjected, "sometimes in life we don't get what we want. You chose your bed, now you lie in it." Before he could open his mouth, I cut the communication.

The silence was beautiful—for the whole five seconds it lasted before the man called back. Seven messages had come in while I'd been talking to Mr. Switch. I programmed the auto-responder, no longer caring that the Captain preferred we give the passengers personal service. No amount of pay in the universe was worth listening to that man.

A steady itch wormed around my eyelids and crawled across my scalp. I ran a thumbnail across the bottom lashes of my right eye and came away with tiny flakes of skin. Damn it.

I headed for sick bay.

●

I sent a message to the captain to let him know I'd be offline for a few hours. I found sick bay empty, but that was all right. I knew my way around and began filling the bathing tub with oil.

It was about three-quarters full when Dr. Holloway entered, complaining about attending hypochondriacs with cases of cabin fever. She stopped when she noticed what I was doing. While she took over the preparations, I undressed.

In the time since I'd stepped into sick bay, the Peel — and its incessant itch — had already spread across my face and down both arms and legs.

She asked when the Peel had started.

"Probably an hour ago," I told her.

She wanted to know what I was doing then.

"Just some work for the Captain," I said.

She reached for her pad, so she could pull up my file and add to her notes. Her dark hair fell in front of her face; she pushed the locks back, tucking them behind her ear. She had some grandiose idea that she could cure me — something about finding the Peel's triggers. I had tried to set her straight; my immune system had been altered by alien DNA. There was no cure, no reset button, no off-switch. But I guess it was in her nature to keep trying.

While she mumbled about stress as a possible trigger, I resumed preparations.

A large mirror hung on the wall next to the tub. I avoided

glancing at it while tying my hair on top of my head. Peeling white layers over scarlet raw skin rapidly spreading over my entire body? No one wanted a view of that. Least of all me.

Dr. Holloway wanted me to elaborate on my work for the Captain.

I suggested her time would be better spent helping me find a new posting — a solo gig so other people wouldn't have to look at me. I'd made the suggestion before, but always with a laugh. Not this time. Even I heard the vitriol in my voice.

Her expression softened to sympathy.

"You don't have to hide." She'd said it before and often. It was easy for her to say.

"If you care about me at all," I said, "please help me find a job where I only ever have to hear the sound of my own voice."

She looked up from her notes. I quickly turned away from her pity and lowered myself into the oil bath.

●

Then

I WOKE TO THE UNMISTAKABLE smell of antiseptic and the steady beeps of monitors. Sick bay. The fog of deep sleep clouded my memories. The last thing I remembered was being aboard the ghost ship. Laughter. We were setting up to haul it back. I'd heard something —

My crew.

My screams competed against the alarms on the monitors.

Dr. Matuzzi rushed over. "Settle," he said, "or you'll tear off your new skin."

"But my crew—"

I fought off the doc. He called for a sedative. I shoved him away from me. He called for the Captain.

The Captain with her short flame-red hair appeared in my view, towering over me, and barked orders for me to settle down.

Expecting to finally get some answers, I did and asked her what happened.

"You were ambushed," she said. Her mouth turned down, brow pinched. "Scanners never picked it up. Should have, but...they missed it. As soon as you saw the alien, you shoved your team out the door. Locked them out of the bridge."

"They got out? They're okay?"

"Thanks to you."

Relief flooded my body and I fell back against the pillow. They'd got out.

"The alien?" I asked.

"Dead. You took care of that right away." Her eyes lit with pride. "The crew came back for you as soon as they'd put on contamination gear, but by then it was too late. You'd already started to peel."

"The crew of the other ship—is this what happened to them?"

The doc chimed in. "No, no. They're gone. Eaten by the alien, from what we can tell. You have a nasty virus. Probably from when you killed the alien and its guts splashed over you.

Took off all your skin. Every layer. We had to sedate you and wrap you in oil-soaked cloths until you grew a whole new set."

A whole new set of skin? That kind of shit didn't happen overnight.

"How long?"

"This kind of thing isn't my specialty." The doc turned away. Probably so I wouldn't strike him again.

I turned to the Captain. "How long have I been out?"

She shifted like she wasn't going to answer, but dammit. I needed to know. How long had I been knocked on my back? How long had I been lying here instead of working—instead of saving for my own ship?

"How long?" I demanded again, pushing up against the bed, trying to rise but failing. I flopped against the mattress.

She wouldn't meet my eyes. "Three weeks."

"And it will happen again," Dr. Matuzzi said from across the room. "Looks like the virus has altered your immune system. I suspect this is only the first symptom. But like I said, not my specialty."

It hit me then, the cold chill of reality, that this was my new life, that my career was over. "Fix me. Fix my DNA. Get the alien out of me. Get it out of me!"

They exchanged a glance but offered no course of action. The doc began to mumble about the impossibility of disentangling DNA strands—

"Fix me!"

Anger rose up. I wanted to punch the pity off their faces. Even made a valiant attempt. But the doc finally had that sedative in his hand.

It was over. It was all over.

●

Now

I WOKE IN A PRIVATE room in sick bay to Dr. Holloway's tuneless humming, a sign of her being engrossed in her reading. She was curled up in the chair next to my bed, a blanket pulled over her long legs. I wondered if she'd been dealing with more cabin fever complaints. I wondered if we were moving yet.

The humming stopped when I stirred and stretched. "Best bed on the ship," I said. "Good reading material?"

"Science journal. You would not believe what they're able to do with DNA these days. I'd like to take a sample of your connective tissues—"

"No."

"Why not? Your sample could make the world of difference for someone else—"

"I said no."

"And I said why not?" She locked her determined brown eyes with mine. "I don't need your consent. I could order you to do it."

"But you won't."

"Fine." She put down her pad. "Some of us have work to do." She got up from the chair and began clattering instruments on the table.

Was she mad at me? Because I didn't want to be poked and prodded and experimented on?

I failed in my attempt to achieve a sitting position, my arms buckling under me. My joints needed a good greasing.

"You don't have to sit with me through treatment."

"No? So I should let you drown in the oil bath? Let you wrap your own bandages, then?" She turned up the lights.

Yep. She was mad at me.

I rolled onto my side and slipped my feet over the edge of the bed. There. Sitting accomplished. I blinked against the bright lights.

Dr. Holloway was the best doc in the Galactic Navy. What's more, she took an interest in my case. For my efforts with the ghost ship retrieval, I didn't get my own ship, but when I asked to be posted with Dr. Holloway, the Navy didn't hesitate.

In the past year under her care, my skin regrowth had been reduced to a mere twenty-four hours. And yeah, I could run my own bath and wrap my own bandages.

Doc's orders were to wear silk pyjamas for forty-eight hours after treatment. They'd cost a pretty penny, but felt nice against my tight new skin as I dressed.

"I found you a posting," she said, keeping her back to me, "and forwarded it to the Captain. Monitoring an asteroid field. Solo mission, just like you want."

I muttered my thanks, unsure it was the right thing to say.

She told me the Captain wanted to see me, so I nodded and headed for the door. I thought to ask her if there was something I could do to make her understand that I didn't want to be a walking science experiment. But then thought better of it. Doing so would only tip off a fight. Lately the treatment — or maybe the disease — left me feeling like I'd been rolled out and stomped on, so for once, I didn't feel like fighting.

●

THE VIBRATION OF THE MAIN thruster engine chugged through the walls and the floor under my feet. That was good news. We were moving.

I'd taken the time to change into a full service uniform; no way was I going to let the Captain see me in my pyjamas.

The Captain was on the bridge and when I entered, he waved for me to follow him into his office. He made a remark about how I must feel like a new person. It was the same joke he made after every one of my treatments.

We sat on opposite sides of his desk.

I figured this was about my request for a new assignment. I confessed to him what I couldn't tell Holloway even though she suspected; job stress was causing more frequent flare ups of the Peel.

"Job stress?"

"Passenger stress," I amended. If I were to get the solo assignment, I needed him to understand I was capable of doing the job, that the Peel wouldn't stop me.

I expected him to make a joke, not measure me with his eyes. Where was the suave, charming captain we all knew?

He told me Dr. Holloway sent the recommendation because

I insisted, but her report suggested this wasn't the best course of action.

"Probably doesn't want to lose the funding," I said. Since I'd come aboard, she'd published her findings about my condition in medical journals and secured grant funding. She told me the whole medical community was impressed by my progress. That was fine for her, but I didn't want to spend my life being someone's science project.

"Is that what you really believe?" he asked. "There couldn't possibly be any other reason?"

My mind clouded over with the memory of her being angry with me. "I don't know what you mean, sir."

He waved a hand. "Not my place to get involved," he mumbled. He drew in a breath. "I have to say I was surprised by your request. Having someone with your knowledge and experience on my crew is mighty valuable."

Probably didn't want to handle the passenger complaints himself. "Thank you, sir."

"You should take some time to think about it, and you should probably discuss this further with Dr. Holloway."

"I feel I've already spent plenty of time thinking about it, sir. And there's nothing to discuss with Dr. Holloway."

I could handle my treatments myself and besides, if I was on a solo mission, no one would care if my skin was peeling or not. I only had to worry about how I felt and not that my appearance was horrifying passengers or crew mates.

A message from the bridge beeped, preventing his reply. The thruster engine had stalled out but was back online, still at half-power.

I jumped to my feet. "I'd like to have a look at that, sir." Do something useful for once.

He consented. "Take Omesh with you."

Finally. Something I could do.

●

WE ALL HAVE OUR LIMITS. About six years ago I'd been serving onboard a freighter that was nearing the end of its service life. We were transporting some ore and building materials for one of the new colonies when the thruster engine petered out. We'd spent two days crawling around the engine before I found a crack in the expansion chamber. Once the crack was found, the repair had been easy.

I was explaining this to Omesh on our way to the engine. As we were about to pass sick bay, I had the sudden urge to check in with Dr. Holloway. I told Omesh to wait for me.

Dr. Holloway appeared to be logging samples or checking measurements or something. The pale light of the refrigeration unit passed through her hair, giving her a halo, and my breath caught in my throat. She glanced up when she heard me cough.

She asked if something was wrong. I shook my head, uncertain why I'd even bothered to stop in here in the first place.

"You're rubbing your shoulder," she said. She put down her tablet, moving to come take a closer look.

I assured her it was fine. Just leftover stiffness from lying still for so long, a side effect of the treatment.

She got that look in her eye again—the one that said she was about to start asking me all kinds of questions, taking samples and examining them under the microscope.

"You opposed my assignment request," I said. "Why?"

She froze for a moment, but blinked it away. "You're so close to remission," she said. "It would be a waste for you to give that up now."

"Remission?"

"If you keep up the treatments, yes. I believe it's possible."

I imagined a life of clear skin, to never have the Peel again, to never have to see the look on people's faces when my skin turned bright red and started falling off. But that life meant serving aboard this ship, continuing to serve another captain.

"It's not that I'm not grateful. I just want my own ship. It's what I've always wanted."

"Now?"

Now was my chance. Before other symptoms confined me to this ship.

Dr. Holloway seemed to be waiting for me to say something, and it suddenly occurred to me that if I took this assignment I would miss her, and maybe she would miss me too.

"You could come with me," I blurted.

"To monitor an asteroid field?" She frowned and shook her head.

Yeah, it was pretty stupid of me to think she would give up all this—the lab, the research, the patients—for a monotonous assignment. I suddenly felt too hot and the sick bay too small. I backed away and exited like a dog with my tail between my legs, not even turning back when she called my name.

●

"THE CRACK MIGHT ONLY BE as long as my thumb," I explained to Omesh. My voice echoed across the chamber.

We'd already shut down the thruster engine and put a technician on guard to make sure no one switched it back on while we were working on it. I was just explaining how we could make a repair that would hold long enough until we could replace the expansion chamber, when I stopped.

"You hear something?" I asked Omesh.

He raised an eyebrow.

The thruster engine room was heavily insulated from the rest of the ship. I could hear Omesh's every exhale echo off the walls. Cold fear wormed around my spine.

That was another time, another ship. An isolated incident, they said. Cracks in the thruster engine were happening all over space—the fault of the manufacturer. It was years ago and the engines had been recalled and replaced.

I dismissed my fear and resumed the search.

"How's things with the Doc?" Omesh said casually.

"What things?"

"I've seen the way you look at her," he said playfully. "And the way she looks back at you."

Was that...did *feelings* have something to do with why she was mad at me? Maybe it wasn't just about science funding.

I frowned. "She's my doctor. I'm her patient."

Omesh laughed. I started to ask him to elaborate, when just

outside my peripheral vision something skittered past.

"Do you have your sidearm?" I asked softly.

"Of course. Standard uniform —"

"Get it out."

Omesh didn't hesitate.

A high-pitched scream pierced my ears.

Omesh's eyes went wide, his jaw slackened.

A shadow rose up between us.

My entire body suddenly felt like it was burning up from the inside. I fumbled with the holster strap, my knuckles feeling stiff and swollen. I tried to flick off the safety, but my weapon clattered onto the floor.

The alien slid closer.

I took a step back, hit the wall and my knees buckled under me.

Omesh fired but missed. A gurgling sound escaped his mouth. I felt around for my weapon and yelled at him to get to the door. My barking got through to him and he followed orders, scrambling to get out.

I found my weapon, but my knuckles had swollen up — stiff joints, the side effect. I couldn't squeeze the trigger.

The shadow slithered closer. I back-peddled across the floor, pulling myself toward the door. Shots rang out again. The alien exploded, showering us in contamination.

Omesh.

Shit.

He hadn't made it out. He'd stayed to save me.

•

ONCE AGAIN I FOUND MYSELF delivered to sick bay in a containment unit. At least this time I was awake for it.

I was able to communicate to the Captain that the aliens must be causing the cracks in the expansion chambers, perhaps hiding in there, hibernating in the combustion from the thruster engine. Crawling out once they'd caused the engine to break down. Word needed to get out to the rest of the Galactic Navy. He promised it would.

On the bed next to mine, Omesh fidgeted and squirmed. His eyes were wide and terrified.

"You're in good hands," I said, trying to be assuring.

I don't think he was convinced. Can't say I blamed him. No one wanted alien DNA under their skin.

When Holloway came over to examine me, I asked her if Omesh was going to be all right.

"He's going to be alone." Maybe it was her level gaze and sharp tone, but I got the impression we weren't just talking about Omesh.

I still wanted my own ship. I would never stop wanting my own ship. But the reality was my body was breaking down, system by system — skin, tissues, joints and whatever came next. Did I want to be alone for that? Alone for the rest of my life?

That was the question, wasn't it?

I let out a long slow breath. "No, he's not."

Was it just my imagination, or did I detect the faintest hint of warmth around Holloway's eyes when she saw I was earnest?

"I'm cracked, flawed, unfit to be around people," I said. Though it seemed some of them still wanted to be around me. Why, I didn't know.

"We all are," she said. "But we have each other to help us manage."

Now, maybe she was offering to assist with my treatments, but I didn't think so.

There was only one way to find out.

"You still want that tissue sample?" I asked.

Holloway held me steady in her gaze. "It's a good for a start."

Well, geez.

Were Omesh and the Captain right? Were *feelings* involved here?

Only one way to find out.

I drew in a deep breath. "You got a date for the G-Navy Ball, Doc?"

She smiled.

_____

Sara C. Walker writes urban fantasy novels and speculative fiction and poetry. Her work has appeared in *ON SPEC* magazine and anthologies published by Exile Editions, Tyche Books, and others. She's a member of SF Canada. When not writing she enjoys hiking through the forests of Central Ontario.

https://sarawalker.ca

An Unexpected Taste of Home

by Terry Mixon

"I DON'T SEE WHY *I* have to come up with a plan," Zig complained. "He's your friend. Shouldn't you be figuring out a way to get him out of his bind with the loan shark?"

Zag grinned at his young partner as he piloted *Razor* above the surface of Oceana. Her tone alone would've revealed the fact that she was an adolescent human female, even if he'd been blind.

"I *do* have a plan, but I still want to hear what you'd do if you were running this," he said. "Think of it as part of your bounty hunter training."

His partner rolled her eyes dramatically. "Oh, I'm sure you have a plan. The problem is that it's going to revolve around fists, guns, and us running for our lives, based on my experience.

"Don't you think your friend—who still has to live here when we're done—would want something a little less dramatic? We shouldn't make his situation worse than it already is."

Zag had to concede that his partner was right. His plans did tend to involve violence, and sometimes things went sour, but that was because he was a bounty hunter. Targets rarely came willingly or did what one would expect when confronted. She'd figure that out as her training progressed.

When he'd contacted Utag to do the work *Razor* needed to house him and Zig in somewhat more comfort, his friend had agreed to do the work at cost if Zag could fix a little problem for him.

It seemed that Utag owed a large sum of money to a loan shark. Not an exorbitant sum for someone who owned a shop that repaired and modified spaceships, but more than he could pay back at this particular moment. He hadn't fallen behind in his payments yet, but he was up against the wall.

Considering the scale of the modifications Zag was considering for *Razor*, it was worth his time to help Utag strike a deal. Getting the work done at cost meant he could get more done for the same amount of money, and this might be the only opportunity he had to get it done.

Bounty hunting meant always being on the job, and he couldn't afford to take weeks off very often and still pay the bills. Particularly now that he had two mouths to feed. Despite her small size, Zig ate more than he did.

Okay, not really, but it sometimes felt that way when he saw the food bill. Teenagers.

Razor was a solid ship, but she'd been built for humans, not Borelians. Being two and a half meters tall with horns a meter wide made for an exceptionally cramped cockpit. The cost of ripping out all the control systems and redoing everything would be…considerable, and that didn't add in the other modifications he needed.

The deal his friend had offered was more than enough for him to agree to the favor. Now he just needed to make it work.

"When I found you on Norvas, you'd made a successful life for yourself running a gang of street rats," Zag said as he adjusted their course slightly. "My plan is to tap that know-how because you've dealt with people like loan sharks before. Maybe not personally, but you know how to strike a deal. You can give me advice on how to approach somebody like that."

Zig sighed and shook her head. "What worked for me isn't going to work for your friend. All I had to do was fork over a cut of the profits to the people whose territory we were working in. It wasn't that complicated.

"Your friend owns a large repair shop that works on spaceships. He's probably paying protection money to some organization because that's just how things work, but the loan shark is a different deal. Borrowing money is something completely new to me. If we ran short, we did without."

"So, you're saying that you really don't have any ideas."

"I don't think your friend would be willing to pass on a percentage of his ownership stake to the loan shark, so that's out. And, honestly, that's not the kind of person that you want to get in bed with, either literally or figuratively."

He frowned at the girl. "You don't know anything about literally getting into bed with anyone. At least you'd better not."

She laughed. "What are you now? My mother? Which, for the record, I did have one, and she was a prostitute. So, I know far more about what literally goes on in a bed than you do."

It was a good thing he had thick fur because if he'd been human, he'd have been blushing. Borelian society was different than human society. Most males never had the opportunity to be with a female, and he was no exception.

Not that he'd have ever considered telling Zig that. Knowing how humans reacted to male virgins, it was best to change the subject.

"I supposed that we'll have to figure it out when we get there," he said glumly. "We're almost to the floating city where his shop is. Make sure your harness is tight, and let's get *Razor* onto the appropriate pad."

During the first part of their landing pattern, his partner stared out at the vast expanse of water below them in something approaching awe. Having grown up on a desert world, she'd never seen that much water in her life.

Of course, even as an adult, he felt the same way, but he had a lot more experience than she did at visiting strange new worlds. He just knew how to hide his wonder better.

As the city grew larger in front of them, Zig leaned forward in her acceleration couch and stared in amazement. "Holy crap! Just take a look at that place."

It was a sight. The city looked like some kind of colossal lily floating on the surface of the water. The floating platform it was built on was probably twenty kilometers across and had piers and docks extending for at least five kilometers beyond that.

Considering the lack of building materials on a water world, it was a huge investment. The locals paid for it by mining rare ores from the ocean floor deep below the surface. Zag repressed a shudder just thinking about it.

None of the buildings rose very high. Even those in the city's center were relatively short compared to the metropolitan areas of other advanced civilizations.

The problem with having your city on a floating platform was that you always had to be conscious of the stability of the structure itself. There was only so much give a tall building had when a major storm came along and the "ground" underneath it moved and flexed.

Traffic control updated his course and confirmed the landing pad he was assigned. The pad would be relatively close to the city since the ship had to come into the shop to be worked on. Thankfully, since the city was situated on water, having the pad towed in was a lot simpler than it sounded.

Zag brought *Razor* around the city, tilting the ship so his partner got a good view of the city as they circled it. She said nothing, her attention raptly focused on the sight before her.

He had to admit that the first time he'd come here, it had been a shock to his system as well. Borel was mostly savanna with some hills and forests. The biggest body of water he'd ever personally seen before leaving his home world had been a massive inland lake, though his world did have oceans.

Big surprise, Borelians weren't avid swimmers, so being above so much water was a nerve-racking affair. Anytime he had to land his ship on a water pad, he worried that something would go wrong, and he'd end up having to escape a sinking ship, only to sink himself.

His anxiety wasn't quite to the level of a phobia, but he certainly didn't enjoy the prospect of falling into deep water. Not at all.

Thankfully, just like every other time he'd made this particular type of landing, everything went smoothly. He brought *Razor* to a hover above the pad and settled her onto it as gently as he could.

As soon as he cut the jets, he could feel the pad gently rocking on the water, making him queasy. Still, he knew it was stable because the pad was designed for ships bigger and heavier than his own. It would be fine.

Under normal circumstances, he'd have had to wait for the pad to cool before they could exit, but with all this water around, it was a simple matter for their hosts to shoot water over the hot surface. That meant they'd only have to wait five minutes before they could leave the ship.

That gave him five more minutes to come up with a workable plan. He wasn't holding out much hope, but maybe inspiration would strike. If not, he'd bull his way through the situation like he always did.

●

IN FACT, THEY DIDN'T EVEN have to leave *Razor* if they didn't want to, because the tugs were already there to tow them to the repair shop. That was just one more charge he'd have to pay, but it was worth it. He'd put up with the inconvenience of cramped bridge controls and tight corridors for long enough.

The prospect of refitting *Razor* so he didn't have to deal with some of those issues was a lot more enticing than he'd ever admitted to Zig. As a small being, she didn't have to deal with problems like that, though she did lack quarters of her own.

She'd been sleeping on a salvaged mat in the engineering area, and that wasn't enough for someone on the brink of adulthood. He didn't want to be anywhere close to her when she hit puberty, so a room he could banish her to was an absolute necessity for his sanity.

He'd pay extra to make sure that happened.

Being towed to the repair shop wasn't nearly as exciting as it sounded. The tugs moved the pads slowly to avoid any upsets. Watching from the bridge quickly bored Zig, so she excused herself to get something to eat before they left the ship.

Considering that he had no idea how long this meeting would take, eating was probably a good idea. He followed her to the galley and waited his turn. The galley could stand a little bit of redesign, too. Just one more thing to be looked at.

There was no way his friend would be able to enlarge every single area of the ship. It was a zero-sum game — something had to be made smaller for every bit that was expanded. Everything was a compromise.

Zig finally retrieved one of the ration bars she preferred and made way for him.

He shook his head at her choice of meals. "How can you eat that stuff? It's like chewing grass."

She raised an eyebrow meaningfully as she peeled the wrapper back and took a bite. "It's not grass, it's oats, and they're pretty good. Besides, didn't you tell me that Borelians are generally herbivores? I understand that *you* eat meat, but surely oats aren't off the menu back home."

"Oats don't taste good," he grumbled. "Yes, my people eat something similar, but it's not the same. Take my word that oats just aren't that tasty to us. Not even when you add honey, since I know that's where you're going next."

She closed her mouth, confirming his guess that it was what she'd been about to say. While she pondered where to take the conversation next, he opened a different cabinet and pulled out a wrapped piece of beef jerky. They were made to last a long time, and frankly, they suited his taste buds better than plants and vegetables.

Borelians were almost exclusively herbivores, but he was an omnivore. His secret love of meat was another reason he'd left Borel. There, they lumped meat-eaters in with the predators who had once kept the herds trimmed, so to say they took a dim view of people like Zag was something of an understatement.

He knew Zig liked the taste of the jerky, too, because he'd had to buy extra to make up for what she'd been eating. Once again, he couldn't blame her because she was growing. She needed the calories to keep up with what her body was doing.

Food storage, he reminded himself. One more thing that could do with a bit of adjusting. Right now, he was using a parts bin in engineering to hold extra food supplies. The galley just didn't have enough space for everything, so they'd had to play games with where they put things.

It was like hide and seek, but with calories.

At this rate, maybe he should just sell *Razor* and buy a bigger ship. Not that he had enough money to do that. Well, they'd just have to make do with whatever they could arrange. Anything would be an improvement.

Grabbing a second chunk of beef jerky, he led the way to the ramp and hit the control lever to lower it. For a change, it went down smoothly all the way to the surface of the pad.

"See?" Zig poked him in the ribs. "I told you I had it working. All it took was replacing that hydraulic cylinder and a little bit of maintenance on everything else. Now it works like a champ.

"Contrary to what you seem to believe, a little bit of tender loving care will make your machinery last longer and work better."

Zag walked down the ramp without responding and looked out over the water toward the city. They still had a little way to go to the shop. He made certain not to get anywhere close to the edge of the pad. Safety first.

Worries about the water didn't stop Zig from drinking in the view while hanging onto one of the safety ropes. "How deep do you think it is here? Is this city perched on some kind of geological formation or free-floating?"

"I have no idea," he admitted. "Even if it is free-floating, it could be a couple of hundred meters down or a couple of kilometers. Maybe more. Honestly, when you get past ten meters, does it really matter?"

She shot him a look of disdain. "Of course it matters. Maybe we should go diving. That would be fun, right?"

"I'm pretty sure that you can't swim. If you fell into the water, you'd flop around for a minute or two and then sink straight to the bottom."

She crossed her arms over her chest and considered him. "You're afraid of the water. Is that because your people don't swim? You're big and muscular, so maybe your density is higher than mine. I bet that if you went into the water, you'd sink like a rock."

"Pretty much. Some Borelians like going into the water, but they use artificial flotation devices to increase their buoyancy. Me? I'm much happier staying on solid ground. If any of your plans involve going into the water, count me out."

"Spoilsport."

The two of them stood in silence and watched the tugs nudge their pad up beside the repair shop. The pad automatically latched on, and their footing became noticeably more stable. For all intents and purposes, they were now standing on the city platform.

Utag was waiting for them. The Uchmet was something of a cross between an upright seal and a hippopotamus, with stubby antlers thrown in to confuse the issue.

Unlike Borelians, they were more than happy to go into the water. In fact, they needed a certain level of hydration to maintain their skin, so it wasn't unusual to find them on worlds like Oceana.

For someone who weighed as much as a Borelian, his friend was only about two-thirds of his height. Others might call Utag's people fat, but the layer of blubber beneath their thick skins allowed them to deal with the cold water without issues. On the whole, Zag thought they were well suited for this environment.

Utag walked over laboriously, with his hand extended. "It is good to see you again, my friend. I'm quite pleased that you've decided to visit."

"Less a visit and more a meeting to work things out. Like I told you from orbit, I'm looking to have the internal layout of my ship completely redone. It's tough for me to do things in a ship made for humans.

"I have no idea how intensive that kind of work will be — or even if it's possible — but as soon as I decided that something like this needed to be done, you were the one I thought of.

"And considering how expensive it would probably be to get that kind of work done paying full price, I have to say that I'm definitely looking forward to the opportunity to make your life a little easier with the person that you borrowed the money from. If I can."

Utag nodded seriously. "I appreciate that, but I would prefer to speak of this matter in my office, where we can have some privacy. Come."

Then Utag blinked and looked past Zag. "I'm sorry. I did not realize you had an associate. This is unusual, no? I thought you worked alone."

"I used to, but now I have a partner. This is Zig."

Zig stepped forward with a smile and raised her hand up to Utag. "It's a pleasure meeting you."

The Uchmet stared at her curiously as he shook her hand. "You are small for a human. Are you a child? Are the bounty hunters allowed to use children as labor?"

"She's an apprentice," Zag said smoothly. "While there might be work involved, it's toward getting her certification. And don't let her size fool you. She's clever and resourceful. Anyone she comes after will deeply regret underestimating her."

Zig shot him a look, seemingly trying to tell if he was being facetious. When it became apparent to her that he was complete-

447

ly serious, she smiled even more widely and bowed with her hand over her heart.

"Zag and I complement each other. The two of us working together can accomplish things that neither of us could do separately. And that's how we're going to fix your problem."

He wanted to kick her for making promises he didn't know they could keep, but he'd already laid out the caveat. Still, it was best to make it clear.

"As I said, we'll do the best we can," he added, "But it's really going to depend on how adamant the other party is."

Utag sighed as he led them toward the large building, where Zig could see a partially disassembled spaceship with various beings crawling over and through it. "The lender is a confusing mix of different personality types to me," Utag said, "but I'm hoping that you'll understand her better than I. In some things, she is pretty flexible, but when it comes to money, she is not forgiving of those who do not pay on time.

"The only reason that I have gotten any leeway at all is that one of the nearby stellar systems is under blockade, so our trade is down. That means that there are fewer ships for me to work on. She's made allowances for that, but her patience has grown thin.

"The interest payments are becoming prohibitive, and I need to come to some kind of restructuring agreement. I need lower payments for a longer period of time.

"I don't want to deny her what is rightfully hers, as I made a deal, but something has to change. That's why I knew it was a sign from the sea gods that you came. It can be nothing else."

Zag frowned as they entered his friend's office. "Why is that?"

Utag smiled at him. "Because while females of any species are difficult for males to comprehend, you are unique among my acquaintances. What are the odds of another Borelian coming to see me now?"

Zag came to a screeching halt, his brain seeming to stop as well. "Excuse me? What did you just say?"

"Simply that the lender is a Borelian female. Fortuitous, yes?"

●

"I DON'T GET WHAT YOU'RE SO torn up about," Zig said as they walked into the city after the meeting with Utag. "This seems like the luckiest break ever. You're going to have insight into this woman that no one else could possibly have. That's going to give you an edge."

Zag fought the urge to rub his face with his hands. "Did you ever have something about the society on Norvas that you just couldn't seem to escape, even though you've really tried? You have no idea how ingrained certain behaviors are among my people, and if you think this is going to be an easy-breezy talk where I just flex my muscles and get my way, you're sorely mistaken."

She tilted her head slightly as they walked and considered him more closely. "Something about this situation has you off your game, and I don't understand it. Look, I'm not trying to make fun of you, but I can't give you any kind of advice if you don't tell me what's wrong. Why does the idea of talking to this woman have you running around in circles, biting the small of your back?"

He sighed, not really wanting to explain the situation but lacking any other option. No matter what happened, Zig was going to find out more than he felt comfortable sharing no matter what he did, so he might as well lay everything on the table.

"It has to do with the way males and females interact on my world," he finally admitted. "There's no real comparison to human society. Borelians are herd creatures, and so reproduction revolves around the herd.

"The only males who are allowed to breed are the top-tier specimens. They are led by an alpha, who is the titular head of any particular herd. He's got a group of males underneath him who are also allowed to breed.

"All the females in the herd, well, they have relations with whatever top-tier male catches their fancy when the mood strikes. In fact, them having relations with a male is what raises the male to the top tier."

"Nothing wrong with a gal choosing who she beds, but I get you. That is a little convoluted. There has to be some kind of disparity in the number of males versus females, or that wouldn't work. Or, if there's no disparity, then there's a lot of women making a fuss over just a small number of men. Which is it?"

"There's a surplus of males in our society," he clarified. "There is constant jockeying for position among those who aren't in the top tier. That means fighting and doing other things to catch the attention of the females who might elevate one's place in society.

"Honestly, it's one of the biggest reasons I left Borel in the first place. I couldn't stand the idea of wanting things I would never get. I hate to call the vast majority of males on my world drones, but there's something to that. That wasn't the life for me."

She opened her mouth to say something and then blinked. She closed her mouth and stared at him intently. "Excuse me, but did you just say that you're a virgin?"

"Out of everything I just said, that's the one thing you heard? This is why I don't talk about my past. Being a virgin isn't the same thing in my society as it is in yours.

"Believe me, it's not because I lacked the desire, but the competition for selection is fierce. Basically, you're a piece of meat, having to prove you're strong and fit enough to breed top-tier offspring.

"Not only that, but the females play mind games with you. They lead you to think you might have a chance, to make you dance to their tune, then they walk away laughing. It's degrading.

"Don't get me wrong. I chased that dream with all my heart when I was younger. Then I finally understood just how futile it was. When the opportunity came for me to leave Borel with a visiting bounty hunter, I never looked back."

Zig put a hand on his arm, forcing him to stop. "Just because I asked the question doesn't mean I'm judging you. I'm not going to tease you over something like that.

"I've seen that kind of behavior play out firsthand with some of the older kids on Norvas. I saw groups torn apart by fighting because someone had slept with someone else and then broken up. The hormones in young people are just unbelievable.

"And, just to be clear, I'm not excluding myself from that. I know that my time of being an unreasonable teenager is coming. My apologies in advance for the intense frustration that I'm going to heap on you.

"What I want you to know right now is that whatever you decide to do, I'm your partner, and I've got your back. If you decide that this mission isn't for you, I'm not going to judge you. If you decide to go play pinch and tickle with some gorgeous Borelian woman, I'm not going to judge you about that either, though I reserve the right to tease the ever-living hell out of you for it.

"Bottom line, we're in this together, and we'll make it work. Just keep any icky details to yourself."

He snorted and raised an eyebrow. "And that from a girl whose mother was a prostitute? I thought you said you already knew all the icky details."

"I know the icky *human* details. I don't need to know *anything* about my partner's sex life. Some things are meant to be a mystery, so just keep that kind of stuff to yourself."

"Got it. No talking about who gets to wear the cowbell."

Zig rolled her eyes hard and walked away with a shake of her head. "I should've known that you weren't going to take this seriously. You're incorrigible."

He laughed and quickly caught up with her.

Frankly, he couldn't understand why a female had left Borel. They quite literally had a life that he could barely imagine. They were the aristocracy of his people. Why would a noble leave all that behind?

Zag had basically been a peasant, so leaving hadn't been a difficult decision. Not many of his people would follow in his footsteps, but that was hardly unusual. Everyone got into a rut, and they never even thought about the kind of world they lived on. Not really.

Whatever this woman's story was, it would be unusual, and she would be different from the females he'd seen when he was younger. Had she been exiled? Had she left on her own?

Well, he supposed he'd find out soon enough.

Zag wondered how the woman had been able to afford to become a loan shark in the first place. It required a great deal of money. While the females on his world lived well, their wealth wasn't something which could be picked up and taken with them if they decided to leave.

He only hoped she didn't still have the attitudes his people held dear. Otherwise, this would be an unpleasant conversation, and he wouldn't be doing his friend any favors.

That made him sigh. He was here as Utag's representative, and he couldn't do anything to make the Uchmet's life worse simply because this woman and he shared a complicated societal past.

He'd have to find a way to be a delicate negotiator and not let his emotions lead him down the path to conflict. While he could leave this world at any time, his friend didn't have that luxury. Zag couldn't screw this up.

●

THE BUILDING HOUSING THE LOAN shark was low and wide. It looked like an old hotel. Not that it was ancient or anything, simply that it was set up like a hotel that had been converted to a different kind of business.

The entry foyer took up a significant portion of the front room. He could envision the area with small groupings of chairs and tables to promote intimate conversations between the guests. The floor was made of polished stone that would've done any hotel proud.

The far end of the room was where the hotel's front desk would have been, but now contained a modern security and secretarial desk. The three beings behind it were of different species, and Zag's experience as a bounty hunter allowed him to immediately spot that they were armed.

He and Zig hadn't taken more than a few steps toward the security desk when he saw their eyes widen. His step almost faltered until he realized that their reaction had to be because they weren't expecting to see another Borelian.

"Good afternoon," he said evenly, when they arrived at the desk. "If at all possible, we'd like to speak with your employer about one of her clients."

One of the beings—an amphibian of some kind—shook his head, his wet skin glistening in the light coming through the expansive windows. "Our employer only sees people via appointment. Do you have an appointment?"

"I do not. Could you make one for me?"

"Identification?"

Zag pulled his bounty hunter's license out of his harness and slid it across the counter. "My apprentice is covered under my license."

The being examined it before looking back up at him, his eyes narrowing. "Are you interested in our employer in a professional capacity?"

"Does she have a bounty on her head? Not that I'm here for her; I'm just curious."

The man slid the identification back to Zag. "Our employer may be unwilling to see you. Come back tomorrow, and I will have an answer for you."

Zag considered arguing but decided it wasn't worthwhile. He needed goodwill from their employer, and bulling his way through her security would do the exact opposite.

"Very well," he said in his politest tone. "Please let your employer know that if she does have a bounty on her head, I'm not interested in it. As the saying goes, there are plenty of fish in the sea, and I don't feel the need to hunt those from my home world."

He turned and led Zig back toward the door.

"What are you doing?" she asked in a fierce whisper. "You're just going to let them put you off like that?"

"We're not here to cause trouble. We've got time to find a solution to my friend's problem without causing a stink. I'll come back tomorrow and see what happens."

"Wait," a voice said as they reached the door.

Zag turned and saw a human he identified as a high-end bodyguard coming through a door at the back of the room. He was tall, muscular, and well dressed. Armed, too.

The man strolled over to them and stopped a few meters away. "My employer has decided to grant you a meeting immediately. That is contingent upon your cooperation, however. I'll need your weapon."

"I'm a bounty hunter, and I don't turn my weapon over to anyone. I've already told your people I'm not here for your employer and I have no intention of pursuing any bounty she may have on her head."

"Then we are at an impasse."

"Why don't you let me take your weapon, and I'll go back to the ship?" Zig asked. "You're just here to talk, so why not make that concession?"

He mulled her suggestion and slowly nodded. He was stubborn by nature and having anyone ask him to turn over his weapon always raised his hackles. Still, in this case, it might be warranted. "Okay."

He removed the holstered weapon from his belt and handed it to Zig. It was ludicrously large for someone her size, but he had big hands and the body to support a powerful weapon.

"Head straight back to the ship," he told her. "If I haven't come back in a couple of hours, contact the authorities and let them know where I am. If I'm going to be delayed, I'll call and use the appropriate code phrases."

They had code phrases because there was always the possibility that someone would get the drop on one of them. They needed a way to tell the other what the situation was without using plain language.

"Don't let this get to you," Zig said softly. "You're not on Borel anymore. Be yourself and do what you need to do. Whatever the outcome, we can live with it." And with that, his partner walked out the door.

The bodyguard led Zag deeper into the building. Zag was impressed that everything had been redone to allow a Borelian to walk down the hallway without ducking their head or dodging any of the light fixtures. The corridors were even wide enough for him to move through and still leave space for others. That was something one didn't see very often in the Confederation. Like ever.

They went down a set of stairs and into a room beneath the surface of the city. It was filled with wide furniture, soft pillows, and a view of the ocean life circling the area that made him a little queasy.

Zag took that in with a glance before the woman lounging on one of the wide chairs captured his attention. He hadn't expected to ever meet another Borelian once he'd left Borel, much less a female of the species. The emotional impact was just as powerful as he'd feared, and he felt almost compelled to lower his head in submission.

Instead, he forced himself to stand tall, but restrained himself from snorting or trying to assume any kind of dominant posture. He wouldn't play their game. He was done with Borel and its idiotic customs.

As his shock at seeing her wore off, Zag realized another unsettling fact. He *knew* her. He wracked his brain and it eventually coughed up a name: Lisihana.

They'd been in the same herd, though she was more than a decade older than him, and far above his social strata. Not that she'd have ever heard his name, and likely couldn't have pointed him out in a lineup.

She rose to her feet and smiled. "Welcome to my home, Zagarathan. I never expected to meet another of our kind after leaving Borel, yet here you are."

Zag goggled at her for a few seconds, trying to imagine how she'd discovered his name. He didn't use it anymore. He'd gone by Zag from the moment he'd left Borel. She couldn't know him.

Yet she did.

Then he tried to regain his composure. This wasn't the first time he'd been surprised by an unexpected situation, and he knew better than to let it knock him off his game. Time to get down to business.

"Lisihana," he said, his throat feeling constricted. "You're a long way from home."

"And getting farther away every day. Sit. We have much to discuss."

She resumed her seat, saying nothing as he took the chair across from her, then examined her closely. She was shorter than him by roughly a head and her horns weren't as wide, as was common in Borelian females. She was slender, though still muscular, and her fur was bright, without any sign of gray.

In all, she was an extremely beautiful woman.

"I apologize for intruding, but I'm here to speak with you on behalf of one of your clients," he said politely. "He wishes to renegotiate the terms of his loan so he can continue to operate his business while still paying you the money he acknowledges he owes you."

She pursed her lips. "I'd much rather talk about *you*. Since you left Borel quite abruptly and never returned, you're probably unaware of the stir your departure caused. You weren't shy about pointing out what you saw as the failures of our caste system and how things were unfair to the vast majority of males.

"Admittedly, almost everyone ignored your tirade and continued on as they always had, but I thought long and hard about what you'd said and took a closer look at the life I was living.

"Eventually, I decided that you were right. So, in a way, you're the reason I'm here with a bounty on my head."

Zag blinked in shock. A woman of her station paying attention to a lowly male? Listening so closely that she decided to leave their home world? Unthinkable.

Yet here she was.

"So, was leaving home enough to get a bounty on your head?" he asked, trying to buy himself time to think. "That seems a little much, don't you think?"

Her smile widened. "That *would* be a little bit outrageous under normal circumstances, but no. The bounty on my head is because I took a fair portion of the herd's liquid assets with me when I departed.

"As long as I was going to make the alpha and other females angry, I figured that I might as well make an exit to match yours.

"I have to tell you that it's refreshing to see someone speak up on behalf of one of their friends, but money is important to me, and the negotiations are unlikely to be simple or straightforward.

"Tell me who the client is and what he would like to see happen. If this person has been dealing with me fairly, I might be open to renegotiating our agreement. Maybe."

Zag explained about his friend, his business, and his desire to fulfill his obligations even though the lack of traffic was causing a significant impediment to his ability to do so.

He didn't try to embellish the story. He wasn't here to make Utag's situation sound worse than it actually was.
Lisihana listened closely, then after a few moments, she nodded slightly. "Utag has always dealt with me honestly, and I've been willing to show him leniency because of the situation Oceana has found itself in.

"Unfortunately, simply because he's doing poorly doesn't mean I don't need the money he owes. Yet there may be a solution that allows your friend the breathing space he needs. It really depends on how willing *you* are to make sacrifices for your friend."

Zag blinked and then frowned. "I don't think I understand."

"If you think about it a little, I think you'll understand. I've been gone from Borel for many years now, and there are things I miss that I can't get here. An unexpected taste of home, if you will."

He was about to say that he didn't have much in the way of Borelian cuisine when he realized she wasn't talking about food.

For several seconds, they just sat there staring at one another as he struggled to overcome the complete and utter shock of being propositioned, with his friend's livelihood on the line. Then his emotions came back to life and he got truly angry.

"I am not willing to barter myself or my self-respect for anyone," he said coldly. "I left Borel to get away from this kind of thing. My body is my own and I will not be coerced into being someone's plaything, not even to save a friend. You can't extort me this way."

Rather than becoming angry, she cocked her head and considered him. "Do you not find me desirable?"

"I've never seen a more beautiful woman, but I will not submit to you or anyone else. My days of doing anything to gain the notice of females or desiring elevation in the herd are long past."

He rose to his feet and bowed shallowly. When he straightened, he looked her in the eye and shook his head slightly.

"We've both come a long way, but I'm not sure you've truly left Borel at all. It certainly hasn't left you. I regret that we part under these circumstances but still wish you all the success you can find in life."

"I apologize," she said, bowing her head. "What I demanded was out of line, but I needed to hear how you'd respond. I won't say I would've objected to such a dalliance, but I needed to test the strength of your character. Now I know you are more than worthy of my respect. I had to know.

"Now, I'm a reasonable woman, so I'll have my people speak with Utag and rewrite the terms of our agreement. It's in my best interest that he stays in business, and he hasn't tried to weasel out of his obligations like others have attempted to do. He has honor, so I shall behave honorably toward him.

"With that out of the way, I would like to ask you to remain and have dinner with me with no strings attached. I want to hear about your travels and get to know you better. Perhaps much better, if the mood strikes us both. You're free to say no, though I hope you say yes."

His anger flowed out of him, leaving him feeling almost deflated as he sat back down. He considered her and then nodded. "I think I'd like that."

Zag didn't know exactly what would happen this evening, but he was willing to take a chance. If he did end up staying beyond dinner, he'd have to call Zig and let her know what he was doing in the most general terms so that she didn't make teen girl noises.

Then he'd have to deal with her incessant and annoying teasing when he finally came home.

Zag had to admit that the prospects excited him now that his self-respect wasn't at stake. He'd see what happened and do what felt right.

An unexpected taste of home indeed.

#1 Bestselling Military Science Fiction author Terry Mixon served as a non-commissioned officer in the United States Army 101st Airborne Division. He later worked alongside the flight controllers in the Mission Control Center at the NASA Johnson Space Center supporting the Space Shuttle, the International Space Station, and other human spaceflight projects.

He now writes full time while living in Texas with his lovely wife and a pounce of cats.

https://terrymixon.com

Symphony

by Douglas Smith

FAST FORWARD: Third Movement, Danse Macabre (Staccato)

THEY HAD NAMED THE PLANET Aurora, for the beauty that danced above them in its ever dark skies. At least, it had seemed beautiful at the time. Now Gar Franck wasn't so sure.

Gar huddled on the floor, shielding his two-year-old son, Anton, from the panicked colonists stampeding past them in the newly-constructed pod link.

"Damn you, Franck! When will you make it stop?" a man cried from across the corridor. A woman lay in the man's arms, convulsing as her seizure peaked. She was dying, but to Gar's numbed mind her moans harmonized with the screams of the mob into a musical score for his private nightmare.

Anton sat on the floor, a broken comm-unit held before his blank face. The child let it drop to strike the metal surface with a dissonant clang. More people fled by. The child ignored them. With morbid fascination, Gar watched Anton repeat the scene. Pick up the comm-unit, let it drop. Pick it up, drop it. Again. Each clang as it struck the floor was more chilling to Gar than any cry from the dying.

This attack had blown the colony power grid. The only light now came through the crysteel roof. Gar looked up. The aurora blazed and writhed in the night sky, a parody of the chaos below. Greens, reds and purples shimmered strobe-like over the corridor, turning each person's frenzied flight into a macabre dance.

"God no!" the man cried. The woman stiffened then fell limp. "No!" The man pulled her to him, sobbing.

The rainbow lights of the aurora dimmed and the flickering slowed. The screaming died. Gar stood and looked around, dazed. People were shaking their heads, helping up ones who had fallen, poking at bodies. The man still sat holding the dead woman, his eyes hard on Gar. Other colonists stared at Gar too.

Gar swallowed. Picking up Anton, he walked past accusing faces toward their dorm pod. Anton squirmed in his arms. The child didn't like to be touched, let alone held.

Someone whispered as he passed. "How will he talk to this *thing* when he can't even talk with his own son." Gar pulled Anton closer, smothering his sobbing in the child's sleeve.

●

REWIND: First Movement, Prelude (Agitato)

SIX MONTHS AGO. ANTON WAS eighteen months old. Their ship, *The Last Chance*, had just dropped out of the worm-hole, leaving a poisoned Earth and the plague behind. Earlier probes through this hole had identified a G2 star with planets within range.

The plague had forced the *Last Chance* to launch before completion of its biosphere. The ship was only partly self-sustaining. They had only a year left to find a new home. It wasn't called the *Last Chance* for nothing.

Gar lay exhausted on the wall bed of the small ship cabin

that he, Clara and Anton shared. Clara's latest holographic sculpture spun suspended before him — shifting geometric shapes in greens, reds and purples. Vivaldi filled the room, wiping words from his head like rain washing graffiti from a wall. Gar lived with words all day. He'd had enough of words.

The jump had flooded MedCon with hyper-space shock cases. Gar was logging eighteen hour days translating between colonists and doctors. Fluency in ten languages and a name in computerized speech translation had won him his berth as Communications Officer. With over six thousand refugees from all over Earth, both human and automated translators were invaluable.

Gar rubbed his eyes. Overtime was at least an escape from the routine of translating the captain's messages to the crew and passengers. And from the growing tensions of his family life.

He checked the time. Clara worked as a laser and photonics specialist in TechLab. Her shift should be over by now.

Anton sat on the plastek floor, flapping his hands, staring. At what Gar could not say and a fear grew in him each day that Anton did not know either. Gar got down in front of the child. "Hey, big guy. What're you doing?" Anton looked right past him.

"He stared like that for twenty minutes today." Gar turned. Clara stood at the door, her lip trembling. "I measured it."

"Clara..." Gar felt himself tighten up.

"These spells just seem to blend together now."

"Maybe it's the jump," he said, not believing it himself.

"He was like this *before* the jump, Gar."

"He's just slow developing. How was your shift?"

"Most children are speaking by a year," she said.

"He walked on time, right?" Gar turned up the music a bit, not looking at her. "I just did a translation. They've found the system. We'll be there in four months."

"He never looks up when we speak, Gar."

"We'll have his hearing tested again."

"He won't let me hold him." Her voice broke and Gar turned back to her. She was leaning against the wall, her arms wrapped around herself, sobbing. "I can't hold my own child, Gar."

Gar swallowed. He walked over and took her in his arms.

Clara pushed away from him. "I want Ky to look at him."

Ky Jasper was MedCon Leader. "He's too busy," Gar mumbled.

"He owes you for all the overtime. Talk to him."

Gar looked at Anton. The child sat with his hands over his ears, rocking back and forth. The Vivaldi, calm and soothing in the background, gave the scene a surreal feeling.

"He's disappearing, Gar. Disappearing into his own world."

Gar closed his eyes to shut out both the scene and his tears. He nodded. "I'll ask him tomorrow."

●

First Movement, Finale (Largo)

IN THE SHIP'S DARKENED MEDLAB, a hologram of Anton's brain spun glowing and green, areas of red flashing within it. Gar stood stunned beside Ky Jasper and Clara. The imaging unit beeped musical tones as Ky outlined a red area in purple.

"...repetitive mannerisms and actions. Autistics are neuro-logically overconnected, as in this area of the cortex that handles hearing. Their senses are so acute they can overload. A touch is painful. Speech scrambles. Soft sounds are like explosions. One overloaded sense can shutdown the other four."

"So he covers his ears. And won't let us hold him." Clara spoke in a monotone, face blank. "Why won't he talk?"

Gar shook his head. This wasn't happening.

Ky sighed. "Autistics are blind to other minds. Anton doesn't know we're fellow beings with thoughts and feelings. To him, we're just things, moving through his world at random."

"Is there a cure?" Gar asked. Clara's sobs and the beeping of the imaging unit played like a discordant sound-track to the scene. Ky turned to him, his face half in darkness, half in green from the hologram. He shook his head.

●

Second Movement, Main Theme (Accelerando)

THEY WERE LUCKY, THE CAPTAIN had said on reaching the system and finding a habitable planet. Breathable atmosphere, 0.95

Earth gravity. Hotter than Earth, but a polar temperate zone held a suitable land mass. The axial tilt meant they'd be in night for the first 2.4 Earth years, but that was a small issue. Besides, the polar zones offered spectacular auroral activity.

Lucky, the captain had said. Still reeling from the news of Anton, Gar hadn't felt very lucky at the time. Now no one did.

On first seeing the aurora on orbital displays, Gar had felt a dread he couldn't reconcile with its beauty. He had assumed he was subconsciously linking its colors to those of Anton's Med-Lab hologram. Now he wasn't sure. Now people were dying.

Walking through the main colony dome, Gar noted without surprise that all ceiling panels had been opaqued to block any view of the sky. He cranked up Mozart in his translation headset and tried to relax as he neared the newly-built dorm pod.

The construction of the colony on the planet had gone well in the beginning. Gar had made planet-fall with the first group. To translate between engineers and work crews, he had said. Both he and Clara knew he was avoiding the situation with Anton.

Clara had accepted the diagnosis quickly. During the trip to the planet, she had buried herself in researching autism and working with Anton. Gar just couldn't. So he hid in his work.

At their dorm unit, Gar hesitated then stepped inside. Clara sat with Anton, one of her light sculptures hovering before them. Anton rocked back and forth, eyes on the floor.

"Is that a new sculpture?" he said, forcing a smile.

She looked at him and his smile died. "Old one. New colors." Gar noted the absence of greens, reds and purples.

"Autistics think visually. Words are too abstract," she said. "I hoped the shapes and colors might prompt a reaction."

Gar noticed she wasn't in uniform. "Did your shift change?"

"The captain needs to see you about an announcement. He asked me to brief you." She spoke a command. The hologram disappeared and a MedLab report appeared on a wall screen.

Clara led a photonics team analyzing the aurora. Gar had no idea how her work had been going. They didn't talk much lately. He scanned the report. "…high amplitude gamma waves in the brain, resulting in massive and prolonged epileptic seizures. Most victims are adult females. Attacks match peaks in aurora activity. Shielding attempts have failed."

"So it *is* the aurora," he said, as he finished.

"This thing isn't an aurora." She didn't look at him.

"What do you mean?"

"This planet's magnetosphere is too weak." She stared at Anton. "So are the solar flare levels. Besides, the timing of the attacks doesn't even match the solar wind cycle."

"Then what's causing the aurora? Or whatever it is?"

Clara reached out and stroked Anton's hair. The child began shaking his head violently and she stopped. "We think we are."

Gar felt a chill. "What?"

"The aurora was stable until our planet-fall. It's grown steadily since. We think our arrival prompted the attacks and our continued presence is causing their escalation."

"Attacks?" He wished she'd look at him.

"It's not a natural phenomenon. The electron flow doesn't even follow the planet's magnetic field. It appears to go where it wants to, and it seems to want to be over our settlement."

"But why?"

Clara finally looked at him. "We believe we're dealing with a sentience, Gar. An alien intelligence. The Captain wants to try to communicate. He's asking you to lead that team."

•

FAST FORWARD: Fourth Movement, Nocturne (Allegro)

GAR LEANED AGAINST THE WALL of the main colony dome, staring at the fire raging above. Out here he was at least alone in his misery. No one else could stand the sight of the sky any more. Gar preferred it to the accusing stares of his fellow colonists.

All their attempts to communicate had failed. His team had used ideas from the ancient SETI project, transmitting universal mathematical concepts. For six Earth weeks, they had broadcast over the full range of EM frequencies detected in the aurora.

If any message had been received, it created no visible effect. The deaths continued. The aurora still burned the heavens, and he could no more tell what message it held than what was in his own son's head. Standing, he started to walk.

She sat slumped against a boulder crying, Anton in front of her. The child had his back to her, rocking gently. Gar sat down and pulled her to him before she realized he was there. She pushed away at first but then collapsed against him. Her sobs stopped, and they held each other for a long while.

"Do you know why I came out here?" she asked finally.

He paused. "You hoped the aurora might reach Anton."

"In a way," she said. Gar had never seen her face so sad.

"Well, it's quite the light sculpture," he said.

"Gar, I came here... so this thing would kill our son."

The words ran around his head as he tried to pull some meaning from them. "Clara..."

"Practically every victim's been a woman," she said.

"That doesn't..." He stopped. He understood.

"What will happen to him then? You won't..." She turned away, not finishing. He sat there, his face burning, realizing what she had been living with, and living with alone.

"I'm sorry," he whispered.

"Promise me you'd take care of him, that you'd love him."

"I promise," he said. They made love then, there on the ground, Anton as oblivious to their passion as he was to the monster rampaging above. After, they lay gazing at the aurora.

"I realize now how Anton must feel," Gar said.

"What do you mean?"

"Blind to other minds. We've been blind to this thing. Now we're shouting, 'Hey look, we're alive' and it doesn't hear us."

She looked at Anton. "Maybe he's shouting too." Clara stared at the sky. "Words, mathematical symbols are too concrete, too cerebral for this thing. We need something more abstract. Something with emotion. I can feel it."

"'Music is born of emotion.'"

"That sounds like a quotation."

"Confucius. Music can express ideas, subtleties, and emotions that words can't. The language areas in the brain show activity when we listen to music. Too bad the sky has no ears."

Clara smiled. "You and your music. That's what first attracted me to you, when we met after the launch."

"Really?"

She nodded. "The first crew briefing. You had Bach playing in the room. I remember the colors—all golds and reds."

"Music helps to... wait a minute. Colors?"

She looked embarrassed. "I'm a synesthete. Sounds make me see colors. That's why I always have music playing when I work on my light sculptures. Inspiration."

"Synesthesia. You've never told me about this."

"I once worked in a laser lab with another synesthete. With her, light prompted sounds, even tastes and smells. It was so distracting for her that she had to quit her career. So when I applied for a berth on the ship, I kept quiet about it."

"No need to be ashamed. Lots of creative types have been synesthetes. Scriabin even built a 'color organ' for *Prometheus: Poems of Fire*..." He stopped and stared at the sky.

"Too bad my synesthesia isn't like that. I could tell you what kind of music the sky is playing..." She stopped too.

They looked at each other.

"We could use colors for different pitches," he said.

"You mean, correlate the spectrum of EM frequencies displayed by the aurora with sound frequencies of the music."

"That's what I said."

"Rhythm can just stay the same. Brightness for volume."

"What about orchestration? The timbre of each instrument?"

"Holographic images. Different shapes for each instrument."

"Your sculptures! We could adjust sizes too."

"Small shapes for high notes, larger for the bass range."

"And add more shapes for more volume as well," he said.

"What about harmony? Melody?"

"Tough one. Don't know what colors or shapes go together."

"You'll figure it out." She stood and picked up a wriggling Anton, giving him a hug. "Come on. We've got work to do."

•

Fourth Movement, Finale (Crescendo)

GATHERED UNDER THE SEA OF swirling light, the entire colony seemed to hold its breath as Gar spoke the command. Lasers flared into life, and Schubert's 8th Symphony danced in cubes and stars and dodecahedrons of rainbow colors across the sky. Gar had always thought the Unfinished was music for the end of the world. A fitting epitaph for the colony if they failed.

A computer controlled the shapes, colors and other aspects of the display, monitoring the aurora and repeating patterns that prompted lower EMR levels. "Audience feedback," Clara called it.

The music of the lights played. The colors and shapes of the music kept changing and the colony kept waiting. Ten minutes. Fifteen.

The aurora seemed to slow, to drop in intensity. A murmur swept through the crowd, and Gar's heartbeat quickened.

Someone screamed.

Gar spun around. A woman trembled on the ground. Another fell. Then a man. More dropped. Gar's ears buzzed and his head throbbed. "Gar!" Clara fell to the ground, hands stretched toward him, twitching. Anton still just sat, staring at the sky.

Gar moved to help Clara. Pain flamed in his head and he fell. The air seemed thicker, misty. Then he understood.

The aurora had dropped from the sky. It enveloped them, a swirling cloud of colored sparks and flashes. Electric shocks stung his skin. Saliva trickled from Clara's mouth. The comm-unit to control the display lay before him. He forced his hand forward. The screaming grew louder as he clawed the unit to him.

His lips began to form the command to kill the light music when he saw Anton. The child still sat but his eyes...

Gar felt a thrill of joy as for the first time Anton's eyes focused on something in this world. Clara's sculptures danced in the sky to Gar's music and their child followed every pirouette.

Twisting his head, he saw that Clara was watching too, the happiness in her face shining through the pain.

Whether it was the sculptures or the music or the aurora, Gar neither knew nor cared. He let the comm-unit slip from his fingers. This scene would play itself out.

He reached out to clasp Clara's hand, wondering with a strange calm if they would survive. Together they lay in the dirt of that alien world and watched their son turn to look at them — and smile.

Douglas Smith is a multi-award-winning Canadian author of speculative fiction, published in twenty-seven languages and thirty-five countries. His short fiction has appeared in top professional magazines, including *Amazing Stories, InterZone, Black Static* (formerly *The Third Alternative*), *Weird Tales, Baen's Universe, Escape Pod, Postscripts, On Spec*, and *Cicada*.

His books include the novel The Wolf at the End of the World, the collections Chimerascope and Impossibilia, and the writer's guide, Playing the Short Game: How to Market & Sell Short Fiction.

Douglas the three-time winner of Canada's Aurora Award and has been a finalist for the Astounding Award for Best New Writer (formerly the John W. Campbell Award), the Canadian Broadcasting Corporation's Bookies Award, Canada's juried Sunburst Award, and France's juried Prix Masterton and Prix Bob Morane.

http://www.smithwriter.com/

Did you enjoy this book?

How to make a big difference!

Reviews are *powerful*.

Honest reviews help bring books to the attention of other readers. If you enjoyed this anthology, we would be grateful if you could spend just a few minutes leaving a review (it can be as short as you like) on the book's page where you bought it.

Thank you so much!

About the Editor and the Publisher

Stories Rule Press is a family-run micropress in Alberta, Canada, working as a cooperative to bring great story-tellers together and assist them with publication.

Editor Tracy Cooper-Posey is one of the original authors with Stories Rule Press. She writes across several fiction genres, including space opera under two different pen names, and grew up reading classic science fiction.

Find SRP's fiction at https://StoriesRulePress.com.

Science Fiction
Thrillers
Fantasy & Urban Fantasy
Romance

Other SRP Anthologies

Previously Released:

Space Opera Digest 2021: Fight or Flight
Christmas Romance Digest 2021: Home for the Holidays

Stories Rule Press will be releasing genre-theme anthologies every quarter. Watch www.storiesrulepress.com/stories-rule-press-presents for news of upcoming titles.

CPSIA information can be obtained
at www.ICGtesting.com
Printed in the USA
LVHW021043050222
710251LV00015B/601